MW01596633

CRITICAL PRAISE FOR SAMMY JULIANO'S SECOND NOVEL, *IRISH JESUS OF FAIRVIEW*

"Move this Book to the Top of Your Reading List! The universal themes of love, loss, and the sharp turns life can take are woven throughout the pages, making this astonishing piece of storytelling mesmerizing, relatable, and profoundly affecting. After breaking the reader apart, Juliano reminds us that we can be put back together again, stronger and wiser than before."

–**Laurie Buchanan**, award-winning author of the Sean McPherson novels *Indelible, Iconoclast, Impervious, Iniquity*, and the upcoming *Illusionist.*

"A Fantastic Work! Fairview, New Jersey native Sammy Juliano's second novel, Irish Jesus of Fairview, is a perfect follow-up to his debut work, *Paradise Atop the Hudson,* and that says a lot. The multi-characters are brilliantly written and fully developed. The author superbly sets the time, place, people, and atmosphere of days long gone by and how the town faces changing times. It's a passionate and masterful must-read filled with pop culture references and a wide range of emotions.

–**John Greco**, acclaimed author of *Transgressions, Dark Secrets, Brooklyn Tales, Harbor House, Bitter Ends,* and *The Late Show.*

"Fairview's George Elliot strikes again! Sammy Juliano takes on the problems of coping with gender expectations in the context of a larger

community. The surrounding community of Fairview, New Jersey, and the pop culture of the seventies practically take on the role of additional characters. The best comparison I can think of is *Middlemarch*. Adam Furano's compassionate nature and his frailness run into the toxic masculinity of a working-class New Jersey town much in the way that Dorothea Brooke's grand ambition ran into early Victorian views of womanhood. And then there is the setting. James Joyce said that if Dublin were to disappear from the Earth, you could reconstruct it from *Ulysses*. Having never finished *Ulysses* (or gotten very far) and not having spent much time in Dublin, I don't know about that, but having spent my youth walking the streets of Fairview, I can tell you that you will be able to experience Fairview in the sixties and seventies from this work and its prequel, *Paradise Atop the Hudson*.

–**Peter J. Reilly,** acclaimed author of *Reilly's Laws of Tax Planning (& Life!)* and co-founder of CCR LLP, which grew to be one of New England's largest regional CPA firms.

"In the captivating sequel to Sammy Juliano's debut novel *Paradise Atop the Hudson*, we continue to follow the fortunes of Adam Sean Furano. Adam's journey is filled with introspection, challenges, and personal growth. Juliano's narrative deftly explores the themes of family, faith, identity, and forgiveness. *Irish Jesus of Fairview* is heartfelt and engaging.

–**Tony D'Ambra,** Sydney, Australia-based literary and film writer, noir specialist, and founder of the net's premier noir site, *films.noir.net*.

"Powerful follow-up to Paradise Atop the Hudson! *Irish Jesus of Fairview* is a gripping sequel to Sammy Juliano's *Paradise Atop the Hudson,* chronicling Adam Furano's trials and tribulations during much of the 1970s. I'll admit I slightly preferred the first book, but Irish Jesus has much to recommend. The highlight this time is Adam's brother Mikey, who takes center stage at various points, and becomes a pretty complex character as the book progresses. (ditto adopted brother Jay).

–**Brian Paige**, esteemed Kentucky-based author of *Salvaged from the Flood.*

"As Sammy Juliano is a devout Catholic who exemplifies many of the most outstanding qualities of the religion – empathy, kindness, generosity – it came as no surprise to find his brilliant follow-up to *Paradise Atop the Hudson* homes in with tender precision on the way true character is revealed by tests of faith. Evocative details abound that will have readers salivating for the sweet smells and aural pleasures of warm summer nights on the New Jersey boardwalk. But what will stay with you long after you turn the tale's final page is how the author integrated his deep love and understanding for the characters he's created into how they relate. *Irish Jesus of Fairview* was a sincere pleasure!"

–**Jay Giampietro,** writer, director, actor, and musician whose short films have played at the New York Film Festival, the Maryland Film Festival, BAM Cinema Fest, the Montclair Film Festival, the Sidewalk Film Festival, and the Rotterdam Film Festival. His films, *Unpresidented* and *Quarterbacks,* were selected as Vimeo Staff Picks.

ABOUT THE FRONT COVER

Illustration and Art Direction by Andrew Castrucci
(oil on canvas, 2024)

November 10, 1985: The oil on canvas painting depicts a plane crash above the communities of Fairview and Cliffside Park, hitting a four-block radius. Cliff, Kamena, Fifth, and Walker Streets were adversely impacted by the crash of two planes above Teterboro Airport, one flying out of the airport and the other arriving from Caldwell, New Jersey. Six people died, one on the ground, and eight were injured. A telephone pole caught fire, and witnesses reported "fireballs hurtling through the sky." The painting was based on the artist's memory; no photographic reference was employed. The tapestry is a dream state/surreal evocation, including the cliffs' foreground. Artist Castrucci wanted to show the plane seconds before impact, purposely avoiding showing buildings on fire or smoking. Castrucci stated that he also wished to establish a symbolic connection with the political chaos of the present day.

Mikey's Absolution

Sammy Juliano

Edited and Formatted
By Rob Bignell

Cover Art by Andrew Castrucci
Graphic Design by Daniel Velle

ISBN 9798303451513

Edited and Formatted by Rob Bignell

Cover art by Andrew Castrucci
Graphic Design by Daniel Velle

Printed in the United States of America

DEDICATION

Mikey's Absolution is dedicated to the late Fire Chief John Mesisca and the Fairview Fire Department. Mesisca, a beloved community activist, wore many hats in his distinguished service to the Borough of Fairview. He worked as a fire inspector and served as President of the Fairview Little League, an institution where he coached. John passed in July 2014 at 57. He served as President of the Fairview Board of Education, Our Lady of Grace CYO basketball coach, and the Borough of Fairview recreation director. He was dubbed "Superman" by his family for his long and courageous battle with cancer. In a novel featuring a real-life plane crash over Fairview and Cliffside Park, John orchestrated a yeoman response to the disaster and is depicted in his leadership role in the fictional narrative. John was Karen's beloved husband for twenty-five years, son of Queenie and John Mesisca, and father of Nicole Turro and Frank Del Vecchio, as well as their spouses, Kim and Charles. John was the cherished brother of Michael and his wife Patricia and uncle to their son Michael John.

Comprised of three companies in a town smaller than a square mile – Grandview, Tiger Hose, and Walker Street – Fairview's fearless firefighters have served as pillars in a community with a time-honored tradition of safety and assistance for residents of the borough and neighboring communities. For decades, the Fairview Fire Department has been at the center of town events and once sponsored a famous bazaar that attracted overflow attendance. Most recently, the Fairview Fire Department has faithfully stood beside family members and residents during the Borough's annual 9-11 ceremonies.

"I don't want sunbursts or marble halls; I just want you."
–Anne to Gilbert in *Anne of the Island,* L. M. Montgomery

CHAPTER 1

Nungesser Lanes

July 12, 1980

"Daddy, those little stone squares at the top look like wheels," said seven-year-old Saoirse Furano, pointing diagonally upward to circular designs encased in a brick rectangular extension at the top of a building with a grey façade that was the home of Nungesser Lanes bowling alley.

"Beauty, I asked about the history of the place. I was told it used to be a trolley barn. I think they may have fixed the wheels of the trolley cars here," answered the youthful parent, Adam Sean Furano.

"But Daddy, if it was a barn, wouldn't animals live in it, too?"

Grinning broadly, Adam leaned over and kissed his daughter on the head.

"Honey, the word barn, usually refers to where farm animals or feed are stored. You are right to think that. But a barn could also be a large building. It is also a word that is not meant to be literal."

1

"I think I know what you mean, Daddy. The White Castle isn't a castle, either."

Adam guffawed.

"That's right, beauty, and all the Pizza Huts around the country aren't *huts* either. Let's head in so you can bowl for the first time. You're going to have so much fun; I guarantee it."

On this warm Saturday, more than a week after Independence Day, Adam held Saoirse's hand as he pulled on a glass door. A step later, he opened another one, leading to a lobby where a food bar operated on the right, just a few feet before a wooden phone booth.

"How about if we get a hot dog or hamburger and fries when we're done, beauty? And your favorite orange soda, too! They even have the squirting plastic ketchup bottles."

"Daddy, I like the orange crush at the White Castle better. And their cheeseburgers are the best!"

"I guess I know where we will be going for lunch today," Adam announced, smiling with resigned but gleeful anticipation."

"We can't compete with that place," the short, stocky counter-woman said. "How about one of these?" she asked, holding a red lollipop for Saoirse.

The girl was tentative, but the woman pushed it, adding, "Please. It's on me. Next time your dad takes you bowling, I'll make you a special cheeseburger."

"Thank you so much, good lady," said the beaming adolescent who looked so much like her daddy in looks and the affectionate manner she projected when she addressed others. The woman blew Saoirse a kiss as the father and daughter ascended four steps to enter a final glass door that served as the entrance to the bowling alley proper.

"Hi, Yogi," declared Adam as he extended his hand.

"Hello, young man, and hello, young lady," said the most regularly visible proprietor of the sixteen-lane bowling mecca.

Yogi Rogers was the facility's short, sturdy, and energetic counterman for as long as many younger patrons could remember. The North Bergen resident wasn't the institution's owner – that distinction belonged to Frank Orrico, who sometimes operated the counter or the bar – but he was the face of it. A master organizer, he enacted discipline when matters became unruly among the teenage bowlers and promptly dispatched others, one of whom was the tall, athletic Roy Ghostlaw, to correct lane mishaps and the occasional malfunctions in the mechanical pin replacement system that operated behind and above each lane.

Ghostlaw was also a talented bowler who sometimes honed his craft at the rare times when few were playing. Some locals would later boast to others that they witnessed a 300-game by the right-hander. One regular considered him the Nungesser Lanes' version of Earl Anthony, a famed PBA record-holding bowler, who, like Ghostlaw, was lean, wore glasses, and stood over six feet.

"This is my beauty, Saoirse. She will turn eight over the summer, and I thought it was time she learned how to bowl."

"She has the best teacher in her dad. I'm sure she'll be fine," Yogi said.

"You are too kind," Adam responded. "But I am the worst bowler. Most of the time, my ball finds its way to the gutter. My daughter needs a much better role model."

Yogi grinned but stayed the course. "Keep at it, Adam. You'll get the knack soon enough. It just takes practice."

"Practice makes perfect," said Saoirse.

"See, the young lady knows it too!" exclaimed Yogi. "So, my guess is maybe a size six for Saoirse, and, of course, we already know your size."

"You have the best memory," exclaimed Adam.

Yogi turned around and quickly pulled two pairs of bowling shoes, one each from two labeled square compartments toward the bottom of the wall rack.

After signaling he wanted three games, Adam placed a ten-dollar bill on the counter. Though the total cost was under seven dollars, he advised Yogi to keep the change.

"Oh no! Take your money, young man!"

Adam smiled but hurried away with Saoirse in tow.

"My Lord, who was that? Is he a father? I don't believe it. He doesn't look like, sound like, or act like any man I know," said the macho part-time counter assistant. "What a sissy!"

"Be nice, Pedro. I've known that young man for a very long time. He started coming here when he was a little older than his daughter is now, maybe around 1964, when Adam was about ten. He was always a feminine and delicate boy."

"I'll say," answered Pedro.

"But that's who he is," said Yogi. "I think it was best that he started to show himself this way. There isn't anything he wouldn't do for anyone. Few people I know are loved as much as he is. But he was bullied and brutally beaten for most of his life. I'm sure you don't know something else."

"What's that?"

"Adam is the boy who fell off a roller coaster eight or nine years ago in Palisades Amusement Park. He was in a coma for days and nearly died. Most say it was a miracle he survived. He developed a stammer, but it seems now it is only slight. Sometimes, you can barely detect it at all. For a while, it dominated his speech. I don't think it will ever disappear completely, and I'm sure when he is stressed out, it worsens, but he manages it much better now. I didn't hear it once today."

"My parents spoke about it, but I think I was only about seven when it happened," said the sixteen-year-old Hispanic-American.

4

"Wow, who would have thought? But does his wife dress *her*, I mean *him*, in diapers?"

"Now cut it, or you'll piss me off. His wife is the boss, of course, and she's a rugged woman. She is the one who insists he appears the way he does now. She made the right decision as far as I'm concerned. Adam seems more confident in himself, and from what he told me at The Point Diner a few weeks ago, he will be going on an interview next month for a teaching job."

"Why would they make him wait a month for the interview when school starts in September?"

"Adam told me the superintendent is on a European vacation and won't return till late August. I understand he applied elsewhere, too."

Never one to let go, Pedro asked: "It must be kindergarten, right?"

"It's Grade 10. I think it's wonderful. He knows so much about books, music, movies, and sports. I'm sure he knows a lot about children's books, too. He'll be ideal."

"Yogi, can I say something without you getting mad at me?"

"It depends on what you say."

"I'll gamble," said Pedro. "High school students will eat him alive. They are difficult for even the best disciplinarians. He will be laughed at, and whatever he says will be ignored. The worst students might use their hands on him. He looks like he has the strength of an eight-year-old girl. I wish him the best, but I fear the worst.

"My mom is a teacher in Union City. She always said it doesn't matter how much one knows the subject. If there is no discipline, there is no learning."

Yogi pondered what his worker said.

"What you said seriously concerns me. Adam is a fragile young man. I'm tempted to say something but don't want to dampen their excitement. I'm sure he'll get help from other teachers and administrators."

"I guess he'll be at Hackensack High School. Is that right?" asked Pedro.

"No. I heard he will be at Bergen Tech," answered Yogi.

"Bergen Tech? Do you mean the vocational school on Hackensack Avenue near Route 4? I seem to recall there's a cemetery across the road."

"Yes, that's the school," answered Yogi.

"Adam is doomed," said Pedro. "The kids in Bergen Tech aren't going there to learn English or history. They're looking to take up a trade. He's lucky if he lasts a month."

"If you keep talking like this, you'll be looking for a new job tomorrow!" exclaimed Yogi, bluffing.

"I'm just being a realist. If he's hired, I hope he makes it. I feel sorry for the guy."

"That's better. I'm confident he'll find a way to make things work."

"I'm curious. Is he an only child?" asked Pedro.

"No, he has two brothers and a sister. The older brother, Jay, was adopted. He's a nice guy. The younger brother, Mikey, comes off as a ruffian, but I was told he is more academically gifted than Adam. He's bowled here many times. He's got a terrific personality and a great smile. You'd know him. He's average height, maybe five foot eight, stocky build, blond hair."

After noticing Adam retreating to the men's room at the bottom of a few stairs at the northwestern corner of the alley layout, the manager left three singles and 40 cents in change and a Chunky bar with the young girl.

"Your dad is one of a kind," said Yogi.

The young girl beamed and vigorously nodded her head. "Thank you, sir. Chunkys are my favorite."

"How did I know you loved Chunkys?" Yogi winked at the young girl as he returned to the main counter.

Adam glanced at the two pinball machines in the platform space near the restrooms and resolved to treat Saoirse to a few games. Bally's *Star Trek* and *The Lost World* debuted in 1978. Adam had always complimented Yogi on how the bowling alley kept up with the newest releases. However, at least a few times, he privately mourned when the turnover resulted in eviction notices for a few he adored, like 1972's *Fireball*, the first multiball pinball machine, and the more recent *Eight Ball* from 1977, a release Adam thought perfectly combined the game of pool with pinball. Steve Burke had privately told his daughter Sarah that he planned to surprise Adam on one of the young man's January 4 birthdays with the gift of a brand-new pinball machine. Sarah couldn't believe that her dad would go that far and was deeply moved, though she wasn't quite sure where they would put such a bulky item in the Furano home. Steve asked his daughter to put out feelers on Adam's favorite titles.

Adam gave his daughter a beginner's course on keeping scores. He instructed the young novice to choose a ball from the bowling racks, approach the lane, grip the large sphere, and pitch it down the polished wooden lane.

"Beauty, the scorecard is to be placed over this glass," Adam said, lighting a cigarette. "There are markers in the slots to use. The overhead projector will flash the image on the screen above," he added, pointing to the rectangular board fastened above their alley.

Saoirse quickly understood how to numerically record a strike, a spare, and a compound from frame to frame.

"Thank you, Daddy."

"Do you see that man bowling three lanes to the right?" Adam asked, glancing at a guy of average height and dark brown hair.

"I see him, Daddy."

"His name is Steve Koskinen. He bowled a few perfect games and was once among the top bowlers at Columbia Park Lanes. He's a real nice guy and talented in music, too!"

"Daddy, what is a perfect game, and where is Columbia Park Lanes?"

"Beauty, a perfect game is a 300 score. It means the bowler achieved twelve strikes. In a 300 game, there is never a single pin standing after any frame. Professional bowlers sometimes measure the success of their careers by the number of perfect games they achieve. Columbia Park Lanes is another bowling alley located several miles south of here on Kennedy Boulevard. I'll take you there one day. Columbia Park is so much larger than this one. I recall there are 64 lanes, and an oval bar is right down the middle. There is a pool hall downstairs."

"Wow, Daddy, you're so smart to know all that."

"Thanks, beauty, but your Uncle Mikey is much smarter than me. He was in the top ten students when he graduated high school. I can't shine his shoes. He has it all."

"Yeah, Uncle Mikey is so intelligent. But you are, too, Daddy. But why would you want to shine his shoes? He can shine them himself."

Adam guffawed.

"Beauty, it's an expression that has nothing to do with shoes in a literal sense. It means I can't come close to matching him."

"I understand, Daddy. Anyway, I'm sure you know some other great bowlers in this place."

"Honey, everything I know was told to me by people who bowl here or know much of the area's history. One man, a few years older than me, Ron Skokandich, is called the Don of North Bergen. He is sometimes referred to as the town historian. He's the one who told me about this place being a trolley barn before it was a bowling alley. He also explained that an amusement park was located diagonally across from the White Castle in Hudson County Park many years ago. It was called Little Coney Island."

"Did you go to it when you were younger, Daddy?"

Adam laughed.

"Saoirse, Little Coney Island existed 44 years before I was born. Grandpa wasn't even around to see it. He was born in 1930, about 20 years later."

"Maybe Grandma Delaney knows it."

"Yes, beauty, she was alive and old enough to appreciate it, but she lived in Brooklyn. They had their own Coney Island to enjoy."

"That Coney Island is still there, right, Daddy?"

"Yes, sweet one. Your mom and I need to take you and your sisters there. The Cyclone is fantastic. It has one of the steepest drops of any roller coaster worldwide. And they have Nathan hot dogs and saltwater taffy."

"Daddy, a girl in my class said saltwater taffy is the same as regular taffy. A hundred years ago, a candy shop was flooded by water from the Atlantic Ocean. I think the name stuck."

"Beauty, whoever told you that is right. They are the same. I think some of us just like to use fancier names. But I got off the subject. Many great bowlers have made this bowling alley their home."

"Daddy, do you mean they live here? Where are the beds?"

"Saoirse, you are incorrigible," said Adam laughingly. "They don't live here; they do their bowling here. What I said was a manner of speech. However, one man lived in this building from the early 1960s till about 1968 in the apartments above these lanes. His name is Richard Spanburgh, and he is a member of the Nungesser Lanes Hall of Fame. He didn't just bowl; he also fixed the bowling machines and performed some maintenance."

"Is he here now, Daddy?"

"Not now, beauty. But he is a regular, and everybody knows him. Pete Cimino, Roy Ghostlaw, and Chic Suter are other terrific bowlers."

"Daddy, what else do you know about Mr. Spanburgh and those other three bowlers?"

"Beauty, I'm happy I've piqued your interest, but I'll probably bore you."

"No, Daddy, I'd like to hear about them, especially about Mr. Ghostlaw. I like his name."

"I know why you like his name," said Adam, chuckling. "But what a superstar bowler he is. He has some perfect games to his credit and bowled in a Paramus Eastern Classic tournament. I was told he won the Golden Pins Tournament at Feibel's in Teaneck, a bowling alley a block or two south of the movie theater I've taken you to on Cedar Lane. Roy helps Yogi a lot in this place.

"As to Pete Cimino, he's practically a celebrity. He once appeared on a famous talk show. I don't quite remember the name. I'll have to ask Ron or Steve if they remember. I also know Mr. Cimino is one of the most famous action bowlers on the East Coast."

"Dad, what is an action bowler?"

Adam laughed.

"Beauty, I'll explain it to you when you get older. Anyway, I'd bet my life that Mr. Cimino will be inducted into the Hudson County Hall of Fame. He is regarded as one of the greatest bowlers this building has ever hosted. He has a remarkably high average and has bowled his share of 300 games. He has a lovely daughter named Gloria. I've met her here a few times. She worships her dad."

"Wow, what a man!" exclaimed Saoirse. "What about the last bowler you mentioned?"

"Ah, yes, Chic Sutter. He bowled around twelve perfect games and won two pro-regional championships."

"What else do you know about Mr. Spanburgh?"

"His dad's name is Joe, and he used to be a bartender here in the bowling alley."

"Did that man Ron tell you?"

"No, the guy Steve shared it with me. He is so proud of these men. A chart near the entrance shows the names of all the perfect games. I'll point it out to you when we leave."

"I have one last question, Daddy. Who built Nungesser Lanes?"

"Beauty, you mean, the man responsible for making this bowling alley happen?"

"Yes."

"All I know is that his name was Sid Lipton. Before seeing this place's possibilities, he owned a bowling alley in Jersey City. Sadly, he died young."

"When did Nungesser Lanes open?"

"It opened in 1958, so 22 years ago."

After the protracted history discussion, Adam resumed teaching Saoirse to bowl and score.

A middle-aged woman in the next lane noticed the young girl's fantastic aptitude and addressed the unisex-attired, soprano-voiced Adam.

"Ma'am, your daughter is simply incredible."

Having faced this perception error many times, Adam didn't bother correcting the woman. Instead, he flashed a half-smile and thanked her.

"What is her name?" the woman asked.

"Saoirse," Adam responded.

"Oh, what a lovely name. Saoirse, I'm sure you are thrilled that your mommy is teaching you how to bowl and keep score. I'm sure you will love it," the heavy-set, graying brunette declared.

Like her father, Saoirse was also used to this erroneous im-

11

pression but thought it prudent to play along.

"Yes, I am, and my mommy is a great bowling teacher."

"I am just a bad bowler," Adam added.

"Tut, tut, girl," the woman answered. "Oh, let me introduce myself. My name is Stefania Eagleson. I live on Adams Street here in North Bergen. I belong to a league. We bowl twice a week. My son Bob dropped me off so I could get in some practice games. I usually don't bowl on Saturdays, but I'm so happy I did so I could meet such nice people."

Adam knew he needed to come clean.

"Well, you know my daughter's name, but my name is Adam, and I live with my wife Sarah and our three daughters on Grant Street in Fairview. My mom, dad, brothers, and sister live in the same house as a close friend."

Stefania's eyes widened, but she remained silent.

Adam quickly dispelled the woman's fearful embarrassment.

"Don't worry, fine lady," added Adam. "Most people think the same thing. I am not insulted."

Stefania still apologized, and later on, when her son picked her up, she told him how upset she was over addressing a young man as a girl and the mother of his child.

Adam pondered.

That was the last time I will ever be mistaken for a female. I am fucking tired of it. I have no desire to become a female or look feminine. I gave in to Sarah to please her but went against my feelings. I am male, and I want to look male. I allowed myself to continue because of my inaction. This is about to change. At 26 years old, I need to get my fucking act together. I know just how to get it done.

***

Adam lit a cigarette as he and his daughter crossed the street.

"Sweetie, please wait in that long line while I hang out outside

12

to smoke. It is best not to do it while people are eating."

"Sure, Daddy," said Saoirse as she entered the iconic hamburger eatery.

"Beauty, how many, three or four?" said Adam as he joined his daughter on the line a few minutes later.

"Daddy, I think I can eat four. I want an orange crush, too."

"Of course. And I will order you French fries. I know how you love to douse them with ketchup."

"Thanks, Daddy. I need to use the restroom."

"Sweetie, here is the dime you need to get in."

The White Castle didn't offer bathroom facilities free of charge. Patrons needed to insert a dime in a coin slot attached to the door handle. Saoirse enjoyed turning the mechanism, as when she wedged her coins in the old-fashioned peanut and M&M machines.

Adam carried eight cheeseburgers, two orders of fries, one order of onion rings, an orange crush, and a Coke to a side table within a foot of the south door access.

"Beauty, when I was your age, customers were served while they sat in their cars. Waitresses came out on roller skates and attached the food trays to the windows of the vehicles."

"Daddy, that sounds like so much fun. I wish I were alive back then!"

"Sweetie, you are still living at a great time. You'll manage without the outside food service."

"Jimbo and Uncle Jay are crazy about these burgers, Daddy."

"Yes, they are, beauty," said the young father, staring ahead, thinking about when he treated Jay to a sack of burgers after the young man pushed Adam into the lake.

"Dad, Jimbo can eat ten for one meal."

"I've seen him chow down a dozen, beauty."

"A dozen? Did he get sick?"

"Jimbo has a cast iron stomach. I bet he could have eaten even more."

"Wow! Maybe he broke the record?"

Adam laughed.

"Beauty, you'd be surprised how many some people can eat."

CHAPTER 2

Aerobics and Weightlifting at Club Fitness

July 15, 1980

"Adam Furano?"

Adam stood up and followed the representative of Club Fitness to a cubicle behind the front desk.

"Mr. Furano, what duration of membership do you desire? You can have three months up to a full year."

"I would like the full year."

The short, middle-aged rep smiled approvingly. "We are open seven days a week from 8 a.m. to midnight. Our current special rate is $200."

"I'm good with that," said Adam, pulling cash from his pocket.

"Can I call you Adam?"

"Of course, that's what I want you to call me."

"Adam, are you looking to employ a health coach?"

"Sir, I want to build muscle mass and gain weight. I am mainly interested in aerobics, weightlifting, and bodybuilding. I expect to spend some time doing push-ups and sit-ups as well."

"So, you have no interest in a health regimen? My name is Bill, by the way."

"Bill, I'm a smoker and a drinker. There is no way I will give up those habits."

"I understand Adam. We have many members who are the same way. Even some of the coaches, believe it or not," Bill said, laughing. "One of our best, Dave Mimikos, also indulges in your habits but does great work in the areas you are interested in. I am sure you'll be pleased. Bill is around your age, I think."

"I'm 26."

"He's the same age, then," said Bill.

"I'd like to employ him."

"We would need $25 a month. You can pay at three-month intervals, with $75 down right now."

Adam revisited his pocket for the additional fee.

***

Dave dabbled in drugs and, during his smoke breaks with Adam, enticed his new client with pot.

"Fuck, man, I haven't done this in over two years. I attended a Stones concert and was pulled over by a cop driving home."

"Well, Adam, don't you think it's time you got reacquainted?" asked Dave.

"Fucking A," said Adam.

Wanting badly to alter his image in every conceivable way, Adam indulged, irresponsibly ignoring his addictive personality. He enjoyed the experience immensely and volunteered to pay for the next joint. He looked forward to getting high during every session whenever Dave was present, usually about three nights a week. Adam worked independently for the other session or two. He continually lied to Sarah, telling her he and his friend had caught a snack at The Point.

Despite his immersion in alcohol and illegal substances, Adam vigorously advanced with the bodybuilding program. His lifelong obsessive-compulsive disorder took root in a worthy pursuit aimed at reversing Mother Nature's longtime constraints on the young man.

***

"Adam, I've coached a few others who came here unable to bench press less than half their weight," said Dave during a smoke break two days into Adam's reinvention. "One short guy from North Bergen was the ultimate wimp. After nine months, he was unrecognizable. I felt sorry for anyone who tried to meddle with him. There's no reason for me to believe you won't transform yourself in similar terms with the proper application."

"So you are saying, where there is a will, there is a way, is that right?" asked Adam.

"Pretty much," said Dave. "I see unlimited potential with you. Motivation is the key."

"Davey boy, I couldn't possibly be more motivated. Some people did me great wrong in my life. Even my adored wife was complicit. One day, I'll explain the shocking story to you. My new image will be perfect for the profession I hope to debut in soon."

"Which is that?" asked Dave.

"I am certified to teach. I recently graduated from Jersey City State."

"You are a teacher? Wow! Somehow, I would have expected teaching would be the last profession I'd associate with you."

"Fuck man, am I some derelict? You better apologize!"

"I'm sorry, guy. Please don't take it the wrong way. I tend to think of teachers as wimpy, bookish types. You are a macho guy."

"You are right, Dave. Many are like that. But what subject do you associate with male teachers?" asked Adam, lighting a cigarette.

"I think of them teaching gym. As far as the academic subjects, maybe history."

"Dave, I'm a big movie fan. Have you ever seen *Annie Hall?* It came out two years ago and was directed by Woody Allen."

"Adam, I have seen a few Woody Allen movies. I loved *Bananas* and *Sleeper.* But sadly, I haven't seen *Annie Hall* yet. I know it won all those awards."

"In *Annie Hall,* Woody Allen said: *Those who can't do, teach. And those who can't teach, teach gym,"* said Adam.

"That's hysterical," said Dave, chuckling. "So gym teachers are rock bottom!"

"Yep, that's the implication. Maybe you'll be surprised to learn that my major is English."

"Surprised isn't the word! You speak very well, so maybe I shouldn't be, but I don't connect you with a subject like that."

"Dave, I haven't been hired yet, but if some school system decides to take a chance on me, I'll use novels and short stories in abundance."

"Sounds like you are a big reader."

"You got it. I have read a ton since elementary school. That's one of the only good things I care to remember from my terrible childhood and adolescence."

"Cool! Somebody's got to get you in a classroom!"

"Hey Dave, maybe I should teach them about some of the things you and I do together."

"You also have a fantastic and cynical sense of humor, Adam!"

"Let's head back inside," said Adam. "I'm ready to do some squats."

"Now you're talking, guy!" Dave exclaimed. "Squats hit the most muscle groups in the body. I always recommend barbells. When you are ready, we'll proceed to the deadlift."

Within a few weeks, Adam and Dave became close friends. Inspired by personal connection, Dave worked harder on Adam's behalf than he had for any other client. Their mutual affinity for illegal substances further bonded them. They spoke on the phone daily when not meeting at the gym. Never losing his obsession with ranking, Adam told Dave he was the best friend he ever had.

"Adam, I feel the same way about you," said Dave.

CHAPTER 3

A New Image

August 21, 1980

"Susan, Adam is changing."

"Sarah, I assume you mean he is regaining his confidence from years ago. I have noticed he seems more assertive than he was," said Susan Clarke. "Anyway, everyone changes, some dramatically."

"You are right about that, Susan. But that isn't the change I was referring to. Adam has developed a ferocious temper. He is sometimes irritable and has incorporated foul language into his vocabulary. I've heard him use the F-bomb and the C-word in front of our children numerous times. He employs all the other standard curse words as well. I have resisted confronting him as I don't want to instigate family dissent, but to say I am deeply concerned is an understatement. I've witnessed him punching the wall and flying off the handle in tame conversations."

"Give me an example, Sarah."

21

"Last week, he complained about the food we had delivered to the house. Granted, it wasn't model health food, and I'm not a big fan of Kentucky Fried Chicken, but Adam's reaction after a few bites of a leg was revolting. He exploded in front of the kids."

"What did he say?" asked Susan.

"He got up from the table and tossed the rest of his food into the garbage, yelling: *This fucking food sucks. Sarah, don't order this shit anymore. I told you to call the Yankee Tower!*"

"I'm shocked. But then again, I shouldn't be."

"What do you mean, Susan?"

"Sarah, it is not uncommon for men to develop anger management issues as they approach middle age. Adam is only 26 but is still old enough to have IMS."

"What is IMS?" asked Sarah.

"Irritable Male Syndrome. It's a condition defined by anxiety, frustration and anger. Professionals say it is associated with biochemical changes, hormonal fluctuations, stress, and – now get this, Sarah – loss of male identity. He is undergoing stress and a degree of self-loathing. As to his use of vulgar language, that's part of him. I think it is sad that the kids heard him talk like that. My dad was the same way."

"So, you think he's angry because his maleness is disappearing?"

"Sarah, he is rebelling. You, I, and many others have read him wrong for years. He doesn't want any part of a partial female identity. Because of this change, we know he identifies as male completely and will now do everything within his means to become as macho as possible. He seems to have been a slow developer."

"He has become so moody and distant," said Sarah.

"Honey, I've known that for years. I'm fond of him, but he is hugely problematic and significantly flawed. We knew his best

22

qualities made him unique, but most people change. Considering who he is and what he perceives himself to be, we shouldn't be surprised. Have you detected other deviations from the norm?"

"I don't think I mentioned this to you, but he joined a gym on Bergen Boulevard almost five weeks ago. He runs on a treadmill, does push-ups, sit-ups, and lifts weights. He spends at least 90 minutes four nights a week. He is working hard to build muscle mass in his biceps. I can already tell he is stronger and flaunts his physique to our daughters."

"Ah, you confirmed my diagnosis. The new Adam will be the polar opposite of the old one. Get ready, Sarah. I fear some unthinkable extremes. I am loathe to say them. So this is a health club?"

"I could hardly call it that. Adam smokes like a fish and drinks every day. We try to help him with his diet, but he fluctuates between healthy meals and junk food. He likes broccoli, carrots, and blueberries and is getting plenty of exercise now."

"We all have those problems," said Susan, a smoker and veteran of drinking issues. "But it sounds like he's eating some good things."

"He's also partial to Raisin Bran, is consuming plenty of protein drinks, and is gaining weight."

"Well, those are positives," said Susan.

"Susan, on the downside, my husband and my father are alcoholics. We've tried to help them."

"I understand, Sarah. The problem will always be there, I'm afraid. I guess they drink together, right?"

"All the time," said Sarah.

"Sarah, I have to say that Adam never seemed to pay much attention to his frame. He wasn't born with a permanent condition that would prevent him from altering his physiology. Hard work can do wonders for the human body. The wimpy Adam of the past is history. He's your husband, Sarah. Unless you or your children are threatened in any way, this could be a positive development."

"You are right, Susan."

"Has he done anything significant with his appearance?"

"Yes. He is growing a goatee, and he has removed his hair dye. His hair is turning jet black again, the same color at birth. His natural black always looked better, accentuating his light skin. He looks more and more like his dad now. All of a sudden, he is proud of his Italian heritage."

"His goatee puts to rest any notion that I wasn't a hundred percent correct. Adam wants to move as far away from feminine looks and mannerisms as possible. Expect an arm tattoo next."

"I don't know if he is planning that, and I don't know if there will be other surprises," said Sarah. "More importantly, Adam told me he is attending a job interview next week. He's playing coy, however. He said he would tell me all the particulars on the morning of the interview."

"You know I am vested in the interview, so please keep me fully abreast," said Sarah. "Are you holding anything back from me, friend?"

"You are a clairvoyant, Susan. He's met with a speech pathologist and plans to work with a voice coach. He begged me to pay for it. Dad helped me. Adam wants to lower his register. Also, he has become best friends with his trainer, Dave. He's constantly on the phone with him."

"Of course. I should have figured that out. He wants a masculine voice. And he'll get it. Those specialists work wonders. I have a feeling Dave isn't the most reputable person. I hope I'm wrong. My friend, your life is about to change, and I'm not sure you'll be pleased."

"Out of the clear blue, a few days ago, he told me he wanted to find our old high school classmate Helga and smash a blueberry pie in her face."

"Sarah, that's one of the oddest things I've ever heard."

"Susan, shortly after we started dating, Helga attacked Adam in our Cliffside Park High School cafeteria. She grabbed the piece of blueberry pie on his tray and crushed it in his face."

"This paints an even scarier picture, my friend. Adam has added revenge to his agenda. I hope I am wrong, but I see some violence in the cards for him."

"It could have been worse. She also viciously attacked him in the hallway and nearly strangled him to death outside the gym."

"This picture is terrifying, Sarah. Hang in there, friend. I'll call you tomorrow."

CHAPTER 4

Job Interview at Bergen Tech High School

Tuesday, August 26, 1980

"Adam Sean Furano, please follow me," announced a tall, middle-aged brunette in an office waiting room at Bergen Vocational-Technical School in Hackensack.

Adam, who sat with other job applicants, rose. He followed the secretary to Dr. John Grieco's office.

"Please take a seat, Mr. Furano. Dr. Grieco will be with you shortly."

Adam looked in awe at all the plaques and certificates on the walls. He read some before a bespeckled, black-haired man in his late thirties entered. Adam rose to accept an energetic handshake from the smiling superintendent of schools, who wore a violet buttoned shirt, black pants, and a dark purple tie.

"Sit, Mr. Furano. Let me get your paperwork."

27

"Please call me Adam."

Grieco smiled and returned with an overstuffed manilla file folder and continued.

"Adam, your application revealed that you waited a few years after high school before attending college. I'm rather delighted you started at Bergen Community College. As Bergen County residents, many of us are proud of our local two-year institution. Presently, it is highly underrated. Still, I'm sure its reputation will continue to grow as more and more students realize it is an economical and high-quality option for those who would prefer to stay close to home while deciding on what degree they would like to pursue. I see you received your degree at Jersey City State College, another institution I hold in premium regard. The president is Robert Maxwell, a visionary administrator and a personal friend."

"Dr. Grieco, I remember him from the day of my graduation. He delivered a wonderful and moving speech."

"I'm not surprised, Adam. He is one of the finest speakers I've ever known. Getting back to your records, I have to say that I am impressed with your grade point average at both institutions. Only math held you from the perch, but that's typical for an English major."

"Mathematics has always been my biggest challenge. My younger brother aced it but was tops in every subject. Mikey is our family's genius. He achieved a class rank of number 6 in his high school graduating class."

"You have nothing to regret, Adam. Your grades were excellent."

"Thank you so much, Dr. Grieco."

"Adam, if past grades were the only criteria in determining the hiring of teachers, you'd be in the top group for consideration. But there are other factors. After exploring your credentials and personal information, I find you an even more appealing candidate."

"I am deeply appreciative, sir," said Adam, blushing.

"Adam, I must tell you, and I'm sure I won't surprise you, that I don't consider you the archetypal applicant for a teaching position. I am not referring to your academic prowess but something else."

"Is there something wrong about my appearance, Dr. Grieco?"

The superintendent grimaced. "Oh no, Adam, I'm sorry I misled you. I like the way you present yourself. Your goatee is a fine choice, and your short haircut is perfect."

"Thank you, sir. I recently joined a gym, where I do aerobics and lift weights."

"Excellent, Adam. It is always best to stay in the best physical shape."

"Many thanks," said Adam.

"I know you have two certifications, elementary and secondary. Despite your expertise in American and English literature and film, I would have thought your best bet as a first-year teacher would be in the lowest grade levels. High school students are perhaps the most difficult to discipline, especially in this school, where most want to learn a trade. Is there a particular reason why you applied here?"

"Dr. Grieco, I submitted about a dozen applications to elementary schools. This is the only secondary school I applied to. So far, you and a principal in a Demarest elementary school have notified me."

"Adam, have you gone to the Demarest interview yet?"

"No, Dr. Grieco. It was scheduled for next Monday."

"Let me get back to what I said earlier when I said you are not an archetypal applicant."

"I am listening, good sir."

"I found out about your accident at Palisades Amusement Park. I believe it happened about a decade ago."

"Nine years, to be exact," said Adam.

"My secretary recognized your name immediately after she received your resume. She said she remembered the incident as if it were yesterday. I researched the news stories and was captivated by what I read about you. Your unlikely survival from that terrible accident inspired many people. Even before this interview, I had leaned toward giving you a chance. If it doesn't work out, I pledge to find you a spot in the primary grades. I have many friends and contacts in education. You should probably experience teaching older kids, even if the younger ones are your future. Then again, who knows?"

"My gratitude to you is boundless," said Adam.

"Young man, you'll need to complete a ton of paperwork. You know what I mean if you've ever leased or bought a new car. You'll be here a few more hours."

"I am in seventh heaven. If it were ten hours, I wouldn't mind." Grieco beamed.

"I see. Let me be honest with you, Adam. Though I know little about you, I'm not confident you will control high school students. Call it a vibe. I might think differently if you had even a single year under your belt. I think your teaching skills and knowledge of your subject are probably impeccable. But there can be no teaching without discipline. I have serious reservations about taking a chance on you. If it doesn't work out, we'd need to start again with another person for your position."

Adam breathed heavily.

"Please don't get upset, Adam. Based on additional comments you made on your application, I see you are a big movie fan. I'll quote a line from the Biblical epic, *Ben-Hur.* Do you know the film well?"

"Dr. Grieco, it is one of my favorite films. I must have seen it over 20 times, and it's quite long."

"I love your passion, Adam. You are my kind of guy. In the scene where the consul Quintus Arrias appears before Emperor Tiberius to plead leniency for Judah Ben-Hur, the Roman monarch's initial comment leads Quintas Arias to believe there can be no hope for Judah. But the Emperor tells his consul, *Give us a chance to be compassionate,* before turning Judah over to Quintas Arias. Adam, I am ignoring my better instincts by hiring you as an English teacher."

"No level of appreciation could be enough, Dr. Grieco," said Adam, tearing up.

Grieco guffawed. "Adam, you may want to take a break. Do you smoke?"

"Oh yeah."

"Then go outside and take your time."

In his car, Adam smoked while listening to a classical rock station. When he returned, Grieco asked the young man to sit.

"Adam, though I will recommend you, you won't be officially hired until next week at around the same time when you are scheduled to interview for the job in Demarest. The Bergen County Board of Education will need to approve my recommendation, though I have no doubt they will. I advise you to call Demarest tomorrow and inform them you are strongly being considered for another position. Let them decide if they still want you to come in. My secretary will show you what you need to do. You will get a phone call the morning after the board meeting, and if it goes as I expect, you can set up your classroom any day after that. It would be premature to say, *Welcome aboard,* but I expect to extend that term to you soon. Otherwise, I wouldn't have you filling out all this paperwork."

"Thank you for all you have done on my behalf."

31

"My pleasure, young man. I wish you the best."

"Dr. Grieco, I have one more question. I just wanted you to confirm that the position is Grade 10 English. Is that correct?"

"Yes, Adam. There is an opening on that grade level because of a retirement."

"I didn't realize there was a specific opening when I applied. I sent many applications, hoping one would be considered because of a vacancy."

"All's Well That Ends Well, as the Bard wrote in titling one of his comedies," said Grieco. "Speaking of Will Shakespeare, I trust you are a fan, no? He was always my favorite."

"There is no writer in world literature I love more! Two of my favorite college classes covered all his plays. They were taught by a brilliant professor named Margaret Croyden."

"I'm impressed, Adam! I know Margaret. She made her mark in theater criticism, and her expertise in Shakespeare is impeccable. I'm not sure if you know that she was one of the hosts of *Camera Three,* a popular CBS Sunday morning arts program from the 1970s."

"Dr. Grieco, I never watched it. Wow! Professor Croyden seemed to be a modest person. She never told her students."

"I'm sure, Adam. She isn't a boaster. Her guests on that show included George C. Scott, Dustin Hoffman, Joseph Papp, Vanessa Redgrave, Lee Strasberg, Irene Worth, and others whose names presently escape me."

"Oh, Lord! Her fame is far more extensive than I could have imagined. She's a celebrity."

"You could say that, Adam. She is also a distinguished author. I have a copy of her work on the development of the avant-garde theater."

"I knew she wrote several books. The English Department chairperson mentioned it when I made my schedule."

Grieco smiled and nodded.

***

"Sarah, I don't believe it," exclaimed Susan Clarke into the receiver. "Nobody is in the same position as me in judging Adam's prospective abilities as an educator. I like him and don't want to drop cold water on all the excitement and enthusiasm, but he will never be able to control kids that age. They will abuse him and cause extreme mischief. Though Adam's knowledge and passion for his subject are second to none, he is much too easygoing and never wants to do or say anything that might hurt anyone's feelings. If he takes this position, we have a recipe for disaster. I don't think he could control the second grade, but putting him in front of high school students is utter insanity."

"Susan, I respect your position. But who can he lean on if Adam can't depend on his wife for support? He is as happy now as he's been at any time. He's been compiling lists of the books he plans to teach, placing orders for teaching guides, and working on the plan book he received at the high school. We can't be sure he will have problems. His excitement has spread to all of us."

"Sarah, I think Adam's enthusiasm is fantastic, and I am pulling hard for him, but I fear there could be a crushing letdown. I didn't know Adam had applied to high school. I thought he planned only to submit applications to elementary schools."

"Adam only submitted this one application to a secondary school. He said he was sure he wouldn't be called and expected to end up teaching elementary. He was surprised they called him in for an interview. Susan, you know what I always said about destiny. There was some force pushing him to apply to this high school."

"Well, when you apply, there's always a chance. I chided Adam for obtaining a secondary certificate. I informed him that there wasn't any point since he would only ever teach the lowest grades. He agreed with me, but he still went ahead and secured it. He told me he wanted to expand his horizons. Had he not procured the second certification, we wouldn't have this discussion now. But I do hear you on the matter of destiny."

"The superintendent was quite impressed with Adam."

"Sarah, I don't know Dr. Grieco personally, but I've met him several times at events. He commands a vaunted reputation. He has worked miracles at the vocational high school. I assume he was impressed with Adam's grades and overall interview."

"Yes, he was. There was one other thing. Dr. Grieco told Adam that he knew about the accident at Palisades Amusement Park."

After a silence, Susan said, "Now I understand. I should have already figured it out. If I were in Dr. Grieco's shoes, I, too, would have factored Adam's preternatural recovery into my decision. I will do all I can to help. There will be great difficulty, but I am eager to impart advice based on years of experience. I want to visit you as soon as possible."

"Susan, you are welcome to come at your convenience. Adam needs you."

"How about tomorrow night?"

"Perfect. We look forward to seeing you, great friend."

***

"The best advice I can give you, Adam, is to resist becoming friends with any of your students," said Susan, seated at the kitchen table. "You would lose all respect as an authoritarian figure. Should it reach that point, you cannot salvage any discipline in the classroom. I know other teachers who thought they could win over their students by showing them compassion and trying to win their loyalty. The strategy failed miserably. You are there to teach them and to maintain order. It would be best to stay as far away from them as possible. I must repeat that should you lose control, you'll never regain it. I know some teachers who became so frustrated that all they could do was yell. Once it reaches that point, even the students realize they can and will do as they wish. When the volume of a teacher's voice increases, the students know they have won."

"You are saying I should be mean and inflexible?"

"Adam, I am not saying you should be mean, but an unwritten rule in the profession states it would be best if you didn't crack a smile until Christmas. Teachers, especially first-year educators, should distance themselves from personal interactions. The message you must send the kids is that you are all business and unwilling to make the classroom environment more humanist until expectations are met. Machiavelli once said it is better to be feared than loved, and it is far easier to begin strict and become kind than to start kind and become strict."

"But Susan, isn't something positive to be said for being approachable? Wouldn't a smile tell the students more than I could verbalize? Wouldn't it show I respect them, wish to foster a positive environment, and am happy?"

"Well said, young man. You persuasively pose the attributes of an eternal smile. We can't forget that a positive tone and demeanor encourage happiness, kindness, and respect. If you weren't who you were, I would set aside the earlier advice to be super-tough, but my dear Adam – and please look at me – this isn't you. You don't have a contentious bone in your body. Your natural inclination always defaults to kindness and trust. Yet, the teaching profession is demanding, and only those willing to make the hardest decisions are successful."

Sarah poured coffee into a mug, placed it in front of Susan, and set down a dish of butter cookies. "Cream or milk, Susan?"

"Cream, thank you."

Sarah opened the refrigerator and pulled out a quart container of cream and a can of Budweiser. She placed the beer before

35

Adam and poured the cream into Susan's java. Susan added two spoons of sugar and stirred.

"Hi, Professor Clark!" exclaimed Saoirse, arriving from her basement room.

"Why hello, sweetheart! Please call me Susan!"

"I love you, Susan," said Saoirse.

"If you aren't the sweetest young lady I know, I can't imagine who is," said Susan about the affectionate eight-year-old she embraced. "I love you too, honey."

"Thanks for helping my Daddy."

"Sweetie, there isn't anything I wouldn't do for him or any of you."

"Honey, try and keep the twins occupied," said Sarah. "We have a personal matter to discuss."

"Sure, Mommy," said Saoirse as she grabbed two cans of Coke from the fridge.

"Don't you need three, young lady?" asked Sarah.

"Carol and Michele want to share one," responded Saoirse, clasping two red plastic cups from a stack on the countertop.

Susan continued. "Adam, I don't think you can change your nature. You are who you are, and your natural inclinations will surface in any situation involving your relationship with others. But because I want you to succeed so badly, I will do all I can to guide you in the right direction. If you don't at least meet me halfway, I am fearful."

"Susan, I'd be eternally grateful."

"It would be best if you pulled in the reins by not being overly generous. You need to set up some fundamental regulations at the outset. Bathroom visits should be limited to emergencies. I assume the periods are one hour, is that right?"

"Dr. Grieco told me they are 50 minutes, so practically an hour."

"Ah, yes. Students would have 10 minutes to get to the next

class. Some use that time for bathroom visits or to sneak a smoke. It would be best if you held steadfast to any rules you introduce. Never bluff. Always follow through. A common violation is tardiness. Some schools require late students to report to the attendance office to secure a pass for classroom admittance. Always keep an efficient record of lateness in your roll book."

Adam took a swig from his can and nodded.

CHAPTER 5

Teaching High School English

Sarah had recently returned to her secretarial position in the Cliffside Park school system. On Wednesday, August 27, she took a personal day to help her husband set up. The first-floor classroom faced the parking lot on the north side of the sprawling institution, a short distance from the Coach House Diner and Highway 4, and across Hackensack Avenue from two cemeteries.

The Furanos were greeted at the main office by Joseph Volpe, the head of the English Department, who walked down the long hall with them to Room 106.

"We have an extensive collection of materials, novels, short story collections, and classroom supplies on the teacher's room shelves. You are welcome to use whatever you wish. The books are paperbacks. There are about 130 copies of each title."

Adam and Sarah brought in the items they purchased at Bosland's Learning Plus in Saddle Brook the previous day. After Adam's motivational conversation with Dr. Grieco on the Bard, the maiden educator reserved the giant board at the back of the room for a striking collage of famous phrases from Shakespeare's tragedies. Advanced grammar charts and a classroom rules placard were utilized, and on a board in the front of the room, Adam stapled a '10 Writing Tips' poster that featured the steps in outlining a composition.

"Adam, perhaps you should claim the copies of the books you need from the teacher's room," said Sarah. "I recall you saying the author of the book you are interested in is John Steinbeck."

"Yes, *The Pearl,* Sarah. I am equally fond of the author's other great novellas, *The Red Pony* and *Of Mice and Men*. I'm still uncertain what other titles I will settle on, but I am leaning toward *The Chocolate War* by Robert Cormier as the title I will teach after *The Pearl*. I saw a bunch of copies of that one as well. I will also use at least one novel by S.E. Hinton, probably *The Outsiders.*"

"Sweetie, I never heard of *The Chocolate War.*"

"Sarah, the author's other famous novel, *I Am the Cheese*, was published a few years after *The Chocolate War.* Both books reflect Cormier's pessimistic outlook on life."

Sarah sat in the chair behind the teacher's desk.

"Tell me more, sweetie. You are so fascinating when you talk about literature."

"Shit, Mikey is much more fascinating and knowledgeable than I am," said Adam, smiling. "I think young people will relate to the book, but I'll admit it does contain strong language, sexual content, and violence."

"Adam, I'm surprised this high school allows it in the curriculum."

"Dr. Grieco told me the institution is progressive. But I have not heard anything about *The Chocolate War* being banned anywhere. Besides, it bears a few similarities to *A Separate Peace* and *Lord of the Flies*, two other books I love. They, too, present the darker side of human nature."

"For someone who is usually upbeat, positive, and happy-go-lucky, it is hard to believe you have always loved the gloomier works."

"I love many positive and uplifting novels, too, Sarah. But I will admit I do gravitate to the darker ones."

"Mikey is wild about *A Separate Peace*, but I never heard him mention *Lord of the Flies* or *The Chocolate War.*"

Adam guffawed.

"Mikey knows more about *A Separate Peace* than the book's author does! Maybe I'll enter a request for him to teach a unit on it."

"Sweetie, I don't think the administration will take too kindly to such a suggestion, but you are right about your brother. He is so brilliant. I suspect he will also become an educator, likely in your subject. I'm expecting he'll be attending college soon."

"I have no doubt he'll be a university professor one day, Sarah. Getting back to the books, I know Mikey read *Lord of the Flies*. He loves it and the 1963 film adaptation. There are copies of the novel in the teacher's room, but I thought using a less well-known book might be a more interesting idea."

"Sweetie, what about *To Kill a Mockingbird?*"

"Sarah, I'm guessing many students have already read it, perhaps in junior high school. But I will ask Mr. Volpe. I know the books are there. We all adore it."

"Of course, Adam Sean," said Sarah, smiling. "How about *The Catcher in the Rye* by J. D. Salinger?"

"Nice, Sarah. *Catcher* is controversial, but I must find a way to use it! I am unsure if there are copies, but I'll get them one way or another. I also wrote down the titles of three other works on the shelves: *The Pigman* by Paul Zindel, *Death Be Not Proud* by John Gunther, and *The Diary of Anne Frank.*"

"*The Diary of Anne Frank* is one of my favorite books. The story behind it always devastated me. But I don't know the other two."

41

"*The Pigman* is an authentic depiction of teenagers with a fascinating dual perspective of one character, an elderly widower named Angelo Pignati. The teens, Lorraine and John, have opposite personalities, and together, they present a thought-provoking narrative. Like *The Chocolate War,* the book contains sexual themes and offensive language. *Death Be Not Proud* is one of the saddest books ever written. It isn't a novel but a memoir written by John Gunther, a journalist whose son John Jr. died of a brain tumor at 17. The boy was brilliant and fought a brave battle."

"Sweetie, I don't think I could teach such a work. You have courage."

"I don't know how it will go, but I refuse to believe anyone won't be moved to tears."

"I'm going to read it this week, sweetie," said Sarah. "You have me intrigued. Adam Sean, do you have any other definite plans for each period?"

"I will be giving a vocabulary test once a week on Fridays. I will recite 20 words on Monday and instruct students to write the definitions."

"These sound like great plans, sweetie."

"All the credit belongs to Mr. Shelley. I had him in the eleventh and twelfth grades, and vocabulary tests comprised one-fourth of the grade. Aside from a few reports he asked us to complete, the remainder of the grade was based on how many pages we read."

"Sweetie, why don't you try that?"

"They expect me to follow the curriculum. I don't have Mr. Shelley's confidence, and I believe only a person with complete control of his students could succeed with such a personalized approach."

"What you say makes sense, sweetie."

"Sarah, I need to go outside to smoke. Unless you want to join me, would you carry the copies of *The Pearl* to the classroom?"

"I'd love to get the copies," said Sarah. "Maybe I should include *The Chocolate War.* How long do you plan for your novel units?"

"I'm estimating it will take three to four weeks. It will all depend on the students. I need to learn their pace and capabilities, but I think bringing copies of *The Chocolate War* is safe. If another teacher asks about them before I launch the unit, I will surrender the books and use the title later in the year."

After nearly six hours, Adam was confident Room 106 was ready. As soon as Sarah completed stocking Adam's desk with supplies, they departed, using Route 4 East to Grande Avenue.

***

On the morning of the first day, Volpe told Adam to stand at the doorway when the students for his first-period class arrived. A well-built, medium-height, dark-haired, handsome teenager, Brian Fischer, a Garfield resident, spoke.

"Hi. Are you Mr. Furano?"

"Yes, I'm Adam Sean Furano. I am your English teacher. Please come in and sit where you wish."

"Cool," said Brian.

Adam had already committed two mistakes. He announced his first and middle names to a student who only needed to know and address him by his surname. The second slipup, an even more enormous blunder, occurred when he invited the boy to sit anywhere. By staying loyal to his nature, Adam disavowed proper student-to-teacher respect and classroom protocol that should always include assigned seats. The Fischer boy signaled other students entering the room to sit near him, whispering to one:

"No assigned seats. Everyone sits wherever they want."

Adam continued his reckless strategy.

"I would like to explain a bit about myself to the class. This is my first teaching job. I attended Bergen Community College and received my B.A. in English at Jersey City State College. I live in Fairview with my wife Sarah, three daughters, Saoirse, Carol, Michele, and other family members."

Adam handed out a one-page syllabus defining the class's aims, a list of the readings, an explanation of the weekly vocabulary tests, periodic creative writing topics, and the chapters planned from the grammar textbook. He then called the roll, giving him the first opportunity to pronounce the students' names. His elocution was excellent, save for the name of a football star, James Beauchamp, who angrily objected to Adam's mispronunciation.

"Adam, my name isn't pronounced Bo-Champ. It's Bee-Chum. You got that?" James asked threateningly.

"I'm so sorry, James," said Adam, unfazed by the student's disrespectful use of his first name. From that moment forward, every student in the class called him Adam. When the word got around to the other tenth-graders, they followed suit. Adam taught five classes. His schedule included lunch at noon and a study period. The first-year teacher had sown the seeds of his demise by doing what Susan had strongly advised him to avoid at all costs. Still, the first day, occupied by introductions, materials distribution, and syllabus explanation, didn't devolve into anarchy. Adam didn't divert from how he approached the first class with the four that followed. However, what the students learned about their new teacher was likely to ensure a breakdown in discipline was near at hand.

***

"Do you feel you said or did anything you regret?" asked Susan at the kitchen table in the Furano home later that evening.

"No," said Adam. "Well, maybe when I spoke a little about myself. I may have been too open."

Susan glared at Adam and then shook her head at Sarah.

"Honey, I'm afraid to ask you what you meant by that," Susan

44

said.

"I announced my name, hometown, and teaching experience."

Susan feared the worst.

"You told them you were a first-year teacher?" she asked apprehensively.

"Yes. I wanted to be honest."

"Adam, honesty isn't always the best policy, contrary to what the term often means. Did the students address you properly after your introduction?"

"They all called me Adam. But they always raised their hands."

Susan stood up, approached Adam, and exclaimed.

"No! How could you, Adam? How dare you tell them your first name!"

Adam looked downward. Susan and Sarah couldn't see him grit his teeth.

Susan quickly backpedaled.

"Honey, I'm so sorry I raised my voice. All I want is for you to succeed. But there is too much disconnect by the students calling you by your first name. From the first day, you have greatly lessened the chances for teacher-student respect."

"They didn't disrespect me," said Adam haltingly. "They were friendly and cooperative."

"Oh, honey," said Susan resignedly. "I am happy to hear you were pleased with the reception. I didn't mean to generate negative energy."

"Dear Susan, you've been incredibly supportive. I am going downstairs to talk to the girls. Saoirse made me promise I would tell her how the day went. I will be back in a few minutes."

"Of course, honey. Sarah and I will chat until then."

After Adam departed, the two women shook their heads in unison.

"I feel like he is my child," said Susan. "I apologize for upsetting him. But I see a looming disaster. In what high school do students address their teacher this way? The lack of respect is certain to snowball. I'm frightened he could eventually be physically harmed. He is much too kind and friendly for this profession. Or at least he *was* kind and friendly. I know well how much he has changed. Anyway, he is incapable of executing sage advice. I was afraid of this happening. He will follow his nature. Now, he is at the mercy of his students. There is a slim chance they will be compassionate, but much more likely they will be abusive. Teenagers can be brutal. Sarah, we must continue encouraging him, imparting advice, and hoping for the best. I am loathe to think where this all may go."

"Susan, as you know and have said yourself, Adam is not the person he was six months ago. He will not be physically harmed. If anything, his students will be harmed. You are giving him excellent advice, but I am not seeing the same result."

"Sarah, I respect your opinion, and I do realize Adam is in the process of transforming. He's a work in progress."

Carol entered the kitchen.

"Mom, what is Adam's biggest flaw?" Sarah asked.

"We have always agreed he is as stubborn as an ox. He was that way as a child, and to this day, he is the same."

Sarah nodded.

"Susan, my son listens to a voice in his head," Carol added. "No advice from anyone is likely to be honored. He is also an expert at giving lip service. He always tells people what they want to hear."

"He isn't always truthful, either," said Susan. "In his crusade to make others happy and content, he sometimes lies and gives false assurances."

All three women nodded simultaneously.

"We love him dearly, but my son is far from perfect. Sarah defended some of his lies. Our family has known this for years. He'd give you the last penny in his pocket, but he has a dark side, does he not, Sarah?"

Sarah nodded rather than contest some of her mother-in-law's false assertions from years ago.

"Adam Sean did what he wanted to do," said Susan. "I'm sure he didn't even tell us everything. As I said earlier, he could still get by if the students don't take full advantage, but he has little hope for that to happen. We will continue to coach him and hope a few suggestions are utilized."

Carol rose to brew coffee and get a package of Stello Doro cookies from the pantry.

Around ten minutes later, Adam returned. He opened the refrigerator for a beer can, pulled on the tab, sipped, and lit a cigarette.

"The beauties are so excited," he said, exhaling. "They want me to take them to the school when class isn't in session. Of course, Michele has some ideas of how she would decorate."

"Naturally," said Sarah. "Give her a few packs of markers and crayons; there wouldn't be any white space on the boards."

Everyone guffawed.

"Adam, did you complete seating charts for the five classes?" asked Susan.

"Yes," said Adam, looking downward.

"Did you bring the lists home?" the academic asked.

"Susan, I'm sorry. I lied. I thought it was best to let the students sit where they wanted. Tomorrow, I will make the charts based on those preferences."

Susan Clarke nearly stormed out of the house.

Carol flashed a vindicated smile.

"Adam, it is always best to decide where they sit," said Susan. "Otherwise, friends will gravitate to adjoining seats, and you will have more difficulty controlling the class."

47

"Maybe I can do that tomorrow," said Adam.

Susan nodded, deep in thought.

He's lying to my face, telling me what I want to hear, and will not change anything tomorrow. His prime concern is making the kids happy. I've never encountered a new teacher so irresponsible. He will teach at this grade level for one year. There isn't a path for him to be rehired.

"A boy in my first-period class was so friendly," said Adam. "He said he was willing to be a classroom helper. His name is Brian Fischer."

"Adam, classroom helpers are ideal for the lowest grades. In high school, they can only impede your efforts at maintaining order. I don't advise using Brian. It would be best to keep your distance. I'm sure he is a fine young man who means well, but you should stay clear of this proposal. I can't repeat myself enough when I say that close friendships between teachers and high school students are taboo."

"Thank you, Susan. Tomorrow, I will re-evaluate this idea," Adam said, crushing his cigarette. Again, Susan thought:

Translation: Thanks for the advice, Susan. However, I will still use Brian as a classroom helper. I have learned today that my dear Adam is a pathological liar. It is more vital for him to do as he wishes than be honest with those who love him the most.

***

Susan's predictions came true, though they happened much sooner than expected. Adam completely lost control of his classes on the third day of the third week after he defied another vital suggestion – don't allow students to leave the room indiscriminately. The high schoolers established their authority by leaving the room without permission and staying out for longer intervals. Volpe approached Adam in his classroom at the end of the day.

"Mr. Furano, I am rooting for you. But there are some danger signs I need to point out. Some of your students were caught smoking in the restrooms. We allow smoking on school grounds but not anywhere in the building. When one of the smokers, Brian Fischer, from your first-period class, was asked what room he was excused from, he responded: *Adam's room.* Mr. Furano, I've taught at this school for sixteen years, and I've yet to come across a student addressing a teacher in such a manner. I don't know who prepared you for this assignment, but I greatly respect Dr. Grieco, who was enthusiastic about your hiring. To succeed, you need to distance yourself from your students. They will control your classes if they see you as their friend. This is the most fundamental rule about this profession. I've stood outside your door without you knowing it."

"My advisor, Susan Clarke, is a friend. She was my professor at Jersey City State College. She gave me plenty of advice. I respect her, but I have some ideas about the best chance of success, depending on my personality and style. I didn't think I should alienate myself from my students and thought the best results would happen if there was some affection between the teacher and students. I'm sorry about the smoking. I understand the need, though, since I am a smoker."

"Mr. Furano, I smoke as well. Half of the staff does. But we are teachers. Students have to follow the rules. They can do it outside, not in the restrooms. Allowing students to leave your room with abandon encourages this violation to happen repeatedly. Other teachers are complaining to me. Your name has been mentioned many times. The last thing you need to do is lose favor with your colleagues. Do you understand you are here to teach kids, not to use the school to make new friends? Do you understand, Mr. Furano?"

Adam slowly nodded.

Volpe softened his tone.

"Can I call you Adam? You've clarified that you prefer to be called by your first name."

"Yes, of course, Mr. Volpe," said Adam.

"Adam, I respect and even applaud you for wanting to do your own thing. There can't be any personal satisfaction if you constantly follow orders, and you are right when you say that what works for one person doesn't necessarily carry over to another. But you would significantly improve your odds if you adhered to some basic rules, which are no-brainers."

CHAPTER 6

A Sullen Mikey

September 2, 1980

"Mom, there must be something going on with Mikey," said Jennifer. "When he returns from work, he heads straight to his room and only leaves it for the bathroom. He doesn't talk to anyone and looks pretty depressed."

"I know, Jen. This has been going on for months. He stopped joining me for our late-night chat and coffee. Whenever I ask him if everything is all right, he says it is, so I don't inquire further. Even today, his 20th birthday, he didn't say two words to me. We have a cake for him. I hope he'll leave his room to blow out the candles."

"He seemed to have recovered from that awful business with Sarah and the disclosures, and he is long over Olivia."

"Jen, this has nothing to do with Olivia. I have surmised it is a personal matter. Yet, Mr. Blakely told Adam that Mikey is one of the best workers he's ever employed. Mikey is the produce manager now. He did say he is reticent, though."

"Blakely said the same thing about Alejandro. Maybe Mikey's unhappy with that dead-end A&P job," opined Jen. "He should be in college. I mean, he was a pretty good student in high school."

"Jen, he was a lot more than pretty good. He earned higher grades than Adam, and it wasn't even close. This was true in grammar school and throughout high school. Mikey's class ranking at his Cliffside Park graduation was sixth. Adam's was 73rd. I think there were 260 graduates in Adam's class and a bit more in Mikey's. You must have been in your own world when all that business about a scholarship came up."

"What happened with that? I think I remember Mikey saying he didn't care about something."

"You only heard part of it, Jen. Mikey did his best to suppress any conversation about it. His high school guidance counselors were beside themselves, trying to get him to take advantage of numerous scholarship offers. He could have gone to some of the best colleges in the country. Adam tried to convince him, but Mikey curtly told his brother to mind his business. One of the counselors, a lovely Irishman named Jim Ferrie, was at the house three times. He loved Adam and developed the same feelings for Mikey."

"Wow, he traveled to Fairview to speak with Mikey?"

"Mr. Ferrie lives a few minutes away in Edgewater. His house is appropriately next to a church. He reminded me of your grandfather – always jolly and liking his drink. I think he lives with his sister. There wasn't anything that man wouldn't do for you. Your dad liked him a lot."

"I can't believe I am Mikey's sister, and I never knew of this."

"Jen, we have a wonderful family in some ways, but in others, everyone is caught up in their affairs. Mikey was deeply troubled that year. He wasn't nice to Adam and told me he had a deep-seated personal matter that he wasn't willing to discuss with me.

I pressed him once, but after he cried, I backed off. I assumed it had something to do with Olivia. My first fear was that he got her pregnant."

"I saw how he treated Adam, but I also knew he loved him. He still loves him. Mikey was so complicated back then, but he still is now. Mom, did he say he would eventually attend college?"

"Yes, he did, Jen. He said he would submit his applications after he had solved his issues. As you know, your dad and Mikey had a strained relationship, so Mikey didn't get pressured by him. But your father was so sad about it. He couldn't understand how someone so brilliant could delay a college education."

"Wow, I never realized that, Mom. "I always thought Adam's excellence in literature and the arts made him the brighter student. I didn't know we had a scholar of that caliber living in this house."

"Jen, Adam wasn't too far behind Mikey in English, history, and the arts, but in algebra, science, and physical education, Mikey was ahead by miles. Adam barely passed those subjects. Of course, he did graduate in the upper quarter of his class, but Mikey was among the elite few. Adam always said Mikey was extremely gifted and much more intelligent than him. Mikey's teachers always praised him. His mischievous ways made some people think he wasn't academically inclined. But his perform-ance proved just the opposite. He is a great speaker, and his vocabulary is outstanding. We have long known this, especially hearing his devious manipulation of us in our late-night chats about Adam."

"I remember that Mikey was a great student in Lincoln School as well," said Jennifer.

'Oh, yes. He wasn't far from getting the valedictorian. A few teachers there didn't care for his reputation as a bully. The award went to an Asian girl, and an Italian-American girl won second place. Mikey had the third highest average, overall."

"Salutatorian is second place," said Jennifer.

"Yes, that's it. I had forgotten the name. For the most part, Mikey was liked in Lincoln. His teachers were charmed and predicted he'd land a high-paying job."

"Wow, he was third in junior high and sixth in high school! Mr. Shelley had Adam and Mikey in his classes. What did *he* say?" asked Jennifer.

"Mr. Shelley is crazy about Adam. They are the closest of friends. But he told me at the senior year Parents' Night that studies came naturally for Mikey and that he thought he was far more well-rounded. He told me a nice Irish boy like him should attend Notre Dame. But of course, we all know Mikey tuned out after he graduated and said he wanted to take a year or two off before going to college. It has been almost four years, and no college is in sight for him. It's such a waste."

"Mom, he spends all his free time listening to his records and reading. Of course, he smokes cigarettes and drinks beer a lot, too. Maybe he will eventually return to school."

"Have you noticed what he's been reading, Jen?"

"When he's at work, his door is usually locked. But sometimes he forgets. Sometimes I turn the knob. Last week, I saw a copy of *Anne of Green Gables* on top of his bureau. The bookmark was wedged about two-thirds in," said Jennifer.

"Adam loved that book. There are a bunch of sequels. I bet he recommended it to Mikey. But I never would have figured Mikey would be interested in it. I think its core readers are girls. I wonder what type of music he's been listening to lately?"

"Mom, he usually keeps the volume low, but I heard Fleetwood Mac's *Rumors* the other night. And I believe I also heard songs from the soundtrack of *My Fair Lady.*"

"The *My Fair Lady* soundtrack is a curious choice. It was so perfect for Adam, but for Mikey, no, I couldn't have predicted it. Still, tastes do change over time. "

"Mom, do you think Mikey may have turned gay?"

"Positively not, Jen. From when he was 14 and up to the present time, his stash was always of women, clothed or nude. He hasn't ever shown any interest in boys or men. I think this would have been evident a while back if he did. Mikey is crazy for girls and women. And then there was Olivia. She was far from the best partner, but he had fun with her. She physically abused him, though."

"His changing tastes are surprising," said Jennifer.

"Jen, I'm not sure we ever knew Mikey's tastes. He kept them private. All we saw or heard was bluster. We knew only what he wanted us to know. That's the kind of person he always was. On the other hand, Adam has always been an open book."

"Mom, I believe Mikey is lovesick. He left a copy of a poem on the couch in the living room. I found it there last week and have held on to it since then. Let me get it," said Jennifer as she left for her room.

"Here it is. The title is *Love's Philosophy.* Percy Bysshe Shelley wrote it."

"Percy Shelley is one of the great poets. That much I do know," answered Carol, quickly scanning the poem. "It is so beautiful. Those last four lines suggest the poet yearns to be kissed."

"I think Shelley meant that no matter how beautiful things were, the romance must happen, or nothing matters," answered Jennifer. "Shelley's wife was the woman who wrote *Frankenstein.*"

"Yes, I remember," Carol answered. "So, who is Mikey in love with? He never goes anywhere. Is it possible it could be someone at the store?"

"Mom, it is possible, but I think it's doubtful. Mikey is the type to act, not wait. Anyway, the only people he sees otherwise live in this house. Everyone is either related to him or already taken. But of course, there are only Sarah and me." Jennifer chuckled.

Mikey started working in the A&P at the beginning of 1980. His dad offered him a position at the Clifton security office, but Mikey declined, insisting he preferred to work locally. Sometime after he asked his brother about any openings at the supermarket, Adam contacted the store manager, Harold Blakely, who advised him to have Mikey come in and fill out an application. Adam had continued a friendship with his former boss, even after leaving to take his teaching position, and sometimes stopped at the store to say hello and briefly chat. A month later, Mikey was hired in grocery. He was transferred to produce after that department became short-handed because of a termination. Mikey felt comfortable stocking the bins with fresh fruit and vegetables and was often complimented for maintaining clean and aesthetically pleasing displays. After a few months, he was entrusted with organizing inventory in the stockroom. He unloaded delivery trucks, but Blakely preferred he supervise those undertakings rather than participate.

CHAPTER 7

Exploding on Susan

A week after Susan Clarke discovered Adam was a bullshit artist, she resolved to be even firmer in a follow-up visit to the Furanos. If she needed to bully him, so be it. Wearing kid's gloves with Adam was a losing strategy.

"Adam, we need to schedule a meeting with Dr. Grieco. Sarah told me you've been having serious problems, much as I predicted you would."

Sitting at the table drinking a Bud, Adam exploded.

"Susan, I don't give a fuck what you say! I'll decide what needs to be done. I've had enough of your negative energy! There will be no meeting with Dr. Grieco!"

Susan rose.

"Goodbye, Adam. I wish you the best, but don't expect to see me again. I'll still communicate with Sarah over the phone, but I think I best stay clear of this house."

"Fuck you, Susan! Don't let the door hit you on the way out, asshole!"

With tears rolling down her face, Susan thought as she descended the stairs.

I have long favored the wrong brother. Carol was right all along. I'm glad I finally found out who he is. Adam is vulgar, selfish, and ungrateful. I hate him and never want to see him again.

"How dare you talk to Susan like that!" Sarah yelled. "How dare you! Susan is one of your best friends. She's one of *our* best friends! Seeing you succeed has obsessed her for the longest time!"

Hearing the commotion, Saoirse ascended the stairs.

"Saoirse, you missed the terrible words your father used against our dear friend Susan!" exclaimed Sarah. "He should be ashamed of himself!"

"Beauty, Susan is a bad person," said Adam. "We are all better off not seeing her anymore."

"I should leave this room now," said Sarah, bolting to her bedroom.

"Adam Sean, your behavior is deplorable. I never expected to witness anything like this," said Carol.

"Daddy, I like Susan a lot. Please tell her you are sorry. She loves you, Daddy."

"I'm sorry, beauty," said Adam. "I said some words I didn't mean. I wish I could take them back. I'm not happy with Susan's involvement with my teaching career. She needs to mind her own damn business. But I was too harsh."

"Susan is as invested in your teaching position as you are," said Carol. "Anything she tells you is for your good. Do you think she would say anything to hurt you deliberately?"

"Mom, I know she tried to help. But I thought she was too forceful," Adam said, lighting a cigarette.

Saoirse left to speak to her mom.

"I'm sorry, Adam Sean, but sometimes the only way to get through to you is being forceful," said Carol. "You have been stubborn since you were a child. When you get it in your head to do something, nobody can change your mind. We were forced to go along with you on your every whim. Luckily, it all worked out. But school is a different story. If you don't do your job, you will be replaced. You can't expect education professionals to go along with your carelessness."

"Mom, that's bullshit, and you know it. They hired me to do a job. Everyone has a different style. I'm confident with mine. I'm sorry I spoke as I did to Susan, but she should go her way, and I'll go mine. She's showing me disrespect, and I don't fucking like it one bit!"

"Adam, I don't know what to say anymore. You've changed. You're aggressive and always use foul language. You can't take criticism anymore. I fear you've developed bipolar disorder. First, the stutter, and now this."

"Mom, if that's the case, I welcome the change. I need to stand up for myself. So Susan doesn't like it. Tough shit for her. She's not my fucking wife!"

"No, but I'm your fucking wife!" screamed Sarah, reentering the living room. "I'm not a fan of the new Adam, and I won't tolerate you speaking like that to Susan. She's not a piece of shit. You embarrassed the family today. I fear she will stay away a long time."

"Who gives a shit? I don't," said Adam, his anger rising again. "She should mind her fucking business!"

"Daddy, I thought you said you were wrong," said Saoirse.

"I guess I was wrong, beauty. As I've gotten older, I've developed a bad temper. Susan will never forgive me for what I said, so I need to move on. I won't ever forget all she did for me."

Adam flipped the tab on another Budweiser.

"You smoke and drink too much, Daddy."

"Beauty, I enjoy my vices. Still, I hope *you* won't take them up

59

when you get older. Our family is partial to these habits."

"Yuck," said Saoirse.

"Adam Sean, you know damn well Susan is a forgiving person. So stop talking shit," said Sarah, whose vulgarities were encouraged by Adam's regular use of the words. "Tomorrow, I will drive you over to her home. You will apologize."

"I can't do that," said Adam.

"Adam, you must. There is nothing more to be said."

"Sarah, I will never apologize to Susan! Never! I want that cunt out of my life!" he exclaimed, immediately backpedaling on his assurances to Saoirse. "Now, end this!"

"You are a monster, Adam! Please don't come to our bedroom! Good night!" Sarah yelled, storming out of the room. Adam's daughter witnessed his foul language explosion, as did Jay, who listened at the bottom of the stairs and watched Susan leave the house.

"Adam, is everything all right?"

"I'll be right down, Jay. Let me get a few beers. Beauty, I'm sorry you had to witness this disagreement. Please comfort your mom."

Saoirse kissed Adam. "I love you, Daddy."

Adam returned the kiss, grabbed his cigarettes, lighter, and a six-pack from the fridge, and headed downstairs.

"Hey man, you lost it on the professor," said Jay. "What an ugly scene."

"Jay, I've had it with that fucking cunt," Adam exclaimed, lighting up and pulling the tab on his Bud. "Take one, brother."

Jay dislodged a can from the plastic ring and placed the other four Budweisers on the table.

"You need to calm down, bro. Nobody wins here."

"Jay, that bitch meddled in my business for the last time," said Adam, taking a deep drag on his cigarette. "I am putting my foot down with Sarah. Susan is not allowed in this house again. If I see her here, I'll file for divorce."

"Man, you have changed so much. Don't get me wrong, I love the change. And I love that the real you emerged," said Jay, raising the can to his mouth. "But, you and Sarah have the perfect marriage. I never heard you talk about divorce before, even jokingly."

"Years ago, you said the real me was a girl! How fucking sick was that?"

"I regret what I said. I was misled and ill-informed. You are a proud macho guy."

"Anyway, Sarah is insisting I apologize to that bitch."

"Maybe Sarah is right," said Jay.

Adam's face contorted with anger.

Jay added, "I'm sorry, man. I don't know the whole story. You probably have a good reason to be furious."

"I do, Jay. Susan attacked me on my teaching methods. She made me feel fucking worthless. She thought she was trying to help me but came off as arrogant. She was always that way."

To disuse Adam's anger, Adam told his brother what he wanted to hear.

"I've always thought so as well. Man, there is no reason why you should accept disrespect from Susan or anyone. I'm with you, bro. But please don't lose your head over this. Sarah comes before everybody."

"You are right about that, Jay. I need to give her space to cool off. Can I crash on the couch?"

"Sure, I'd be honored. You're looking fabulous. That gym is doing wonders."

"I'm bench pressing my weight now," said Adam.

"Wow! And you gained. How much do you weigh?"

"One-hundred-sixty-five, the most I've ever weighed."

"I weigh 160," said Jay. "Come on, tough guy, let's arm wrestle at the table. I'm sure you'll enjoy trying to get revenge on me for past years."

"Sure, I'm game," said Adam.

"Ready, go!" exclaimed Jay after the boys lined up, clasping hands. Jay gained the upper hand immediately, but Adam rallied. Twenty seconds later, he took Jay down.

"I never thought I'd see this day," said Jay, admiringly.

Adam grinned. "I couldn't have done it without weights and the exercise coach."

"Don't fool yourself, brother. You always had this ability. It lay dormant because you lacked self-confidence. Any weakling can become strong if they work at it. Well, not quite anyone, but over half, I surmise. This will be the last time I ask you to engage with me in arm wrestling."

"You mean because you might lose to a girl? Remember what you once said about me? Do you fucking remember, Jay?"

"Man, I'm sorry. That's the past. Your body physique is becoming more and more muscled every day. I'll make this prediction. In four more months, you'll bench press 30 to 40 pounds more than your weight."

"Shit, I don't know about that, Jay."

"I do. Your current development proves it's working. I know you are fiercely committed to it, right?"

"Five nights a week," answered Adam, dragging on his cigarette. "I have a great coach, too. He has become my best friend."

"He must be a Superman type."

"Dave is nothing like that. I'm stronger than him overall, and I bench press more. He's afraid of me."

"Does he give you a hard time about the smoking?" asked Jay.

Adam laughed.

"Fuck no!" he smokes, too, exclaimed Adam. "We go out together on our breaks. He also loves his brewskies. We share something else, too," said Adam, squeezing his fingers to his lips to denote the illegal practice.

"Cool, man!" exclaimed Jay. "Be careful. The Fairview cops might bust you."

"We smoked in his car, parked behind a fence in the back of the building. I also did lines of blow with him at his apartment."

"Cocaine? Wow, I don't believe it! You better be careful. You could have a panic attack. I feel scared. Adam, this is terrible. I've only smoked pot once. Does this guy live in Fairview?"

"You don't know what you're missing, Jay. No, he lives in North Bergen."

"Does Sarah know about this?"

"Yeah, I told her everything. She said I was hopeless and wasn't surprised. Sarah said I have the most addictive personality of anyone she's ever met. But she made me promise I wouldn't go beyond pot in the future."

Adam opened another Budweiser.

"I am thinking, Adam. Wouldn't it be great if you kicked Jimbo's ass for what he did to you? You'd destroy him."

"Jay, I would never hurt him. He has been my friend for so many years."

"But you have finally admitted to yourself what he did, right?"

"Yeah, he tried to fucking kill me! He wanted me dead! You think I don't know that?"

"Oh man, I'm so sorry I brought it up, brother," said Jay, rushing over to embrace Adam. "Please forgive me. What I said was so terrible."

"How could I have said those terrible words to Susan? Jay, I am a fucking piece of shit. Please help me."

Jay helped Adam from the table chair to the couch. He wedged a pillow under the intoxicated man's head. Adam closed his eyes and whimpered. Jay dashed up the stairs and knocked on Sarah's door.

"Sarah, he's crying his eyes out."

"He's drunk, right?"

"Of course. He had five cans so far. He said he can't believe he said such terrible things about Susan."

"I expected this," said Sarah. She turned to Saoirse. "Sweetie, go down by your sisters. Maybe you can play a game."

"How about Parchesi, Mom?"

"Good choice, honey."

After Saoirse departed, Sarah used the bathroom and then followed Jay downstairs.

She pushed Adam's head so it rested on her lap.

Adam opened his eyes and blubbered.

"I'm so sorry, Sarah. What I said to Susan was so horrible. Sarah, please forgive me. What am I going to do? Sarah, I did a bad thing. I'm different now."

"Yes, Adam Sean. The way you are now is who you are. You just took a little longer to get there. You did an awful thing. We will go to Susan's apartment tomorrow, and you will apologize."

"Will you give me my cigarettes?" asked Adam.

Sarah handed him his lighter and pack of Marlboro.

"Maybe Susan will turn me away."

"Oh, Adam, Susan loves you. But I'm sure she is deeply hurt. I'm certain no other person has ever talked to her like that. When you finish your session at the gym, pick me up. Are you interested in attending mass tomorrow? You haven't gone in a month. That's another old routine that seems to be fading."

"Sarah, how about if I go next week? I miss chatting with Father Peter on the church stairs after mass."

"Next week will be fine. Mom and I will be going food shopping before twelve. The girls would like you to play some games with them."

"I would love to. Please get four six-packs," Adam said. "There isn't a can left."

"Of course," said Sarah, puckering her lips. Jay slowly shook his head.

***

"My dear friend, Adam Sean, cried himself to sleep last night. He wants to apologize for the monstrous things he said to you," said Sarah into the receiver.

"Sarah, I'd be lying if I told you I wasn't extremely hurt," Susan answered. "Nobody ever said those words to me, not even my dad or my brother. Adam is vulgar. I am unsure I wish to speak to him."

"This is what he has become, Susan. Would you be willing to forgive him?"

"Sarah, honey, I've always been fond of Adam. But last night, when I left your home, I told myself I hated him. I wasn't lying, but I later knew it was my anger talking. I know now that he will do as he wants, but maybe I could convince him to compromise. In answer to your question, I will forgive him, of course. Your family is a major part of my life. I have so many wonderful memories."

Sarah sniffled.

"Susan, you were the last person who deserved what happened to you last night. Adam has a mean temper."

"Sarah, let me guess. Adam's good side came out after he got drunk."

"Bingo."

"So sad. Having gone through it myself and sometimes allowing it to return, I am not the best one to point fingers."

"He is exactly like my dad," Sarah said.

"Honey, it seems you were destined for these kinds of people. My crystal ball tells me there will be a major change."

65

"Susan, you mean Adam will stop drinking?"

"Hardly, Sarah. I'm afraid there is zero chance for that. Adam has an addictive personality. Alcohol is a major part of his life. The best you could hope for is some measure of moderation or control. I foresee his teaching job helping him to focus. I'm not sure what the change will be. Maybe I'm just talking out of my, you know what. And since you never had the problems Adam and I have had with drinking, you can't possibly understand them."

"Susan, I've tried to understand since I was a child. Dad used to get plastered with his Wall Street buddies after work. He missed some days, but his supervisory position ensured he wouldn't be penalized."

"I understand," Susan said. "Adam doesn't have that luxury. He must appear every day before his classes."

"Susan, I've waited to tell you one other thing, which is important. I feel Adam was wronged by several people, myself most prominently. He may have been right to rebel and to move as far away from what he was as possible. He may now be seen as extreme, but given all that happened, can anyone fault him?"

"Sarah, I'm sure I won't care for the new Adam, but I fear you are right."

CHAPTER 8

Taking Control at Bergen Tech

On a Monday morning in October, Adam resolved to take control of his classes. After the students in his first-period class arrived, they typically milled around, in no rush to sit.

"I want everyone to get in your fucking seats right now!" the teacher shouted as he opened the top drawer of his desk and pressed the start button on a tape recorder.

Some of the female students looked at each other with half-smiles. The boys were turned on by the audacity of a classroom teacher using vulgarity since they assumed its use, by extension, would allow them to talk similarly.

"I have a story to tell you all," said Adam. "I expect your full cooperation. Anyone interrupting me will be fucking evicted and sent to the principal's office. I won't take bullshit from anyone, you got that?"

The class liked where the talk was going. Any teacher who risked getting terminated for using inappropriate language in a classroom was a cool dude.

"As you all know, my name is Adam Sean Furano. But none of

you know anything else about me besides that this is my first year of teaching and that I am married and have three daughters. Some of you think you can do as you fucking please. You can forget that shit. It won't work anymore! You see, Bergen Tech sophomores, your English teacher almost left this world in 1971 at age 17."

The students stared ahead after hearing such a shocking revelation. Many assumed their teacher had contracted a sickness. A few thought he may have been a victim of violence. Either way, they were spellbound.

"As a teenager, I lived close to Palisades Amusement Park. I thought I was a lucky teen to have such a place at my fingertips for fun and games. During the week before the park closed, I decided to ignore the advice of my girlfriend, now wife, and spent a weekend day with my best friend, Jimbo. We hung out, went on the rides, smoked cigarettes, and played some chance stands. At that age, I was a fucking wimp. I was frail and uncoordinated. Though Jimbo was my best friend, he bullied me. A fateful event occurred in the amusement park that day. From what I was told, it was an event plastered all over the newspapers and television stations that night and for a week afterward."

The students' eyes widened.

"Jimbo and I went on the Wild Mouse, a small roller coaster next to the Funhouse. We sat in the front row of a car. Two girls sat in the back. When the coaster reached the top, we made a sharp turn, and I was thrown from the car. My body flew through the air, and I landed in a grassy patch near a wooden foundation."

A female student shrieked.

"Holy shit!" yelled one of the males.

"I found out a short while later that my friend purposely unbuckled the belt. He wanted me to fucking die because he was jealous that I had a wonderful family, and his own was a broken one. Today is the first time I ever admitted the truth about what caused my accident."

A girl in the front row sniffled.

"I was later told that my girlfriend – who became my wife a year later – arrived just about the time I fell off. They rushed me to Englewood Hospital in an ambulance. She insisted on taking the ride. I was informed she screamed the whole way, but I didn't hear her. I was in a coma."

Two female students wiped tears from their eyes. A male covered his face with both hands.

"I remained in the coma for nearly a week. For two days, doctors told my parents it was likely I wouldn't make it. When I regained consciousness, the medical professionals likened it to a miracle. The event traumatized me. I receded into myself. I later developed a severe stutter. My depression led me to drink heavily. Around that time, I got married because my wife got pregnant. I was only 18 when Sarah and I tied the knot. She was 19. I spent some time in rehab because of my heavy drinking. I started college, and after four years in Bergen Community and Jersey City State, I received my degree. But my time there was difficult. My body was slow to develop, and my voice was high-pitched. I was seen as a femboy, and my physical appearance reflected this. My taste in books, movies, and music supported this perception. But guess what? I didn't want to be a fucking femboy! My family read me wrong. All of us go through changes. My tastes sent the wrong signals. In the beginning, I accepted it. An appointment was made for me at a salon, where a woman tortured me and gave me a nose ring. I better never meet that fucking bitch, or I'll give her a crew cut!"

The class cheered and was anxious to hear more.

"The worst thing you can do to a man is emasculate him. I don't blame Sarah. She misread me. But she was far from faultless. A year after we had Saoirse, my wife gave birth to the twin girls,

Michele and Carol. Shit, there was no fucking way my family would end up being five girls. Recently, I started working out at a gym. I do about two hours a night for five days. I lift weights and am working with a trainer. With aerobics and bodybuilding, I'd forever put to rest who I am. I've been looking at bikes recently and dream of purchasing a Harley. Have I rebelled? Fucking A! If I can survive falling off a roller coaster and the misguided attempts by others to alter my gender perception, I can tell you that teaching English to high school students will be the easiest thing I've ever attempted. Whether you become a carpenter, plumber, electrician, or take up culinary arts, you need to be literate, and you need to appreciate literature and develop a good vocabulary. My mission is to make you the best you can be, and I'm not taking any shit! You will address me as Mr. Furano while you are in the classroom. I am a proud Italian-American who likes hearing my last name spoken. You are free to call me Adam outside the school."

The class erupted. Adam's calculated risk reaped immediate dividends, though he could have been fired on the spot had a school official witnessed his vulgarity. Based on one speech, the tenth graders concluded they were lucky to have the coolest teacher ever and a person with a storied past. After he stayed on the script with the other four classes, it was clear that respect for him was uniform. No other teacher ever revealed intimate personal information about themselves as Adam did.

The next day, Adam explained that he was changing how the class would be taught. He presented an extensive reading list. Students were instructed to read any novels or plays on the list and to prepare for interviews on Fridays every week. Students raised their hands and sat in a chair next to the teacher's desk after being recognized. Adam would ask about six or eight questions to be sure the student read the book and wasn't trying to bluff his way through the interview. Adam wrote down the page total of the book on index cards he had made for each student. At the end of the marking period, he added page numbers for each student. Any student reading 2000 pages earned an A. If they read 1700, they received a B. If they read 1300, they'd get a C. The grade for reading comprised three-quarters of the final grade for the class. The other quarter was the cumulative test average for the vocabulary tests and some grammar homework grades.

"I will give you all a participation grade for the discussion following my film showings. Up until a few years ago, I was a fanatical filmgoer. Much of my personal life is different now, so I rarely go to movie theaters anymore, but frankly, other activities interest me more. As some of us get older, our tastes change. As a teenager, I liked romantic songs and show music, but now I'm into heavy metal, which is real music. I can't believe I used to enjoy such crap in my early years. I once serenaded my wife on a seashore vacation with John Denver's *Annie's Song*. And I got teary-eyed when I sang Jim Croce songs. I am embarrassed to admit I sang songs from *The Sound of Music* in the shower. I was misguided in those years, but somebody up there was watching and helped show me the error of my way."

The students smiled approvingly.

"Still, I've retained a passion for the film classics and am preparing a shortlist of the films I might use. Most correspond to the books on the list. I aim to use two each semester, meaning eight for the school year. The films will be watched on a television screen with the signal from a VHS cassette player."

The students became competitive and read more to surpass their classmates. Before long, parents expressed delight that their kids were becoming voracious readers, especially since many had never shown any aptitude for academics. Womrath's Bookstore on Main Street in Hackensack posted Mr. Furano's reading list on the wall behind the register, a courtesy that turned into a wise business decision. However, it was a nightmare for attendance office secretaries who always handed late passes to students arriving late from the prep period excursions to the store, half a mile south on Hackensack Avenue. The school eventually banned students from leaving the building. Still, brisk sales continued on the weekend when Mr. Furano's teenagers used buses to reach the spacious two-story shop that featured a basement literature section in a rectangular pit below the floor.

***

Adam conducted interviews on Friday of the third week, and Brian Fischer appeared before him. The boy read S. E. Hinton's *The Outsiders,* a young adult novel about two rival Tulsa, Oklahoma, gangs of White Americans divided by their socioeconomic status. Following Adam's instructions, Brian brought up the copy of the book, at which point Adam pulled out a card from a stack that contained questions for that title. Sometimes, the instructor asked questions from the top of his head.

"I will start with a general question, Brian. The author has written three other acclaimed novels. Can you identify them?"

"That Was Then This is Now, Rumble Fish, Tex."

"Awesome, Brian! *Tex* just published last year. Who is Ponyboy Curtis?"

"Mr. Furano, he's the book's narrator. He's 14 and an excellent student. Ponyboy is a Greaser and reads a lot."

"Excellent, Brian. I hope you are modeled after him. Now tell me where Sodapop Curtis works."

"He works at a gas station."

"Dally Winston?"

"Dally is the toughest member of the gang. He lived for three

72

years on the streets of New York and carries a gun with him at all times."

"Describe Johnny Cade with as much detail as you can."

"He's 16. He's quiet, and he lives with his alcoholic and abusive parents."

Brian rubbed a tear from his eye.

"Is everything okay, Brian?"

After hesitating, the teenager leaned over and whispered into his teacher's ear.

Adam's eyes hardened and narrowed into slits.

"How long has this been going on, Brian?" he asked in a low tone.

"A few years."

"Brian, don't take the bus home at the end of the day. Could you wait for me outside the north entrance? As for the interview, you aced it. I am so proud of you. I advise that you next read *That Was Then, This is Now.*"

CHAPTER 9

Confrontation in Garfield; Susan's Reaction to Tape Recording

Brian waved goodbye to Hubert Stigliano, a veteran drafting teacher and former Board of Education president who lived on North 8th Street in Fairview.

"Brian, hop in my car. I am driving you home. I have your address on the attendance card. I know Outwater Lane well. That Russian Orthodox Church of Three Saints is beautiful."

"Are you sure this is a good idea, Adam? My stepdad can be mean," said Brian, making good on his teacher's clearance to be called by his first name outside the school building.

"Fuck your stepdad, Brian! Let's see how tough he is," said Adam, his face contorting.

"Adam, do you mind if I smoke?"

"Not at all. Go right ahead. I'll be joining you," said Adam, flicking his lighter on two cigarettes.

Adam took Hackensack Avenue south to the Little Ferry Circle, where he headed west on Route 46. After a brief tie-up near Teterboro Airport, the highway was clear to the Outwater Avenue exit. Within minutes, they were in front of the home, a poorly maintained, dirty-white shingled two-story house in a lower-middle-class neighborhood.

"Adam, I'm scared," said Brian, tearing up. "When you leave, he will hit me. I am much stronger than him, and if I retaliate, I might kill him. I'd end up in jail, and my mom's life would be destroyed."

"Brian, I can see you are powerful. But follow me," said Adam, ascending the four stairs to the front door.

Brian's mom, a husky, graying woman wearing a disheveled light blue blouse and dungarees, answered the bell.

"Mrs. Fischer?" asked Adam, forgetting that Brian's last name was the same as his real father's.

"My last name is Rovelli. My son is Fischer."

"Mrs. Rovelli, I know your son is Fischer, but I forgot you remarried. As you can see, Brian is behind me. I am his English teacher. We need to talk."

"What is your name?" she asked suspiciously.

"I am Adam Furano."

"Okay, Mr. Furano, you can come in. Please sit on the couch. I will call my husband."

"What's this all about?" asked Jim Rovelli, a slim, tallish man with beady brown eyes.

"Let me get straight to the point, Mr. Rovelli. Brian is a student in my first-period English class. I have strong reason to believe you've been abusing him. The boy is only fifteen. What kind of a man uses his hands on a child?"

"Now, who the fuck are you to question how I bring up my children?" yelled Rovelli.

"Who the fuck am I? I will gladly submit your name to school officials, who will notify the authorities. Would you like the police to ring your bell?"

Rovelli looked at Brian with fire in his eyes, causing the boy to sob.

"I show Brian respect. He's my wife's only child, and I have none of my own. His welfare is my main concern."

"I think you are dishonest, but Brian needs some room. He is coming back with me tonight. He will sleep with my family for the next week. If you notify school officials, I will initiate a child abuse case with the Office of Children and Family Services. You can get me in serious trouble, but if you do, I assure you I will do the same for you."

Rovelli knew he was caught between a rock and a hard place.

"Brian, look at me!" he exclaimed. "Is this man your English teacher?"

The teenager nodded demurely.

"Do you have proof of who you are?" asked Rovelli.

Adam pulled out his wallet and showed Rovelli his photo identification from Bergen Vocational-Technical High School, which had the words 'English teacher' printed across the bottom.

Rovelli nodded.

"Fair enough, Mr. Furano. I see you are Italian like me."

"And damn proud of it," answered Adam.

"My wife and I will go along with your plan," he said, answering for his spouse without asking her, even though she was Brian's biological mother.

Adam smiled, appreciating the man's leadership role in the familial decision-making. The teacher decided to throw Rovelli a bone. The next question defused the lingering animosity connected to this contentious affair.

"Brian, how much do you like your dad?"

"I adore my dad," said Brian. "He's my idol."

Jim Rovelli hugged his son and wept as his wife, Denise, wiped her flowing tears.

With one question, Adam Furano did more to foster familial

harmony than years of therapy could have accomplished. For Jim Rovelli, a man starved for affection, it was well worth losing his stepson for a week in return for a public declaration of love he had never received from the boy.

"He's an unconventional teacher," Rovelli told his wife as Adam pulled away. "But I don't trust any of them. They all teach liberal ideas to the kids and try to make them Democrats."

"Honey, you'd be surprised at what I just saw," said Denise. "There were two bumper stickers on his car. One said, Reagan for President, and the other said, Stop Voting for Democrats."

Jim's eyes widened, and then the man smiled broadly.

"I think our boy is in good hands. Maybe we can become friends one day."

***

The Furanos were wholly charmed with Brian, a powerfully built, exceedingly handsome boy of average height with a winning smile, curly dark brown hair, blue eyes, and a dimpled chin.

"So your dad was German?" asked Joseph.

"Yes, as is my mom; I'm completely *Deutsch*," the boy said. "But I hate the Third Reich."

"I can't blame you for that," said Carol. "But I think you must like German chocolate cake. I am going to bake one for you tomorrow."

"Oh my God, I love German chocolate cake. I haven't had it in over a year! You don't have to do that for me!"

"Young man, we will surprise you with some food dishes too," said Sarah.

After seeing others smoking, Brian lit up.

"It looks like you'll be right at home in this house," said Carol, smiling. "Do your parents know you smoke?"

"Yes, I've smoked in front of them for almost a year. They are both smokers. Neither one has given me a hard time."

"This house is a chimney," said Joseph. "I'm waiting for the day when I encounter a non-smoker affiliated with this household."

"Grandma Delaney doesn't smoke," said Saoirse.

"Sweet girl, your Grandma is a former smoker," said Joseph.

The kids fell in love with Brian immediately. He showed them all kinds of attention and enthusiastically honored their ongoing requests to play board games. When he told them his favorite was Clue, they obliged him with a marathon of the Parker Brothers game.

When little Michele asked Brian about his favorites, he answered Colonel Mustard, the rope, and the conservatory.

"Brian, since you love mystery, I hope you will read at least one of the Agatha Christie novels on the reading list," said Adam. "*And Then There Were None, Murder on the Orient Express*, and *The Murder of Roger Akroyd* are among her most popular classics."

"Adam, I have never heard of the last one, but I will read the first two."

"You are in for some treat if you tackle *Roger Akroyd.* It might be her masterpiece," said Adam. "The greatest shock ending ever!"

Brian bonded with Mikey, Rob, and Jay and enjoyed ample interaction with Jen, who thought the high schooler was irresistible. Saoirse encouraged the temporary boarder to interact with the reserved Jimbo. Carol and Sarah spoiled him at supper, always serving the boy elaborate meals.

"I love this family," he said before leaving with Adam on the teen's final day. Brian went to school every morning in Adam's car and rode back to his temporary home in Fairview at dismissal.

"I'm sure you'll be back," said Sarah. "Our kids will be depressed for quite a while."

"I'll be depressed too," said Brian before he tearily departed.

"I'm going to miss him," said Carol.

"Don't worry. Give it some time. I predict he'll live in this house permanently," said Joseph devilishly.

"If he did, what would you say?" asked Carol.

"I'd lay out the welcome mat," said Joseph. "I love that boy."

***

"Sarah, I'm floored," said Susan. "In all my years in education, I've never encountered such a radical teaching strategy," she added, after listening to the tape recorder of Adam's vulgar-laced lecture to his classes. "And yet, if I were a student, I think I'd fall in love with such a teacher."

"Susan, he has them eating out of his hands now. He did it much faster than Mark Thackeray did in the movie *To Sir with Love.* Heck, maybe that picture inspired him. He watched it many times."

"The teacher in that film didn't use vulgarity, but times are changing. This is 14 years later," said Susan. "I suppose the school administrators will turn their cheeks, especially when they get positive feedback from parents expressing delight their kids are reading."

CHAPTER 10

Alejandro and Yolanda's Wedding at the Italian Coop

Yolanda completed the wedding arrangements over the phone in late October with Italian Cooperative Club board member John Sartor Sr, who advised her to choose the smaller basement space because the total number of guests was only 48, two under the minimum for an upstairs hall. The reception date was set for Saturday, November 15, at 6 p.m., a few hours after Father Alvarez would pronounce the couple man and wife at St. Joseph's Roman Catholic Church in West New York.

Josef and Ania's Wallington friends were invited, but his dad was too embarrassed to extend the invitation beyond the few essentials because of Alejandro's surname revision. The two Polish middle-aged couples invited were deeply saddened by Alejandro's repudiation of his birth name. Roughly a fifth of those invited were members of the Furano family, including Grandma Delaney and her three great-granddaughters. Jimbo's invitation boosted the total to eleven 76 Grant Street residents. Yolanda's dad, brother, maternal aunt, uncle, two paternal uncles, their wives, and eight cousins nearly brought the total to 30. Alejandro's parents and friends, Yolanda's West New York *amigas,* and Father Alvarez would fill the remaining seats.

Neither Yolanda nor Alejandro could afford the wedding. Josef and Ania paid half, and Yolanda's dad guaranteed the remaining $1,750. First, a tossed salad and rice, black beans, and sweet plantains would be served. The dinner choices were filet mignon, Chicken Francese, and salmon, each with parsley potatoes and string beans. A dish of *polvorones,* (Mexican wedding cookies) and the chocolate-layer wedding cake from Rudolph's Bakery in Fairview would be served for dessert. Yolanda preferred Hispanic main entrees, but the chefs at the Coop – an institution run by Italians in a community long dominated by Italian-Americans – weren't experienced in preparing Hispanic cuisine. The price also included an open bar, where bartenders would serve everything from traditional Mexican beers and tequila to margaritas and red wine.

***

The wedding day was overcast and dreary. Light rain fell throughout the morning, and though it was predicted to taper off, the afternoon remained damp and raw. Still, the mid-November 50-degree temperature was about the best you could reasonably expect for that time of the year, and it didn't impede outdoor picture-taking atop the cliff along Boulevard East in West New York, where the scenic backdrop of the Manhattan skyline was a photographer's dream. After breakfast, the Wisniewskis discussed their son's big day.

"Jakob, our son hasn't told me in words, but I saw some disappointment when he discussed the wedding plans last week."

"What was bothering him, Ania?"

"When he mentioned that his future wife's brother Alfredo was his best man, I noticed sadness in his eyes."

"Ah, of course. He feels Adam should have been the one, and I understand his feelings. Adam has been his best friend since they met six years ago. But Alejandro made the right decision, Ania. He should always put family first, and Alfredo will be the uncle of our grandchild. I like Adam, but I'm sure our son will become much closer to Alfredo and spend far more time with him. Family should always come first. Alfredo speaks the same language, lives in the same neighborhood, and will surely be a regular in their home. Having good friends is nice, but maintaining a very close male friend at the early stage of a marriage might not be a good thing."

"There is something else, isn't there, Jakob?"

Jacob pursed his lips. "Ania, yes, there is. A few weeks ago, I spoke to Yolanda over the phone. She was concerned about our son staying close to Adam. She felt, and I agree with her, that Alejandro would soon be a father, and she didn't want her husband to copy the way Adam presented himself. She felt the temptation would get stronger, and it would cause problems in their marriage. Yolanda isn't keen on that kind of man. She admires Adam and knows how Christlike he has been, how he and Sarah are happily married, and that he is the parent of three lovely young girls, but he is still a bad influence. Yolanda is right. You understand that, right, Ania?"

"Sadly, I do, Jakob. It is best they didn't continue a close friendship."

"Yolanda was even sterner. She felt that with her influence and encouragement, she could help their friendship fizzle out completely. She thought it would be best for all concerned that Alejandro didn't see Adam anymore. Yolanda is sure that when our son becomes closer to Alfredo and other friends from West New York after their child is born, he will completely forget about Adam."

"Don't you think it is cruel to encourage the end of a loving friendship? Alejandro would have never known Yolanda if it wasn't for Adam."

"Ania, we can't go by that. People meet others for all sorts of reasons. I counter that it was meant for Alejandro to meet Adam so he could find his soulmate in Yolanda. Alejandro doesn't need competition for affection, especially a friend who might compromise our son's fatherly image. Alejandro's family must always come first."

"Jakob, you are right. I allowed myself to go soft because of my feelings for Adam. But our son has endured so much and deserves a good marriage."

"I disagree with Yolanda's determination to make our son forget English completely, but at least I understand its reasoning. She made me promise only to use Polish when we speak. I haven't done that yet, but I think I will from now on. Yolanda feels that not being able to speak English will further distance him from Adam. Besides, Spanish is the only language Alejandro needs, other than our Polish communication."

"Jakob, I see the sense in all that, but wasn't Alejandro supposed to decide the best man?"

"Yes, Ania. The tradition is that the groom chooses. But Yolanda felt she needed to intervene. She said she wasn't even thrilled about inviting Adam and his family to the wedding, but she couldn't go that far and knew it would seriously upset Alejandro and cause problems."

"That would be too much, I agree," said Ania. "But wouldn't it have made sense to make Adam one of the ushers?"

"There are no ushers or bridesmaids. Yolanda decided to restrict the wedding party to a best man and maid of honor. She knew if she had ushers, it would be impossible not to choose Adam as one of them. She made another smart decision."

"I agree," said Ania. "It is sad, but it is the right choice for our son."

"Ania, we must move to West New York soon. This would end the last temptation for our son to see Adam, but more importantly, we must live nearby with our grandchild on the way. I hope Yolanda will allow us to babysit. I've grown to like Fairview, but it's time we moved on. I will inquire at the office tomorrow."

"I never wanted to move here in the first place," said Ania. "I grew to accept it but never cared for it like you did. I'm happy we will be leaving."

"Adam has brought our son much happiness for years, and we were right to move here so he could find Yolanda, but there was some sadness, too, and some of it quite recently."

"What do you mean, Jakob?"

"I didn't want to tell you this, but Alejandro had a meltdown in a movie theater last week. Sarah called me to explain. Adam convinced him to see an advanced screening of a new movie at the Fairview Cinema. The movie was *Ordinary People,* which was about a family torn apart when the older son drowned in a boating accident. There were two sons. The younger one tried to commit suicide, and the parents separated at the end. Sarah explained everything to me."

Ania squealed and cupped her hands over her face.

"How could Adam do such a thing? He had to know what it was about. And he knew about our tragedy. That was mean dragging Alejandro to see it."

"I feel the same way you do, Ania. Sarah apologized and said that Adam wasn't thinking it through. She said that Adam knew what the film was about but didn't know there would be flashback scenes of the accident."

"He used terrible judgment. A mistake like that could set Alejandro back for months or even years," said Ania.

"Sarah said that our son screamed and sobbed loudly. Some people in the theater got abusive and yelled at Alejandro to stop. Sarah said Adam recommended the movie to take his mind off the John Lennon murder. She said that he cried for days after the New York City killing of one of his favorite rock stars."

"I saw the television reports on Lennon," said Ania. "But that doesn't excuse Adam from dragging Alejandro to a movie that will cause our son nightmares. Alejandro doesn't need Adam in his life."

"I like Sarah and the rest of their family. The mom and dad are wonderful people," said Jakob. "But Alejandro must focus on his own family. I feel bad and will never forget the night we visited the Furanos after Pope John Paul II was elected. But we must consider the whole picture and our son's well-being."

"Jakob, you are forgetting one thing," said Ania.

"I know what you are going to say, Ania. He works at a job that Joseph Furano gave him. But who will bother him? He doesn't see any of the Furanos and makes his transportation. When Yolanda doesn't take him, he uses the bus. They say he is a great security guard, perfect for Spanish speakers."

"It seems it will be a little uncomfortable," answered Ania.

"I don't see why," said Jakob. "As long as he does his job, everything will be fine. Maybe he will find something else in West New York."

"Jakob, I'm surprised Yolanda arranged to have the reception in Fairview. Wouldn't it have been better to have found a place in West New York? She's giving the wrong signal."

"I spoke to Yolanda about that in the same conversation I mentioned to you before," said Jakob. "Yolanda reached her decision in late August, and the reservation was made a few weeks later. She thought about canceling it but decided it would be a kind of goodbye to the town, and she didn't want to forfeit the deposit."

"A deposit matters?" asked Ania incredulously.

"I agree with you, Ania, but I think it had more to do with Yolanda not wanting to go through the hassle of finding a new place. But don't worry. After the wedding, I'm confident Alejandro won't return here."

"How many in Yolanda's family know our son is Polish, and his name was changed?" Ania asked.

"From what I understand, only Yolanda's father, her best friend and maid-of-honor Jasmine Rodriguez, and Alfredo knew, and all enthusiastically supported Yolanda on the name change. Father Alvarez also knows the truth. Our future daughter-in-law realizes a secret of that nature can't be maintained forever, even if our son now looks as Hispanic as men born that way. The real challenge will be if their child is a boy."

"Why is that Jakob?"

"Ania, this is something else I kept from you. It is so wonderful, but I know you will get emotional. If the baby is male, his name will be Wojtiech."

Ania sobbed into her husband's arms, though in joy for the deserved tribute to their deceased child.

After gathering herself, Ania spoke.

"It should be Wojtiech Wisniewski."

"Yes, of course, Ania. That decision continues to leave a deep wound. But we need to accept it and move on. It's better to have half a glass than our empty one with Alejandro. There will be questions about a Hispanic child with a Polish first name. Wojtiech Dominguez will probably doom Yolanda's plans to keep everything under wraps, but she could hardly deny her husband this request. Who could?"

"What if the child is a girl?"

"Yolanda wants to name her Rosa after the friend who died of the drug overdose."

"You mean the girl who assaulted Adam in the parking garage? Don't you think it would be a terrible insult to him?"

"I thought the same, Ania, but Yolanda should get the call on the name of a girl child, and Alejandro agreed with her because he always believed the dead should be honored."

***

Father Alvarez delivered an emotional tribute to Yolanda at the end of the Spanish wedding at St. Joseph's. He referred to her as a beautiful girl inside and out, one he had the honor of baptizing.

A white stretch limousine was parked at the curb outside the church's doors. The newlyweds, Alfredo, Jasmine, Alejandro's parents, and Yolanda's dad, boarded, awaiting the final passenger: Father Alvarez. For the first time in his many years as a cleric, he agreed to ride with the couple he married to attend a wedding reception, but Yolanda was a personal friend, one he felt he must fully support. The St. Joseph's of the Palisades pastor was also moved by the groom's name change to his own.

***

"Will everyone please stand up?" asked the young emcee in Spanish. "Please welcome the best man and maid-of-honor, Mr. Alfredo Perez and Miss Jasmine Rodriguez."

Clad in a tuxedo and clasping Jasmine's arm, Alfredo lit the room with his broad, toothy smile. Wearing a green gown and holding a matching bouquet, the maid-of-honor maintained a brisk pace until she reached the stage, where she stood next to her partner, awaiting the main event.

"I want to introduce Mr. and Mrs. Alejandro Dominguez as husband and wife. Please give them a rousing ovation!"

The newlyweds took in the celebratory moment as they strolled to the center of the stage, awaiting the master of ceremonies to call Alejandro and his bride for the evening's first dance.

Ania wiped a tear, not only because her only son had tied the knot but also after hearing the confirmation of his name change.

Father Alejandro blessed the newlyweds and asked them to face each other.

"You have declared your consent before the church. May the Lord, in his goodness, strengthen your consent and fill you both with his blessing. What God has joined, men must not divide."

Yolanda's wedding song choice was a surprise to the guests. *How Deep is Your Love?*, a 1977 hit by the Bee Gees, was as American as apple pie and hardly the selection one would expect from a Hispanic couple at an ethnic wedding. Still, it was Yolanda's favorite song, and she insisted the vinyl be played as loudly as the equipment could allow.

Alejandro rested his head on Yolanda's shoulder, reversing the standard dance technique. Yolanda wrapped her right arm around his neck and spoke softly as she rocked him in a slow dance.

"*No llores mi amor. No llores.* (Don't cry, my love. Don't cry.)"

Everyone applauded after the closing lyrics *When they all should let us be/We belong to you and me.*

Following wedding traditions, Yolanda danced with her dad and Alejandro with his mom. When completed, they sat at the center of the head table to receive a toast and a short speech from the best man. Alfredo held up a glass to his new brother-in-law and told the gathering in Spanish that he was deeply honored to be chosen as the best man for his sister's wedding and was confident his sibling had found her soulmate.

Alejandro and Alfredo lit cigarettes as the disc jockey played Cuban and Mexican wedding standards. Several couples rose and advanced to the dance floor. Alejandro's eyes shifted to Adam's table. Though he didn't question his wife on who his best man should be and thought Alfredo was a fine young man, Alejandro's first choice by far was Adam, and he was suffering mightily over the snub.

"Sweetheart, Alejandro can't stop looking at you," said Sarah. "He looks sad. I know the reason, and I suspect you do as well."

"Alejandro made the correct choice, Sarah. Alfredo is his wife's sister. He'll be the uncle of his children. I've enjoyed a great friendship with him but could hardly expect him to choose me over his brother-in-law."

"Adam Sean, most of the time, the best man is the groom's best friend, not a relative of his wife. Besides, he only met Alfredo a short while ago. Honey, let's face it. Alejandro didn't make this decision. Yolanda did. I don't want to say what else I am thinking. Let's say she purposely didn't have any ushers to ensure you weren't chosen."

"Sarah, why would she fucking want to keep me out of the wedding party? She probably just wanted a smaller wedding."

"Oh, my sweetest, you are so naïve," said Sarah. "You can never think wrong of anyone. I don't want to hurt your feelings, but I'm sure I know what she was thinking. I am deeply saddened to say this to you, but I don't think you will see Alejandro much, if at all," raising her voice to overcome the volume increase when the disc jockey played Stevie Wonder's *Signed, Sealed and Delivered*, another favorite of the soul music-obsessed Yolanda. "Alejandro has a difficult life ahead of him."

"Sarah, I think wrong of plenty of people. I am not the same person I was. If I don't see Alejandro anymore, so be it. I won't be losing sleep over it."

"Honey, I hope I am wrong. You and he have been inseparable these past six years. It would be tragic for it to end."

Having listened to the discussion, Jay threw his weight behind Sarah's speculation.

"Sarah is right. Yolanda will rule Alejandro. He can't defend himself and will go along with everything she wants."

Ania whispered to Jakob.

"What was that you said about Adam? We haven't seen him since August. He has changed a lot."

"Ania, I am shocked. He must be lifting weights."

"I think we made a big mistake," said Ania.

"Maybe we did, but what's done is done," said Jakob. "It is still best for our son to concentrate on his family."

The opening strains of Roberta Flack's *The First Time Ever I Saw Your Face*, one of Mikey's best-loved songs, played.

Mikey approached Sarah. "My favorite sister-in-law in the world, will you accept a dance offer?"

"Mikey, first of all, I am your only sister-in-law. But I will certainly dance with you, dear brother-in-law."

Mikey smiled, holding Sarah's hand as she rose.

He pulled her close, signaling Sarah to rest her head on his shoulder. Mikey sang the lyrics and slowly danced. Carol noticed Mikey's romantic posture.

"I love you, Sarah."

"I love you even more, Mikey."

Something in the deepest recesses of Sarah's mind suddenly surfaced.

This was ordained years ago. Neither Adam nor Mikey remember the past. If my real name was Sally, they might well recall it. At some point, when the time is right, I will reveal the truth.

91

CHAPTER 11

Gill's Tavern

"Jay, how about we try a new place? I've heard some good things about Gill's Tavern in Cliffside. I'm amazed that none of us have been through its doors even once," said Adam, talking to his brother as they sat in the living room.

"Mikey told me he went there. He raved about the burgers."

"I wasn't exactly thinking about the food, Jay. But a nice juicy cheeseburger might be perfect with a mug."

"I hear you, bro. It's all about the brewskies, but as you say, one complements the other. What made you think of Gill's?"

"A friend I see around town occasionally, John Raffaele, recommended I try it. He said he's been a regular there for years. He also said that the woman who runs it, Sophie, is like a member of his family," said Adam.

"Eddie Ryglicki comes off as a family member, too, but it's nice to hear Gill's is the same," said Jay. "I am tired of the Polish-American Club. There are too many old fogies in that joint, though Mr. Wilcox is there a lot. He was my favorite teacher. I love that guy."

"Jay, when you mentioned the Polish-American Club, it reminded me of a funny story. My friend Peter Reilly once told me that back in 1973, when he was 21, he told his mom he was going out. When she asked him where, he said he was walking and might stop at the Polish-American. The mom wanted to know how much money he had in his pocket. He said one dollar. She urged him not to get drunk!"

Jay guffawed. "You could buy five beers for a buck in 1973. So his mom wasn't saying anything unusual. But a decade later, prices have gone up!"

"I don't remember if he went in, but the humor was priceless."

"Oh yes," said Jay.

"Fuck, if we like Gill's, we could make it our Tuesday night hangout," said Adam. "Of course, most importantly, we can walk there. Driving after some brews is chancy, especially if we have an accident. And we can introduce Rob to Gill's if we like the place."

"Adam, is there a place you don't like? You are a champion of all bars and eateries. When people criticized Swanee's, you were the first to mention how great the food was there."

"Jay, Swanee's gets a shitty rap because the inside isn't immaculate."

"Isn't immaculate?" said Jay, laughing. "Now, if that isn't the understatement of the year, I don't know what is."

"Some of the best places look shabby, but the food is terrific. How about that fucking dump Hagler's on Kinderkamack Road in Oradell? Or Harry's Corner in Little Ferry?"

"Those are two great examples, Adam. You and I have a long history at Harry's. What about that White Manna place in Hackensack? I like the burgers there as much as the White Castle sliders. Both are dumps, but the food is great!"

"I love White Manna burgers and like watching how they cook

94

them before you. They put the meatball on the grill and flatten it with a spatula. If you want onions, they mix them in. There's another White Manna on Tonnele Avenue in Jersey City. You and I went there once."

"I remember, Adam. We need to change the subject. I am getting hungry, even though I ate two hours ago."

"We can always try the burgers," said Adam.

Jay smiled as they left the house. Less than fifteen minutes later, they entered the bar.

Gill's Tavern, a famous Cliffside Park watering hole, was long known for succulent broiled hamburgers and the fanatically attentive stewardship of its beloved matriarch, Sophie Kolonics, a pleasant, saucy conversationist who treated patrons like family members. Locals had long started to call the place by her first name. Kolonics began working at the bar as a teenager under the tutelage of her dad, Polish immigrant Adam Gill, who built the bar in 1937 on the front lawn of his white stucco home on Bender Place, just off Palisade Avenue near Gorge Road. For the most part, the tavern was a meeting place for friends, many of whom desired to unwind and chat. Things rarely got out of hand because of intoxication, and a call to the police station – typical for Cliff & Chris, a bar located a few blocks north on Palisade Avenue – was exceedingly rare. The newbies mainly sought to sample the burgers; consequently, some became regulars.

Jay and Adam entered Gill's on a night when attendance was sparse. Four young men, nursing beers at the bar, smoking, and chatting with the owner, paused as they observed the two newcomers sit in two seats on the short horizontal side of the L-shaped seating configuration. One guy stared at Adam, trying to place the young man. Two other patrons greeted the young men with waves as Sophie laid out the red carpet.

"Who do I have the honor of meeting?" she asked.

"This is my brother Adam. My name is Jay. The honor is ours."

"Jay, can I ask how you heard about us?

"John Raffaele recommended you. He said Gill's is the best fucking bar anywhere," said Adam.

"Oh, Johnny! He's been a regular here for so long. I should hire him as our public relations guy. He usually sits where you guys are with his friend, Tommy Boylan. John doesn't mince words. That's what I like about him best. He also has an outrageous and cynical sense of humor."

"Shit, he does," said Adam.

"I am assuming you are from Fairview like John."

"Yes, that is correct, Sophie. John is a few years younger than me. I became his friend when we played softball on the same team," said Adam.

"What can I give you guys?"

"Two tap beers would be great," said Jay. "And we heard so much about your cheeseburgers. We'd each love one."

"People always praise our burgers," crowed Sophie. "Two coming right up. Onions and pickles?" she asked.

Jay and Adam nodded. "Thank you," said Adam.

Sophie opened a small floor-level white refrigerator, grabbed two hamburger patties, and placed them in the mini toaster oven to the right of the cash register. She filled two mugs with Budweiser on tap and slid them in front of the new customers.

Sophie placed a bowl of chips between them as they lit cigarettes.

"These are on the house," the matron declared.

"Thanks, good lady," said Adam. "I dig your holiday decorations," he added, referring to the artificial tree standing near the door, the mechanical Santa Claus on a windowsill, and the garland running between the bottles lined up on a multi-leveled wall display behind the bar.

"Why, thank you, young man. I appreciate that. I usually put them up right after Thanksgiving. Still, I only got to them this morning," Sophie said, referring to the December 2nd decorating, just hours before Adam and Jay appeared on their maiden visit.

"I'd like to put some coins in the jukebox."

"Go right ahead," Sophie said. Three songs 50 cents. We also have a Pac-Man machine and a bowling game available."

"Brother, how about you check out the juke and pick a song or two," said Adam.

"Adam, I'm good with any songs you choose."

"But I'd love to listen to some of your favorites," Adam responded.

"You choose brother. I like being surprised."

"I'm into heavy metal now, but I'll have to settle for the popular singles," said Adam.

Adam chose two recent songs, *All Out of Love* by Air Supply and *Sailing* by Christopher Cross, and a 1977 title, *You and Me* by Alice Cooper. He knew the Alice Cooper song was one of Jay's favorites, as was the *Lace and Whiskey* album it appeared on. Despite his reassurance to Adam, Jay wasn't the biggest fan of ballads, but when Alice Cooper was the artist, he listened raptly.

Adam noticed a Casper the Ghost statue standing near the bowling game. His eyes shifted to observe a couple making out in the darkened corner a few feet from the door to the ladies' room. He didn't care to explore, so his glance was fleeting.

When he returned to the bar, Jay said, "Please don't tempt me with Pac-Man. That game is highly addictive."

A short while later, Sophie served the burgers. Adam spread some ketchup on the inside of the top half of the bun and handed the Heintz bottle to Jay, who shook it until a red mountain formed on the paper plate, from which he could dunk.

"No wonder everybody praises them," said Jay between bites.

"This is so juicy and delicious."

"Fucking A!" exclaimed Adam, chowing down.

"I'm so happy you two young men are pleased," enthused Sophie. "I'd appreciate it if you would spread the word."

"Sophie, we'd be glad to and will, but the word out there is praise. That is what led us here," said Adam.

"Thanks again!" exclaimed the owner-proprietor, watching Jay and Adam finish the last of their food with beer. Both men smiled.

"Thanks for the Alice Cooper song," said Jay. "I need to hit the john."

As Jay entered the men's room, he saw a young woman who instinctively turned when a person approached. Jay thought inside the bathroom while he urinated.

Wow! That was Maureen. Rob's girlfriend. She's making out with another man. I didn't get too good a look at him, but I think he's dark, probably Hispanic. I'm surprised they came to this area. Maureen lives in Ridgefield Park. Maybe her new lover resides around here. But she is taking some risks, agreeing to go to a local bar. Perhaps she is hoping to get caught. I didn't realize she and Rob were on the outs. Then again, maybe Rob doesn't know what is happening and thinks everything is hunky-dory. I'm pretty sure she didn't recognize me.

After washing his hands and wiping them with paper towels, Jay exited, careful not to look again at the lovemaking. He took his seat at the bar.

"Shit, is everything all right, Jay," asked Adam. "You look like you saw a ghost."

Jay leaned over and whispered in his brother's ear. "Adam, I am going to step outside the bar. Please wait a few minutes, and then join me out there. I have something shocking to tell you."

Leaving a ten-dollar bill on the bar, Jay signaled to Sophie that he would be right back.

"Take your time," she said.

"Sophie, I need to speak to my brother. Everything is well. I love this bar," Adam said as he placed another ten next to his mug. "I'll be back in a jiffy."

The proprietor smiled, blowing a kiss.

Adam approached Jay, who lit a cigarette while leaning on a parked car.

"Please tell me nothing fucking bad is happening," Adam said, grimacing as he lit up.

Jay spoke softly. "Adam, Rob's girlfriend Maureen, is making out with a guy in the darkened corner near the bathrooms. I can tell you with all certainty that her partner is not Rob."

Adam squinted his eyes. His mouth was agape. He couldn't believe Jay's revelation.

"Holy shit! How fucked up is that? Jay, how sure are you that the girl you saw wasn't Maureen? I did notice a couple making out when I went to the jukebox. But I couldn't identify them. I didn't want to appear like I was prying."

"I am 99 percent certain. When was the last time you spoke to Rob? Maybe he and Maureen broke up, but he hadn't told you yet?"

"I spoke to Rob two days ago. He mentioned that he had plans to see a movie with Maureen at Ridgefield Park's Rialto this coming Saturday. I even remember the film's title, a slasher, *My Bloody Valentine.* Maureen loves horror."

"How many years have they been dating," Jay asked.

"I think seven. If my memory serves me right, they started in the tenth grade but were close as far back as junior high school. I refuse to believe their relationship is in trouble. They love each other deeply. I can't fucking believe this!"

"Adam, I think fate brought us to Gill's tonight. Someone wanted us to see what I just did. Why did we come here tonight rather than next week, next month, or even over the coming weekend?"

"You are right, Jay. Still, the last thing we want to do is to discuss any of this with Rob. Some shit might be happening between Maureen and him, something I don't know. I always thought they were the perfect couple."

"Adam, what we see in front of us is not always how things are. I've always thought Rob was a great guy, but there might be private issues between them."

"But, if so, why did she fucking tolerate him for so long?" said Adam.

"True, but maybe she's had enough. Then again, we might not know Maureen as well as we thought. It takes two to tango. Adam, I think we should go back inside."

The brothers returned to their seats. Jay signaled Sophie to top off their mugs.

About ten minutes later, Maureen and her lover emerged. They passed the brothers holding hands as they approached the door. A smiling Maureen turned around and looked at Adam.

"Honey, give my best to Sarah and the girls," she said. "I love both of you guys," she added, alternating glances at Adam and Jay before kissing her boyfriend and exiting.

The brothers were too shellshocked at Maureen's bold acknowledgment to respond, though they smiled and nodded at her request. Ten minutes later, they thanked Sophie for her hospitality, assuring her they would be back. They hardly spoke during the walk home, though they said hello to Frank Hiza, who locked the door to his delicatessen at 10 p.m.

Adam told his wife what happened at Gill's.

"So terrible," Sarah said, shaking her head.

CHAPTER 12

Rob and Maureen Break Up

Three days after the surprise encounter in Gill's early Friday evening, Rob phoned Adam.

"Adam, I need to see you in person. I feel like killing myself. Something awful has happened. Please, my best friend, I am at my lowest point ever."

Adam wasn't surprised to hear his friend's anguished plea.

"Rob, I will leave my house immediately and honk the horn when I approach the front of your house."

"Thank you, friend. I can't wait to see you."

Fifteen minutes later, Adam's Mustang arrived outside Rob's College Place home in Ridgefield Park.

"The bitch left me. She has another boyfriend. She's been cheating on me for quite some time," said Rob haltingly.

"Rob, I can't say how sorry I am. Jay and I knew about this, but we didn't want to break your heart."

"How could you have known?"

"Rob, I will explain, but I am only concerned about your well-being right now."

101

"Adam, what am I going to do? My parents want me to leave their home."

"Rob, why would your parents want that? Wouldn't they rather feel sorry for you at such a terrible time in your life?"

"Adam, I struck Maureen a few times during an awful argument. She came over here and informed my parents what I did. She gave me a courtesy I didn't deserve. She could have gone to the police station and pressed charges against me. Mom and Dad were furious and told me I must leave the house in two days. They said they didn't care if I was their son, as what I did was unforgivable. I've never gotten along with them. Today is the second day. Adam, I don't know where to go. I have my car, so maybe I can sleep in it. I took a leave of absence from my job but don't think I will return to it."

Adam pulled Rob against him and petted his hair.

"Did you pack up some clothes, Rob?"

"I filled two large suitcases. At some point, I need to return for my belongings."

"Rob, I advise you to bring the suitcases. One will fit on the back seat and the other in the trunk."

Rob went back into the house and quickly returned with his luggage.

"Where will you take me?" asked Rob.

"I want to stop at my house for a few minutes."

Rob wiped tears from his face and lit a cigarette. He offered one to Adam, who said he would wait until later. The man sobbed during the ride to Fairview. Adam drove with his left arm, holding his right one on Rob's shoulder. Adam returned to Grant Street a few minutes longer than it had taken to pick up his friend because of a minor tie-up on Route 46 East.

"Rob, I will be back in a few minutes. All will be well," Adam said, leaning over to kiss his friend. "Hang tight."

Sarah and Carol squinted at each other after hearing Adam's latest sponsorship of a friend needing a roof over his head. But both women knew that expressing reservations over Adam's humanist plea would be useless. They also were exceedingly fond of Rob and, in this instance, with the young man overcome by sorrow, felt obliged to honor the request.

"Rob, let's carry your luggage upstairs. You will be staying in our house. As you know, the couch near the window has a pull-out bed. You can live with us for as long as you want, even forever."

Rob wrapped his arms around Adam, nestling his head under his friend's chin. A few minutes later, each man carried a suitcase up the stairs. After setting them down, Adam led Rob to the recliner, urging him to rest. The traumatized former athlete buried his face in a cushion and sobbed. Carol heard the meltdown from the kitchen and alerted her husband in their bedroom.

"Carol, I feel sorry for this young man. He's Adam's friend, and I like him quite a bit. He's a former football player, and he's respectful and personable. But we don't have any more room in this house. I would love to help him, at least for a while, but we are so crowded here that we can't even add a pet, let alone a person. I feel bad, but there isn't anything we can do."

"Joe, he's dealing with serious grief. We would be inhuman to turn him away. I know our house is full. But we do have the living room for now. He could sleep on the pull-out bed.'

Joseph shook his head but realized his wife was right. This wasn't the time to ponder the implications. The boy was suffering and in dire need of help.

"I understand, Sarah, said Joseph, backpedaling. "Somehow, we were meant to be good Samaritans," he said, with an edge of sarcasm. "Our role in this world is clear. I don't regret letting Jay and Jimbo into our home, but now we have three grandchildren. After we add Rob, fourteen people will be living under this roof. The situation has practically become untenable."

"But Rob will only be temporary," said Carol.

Joseph sighed.

"It seems few decisions concerning this household are temporary. While I can't imagine Rob wanting to stay here for an extended time, everybody else is in it for the long haul, if you know what I mean."

"I know what you mean, Joe."

"Carol, did Sarah mention anything about Rob's relationship with his parents?"

"Yes, she said it is not good. They never got along. Rob admitted they were always hard on him. Yet, we've never seen a difficult side in him when he's visited our home."

"Carol, are you thinking what I am thinking right now?"

"Yes, Joe. He might be a different person than the one we are familiar with when it comes to living with him."

"Exactly, Carol. But we have no choice now, so we need to be optimistic. We have lost our living room for now, but I think that's a small price to pay for what it means for this young man."

***

Adam decided to keep silent about what he and Jay knew from their visit to Gill's. He surmised it wouldn't change anything and would drive Rob's anger to an eight on the Richter scale.

Rob didn't sleep the entire night. After she woke, Sarah prepared coffee and brought him a mug with milk and two sugars. Rob whispered the standard two words of appreciation but said nothing further. The emotional hit he had absorbed the previous day and the upheaval caused by the unexpected revelation left him benumbed. He opened a window and lit a cigarette as Adam, who had just woken up, entered the living room.

"Sweetie, I'll have your coffee in a jiffy," said Sarah from the kitchen.

"Thanks, Sarah," said Rob.

Adam encouraged Rob to place his clothes in the laundry room's hamper.

"I can't expect Sarah or anyone else in the house to wash and dry my clothes. I will take them to a laundromat. I seem to recall one near the school on Anderson Avenue."

"There are several on Anderson Avenue, but there is no way you will use them," said Sarah. "You are living with us. Carol and I do the laundry in this house. Adding your clothes to the mix is not a big deal. It is our pleasure," she added as Carol smiled and nodded from the kitchen opening.

"But it is not right," Rob persisted.

"Don't think about it again," said Sarah. "You are part of our family when you live in this house."

"What beautiful people, but of course, I've always known this," Rob responded as he set down his coffee mug and stubbed out his cigarette. Then he covered his face with his hands and wept.

"I don't know what to do. It isn't worth living anymore."

Adam rushed over to hug his friend.

"Don't ever think like that, dear friend. Many people love you. You will land on your feet after this temporary setback. There are always some obstacles in life. Shit happens."

"Oh, buddy," said Rob. "You don't understand. I've been with Maureen since junior high. We've been joined at the hip. We were meant for each other. Oh God, how could this have happened? She was my whole world."

Hearing Rob's grief-stricken words from the kitchen as they sipped their coffee, Joseph and Carol shook their heads sympathetically.

"I understand, Rob," said Adam. "You are going through the

worst time of your life. I'm sure Maureen is also having a tough time."

"Adam, your support means so much to me, but Maureen is happy. She's in love with her new boyfriend. I'm the last person she thinks about now. I knew something was wrong since the summer. When we went to Great Adventure, she made several calls from pay phones. She said she spoke to her parents and her girlfriend at work. She never called her parents or her girlfriend. She called Delfin."

"Delfin?"

"Yes, Adam. Delfin. Delfin Lugo, her boyfriend. She said she was calling her friend from work. But her friend was not a woman, but a man. She fell in love with a Hispanic man she worked with for about five years. I don't care if he was Hispanic, black, white, or Asian. Love is love. But I can't deal with the fact that it isn't me anymore and that she kept this relationship from me for so long."

"I know Maureen works at Jacques C. Schiff's in Ridgefield Park," Adam said.

"Yes, in the white stone building on the corner of Main Street and Mount Vernon."

"It looks like a bank," said Adam. "As you might remember, I've collected stamps since childhood. I've lost count of the times I nearly went to see some of their holdings. But for one reason or another, I never made it. My place for new stamps was always the philatelic window at the South Hackensack Post Office on Huyler Street near Teterboro Airport. And I sometimes go to a stamp shop in Palisades Park on Broad Avenue, across the street, diagonally from the Park Lane Theater."

"I know both of those locations," said Rob, rallying. "I think the stamp shop on the corner of East Brinkerhoff also deals in coins."

"Most of his business is in coins, but the proprietor's real passion is stamps. He collected them since he was young," said

106

Adam.

"I think I know why you never went into Schiff's," said Rob. "You knew Maureen worked there, and you didn't want to tempt her into giving you a discount."

Adam lowered his head.

"I'm not so sure that's true," he said.

"I am," said Rob. "Anyway, they've been dating for about six months. Delfin works at a desk in a cubicle beside Maureen's workplace. He sets up stamp auctions. He's a bright guy. I'm sure he'll be a great father to Maureen's children," he added, his voice breaking.

Sarah hastened back from the kitchen and assisted Adam in consoling Rob. They both hugged the sobbing man until his ducts went dry. The last thing Adam wanted to do was to discuss Delfin Lugo anymore, so he made another suggestion.

"Rob, how about a few games at Nungesser Lanes?"

"No bowling until you men have breakfast," Carol exclaimed.

"I think I've lost my appetite, Mrs. Furano," Rob said.

"Always Carol, young man. And I have a short stack for you with butter and syrup. Please try to eat. It's not a good idea to exert yourself on an empty stomach."

"Please," added Sarah.

Rob shook his head but made his way to the table.

Carol laid a plate of two pancakes, each about six inches in diameter, in front of Rob. Sarah brought a Spring Tree maple syrup bottle and a stick of Blue Bonnet butter on a tea saucer. She filled a large glass of Tropicana orange juice and set it next to the pancakes. The women repeated the process for Adam.

"I think you are a bacon and eggs guy, right?" asked Carol.

"Yes, I am. I like my Taylor Ham too, but I don't want to give you any ideas."

"Now we know tomorrow's breakfast," said the smiling Furano

matriarch.

"If I'm hungry, I'll buy my breakfast at one of the stores on the avenue," said Rob. "You've been much too kind already."

"As long as you are living with us, you'll have breakfast here," said Joseph.

"Thanks, Mr. Furano. But this is not necessary."

"I'd love it if you called me Joseph."

Rob nodded and ate his breakfast. When he and Adam were finished, they left the house and headed down Grant Street, crossed Fairview Avenue, and walked past the Part View Diner and White Castle before crossing John F. Kennedy Boulevard to access the glass doors of Nungesser Lanes.

CHAPTER 13

Combatting Depression

All the lanes were occupied, but Adam submitted their names to Yogi, who informed them they were in the second spot.

"Yogi, this is my good friend Rob Murphy. He was a star defensive lineman on the Ridgefield Park varsity team in 74 and 75."

"Pleased to meet you, Rob. You certainly look like a football star!"

"I'm equally pleased to meet you, sir. But Adam is way too kind. I wasn't a star. We had a great team in those years, mainly because of the offense. I guess I was adequate."

"I'm inclined to believe Adam," said Yogi, smiling. "So, how's that sweet princess doing?"

"Ya know, I feel guilty not bringing her," said Adam. "She loves this place."

"How many times has she bowled here?" asked Yogi. "She said the cutest things the last time I saw her."

"I brought her two more times, both on Saturdays. You weren't here in either instance."

"I needed to stay home with a carpenter. He was building an addition in my home. I did arrive here in the afternoon, but you were probably finished."

"Yeah, we always work it out, so my beauty gets her White Castle fix after we bowl," said Adam.

"Adam, I'm sure you look forward to those burgers yourself," said Yogi.

"You know me too well, my friend. There is no taste like them."

"The sauteed onions do it every time. I'm sure your friend Rob is a fan, too."

"You got that right. And I'm always good for eight at a sitting," said Rob. "And a bag of onion rings."

"I can't say I'm surprised," said Yogi. "You are a big boy. Those burgers are addictive, and I know a few skinny young men who wolf down a dozen. Anyway, let's get you guys some shoes. Rob, I guess that you are an eleven, right?"

"You are close," answered Rob. "A ten fits more comfortably."

"Size ten it will be," said Yogi, reaching down to the lowest shelf behind the counter. "And, of course, an eight and a half for my great friend."

"Thank you, but a nine would be better. I don't see any of the ace bowlers around today," said Adam.

"They'll be here later. Their schedules are never the same. Take Lane 1, boys."

"Wow, this is the first time I ever bowled in a lane alongside the wall," said Adam. "Maybe it will bring luck."

"Young man, you don't need luck; you'll do very well," Yogi answered. "Lane 1 will be kind to you."

"Lane 1's gutters are no different than the gutters of the other lanes," said Adam.

"Think positive," said a smiling Yogi.

"I always do, but what happens never conforms with that

mindset."

Rob put on a good show while bowling. He was an emotional trainwreck, thinking everything that happened was surreal. But whenever he came down to earth, he wondered if life was worth living anymore. Maureen was his whole world, and he always put her first. Yet, like Sarah and sometimes Adam, he always thought things were meant to happen. With that train of thought taking center stage, Rob concluded that Maureen took a job at Schiff's to meet her soulmate. He regarded himself as just a temporary companion for Maureen, albeit one who enjoyed a long run with his junior high school sweetheart. He thought they were strongly compatible and shared similar interests. They were both wholly Irish and light-complexioned. But Rob knew he fucked up royally. He pondered.

Maureen had enough of me, and at the same time, she was falling head over heels for Delfin. That's a lethal equation for a break up. But what am I going to do without her?

Adam's first heave, just as he expected, ended up in the gutter, though it came close to clipping the pin furthest to his left. His follow-up pitch reached the gutter much sooner, though on his right side. He returned to his seat with a self-deprecating snicker but rushed over to Rob when he noticed his friend was sobbing. He sat next to Rob and wrapped his arm around him.

"I'm so sorry, dear friend. I can't say I understand how you feel, as I've never experienced such a fucking terrible event. I know you feel your entire life is in shambles. And I've long known how much you've loved Maureen."

Adam's final observation made things worse as Rob sobbed even harder. Yogi heard the commotion and made his way over to the young men. Adam saw the proprietor and rose to head him off, leading Yogi to the space inside the entranceway, alongside all the bowling plaque tributes hanging on the wall. He spoke softly.

"Yogi, his girlfriend, broke up with him a few days ago. They were together for over seven years, though they didn't formally date until high school. He just found out she's been dating someone else. Rob is taking it badly. He's inconsolable."

"Oh, I understand. I feel so sorry for him. I bet you brought him here to get his mind off his grief. You are always there for your family and friends. I feel honored you chose Nungesser's to occupy him. But I suspect this will be a long process for recovery. I've known my share of people who went through this. There was a young man who sold newspapers on Nungesser's corner late at night who committed suicide after a break up. I won't mention his name, but he was a hard worker."

"Yogi, I knew him well. What a tragedy. I took it bad."

"I'm sure you did. A damn shame. But I'm sure you will do everything within your power to get him through what is probably the worst time in his life."

"One day, I'll explain more, but I want to get back to him."

"Of course," said Yogi.

"Oh, I forgot to mention he lives with us now."

"Well, I can't say I am surprised. Young man, you are a legend for helping friends in need and for other reasons."

"Thanks, Yogi. Rob needs our support. Since I met him at Bergen Community College in 1976, he's been one of my best friends. I would never have been able to predict what happened to him and Maureen, but I guess I never knew some things."

"Adam, I hope your friend can find peace sooner. Oh, how are you doing in Bergen Tech? You look like you put on some weight."

"The older kids are tough. But I think I have everything under control. I probably did the wrong fucking thing by making friends with some of the students, but it's my nature. I'm learning the hard way, but so far, I'm surviving. I've been working out at the gym. Aerobics and weightlifting. I have a trainer."

"Wow, Adam, I can already see you are a changed man. I like how you firmly express yourself and see muscles forming on your arms. You'll be some tough hombre in another six months! Now it's your turn to be the bully!"

Wait till I tell that ballbreaker, Pedro, thought Yogi.

"Your help is much appreciated, my friend," said Adam before returning to his seat behind lane #1. He watched Rob throw a strike.

"You have a great backup ball," said Adam, referring to his friend's left-to-right curve, a somewhat unorthodox delivery from a right-handed bowler.

If the backup delivery is successful, the ball initially breaks sharply to the left and then reverses course, usually just before it crashes into the 1-3 pocket. Many bowlers consider the technique harder to control and less consistent than a traditional hook delivery.

"Adam, my ball always breaks in the opposite direction. It's been my style since I was six years old. I didn't bowl enough over the years to work on changing it. Sometimes the ball skirts the gutter before it breaks to the middle, but other times it ends up in the gutter."

"That's my bowling history! Always in the gutter!" exclaimed Adam.

"Bowling is the last thing to worry about, " Rob said.

***

Rob showed signs of recovery after a few weeks at the Furano house. The twins' mischievous antics made him laugh, and he enjoyed the daytime game shows and sitcom reruns in the evenings. After his gym sessions, Adam usually hung out with him for about one hour. Joe convinced him to take a job at the office in Clifton, replacing Alejandro, who had resigned to work at a food emporium in West New York. Rob didn't speak Spanish, but the position didn't require a second language. Rob rode with Joe and Jay, and after a few months, he said that he liked the job and insisted on paying for his food.

"Not once have I regretted allowing an outsider into our home," said Joseph to his wife in their bedroom. "Rob is a terrific young man who strives to help in any way he can."

"Yes, he is a gem," Carol said. "He's accommodating in the kitchen, where he washes dishes and the floor, and he loves doing the food shopping on Saturdays."

CHAPTER 14

Shopping at the Bergen Mall

October 1974

"Mom, would you be willing to drive me to the Bergen Mall?" asked fourteen-year-old Mikey Furano on the morning of the second Saturday in October.

"Let me guess, sweetie. You want to browse Brentano's and Sam Goody's, right?"

"How did you know, Mom?"

"Oh, come on, honey. Those are your places, especially the bookstore, where you could spend a whole day reading at one of their tables. I'll happily drive you there but don't want to stay eight hours. I'm hosting a card game tonight."

"Mom, three hours would be enough if we arrived by 10 o'clock. You'll drop me off and head over to Alexander's. How about you and I grab lunch at Fuddruckers on the way back?"

"Fuddruckers? You know precisely how to win me over, sweetie. Their chicken breast platter is terrific, and you always get their burgers and potato wedges."

115

"You got it, Mom. Those are my favorite burgers. I love White Castle and Callahan's burgers, but nothing beats the oversized ones at Fuddruckers. I love spreading the melted American cheese, adding a few pickles, and drenching the potato wedges with the same cheese and ketchup."

"Honey, it's only nine o'clock, and you're getting me hungry," Carol said, smiling. "Let me get ready; it shouldn't take me long. Sit here and have your coffee," she added before retreating to her bedroom.

Mikey smoked while drinking his cup of java. After dressing in his casual weekend clothes, he left the house and waited by the passenger door of the family's Ford Fairlane.

Carol knocked on Adam and Sarah's door, and after being told to enter, she explained that she was leaving for Paramus but would be back in plenty of time to prepare for the night's poker event.

"I'm ready for the game, Mom," said Sarah.

Carol was convinced that her son – always one to honor her November birthday with a gift – was using his love for books and records to mislead her. She'd be careful not to ask what he bought, though she figured he'd show her only what he wanted her to see.

"I'll see you at one, sweetie. You have three hours."

"Awesome, Mom." Mikey kissed her and disembarked.

Carol couldn't resist watching where her son headed. Sure enough, after he pushed open the glass door to Bamberger's, she knew Mikey would buy her a birthday gift. She admired the boy's resolve to save money from his paper routes, snow shoveling, and delivering food for Hiza's Deli, though he used it on books, vinyl, and, most recently, cigarettes. Carol was generous with her allowances for the teenager; sometimes, Adam would hand him a twenty.

Carol smiled as she drove toward a service road for Route 4, where she would negotiate a U-turn. She found a convenient parking space just outside Alexander's, one of sixteen locations in a department store chain, but a store particularly famous for its 280-panel, 250-ton abstract art mural that measured 200 feet by 50 feet and was, at the time, the largest in the world. For some, the visual allure of the massive painting on glass helped some shoppers decide between the two expansive stores located on opposite sides of the East-West expressway. However, either outlet would have satisfied their needs. Carol aimed to browse the discounted designer clothing.

Mikey made his way to the back of the store, where he browsed the ceramics section. After scrutinizing the earthenware, stoneware, and porcelain vases, a middle-aged saleswoman approached him.

"Hi, young man. What can I help you with today?"

"Hello, kind lady. I want to buy a vase for my mom. I know there are three types. Which variety is the cheapest? I have a decent amount of money but can't afford the most expensive ones."

"I understand," said the clerk. "We have a few items at cut-rate prices."

The woman showed Mikey his choices and recommended a white, translucent, flower-designed porcelain vase sporting a $12 tag.

"This one's a beauty, and it's the last one left," she said, using a famous sales line.

"I'll take it; it is beautiful. My mom will say it is the best birthday present I ever gave her."

"I wouldn't be surprised, young man. If my son bought me one, I'd be so thrilled."

Mikey paid for his vase with cash at the section's main counter. The item was boxed and placed in a white Bamberger's shopping bag. Mikey returned to the woman to thank her. He kissed her on the cheek.

She smiled and thought.

And they say kids are not friendly anymore? What could he be? Twelve or 13? He is so well-spoken and sweet—maybe even too sweet—but what's the difference? I like feminine boys like him. He's a real cutie.

Baby-faced Mikey looked younger than his age.

The teen proceeded to the escalator, where overhead boards informed shoppers which floor the various departments were located. Bamberger's had a basement and a second floor, meaning there were three levels. Mikey saw the cosmetics and women's lingerie departments were on the upper level, so he rode the moving staircase to his destination. The back half of the level was devoted to ladies' accessories and clothing, so the cosmetics were a short distance from the escalator.

He immediately sought help.

"Hello, Miss. Can you get me a tube of ruby red lipstick and some makeup? I am buying gifts for Mom's birthday," asked Mikey.

"Sure, honey. I'll be right back."

The saleswoman, sporting a name tag, was in her late thirties. She approached a co-worker and whispered in her ear. The other young woman giggled as she stared at Mikey. She whispered to her friend.

"They are all the same. The items are always for their mom or their girlfriend. But since when do boys buy such intimate, gender-exclusive items? Yeah, I know some cross-dressers and men who don't hide their activity. I'm sure this adorable teenager is gay and the most extreme kind. He is practically shaking, so this must be his first time. We must indulge him."

"It's always the cutest ones who are that way, and this boy is stunning," Cindy said.

118

"What's his voice like?" asked Amy.

"Feminine," answered Cindy.

"I see. Well, let me get him our best product," said Amy. "Do you mind if I deal with him? These types fascinate me. Don't worry. I'll handle him delicately."

"Sure, hon."

Cindy's coworker was a stocky young woman in her early twenties. Despite her promise to handle Mikey with kid gloves, she aimed to torture him.

"Young man, I have many colors," said Amy. "I know this is for your mom, but the best way we can determine what color you'd think she might like best is to try some on and use the mirror in our dressing rooms."

"Oh, I don't know about that," said Mikey. "I don't need to try on lipstick. You can show me the tubes."

"What is your name, young man?"

"Mikey. Mikey Furano."

"What a cute name. How about if we make sure? We don't want to make a mistake now, do we, Mikey?" Amy asked firmly.

"Well, I guess not," Mikey said, his voice quivering.

"Mikey, follow me to the dressing rooms. They are behind me."

The young man followed Amy to an open fitting room.

"Sit down, Mikey. I'll return shortly."

Mikey sat, covering his face with both hands.

A few minutes later, Amy knocked on the door. After Mikey told her to enter, she handed the trembling young man a tube of ruby-red lipstick and told him to wax his lips. She explained how he needed to pucker his lips and hold up a mirror to look at his handiwork.

"Do you think your mom will like that color?"

Mikey couldn't respond.

"I'll ask you a second time, Mikey. Do you think your mom

would look good in that color?"

Mikey couldn't hold back anymore and bawled loudly.

Amy flashed a victorious smile.

"So you are nothing but a little girly boy, am I right, sissy?"

Sobbing, Mikey looked at the floor.

"Don't make me ask you again!"

"Yes. Yes, I am," said Mikey. "I can't help myself."

"I have a good mind to send you out of this store wearing a dress and heels. I bet you would love that, right, Mikey? Maybe you'll want to try on a bra?"

"Please, don't," Mikey begged.

"Disgusting little pervert. I'd use my hands on you, but I don't want to get sued."

Amy was enjoying herself mightily. But before she could assault the helpless boy even further, Cindy entered. She immediately realized her friend hadn't kept her word. A compassionate woman, she aimed to right a wrong and embraced Mikey. Cindy told Amy to leave.

"Don't cry anymore, honey. We'll keep your secret. I'll ring you up for the ruby red, a pink tube, and a makeup kit. What is your name? I know you told Amy."

"Mikey."

"Do you have a boyfriend, Mikey?"

Whimpering, Mikey answered firmly, "No. I am not gay. I love girls. I am heterosexual. But I think I am a girl myself, sometimes. Please don't have me arrested. I didn't steal anything. Please."

"Ah, I see. You are one of *those* types. Oh, cutie, of course, we won't have you arrested. You didn't do anything wrong. How old are you, Mikey?"

"I turned 14 last month."

"What day?"

"September 2nd."

"You look younger, honey. Did you take a bus to get here?"

"My mom drove me. She's at Alexander's. I told her I wanted to buy something at Bamberger's. She suspects I was buying her a birthday gift. And I did. I bought her a porcelain vase. It's here." Mikey pointed to his shopping bag.

"That's a lovely gift, Mikey. I bet you are a wonderful son. So, we know the lipstick and makeup are for you. Were you planning to buy anything else for yourself in this store?"

Mikey looked at Cindy as he fought back tears. He was unable to answer.

"Honey, maybe I can help you. You are who you are. There is nothing to be ashamed of. I'm sure everybody loves you."

Mikey hesitated but thought it was best to come clean.

"I was going to buy lingerie, specifically panties."

"Oh, panties, of course. What color, if I may ask?"

"Red and pink."

"What size, Mikey?"

"Medium."

"Honey, I will bring a few pairs for you to try on. Just stay right here."

Cindy returned with two packs of ladies' underwear in Mikey's favored colors.

"I will leave so you can try them on, honey."

The two sets of panties were a perfect fit.

"Awesome," said Cindy. "The panties, lipstick, and makeup are gifts from me. I am also including a black bra and some nail polish."

"But I must pay for these," said Mikey. "Why should you pay?"

"Because I want to. You are so enchanting, and it will make me feel so good to give them to you; there is no use for you to argue. I've made my decision."

Mikey put his arms around Cindy, nestling his head on her

shoulder.

"I am going to make a prediction," said Cindy, tearing up. "You will always be a boy, and I reckon you'll be a fantastic husband and father one day, but you have a strong feminine side and must address it occasionally, probably even more often than that. But maybe this is just a fetish that you'll be over in a few months. It isn't easy to call, but I feel this will always be a part of you. Mikey, I am going to give you my phone number. I can't imagine not knowing how everything is going for you. And if I can be so bold, I would love to be your friend. I have a great husband and two teenagers, a boy, and a girl, but I want you in my life."

Mikey bawled. "You are such a beautiful woman. I want to be *your* friend for the rest of *my* life," he said, echoing a line his brother Adam always used before making friendships. "Can I give you my number as well?"

"Of course, sweetie. I'd love that. Here is a piece of paper and a pen."

Mikey recited as he wrote.

"I'm Mikey Furano. I live at 76 Grant Street in Fairview, New Jersey. I have two brothers and a sister. I'm a freshman at Cliffside Park High School. My phone number is 945-4592."

"Fairview? My husband grew up in Ridgefield, your neighboring town. We love the Italian feasts that Fairview stages every year! I know you are Italian by your name, but your blond hair might suggest you are not all Italian."

"My dad is Italian, but my mom is entirely Irish. Everyone says I am her twin. Her maiden name is Delaney. My grandma, who lives with us, has a wonderful Irish brogue."

"No wonder you are blond and light-skinned. If you were a girl, you'd be gorgeous. But you are already beautiful as a boy. Both my husband and I are Irish, too. I'm 100 percent, and he's three-quarters. His other quarter is English."

122

"Thank you, lovely lady," said Mikey.

"Mikey, do you have a girl's name that you might call yourself sometimes, maybe when you look in the mirror?"

"Yes, Mikaela."

"Now that's a lovely name. And a fabulous female version of Mikey."

"I bet you'd be surprised to learn that I was the class bully in my middle school."

Cindy laughed. "You, the class bully?" she said mockingly. "Sounds like someone tried to cover up who he was by acting the opposite way."

"You are right, Cindy," Mikey said, rubbing his eyes. "I am only average strength, but my bluster fooled everyone. I'm sure I'll fool even more people in high school."

"Honey, you have nothing to be ashamed about. Your behavior was perfectly understandable. You exercised defense mechanisms."

Mikey tried to pay but was rebuffed again.

"Can I call you later this week?" asked Mikey.

"There is nothing I'd love more," Cindy answered. She kissed Mikey, and they said goodbye.

***

Mikey put the smaller bag inside the larger one and headed to Sam Goody's, where he purchased the latest Hall & Oates album. He returned to the front of Bamberger's, leaned against the outside wall about twenty feet to the left of the main entrance, and smoked a cigarette.

"Well, we meet again," Cindy said, approaching Mikey as she lit her cigarette. "I'm surprised you smoke, young man. Fourteen is too young. Do your parents know?"

"Yes, they know. I started openly in Wildwood but was sneaking months before. My mom smokes, so what can she say? My dad hates smoking and gave my older brother Adam a hard time when he started at seventeen. But my dad feared me, so he didn't say a word. I smoke in the house now. Does your husband give *you* a hard time?"

Cindy laughed. "No, he smokes too. I caught my sixteen-year-old son smoking a few months ago. I was disappointed, but we permitted him to do it. You are fine, Mikey. Maybe you'll stop when you consider the health consequences. But I know too well that quitting is one of the hardest things to do. I've been smoking since I was seventeen. You'd be so much better if you didn't start."

"You were the same age as Adam when he started."

"Ah, your older brother. I guess he's the tough guy in your house, no?"

Mikey laughed so hard that he nearly stumbled.

"In a future conversation, I'll tell you all about Adam. He is the opposite of what you think, but he is married and has three daughters. He had just turned 18 when he tied the knot."

"Wow, that's so young to be married."

Carol pulled up to the curb.

"Looks like your mom is here," continued Cindy.

"Great lady, would you walk with me to meet her?" Mikey asked. "It will only take a minute."

"Sure, honey. It can be longer."

Mikey and his new friend approached the open passenger side window of the car.

"Mom, please say hello to Cindy. She works in Bamberger's. She helped me with an item. Cindy is one of the loveliest women I've ever met. And she's all Irish."

"Well," said Carol. "That's quite a compliment, but I have no doubt it is true."

"Hi, Mrs. Furano. You have a captivating son. I want to adopt him."

"Cindy, call me Carol. Yeah, Mikey is a sweetheart. I'm so happy you and he are friends, and I hope we see you again."

"Carol, we exchanged numbers. I won't ever let this boy go. Nor you, for that matter."

Carol and Mikey waved as the car headed off.

They didn't see Cindy McNally dab a tear from her eye.

As Carol predicted, they enjoyed a divine lunch at the spacious Fuddruckers and capped it off with ice cream from the desert window inside the main entrance.

***

Before he did anything else, Mikey hid his shopping bag behind a stack of clothes and some footwear in his bedroom closet. Since no person in the household, including his mom, ever had reason to explore the closet, he didn't need to work hard at camouflage. Later that night, the teenager pulled out the bag when everyone was asleep. He laid the cosmetics and lingerie on the bed and placed the boxed vase on the closet floor in the back corner. He folded some outgrown shirts and neatly stacked them over the box. He sat on the bed and nervously examined the items Cindy had paid for. After twenty minutes, wracked by indecision and guilt, the teen held the tube of red lipstick, removed the plastic covering, repositioned himself at the edge of the bed where it was closest to the mirror on the bureau, and waxed his lips. He opened the makeup kit and used the brush to spread a dime-sized amount of primer on the center of each cheek, the lower center of his forehead, and the middle of his chin.

Subsequent brush movements spread the primer over the rest of his face. Mikey moved onto the foundation, patting the sides of his nose, the top of his cheeks, and the thin and delicate periocular skin under his eyes. Over the years, Mikey had witnessed his mom apply her makeup and had no problem recalling the application. Looking at his handiwork in the mirror, Mikey's initial consternation segued into the exhilaration of having accomplished something he fantasized about but always thought outside the realm of possibility. Feelings of guilt and embarrassment ensued as the teenager's hands shook. His thoughts betrayed his once inconceivable actions.

I don't believe what I have done. I haven't an ounce of willpower. Do I really want to do this? I am a boy. I will eventually become a man. If others were to find out about this, my reputation would be destroyed forever. Everyone sees me as a macho guy. Why did I need to act on these feelings? If Mom knew, she'd be devastated. I can't even think what Dad would say. And after all I've done to Adam, I'm sure many will say it is poetic justice. It may well be. I think I am going through a phase. I don't know how long it will last or how often I want to do this. At some point, I might need to seek some therapy.

Mikey first used his lingerie two weeks later, replacing his boxers with red panties.

***

Three weeks later, the phone rang after dinnertime at the Furano household.

"Hello, am I speaking to Mikey?"

"Hi. I'm Adam, Mikey's brother."

"My name is Cindy. I heard a little about you, Adam. I'm happy to hear your voice."

"I'm honored," said Adam. "But I won't hold you. I will fetch Mikey. I think he's in his room."

"Thank you so much, young man."

A few moments later, Mikey picked up the receiver.

"Hello?"

"Mikey, this is Cindy. How are you, honey?"

"I'm fine, good lady. But I am even better hearing your voice."

"Aww, that's so sweet. I'm thrilled to hear *your* voice! Mikey, I

126

have some bad news. My husband was transferred to Chicago. He worked twelve years at the Nabisco plant on Route 208 in Fair Lawn. He worked in corporate offices and tried hard to change the minds of the powerful, but he was too talented, and they wanted to move him up the ladder. Everything happened so fast. A moving van will be taking our furniture and belongings on Friday."

Cindy heard Mikey's sniffles. Overcome, she hesitated before continuing.

"I think it was ordained that we met when we did, right before my move from this area. I am heartbroken for several reasons. My parents live in Teaneck, a town close to where you live. I also have a sister living in Hawthorne with her family. All my friends live in North Jersey. My son, who has many friends, is beside himself, as is my seven-year-old daughter."

"Cindy, you never mentioned where you lived," said Mikey in a halting voice.

"That's true, honey. I never did. Our home is in Glen Rock, where I have lived since our marriage in 1960."

"That was the year I was born," said Mikey.

"That's right, on September 2nd. I'll never forget your birthday, sweetie. I will honor it every year. But we can talk on the phone sometimes, and we can write. I bet you'll write some beautiful letters. Of course, I plan on visiting my parents, so I'll give you a shout-out when that happens. In the meantime, I want to give you our new address. Can you get some paper and a pencil?"

"Yes, Cindy, I have them right here on the table."

Cindy read off her information:

"Cindy McNally, 4618 Barton Avenue, Evanston, Illinois. The zip code is 60201."

"That's the first time I heard you mention your last name."

"I believe you are right, honey. My maiden name is Byrne. I

don't have my new phone number yet, but since it will be a long-distance call, we'd be better off with letters for a while. Maybe we can talk on the phone on Christmas or Thanksgiving."

"Thanks, Cindy. I will write to you. I've only known you for three weeks, but I'll still miss you terribly."

"Don't make me cry, sweet Mikaela. You take care and always be proud of who you are. You are so special. Bye, honey."

Mikey could barely say goodbye. After he hung up the phone, he bawled loudly.

Carol entered the kitchen and embraced her son.

"What's the matter, sweetie?"

"Cindy's husband got transferred to Chicago. She's leaving New Jersey in three days. I might never see her again," he explained.

"Sweetie, this is what life is all about. There are many happy events but also sadness in the mix. Moving away is always difficult. I'm amazed at how close you are to her since you only met her a few weeks ago. You must have made some impression on her, and vice versa. Your relationship with her is so rare but so wonderful."

"Mom, we have an intimate connection. Nothing sexual, of course, as she is a middle-aged woman, and I am a teenager, but I feel spiritual vibes. It is hard to explain, but maybe one day, years in the future, I'll share some feelings and secrets with you."

CHAPTER 15

Letter to Evanston, Illinois

April 19, 1981

Fairview, New Jersey

Dearest Cindy:

I trust all is well with you and your family. You are probably tied up with work and family responsibilities, so reading my letter shouldn't be a priority. But I still needed to write it. I think about you at least once a week, but usually more. I've told you how much you mean to me, and though you are 800 miles away, I always feel you are sitting beside me, watching me and listening to everything I say. I always marveled at how forty minutes of an October day in 1974 continues to haunt me, even at times possessing me. Though I am not romantically attached to you, a lovely lady almost 25 years my senior, I love you as much as a son loves his mom, as much as a brother loves his sister, or perhaps in my case, as much as a sister loves her sister. Whenever I am stressed out or depressed or feel lost, I see your beautiful face and hear your words of endearment. You couldn't have possibly realized then, but you left an impact on me that could never be dulled or erased by time or place. I have long lamented your physical absence, especially over the last few months, which I must tell you were the worst of my lifetime. I am solely to blame for a succession of terrible events that tore my family apart.

As you will recall, I told you in a previous letter that I couldn't restrain my jealousy of Adam. He has always been someone I wanted to be. Instead of slowly emulating or encouraging him, I sought to mock him and actively strove to win favor with my family – especially my mom – who had always liked him best. At one of my mom's card games, I threatened him and told him to leave after he appeared with dyed hair, wearing cosmetics and earrings. I went along with my girlfriend Olivia when she asked me for permission to rough him up a bit in his room. Cindy, I am crying now as I write this. She enlisted the assistance of one of the card players – a woman named Sandra – and they made him bleed. Cindy, I don't know if I fancied her or saw her as a sex partner. I suspect it was the latter, but I've never admitted this to anyone, not even Mom. I was always afraid of Olivia. She beat me up badly a few times. I don't think a romantic relationship should include fear and physical violence. Anyway, it's over. She stormed out of my home after some ugly events unfolded. She used her fists on my sister-in-law and said some nasty things about my family, Alejandro, Yolanda, and me.

I've told you that I am madly in love with Sarah. I thought it was a fetish, but it grew stronger and stronger. I am so frightened. Sarah is my brother's wife and the mother of his three daughters. She is off-limits for me. Yet, my love intensifies, partially because she lives in my house, and I see her daily. I see her face in my dreams. I fantasize about her holding me in her arms and squeezing me tightly. Though she has always been quite attractive, my connection with her is more of a spiritual one. I find this strange, but I feel I've known her for more years than when she first appeared in Adam's and my life near the end of 1970.

So far, I have been able to conceal these feelings from her and the rest of the family, but I know it will only be a matter of time before they become apparent. Holding them in check while dating Olivia was enormously complex. I have always felt Olivia knew something since – please excuse my intimate revelations – I had difficulty in consummating our sex acts. She stormed out of our house on that tumultuous night and exclaimed, "You were never any good in bed. You can't even get it up. I curse the day I decided to date you." Cindy, I am crying again as I write. I credit Olivia for keeping my femininity under wraps. She never learned of my use of cosmetics and wearing lingerie – how I kept this from everyone over several years is remarkable – but she was wise to my mannerisms and movements and more than once told me I was a more giant sissy than Adam and expected one day I would have the operation and become a woman. She even urged me to add streaks to my hair and wear earrings. I resisted but have fantasized about when I could do it. I want to look like Adam once did, perhaps even more femininely pronounced.

Anyway, I have a serious "Sarah" problem. I know this kind of love is taboo in our society, and by not letting it go, frankly, I am unable to; I am violating my brother in the worst possible way. I am sure that when my feelings are finally known, some will say it is because Sarah's parents are wealthy. But I am truthful when I say that I would still obsess over Sarah even if they were penniless. My love for Sarah transcends pedestrian concerns like money. She has moved my soul just by being who she is and by her generosity of spirit. Though her love for Adam is monumental, I know she loves me, too. I see a glint in her eyes, notice how she addresses me, and observe the affectionate regard she exhibits when we chat.

Even when she publicly condemned me for the lies I voiced that fateful evening in our living room, I knew how it hurt her to make such strong accusations. I think she has always loved me, and during the Wildwood trip of 1974, a few months before I met you in Bamberger's, she was deeply affectionate. Still, she belongs to Adam, and he belongs to her. What right do I have to think about her in these terms? I should seek therapy. Lusting after your brother's wife is abnormal and sinful.

Oh, sweet Cindy, I am hurting badly. I feel alone and am thinking that the world is against me. Even Mom is disappointed; as you know, she's been my biggest supporter. I've been drinking heavily since that awful night and expect that, eventually, I'll need to go to rehab. It worked for Adam. He started drinking again but in moderation.

I should be in college by now, but as you know, I put it off and won't be going in the 1979 fall semester or the 1980 spring semester. I doubt I will go the year after that. I've lost interest, though I read often when not listening to music or watching movies. Maybe one day, I will feel different. I am tired of hearing people ask me when I will attend college.

I am thinking about joining the Fairview Fire Department. The Grandview Firehouse is located down the block from my home, and some of Adam's friends are members. I know what you are probably thinking, and you are right. I want to do something that will foster a masculine image to counter the many hidden aspects of myself that are feminine. Cindy, it is either this or working toward becoming a real woman. I haven't the slightest bit of knowledge about what is expected of a firefighter, aside from answering the siren and needing to wear the proper gear, but I'm willing to learn and give it my all. Part of me is afraid of being ridiculed if any members of the department deduce my feminine tendencies, and this is why I continue to hesitate. I'd appreciate it if you would advise me on whether you think I am doing the right thing by seeking membership.

Well, there's only so much I can say in a letter, and I've taken up too much of your time, assuming you've gotten this far. If you come upon some free time and would like to respond, you should talk about yourself and your own life instead of addressing the depression of a nineteen-year-old girly boy whose issues were caused by selfishness and evil thoughts. I probably would not have bothered you if that terrible night hadn't come to pass. I hadn't anyone else to turn to, sweet lady.

Love,

Mikaela

PS: I apply lipstick and makeup in my room two or three nights a week. I have graduated to wear panties every day under my trousers or shorts. I conceal the practice by washing several pairs of boxer shorts weekly to make it look like I wore them. Mom sees precisely what goes into the hamper. I've been experimenting with nail polish, but the removal is a drag. I had a dream the other day that I appeared on a television show wearing a green dress and black sequined heels. – M.

PSS: I must tell you again how much I love you, Cindy. – M.

CHAPTER 16

Cindy's Response to Mikey

April 26, 1981

Evanston, Illinois

Dearest Mikaela:

I received your letter five days ago but cried for several days before responding. My husband and my children asked me what was wrong. I told them that an old friend from Bamberger's made me emotional, but I didn't get specific. Sweetie, I love you too, and I think about you often. You are the only person I still communicate with from that store, and you didn't even work there. I saw you for forty minutes. The rest is history.

I would like to see you face to face, but you'll recall from a previous letter that my parents moved here unexpectedly. They later admitted they couldn't bear being away from us, especially from their grandchildren, but initially, they claimed they were too old to maintain a house. They retained ownership and now have renters. The downside was that I no longer had an excuse to fly back to New Jersey. But even if I could, and I really would have loved to see you again, I am going through some marital problems. One day, I will elaborate, but for now, I can say that both of us are in a bad way. I feel for you, sweetie. Don't be so hard on yourself. Yes, we all succumb to temptation, but your situation is understandable. What you did to Adam wasn't very nice, but that's not the dominant side of you. You've had to suppress yearnings for a long time, and sibling rivalry and the play for affection from parents aren't easily solved. I should know. My son and daughter are competitive. I know how much you love your brother. You just temporarily lost your way.

I am sorry about what happened with Olivia. You deserved much better. All she did was take care of your sexual needs. From what you told me, she made your life more stressful. She physically abused you and mocked you for your gender issues, even without knowledge of your private practices. I fear she may have seriously harmed you if she knew about those. I will never forget the letter you sent me in June of last year after your Rolling Stones concert. Because you were still dating her, I didn't tell you at that time, nor afterward, how terrible she was to threaten and humiliate that helpless, effeminate boy who was then known as Andrzej. Now you told me how she assaulted Sarah. I'm sure this act angered you, knowing what I do of your love for your sister-in-law. Sweetie, Olivia was a poor choice for a girlfriend, and you are better off that she is gone. You can't have a girlfriend who is a physical threat.

You are not sinful, abnormal, or evil in your love for Sarah. Love is love, and it sometimes goes to and comes from the most unlikely places. No, you cannot rightfully expect Sarah to return the level of love for you that you are privately expressing for her. She is married to Adam. There can never be any consummation.

I'm sure she does love you, and maybe a lot, but this can never lead to any married relationship for you. I'd be heartlessly misleading you if I told you otherwise. I'm sure you know this, but it isn't easy because you are so deeply in love with her. I'm sorry, honey. Your brother and his wife contributed to this untenable situation by moving into your house and mixing in with the rest of the family. This kind of living arrangement rarely works for all sorts of reasons. I would advise you to meet someone and try hard not to think about Sarah, at least not in the obsessive way you have been doing. You said that she is taken, and I agree.

You never cease to amaze me with how gifted you are. I don't even think you realize it. You are an eloquent writer with skills and insights atypical for a teenager. I always thought of myself as a reasonably good writer, but I'm not in your league, and I'm forty-three. It is easy to see why you graduated in the top ten of your class. You must be ready to do it, but you belong at one of the best universities. I know you struggle with your gender, but as I've told you a few times, you will one day be a great husband and father with a precious feminine side that I am happy to see you are continuing to maintain and explore. I must say I'm surprised that you've never been discovered. Usually, there is a slip-up, but I guess you've been cautious to a fault. Then again, I could be wrong, in which case I'm sure you'll be a beautiful and successful woman. Part of me hopes for the latter.

I am honored that you are seeking my advice on the fire department matter. Honey, I think you should join! Membership would broaden your experience and foster a sense of community. However, never be ashamed of who you are, and never be concerned about how you are perceived. I can guarantee that you will be accepted and appreciated. While I am slightly concerned about the danger of being a firefighter, the odds are heavily in your favor that you will be fine. There is risk in everything. A small town like yours diminishes it. I think you will serve your company exceedingly well, sweetie.

One day, we need to speak on the phone again. I will always treasure that one phone chat we had two years back. But there is something about a letter that is more intimate and revealing. Don't hesitate to write to me again as soon as you have reason to, or even to lean on me for some advice. You are always in my heart, beautiful Mikaela.

Love,

Cindy

PS: You must try harder to cut down on your drinking. I saved this for last, but it is the most critical matter you broached. My twenty-one-year-old son has battled this problem as well. He's a chip off the old block.

CHAPTER 17

Steve Burke Wins A Free Trip to Aruba

May 16, 1981

"Will Marvin Sommer please come up to pick the winner of our Caribbean vacation?" asked Frank Sodano, president of the Fairview Lions Club. The entire organization would like to thank you for your extreme generosity. Due to the enormous interest in this prize, we raised over $20,000."

Sommer donated a nine-day Aruba trip to the service organization for fundraising. Sarah's dad, Steve Burke, had joined the service organization a decade earlier at the behest of a friend, and though he was marginally active, he attended some meetings. Burke had purchased five $50 raffle tickets for the prize. With over 400 sold, Burke didn't expect his name to be announced, but like everyone else in attendance, he was curious about whose name would be picked. Burke was a multi-millionaire who didn't need to win anything, but the fun and suspense surrounding the competition were irresistible.

Sommer, a Ridgefield engineer and part-owner of the Lee

Theater, ascended to the makeshift stage.

"Thanks for this great honor," he said. "I would like to say that this trip includes first-class seating, lodging at the oldest and one of the best hotels on the island, free use of a Jeep, and $1000 in cash."

Sommer's announcement received rousing applause from the 90 people in attendance.

Sodano grabbed hold of the lever to a raffle drum and vigorously spun it. The orange tickets, each with a person's name and address written on them, scattered in all directions and were seen through the small, rectangular slats that prevented them from slipping through. After about a dozen spins, Sodano stopped and allowed Sommer to turn the latch so the square gate could open. The prize's benefactor inserted his arm into the cage and pulled out the ticket bearing the lucky winner's name and address.

"Steve Burke of Columbia Avenue in Cliffside Park is the winner of the Aruba trip. Come up and get your envelope, Steve!"

After a round of applause, Burke walked up to claim his prize. He shook his head but smiled, uttering that he didn't believe he won.

"I predict something profound will happen on the trip," Sommer said.

Burke smiled and shook Sommer's hand.

"Now you see why I made you join, Steve," said Jim Stafford, Burke's Fairview friend.

"Jimmy, you know I don't need this, and I don't like airplanes. Michele and I will never use it. Maybe I should donate it back to the club."

"Steve, before you do that, think of someone in your family."

Burke pondered for a moment.

"Of course. This would be wonderful for my daughter and her

husband, Adam. My mind isn't with it tonight. For one reason or another, they never had a proper honeymoon. This vacation is a long time coming. Let me look at the dates," said Burke, opening the envelope. "It says Monday, August 25th through Friday, September 3rd."

"Correct," answered Stafford. "Nine days. Roughly three months from now."

"Well, my daughter can take her vacation days, and my son-in-law is good to go since his school year doesn't start until after Labor Day. As I recall, the holiday falls late this year."

"Labor Day is September 6th," said Stafford.

"My daughter will be thrilled when she hears the news."

***

"Sweetheart, my dad won a free 9-day trip to Aruba. He needs to attend to his health, so he isn't keen to go there with Mom. He wants us to go," Sarah said to Adam excitedly, sitting on a couch in the living room.

"Aruba? I can't believe it. How did he win the tickets?"

"They held a raffle at a Lions Club meeting. He said they sold over 400 tickets, and Dad bought five. Marvin Sommer donated the prize and picked one of Dad's tickets from a spinning cage. Are you ready to take the Honeymoon we never took?"

"I think I might be," answered Adam. "I don't know Mr. Sommer, but shit, he seems to be a good guy."

"For sure," said Sarah. She smiled and vigorously embraced her husband.

"I was never one to expect anything for free, but we deserved this!" she exclaimed. "And I have no doubt we will enjoy the time of our lives."

***

"Enjoy your trip, Sarah," said Mikey on the Thursday evening before Monday's plane departure. At 6:30 p.m., Mikey carried a plate of beef stew from the kitchen to his bedroom when he passed his sister-in-law in the hallway.

"Mikey, thank you, but it isn't looking good for the trip. Adam contracted a severe case of the flu. When he gets it, you must figure he's out of commission for at least two weeks. He was cursing his head off when he found out he contracted it. I think he's even angrier because he can't go to the gym for a while. You know how obsessed he has become with bodybuilding and weightlifting."

"I know Sarah. Adam is turning into a scary guy. I never would have believed it, but as they say, the proof is in the pudding."

"Dad will be so disappointed, but I can't go either. I should stay with Adam. Of course, my husband is ranting and saying that some other family member should accompany me. I lost count of the number of times he used the F-bomb. I'm not even sure if the airline will allow a switch. Adam thinks his mom can attend to him, but I don't feel right leaving him when he's sick."

Mikey's eyes widened.

"I think you are right to stay with him, but if you did go on the trip, I'd volunteer to protect you. Going there would be a dream for me. The timing is perfect, too. I get my two-week vacation starting Monday."

"Aww, sweetie, that's so kind of you. I don't think it would be wise to leave him, but I'll let you know if the plans change."

"Thanks, dear sister-in-law," Mikey said, continuing down the hall. "You deserve a vacation."

***

"Sweetie, Mikey showed much interest in going on the Aruba trip," said Sarah.

"That's fantastic news, Sarah! We have the perfect alternative. Mikey can go and keep you safe. You know how much of a fun guy he is. I should have thought of him, myself. "

"Sweetheart, you can forget that instantly. I love your brother but refuse to leave you behind when you are sick."

"Fuck, Sarah, there isn't anything you can do for me. The flu will take its course as it always does. Our parents will help with the girls. If you stay here, you'll fucking catch it yourself. You are taking the same risk by talking to me right now."

"Adam, sweetie, somehow I think it was ordained that you would catch the flu so Mikey would go on the trip."

"What do you mean by that, Sarah?"

"One day, I'll tell you. I don't think this is the right time."

Mikey disclosed his feelings to his mom, hoping she might try to influence Sarah. Initially, Carol was reluctant to intervene since the trip was Sarah's to manage, and she understood her daughter-in-law's desire to remain with her spouse until his illness ran its course. But Mikey's pleading blue puppy dog eyes and tenacious sponsorship gave her pause. Finally, Carol thought the nine days might help her homebody son enjoy quality time outdoors. She conveyed her sentiments to Sarah, who spoke again to Adam.

"Sarah, it would be so fucking stupid to waste the trip. It isn't fair to your dad. If you don't change your mind, I will change it for you."

Sarah slept on it, and after agonizing over the decision in the morning, she decided to go through with the trip. However, there was still one more obstacle to solve before Mikey could replace Adam, and numerous calls to United Airlines throughout Saturday succeeded when a representative asked Mikey to report to a ticket desk. However, there was a $400 surcharge to make the switch, and it had to be on Sunday since the flight was scheduled to leave Newark on Monday morning. Mikey was prepared to pay, but Sarah reminded him of the $1000 that came with the trip.

"Sarah, I can't adequately express my gratitude for this opportunity. But you are not responsible for paying the money to switch the ticket. I am."

"Sweetie, I insist. We'll still have $600 left and whatever cash we bring. Credit cards work, too. We're sitting pretty."

Mikey was teary-eyed while thanking Adam, though Sarah insisted he express his appreciation outside the open door. She had been sleeping in Saoirse's room since Wednesday and planned to continue through the final night before the flight.

The suitcases and carry-on bags Sarah had purchased at the department store Two Guys in Lodi the previous month were used for clothes and personal items. Mikey loaded his luggage and carry-on with personals, books, and hidden items from his closet. Sarah reminded him he didn't need to bring any toiletries since the hotel room was stocked with such items.

CHAPTER 18

Wojtiech's C-Section Birth

May 27, 1981

Wojtiech Dominguez entered the world as a breech baby at Hackensack Hospital. Alejandro waited outside the pregnancy tent until a doctor's assistant confirmed he had a son and allowed him up to hold the little boy. The young father, dressed in blue scrubs with a white head covering, cried as he had his first offspring, marveling over the miracle of birth while shuddering at the sight of blood-soaked towels in a pail on the floor near Yolanda's gurney. After a few minutes, a nurse took the baby and directed Alejandro to announce the birth to the family in the waiting room.

The Wisnewskis, Alfredo, and Yolanda's dad cried and celebrated the 7-pound, 6-ounce boy whose features and complexion resembled Yolanda's.

"He's a Hispanic baby for sure!" exclaimed Alfredo, who seemed anxious to erase the connotation of a Polish first name he despised. Jakob and Ania gave a feigned smile. Shortly after,

Alejandro followed nurses to the section where the babies could be observed behind glass. After the mother and infant returned to Yolanda's room, Alejandro leaned over to kiss his wife repeatedly, which irked Alfredo, who had just entered and picked up the child.

"Leave my sister alone, Alejandro!" exclaimed Alfredo in Spanish. "She just went through a traumatic event. Do you understand?" he added threateningly.

"Entiendo, Alfredo, (I understand Alfredo.)" Alejandro departed quickly. The young father met his parents outside the room, leading them to the cafeteria after boarding an elevator.

"This Polack needs to know his place," said Alfredo.

"Oh, sweet *hermano,* (brother), I'm sure you'll keep him in line," Yolanda said.

"Yolanda, I won't hesitate to use my fists," Alfredo said, signaling the certainty of an abusive marriage.

The Furanos weren't informed of the birth. After Alejandro quit his security job in Clifton, he severed the last connection with Adam and his family. His position at a food emporium on 47th Street was in the dairy department, ironically mirroring Adam's assignment at the A&P.

The Wisniewskis got their wish. After Adam's attempts to reach Alejandro were rebuffed, there was no further communication between the former best friends. Alejandro inquired about the Furanos, but his wife and parents lied, telling him Adam didn't want to speak to him. Alejandro focused on his wife and new baby, and after a while, he never thought about Adam or the Furanos.

"Sweetie, I know you must be so sad about the situation with Alejandro," Sarah said during breakfast on Saturday morning.

Lighting a cigarette, Adam answered, "Sarah, I am not sad. I don't need Alejandro in my life, and he doesn't need me in his. We had a friendship of convenience. If he were interested in maintaining communication, he would have least informed us when his baby was born."

"Well, you have a family, too, and you do plenty of other things," said Sarah.

"Shit, Sarah, you know I'm not a good family person. I never was. I'm selfish. Jimbo is a better father to Saoirse than I am, and I don't do much with the twins."

At least he's honest. He's a poor father, even if he always means well. Though we never challenged it, Jimbo had taken over the fathership role with Saoirse since she was three. Adam barely interacts with the twins. He treats strangers better than his own family. I wouldn't say he is selfish but self-centered, even if he helps others. He suppresses dissent. I won't dispute him. He spends hours at the gym now after he returns from work. I'll change the subject.

"Honey, I haven't asked you this, but are you at least a little bitter that Alejandro didn't insist you be chosen as the best man?"

"Yes, Sarah," said Adam, sipping his coffee. "I am bitter. He could have been firm. But that's the way he is. He will never get his way in that marriage."

"You didn't feel the same way after you found out."

"Sarah, that was then, this is now," quoting the novel's title that he urged Brian to read.

"But you still want to make friends and keep everyone happy."

"Yes, I do. I recently made good friends with my gym coach, Dave. He's my age."

"Oh, you haven't mentioned him. I'm happy to hear it. Maybe he'll work on your bad habits."

"No way, Sarah, he does them all too," answered Adam, lighting Sarah's cigarette, then his own.

"Oh. Ah well. One day, my love, one day."

"Adam, a health nut? There's a better chance of hell freezing over!" exclaimed Rob, stirring in the living room. "I should be the last one to talk, though."

"Three sunny side up and Taylor Ham, Rob?" asked Sarah.

"Over easy," corrected Rob.

"Ah, that's right, you changed. You said you didn't care for the runny yolks."

"That's right, Sarah, I prefer my eggs to be cooked all through. Where's my little man?"

"He's downstairs playing with his brother and sisters. I'll be calling him up any minute for his Captain Crunch."

CHAPTER 19

Flight to Aruba from Newark Airport

August 25, 1981

"I never asked you guys what airline you were using," said Joseph Furano, approaching the toll plaza off Exit 14 of the New Jersey Turnpike.

"Yes, that would help," said his wife Carol, sitting in the passenger's seat of the family's newly acquired light blue Chevy Caprice. "We wouldn't want these two boarding a plane to Ireland."

"Hey, Mom, that sounds like a great idea! How about it, Sarah?" asked Mikey, sitting behind his dad and next to his sister-in-law. Joseph handed the toll-taker a dollar bill and the manila-colored ticket he had received when passing through the entrance plaza in Secaucus. "This might be our best chance. Aer Lingus, please," joked Mikey.

"What? And give up your free trip?" asked Carol, playing along.

"How about Italy?" asked Joseph. "I'll take you to the Alitalia departure level.

149

"Joe, all kidding aside, Alitalia and Aer Lingus fly out of Kennedy. I don't think they operate out of Newark right now."

"To answer your question, Dad," Mikey said, then sang: "*Fly the friendly skies...Fly the friendly skies...Fly the friendly skies of United.*"

"I never heard you belt out," said Sarah. "You are fabulous, just as great as great as Adam. Your voice is so high-pitched when you sing. I never would have connected you to that. You might make a good soprano."

Mikey smiled widely. "You think so, Sarah? I take that as a compliment!"

"Of course, you have nothing on Adam's rendition of Gloria Gaynor's *I Will Survive* and his *My Favorite Things* from *The Sound of Music,*" Sarah answered.

"That's for sure!" exclaimed Carol.

"I can always try," said Mikey in a severe tone.

Sarah and Carol snickered, waving Mikey off with arm motions. They failed to notice his disappointed expression.

"Mikey, United uses music from George Gershwin's *Rhapsody in Blue* in their newest commercials," said Sarah. "I remember Adam telling me."

"There isn't anything he doesn't know," Mikey responded. "I learn something new from him every day."

"When you are ready, I'll help you sign up for some college classes," Sarah said. "I'm sure Susan can help. Jersey City State would be a great choice. And when it comes to intelligence, you are brilliant. You were in the top 10 of your class."

"Thank you. The thought recently crossed my mind."

"Adam will be so thrilled to hear that!" exclaimed Sarah. "But frankly, I'm excited too."

Joseph exited the airport interchange and accessed the circular road that passed the front of terminals A, B, and C. Green rectangular signs on service roads alerted cars to what terminals housed the airlines. United was in A. He followed the sign for the departure deck, located on the top level.

"Our instructions are to check in our baggage at door 8," announced Sarah.

"Door 8 it is," responded Joseph, pulling up alongside a yellow airport taxi as traffic built up. The Furano patriarch popped up the trunk, and after quick goodbyes and kisses, Mikey grabbed two large suitcases while Sarah snatched the carry-on bags.

"I'll miss you two terribly," said Carol. "Have a safe flight and the time of your lives. And make sure you protect my beloved daughter-in-law, young man."

"With my life," Mikey replied. "I'll see you in nine days. I love you, Mom. I love you, Dad."

Sarah followed Mikey through the turnstile door but found many passengers before them looking to check in and surrender their luggage.

"Looks like a long wait, Sarah, and I am dying to smoke," said Mikey.

"You and me, both," Sarah answered. "I bet we have about an hour's wait before they check us in. How about if you go back outside to do it, honey? When you come back in, I'll take my turn."

"Thanks so much, Sarah. I'll be right back."

After both satiated their nicotine addiction, they resumed waiting in line, but surprisingly, it moved along swiftly. The anticipated one-hour wait was reduced by half, aided by their advantage of priority checking. Following their clearance, Sarah and Mikey proceeded to the long outside extension to the main gate. After they were asked to disclose the contents of their carry-ons, both were instructed to sit in the waiting area.

"Isn't it odd that we didn't need to show passports," asked Mikey. "We are entering a different country, after all. I think the island is Dutch."

"Yes, sweetie. Adam said Holland controls it, but plans are brewing to give it autonomy within the coming year."

"I guess Adam gave you a history lesson on Aruba," Mikey said laughingly.

"You know it," said Sarah. "The only thing missing was some knowledge of the Dutch language."

"Give him time," answered Mikey.

"I don't know," answered Sarah. "He is changing. His interests aren't the same anymore."

"Sarah, there is a confectionery and a small snack bar behind it," Mikey said, pointing to his right. "How about a hot dog or a pretzel? Or both, maybe?"

"I feel like a pretzel right now. We can share one. They're usually big."

"And a Coke, maybe?" Mikey asked.

Sarah smiled and nodded.

"Would you like mustard on the pretzel, Sarah?"

"I would," answered Sarah. "You're so considerate, sweetie."

Mikey returned with a jumbo-sized pretzel and two large Cokes. He broke off a small piece of the pretzel for himself and handed most of it to Sarah. Fifteen minutes later, they were summoned to board the plane over an intercom. They sat in the third row of the first-class section behind the cockpit. They settled in premium seats that provided more space, complimentary alcoholic beverages, enhanced food options, and smoking privileges.

They rose briefly to use the overhead compartments for carry-on bags. Mikey had previously confessed to Sarah that he had a height phobia and wouldn't be looking out the window. As she settled into a window seat, Sarah ribbed him.

"A sturdy man like you is afraid of heights?"

Mikey was stocky and five foot eight.

"I've always closed my eyes when crossing a bridge. And I constantly shutter when looking out the window of a building if I am on an upper story."

"Sweetie, we are on the eighth floor at our hotel."

"I know, Sarah. I'll make sure not to look out the windows."

Sarah grinned. "We won't disturb the drapes. Do you have any other phobias?"

"Sarah, I think some things about me would greatly surprise you, but I'll wait for the right time. I am not who you think I am."

"Let me guess. You are a government spy on a secret mission."

"The government would never trust me. I could never keep quiet," answered Mikey.

"Honey, we could always have your vocal cords severed. Remember what Adam said about that *Twilight Zone* episode?"

Mikey protected his neck with his right hand.

"I am happy we can smoke on the plane," he said.

"Me too, sweetie. However, many non-smokers continue to complain. I don't think it will be much longer before smoking is banned altogether on flights. I don't think you can blame these people. They shouldn't have to breathe in other people's smoke."

Shortly after the smooth take-off at nearly 8:30 a.m., an announcement was made over a loudspeaker.

"Good morning, ladies and gentlemen. On behalf of United Airlines, I welcome you aboard flight 796 to Aruba, with service to Queen Beatrix International Airport in Oranjestad. Our estimated time of arrival is 1:15 p.m. EST. Please make sure your seat backs and tray tables are in their full upright position. Ensure your seat belt is securely fastened and all carry-on luggage is stowed underneath the seat in front of you or inside the overhead bins. Thank you."

A few seconds later, a message blared over the intercom.

"This is the captain speaking. I am letting everyone know that a powerful rainstorm has suddenly veered off course and is now headed toward Aruba. It is presently on the western coast of South America and is moving slowly, but it is likely to reach the island this evening. The storm could well be upgraded to hurricane status. This is a highly unusual development for Aruba."

"Wow, that's surprising," exclaimed Sarah. "Just what we need. A hurricane!"

"Sarah, don't worry. No matter where we are, I will always safeguard you," said Mikey, reaching over to hold her hand.

"Sweetie, I wouldn't want anyone else," Sarah answered, smiling wide.

Mikey took out his pack of Marlboro and offered one to Sarah.

"Not right now, but you go right ahead, sweetie."

Mikey flicked his lighter, inhaled, and aimed his exhalation at the overhead vent. When he finished, he used the receptacle next to him to crush the butt and extended his left hand to clasp Sarah's right one.

"You're always so tender, sweetie," Sarah said, tightening her grip. They stayed that way until a stewardess appeared behind the curtain, pulling a food cart on wheels. Sarah and Mikey chose the bacon, eggs, orange juice, and English muffin combination. Coffee was automatically served unless the passenger declined, and a plastic bag of roasted peanuts was given to each traveler.

"We'll take cream and sugar with our coffee," Mikey said. "I know Adam prefers his coffee much lighter."

"Yes, he changed. He used to like it darker, but now he has been using several more creams."

The blonde stewardess handed Mikey six small, portion-controlled tubs of cream with the same number of sugar packets.

"I think the White Castle has the best coffee," said Mikey. "It is the creamiest."

"The Dunkin Donuts coffee is nice, too. The only problem is that

154

you take home a dozen donuts when you go there. The twins are out of control with the Boston cream, and those are Adam's favorite, too. When he attended Jersey City State, he'd stop at Rudolph's Bakery for two every morning."

"I could never even imagine being the parent of twins. I think I would always confuse them," said Mikey.

"Little Carol is far naughtier, but yes, they look so much alike. Still, you never know, sweetie. Your future wife might have twins."

"I'll only love one person for the rest of my life. Until my last day, she will obsess over me and appear in front of me in all my dreams. She is the sun, moon, and the planets to me. She is truly all that matters to me."

"Ah, sweetie, you need to move on from her. She abused you terribly. You deserve the best, and Olivia was so far from that. Still, you express yourself so eloquently. You'd be some catch for any woman."

Mikey gazed at Sarah longingly.

"I've gotten over Olivia. I wish her the best, but we have gone our separate ways."

Sarah was excited since Mikey's admission meant a romantic announcement was imminent. She contemplated:

He is so romantic and affectionate. I had him read correctly from the start. Like most people, he has imperfections and went through a difficult period, but he is so lovesome. Like I once said, he is my Adam with a dark side. But even the darkness in Mikey is diminishing. Adam is darker now. Mikey will make his new girl so happy. I do wish his mom had named him Michael. I love that name. Mikey is too juvenile for an adult.

Mikey cupped his hand over his right breast, rubbed it, and took a deep breath.

"Are you feeling all right, sweetie? Are you feeling chest pain?"

"No, Sarah. I'm not feeling pain, just feeling a little confused."

Sarah gave a puzzled look.

The plane hit a pocket of turbulence, causing the 'Fasten Your Seatbelt' signs to light up. The pilot spoke on the intercom, assuring the passengers that the rough air currents would be short-lived. Sarah noticed Mikey's eyes drooping and thought it was best to let him nap.

Nearly an hour later, Mikey awoke to behold Sarah smoking and sipping a straw from a cup of water.

"Did you have a nice rest, sweetie?"

"I was tired because the alarm woke me up at five o'clock. I'm not used to getting up that early."

"Of course," Sarah assured him. "When our sleep patterns are disturbed, we have no recourse but to compensate."

Mikey lit a cigarette. "If the storm is as bad as they say it might be, I think we might not be getting any sleep tonight either."

"Yeah, you are right, sweetie. I hope it won't be so bad. This is the worst way to start the trip."

A while later, lunch was served. The host asked customers to choose meatloaf, veal parmigiana, or fried flounder. The meat and fish options included potatoes and mixed vegetables, while the veal was served with pasta. Both chose the veal – Mikey because it was covered with his beloved tomato sauce – and Sarah because she said she wasn't in the mood for the other two choices.

"I prefer more sauce," said Mikey as he ate his medium-sized portion.

"You and Adam are so different when it comes to food. Your face and complexion are Irish, but tomato sauce runs through your veins."

"I was always the big Italian food lover in the family. When it comes to food, I love what Dad loves."

"Sweetie, your name is Furano. How could you not be wild for

Italian?"

"Adam has the same last name, but all he thought about growing up were Irish stews and shepherd's pies. I detect he's changing now."

Sarah chuckled. "Adam is unique. His Irish grandfather once said he was the only child who'd ever prefer Barmbrak over a scoop of vanilla fudge. But yes, Adam's food taste isn't so much for the Irish dishes any longer. He's favoring Italian lately."

"What in tarnation is Barmbrak," asked Mikey.

"Irish bread with sultanas and raisins."

"Grandpa, wherever you are, I love you, but I'll take a scoop of vanilla fudge!"

Sarah beamed, "I love what you said, sweetie. And I'm with you on vanilla fudge, but carrot cake rivals it."

"I love Napoleons the best," said Mikey. "The yellow cream on the inside is to die for."

"Sweetie, the glazed black-and-white icing is divine, too. Adam is also a fan."

"Jen, as well," Mikey replied. "Heck, the whole family, though Mom prefers chocolate eclairs."

Smiling, Sarah nodded. "Not to change this scrumptious subject, Mikey, but we are lucky we didn't get an interrupted flight. I understand many have stopovers in San Juan, Puerto Rico. I think the people on those flights would have to wait, sometimes a few hours, before continuing to Aruba."

"We were treated like royalty," responded Mikey. "First-class tickets meant the best service in every sense."

Mikey reached up to the overhead compartment to access his carry-on bag. He rustled through it to withdraw a Bantam paperback of *Jane Eyre*. A bookmark indicated he was about one-third through the novel.

"You are reading *Jane Eyre*, sweetie?" asked Sarah, incredulously.

"Adam loved it, and he also loved *Wuthering Heights,* by the *Jane Eyre* author's sister, Charlotte."

"Oh, I know it," said Sarah. "Adam and I have a spiritual connection to that novel. Over the last year, you have continued to surprise me with your reading choices. What were your favorites?"

"Well, I loved *Anne of Green Gables, Rebecca, Little Women, The Prime of Miss Jean Brodie, A Tree Grows in Brooklyn,* and others."

"*A Tree Grows in Brooklyn,* of course; it's about an Irish family," answered Sarah. "You read so many books about girls and women."

"I forgot to mention *Emma* and *Tess of the d'Urbervilles,*" said Mikey, smiling.

"I think you took a little break from your reading to do some mischief against Adam back in the day, am I right, sweetie," said Sarah, laughingly.

Mikey burst out crying. Before Sarah could react, a hostess rushed over and asked if everything was all right.

"Sweetie, don't cry. I'm so sorry," Sarah said, reaching over to encircle Mikey. His continued blubbering attracted the attention of other passengers. A middle-aged woman turned around, looking on sympathetically.

"I feel so bad for him. Did anyone pass away?"

"Oh, no. Thank God nobody did. This is a personal matter. I think he'll be okay," Sarah answered. "I appreciate your concern."

"He's such a cutie," the woman added.

"Oh yes," said Sarah. "He most certainly is."

"Oh, sweetie," Sarah whispered. "I know how much you love Adam. I was kidding you. I'm so sorry."

After Mikey calmed down, he spoke softly to Sarah, holding her right arm.

"I was a troubled teenager back then. What I did to my brother should have gotten me thrown out of the house. I gave in to envy and that enormous ego I had. I think I am past those issues now. After Olivia left, I took stock of my life. I cried myself to sleep many nights. I'll never forgive myself. And I've been hiding plenty about myself. I think this had a lot to do with my behavior. I've had certain feelings since I was about 13. I had to struggle with them all through high school. I can't hold them in much longer."

"That was the age you started smoking," Sarah responded, trying to divert Mikey from sharing some personal revelations. "I'll never forget the Wildwood trip."

"I did other bad things to Adam on that trip," said Mikey, tearing up again. "I did them to someone I love. I used my hands on him. Oh, God. And then, I allowed Olivia and that terrible lady to rough him up after the card game. I don't deserve forgiveness."

"Sweetie, no. Those days are long gone. I know what happened. That's all water under the bridge. The adolescent mind is erratic, and hormones play a role. You are an adult now."

Sarah mentioned hormones. I want to take them one day. But not male hormones, Mikey thought.

"There can never be an excuse for what I did. I needed to look in a mirror first."

Sarah was intrigued by Mikey's comments about his need to look in a mirror and about feelings he couldn't keep a secret much longer, but she couldn't solve the riddle and frankly didn't want to. Mikey was emotionally distraught, and she thought it best to lighten the conversation. If Mikey aimed to divulge something about himself, he would do so when he was ready.

"All I know, sweetie, is that you are so different now. You are one of the two most affectionate people I've ever known. The other one is in the same family," though he seems to be changing."

Mikey looked at Sarah, simulating a kiss.

159

"I wonder who that may be?" asked Mikey. "For years, people thought Adam and I were opposites in our interests. But I did well in school, always loved music, and with Adam's help and urging, I started reading much more recently."

"Sweetie, you show it. The difference between you in 1974 and now is major. You seem to be another person now. You make me so proud. I envy the girl who will win you."

Mikey observed Sarah wistfully. "I prefer that my future wife or partner be six or seven years older than me," he declared.

"You have fascinating taste in women, Mikey. I hope it works exactly how you want it to, sweetie."

The remainder of the time spent in the air seemed to fly literally and figuratively. After another short nap, Sarah and Mikey accepted the last option from the food cart: Granny Smith apples, cheese and crackers, and a cold beverage. Forty minutes later, the pilot spoke again, informing passengers that they were circling Queen Beatrix Airport and would land as soon as an open runaway materialized. He advised travelers to make sure their seat belts were fastened.

Minutes later, the plane's air speed and rate of descent were reduced to allow for a gentle landing.

"That was a cinch," said an impressed Mikey.

"I'm sure it isn't always that way," answered Sarah. "But I'm happy it was this time."

CHAPTER 20

Hurricane Landfall

A thick leaden blanket of clouds stretched across the sky, obscuring any hint of blue and casting a heavy, grey veil over the world below. Who would have thought something as colorless as water could make clouds so dark? Soon, the drops would turn into endless music, tapping the restaurant's windowpanes, rooftops, and palm tree leaves, much like an old radio coming to life. But like most storms, the increasing volume of the precipitation would transform into discordance and finally into outright meteorological mayhem.

On a television screen in the upper corner to the right of the bar, Sarah and Mikey read words flash across a lower band: *Hurricane-force winds are expected tonight. Islanders are urged to stay indoors.*

"I think you need another rum and Coke, Sarah. We must dull the senses a bit inside while the weather bombards us out there!"

"Mikey, I had three already," said Sarah, slurring her words. "But I feel so good."

"Bartender, one more rum and Coke for my girlfriend. I'll take a gin and tonic with a wedge of lime. Not too much ice."

"Sweetie, you are turning me into an alcoholic," said Sarah. "But I think I want to become one. Why did you ask the bartender to give you less ice? I'm sure the answer is simple."

"Yes, the alcohol gets diluted with more ice," said Mikey.

As the storm intensified, Mikey signaled Sarah to join him in a booth set along a wall behind the main bar, where the view of the outside pyrotechnics was acute.

Mikey braced his arms to push close to Sarah. He draped one over her shoulder and tilted his head to graze hers.

Sarah beamed.

Sara smile/Oh, won't you smile awhile for me, Sara/Sara smile/ Oh, won't you smile awhile, Sara, Mikey crooned.

"That's so beautiful, sweetie. Thank you. I'll repeat it. You have such a great voice!" exclaimed Sarah. "And I love that Hall & Oates song! How could I not?"

"Is my voice masculine or feminine? Tenor or soprano?" Mikey asked.

"You asked me an odd question, sweetie. I think you are in the middle."

"But which way does it lean?"

"Mikey, will you be insulted if I tell you?"

"Not at all, Sarah. I want you to be honest."

"Mikey, your voice leans toward soprano."

"Thanks, Sarah," he said, smiling. "You made my day."

Sarah was taken aback by Mikey's response but attributed it to the young man's unique humor.

Outside, there were few people or cars on the streets. The palm trees creaked, screaming as their limbs strained against Mother Nature's offensive.

"Sarah, did you ever watch that old classic, *Key Largo?* Humphrey Bogart and Edward G. Robinson starred in it."

"Sweetie, I'm afraid that is one movie Adam never had me watch."

"It's a black and white flick from the 1940s. I don't think I've ever seen a better movie about a hurricane."

"Is that what the movie is about? A storm?"

"Well, it's a gangster movie, But it is set in the Florida Keys, where hurricanes are regular occurrences. I think the storm had a psychological effect on the characters."

"Sweetie, you dig so deep when you discuss movies and music. You do need to enroll in college. You finished in the top ten of your graduating class. It's crazy that you are staying back."

"College counselors tried to convince me to forward applications. Mr. Shelley was relentless. But that was about the time I was up to no good. I guess it was more important for me to bully people. I thought I would go within two years. My mistake was to put it off."

Mikey grimaced but then sang.

We had it all/Just like Bogie and Bacall/Starring in our own late late show/Sailin' away to Key Largo.....

"I know that song!" exclaimed Sarah. "Please keep singing."

Mikey sang another stanza from *Key Largo* by Bertie Higgins, a song that reached Number 8 on Billboard earlier in the year. Sarah applauded. "Adam told me you have a better voice than him but rarely displayed it."

"I know Adam loves the song too, especially since it's about the romance in *Casablanca.* But, of course, it bears the same name as the movie title I spoke about. As far as my voice, I think Adam's is better."

"So, what is the most recent song you've been singing to yourself?" Sarah asked.

"You mean on Top 40 radio?"

"Yes, exactly."

"Abra abracadabra, I want to reach out and grab ya," crooned Mikey from the latest hit by the Steve Miller Band. He reached out and grasped Sarah's arm as he continued.

Wholly charmed, Sarah smiled broadly, surrendering to Mikey's affectionate advance. They embraced each other until a manager approached to announce that the restaurant was closing early.

"I'm sorry, but the storm is intensifying. We must shut down to ensure our workers get home safely, though some will stay at the hotel."

"We completely understand," said Sarah. "I will pray everyone gets to their destination safely."

Since the bar section of the restaurant protruded from the building and was encased by glass windows on top and the sides, one sitting inside during the rain-swept deluge might recollect the times they stayed in their vehicle as it was pulled along in a mechanical car wash when splashing water rolled down the windshield and side windows.

"I've worked in this establishment for almost twelve years and have never experienced anything even close to this," said the supervisor, a Dutchman named Bram Jansen.

The blond-haired, light-skinned, medium-height 29-year-old moved to Aruba in 1970, hoping to launch a career in the restaurant business. Jansen spoke perfect English, as did most native workers on the island resort. Everyone knew Americans constituted the lion's share of the tourism trade.

"Sir, I know you are Dutch," said Sarah. "So I'm amazed at how perfectly you speak English. You are no different than a native speaker."

"Thank you, kind lady. My parents have been bilingual since I can remember, and English was the first foreign language we were taught in my Amsterdam grammar school," said Jansen.

"Almost everyone in the hotel business speaks it. I can't imagine functioning without it. Aside from that, the island has mainly been Americanized. American and British culture is dominant, from music to films to art and literature."

"But you still haven't forgotten Van Gogh, right?" asked Mikey.

"Never. Nor Rembrandt, not even the guitarist Eddie Van Halen. I know he is considered American but was born in the same city as me."

"I think you men may have forgotten to mention the most famous Dutch person of all," said Sarah.

"Who may that be? I think you have me stumped," said Jansen.

"I'm baffled, too," said Mikey.

"Ah well," answered Sarah. "Chauvinism reigns supreme. Have you ever heard of a teenager named Anne Frank? My husband is passionate about her diary and uses it in his class."

"Oh dear!" exclaimed Jansen. "Oh, you are so right. I should be ashamed."

"Anne Frank is among the most famous Dutch people and one of the most renowned in world history. I, too, am embarrassed," said Mikey.

"Technically, Anne was German," said Jansen. "She was born in Frankfurt. Of course, we know why her father fled that country and took his family into hiding. It is wonderful that your husband teaches it, but when did you two first read the diary?"

"I read it in my eighth-grade class at Number 6 School in Cliffside Park," said Sarah.

Mikey was even more specific: "My seventh-grade English teacher, Mrs. Angela Penna, at Lincoln School, taught a complete unit on the book. It was one of the most unforgettable experiences I've ever had in any class."

"In Holland, reading was required in *baisschool*, the Dutch name for your elementary school. I've enjoyed our fascinating

165

talk, but I need to close now. Maybe we'll talk again as soon as the hurricane has passed through. How long are you staying?"

"A total of nine days," said Mikey.

"Perfect," said Jansen. "Oh, what state are you both from?"

"New Jersey," answered Sarah. "In Fairview, across the Hudson River from New York City."

"An exciting place to live, I'm sure. You two make a perfect couple. I'm so happy to have met you."

"Thank you," said Mikey, smiling broadly. "Stay safe."

He and Sarah walked down a long corridor to an elevator. After pressing the button for the sixth floor, Mikey wrapped his right arm around Sarah, who nestled her head under his chin. After the door opened, they turned left, following signs to Room 614. Mikey turned the key.

***

"Wow, this is a hotel suite. I didn't realize we were getting something so lavish," said Sarah. "Dad didn't mention any of this."

"They gave us four rooms!" exclaimed Mikey. "Such a big living room, with two couches and a loveseat, a fancy kitchen, gorgeous dining area, and an attached bedroom."

The oversized bathroom included a hot tub and a long black and gold counter.

"I can't believe it," said Sarah.

"These accommodations are fit for a king," said Mikey. "My brother should have been here. He deserves this experience much more than I do."

This was the first of numerous times on the trip that Mikey would reflect on the strange twist of fate that allowed him to enjoy a premium vacation meant for Adam and Sarah.

"I miss my Adam so much," said Sarah.

"I don't know why he isn't here, but I am," said Mikey in a halting, guilt-ridden voice.

"I do," answered Sarah. "It was fate. It was meant to be. Something important in our lives will happen, but I don't know what it might be."

"Maybe we'll meet a friend who will be part of our lives forever. Someone like Alejandro. We saw what happened when Adam met him in Wildwood."

"Yes, brother-in-law, we may meet someone. But my mind keeps drifting back to 1964. That year has a connection to our current trip. I am convinced of it."

"Well, one day, you'll have to explain what you mean," said Mikey.

"I thought of the summer of that year after you first petitioned to replace Adam on this journey. Oddly, I strongly resisted but then reversed myself. I wonder if my final decision was decreed."

Spooked by Sarah's cryptic words, Mikey diverted.

"Sarah, I am close to collapsing. Between the flight and the time we had downstairs, I am spent. I'm sure you are, too. The couch pull-out will be perfect for me. You'll sleep like a queen on the king-sized bed."

"Mikey, I wake up with the slightest sound, unlike your brother, who can sleep through a tornado. With all the crashing and thunder, I don't think I'll catch a wink."

"I hear you, girl. We can always try."

"Night, dear brother-in-law. I'll do my best."

Shortly after 1 a.m., the air-conditioners shut down, and everything turned black. The hotel had lost power. Instinctively, Sarah shrieked. Mikey jumped off his couch bed and rushed into her room.

"I'm here, Sarah. Don't worry!"

Mikey plopped onto the bed and was flush against Sarah when he draped his right arm over her and mildly squeezed her while resting his head against the back of hers.

167

"Oh, Mikey, thank you, sweetie. The storm has caused a blackout. What a mess."

"I won't leave you, Sarah," he said, pulling the sheet over them and encircling her with his arms. "I love you, Sarah. I've always loved you since the first time I set eyes on you. You are so beautiful inside and out. And I will be right alongside you while the room is dark."

"I love you too, Mikey, but..."

"Please, Sarah, let me keep you safe and warm."

Sarah sniffled but surrendered.

Mikey squeezed her harder. "I love you so much. You are the brightest star in my life, beautiful girl."

"Oh, Mikey," Sarah said cryingly. "What am I going to do with you?"

Their shared breathing was mutually intoxicating. After about 30 minutes, they nodded off, bodies against each other and legs interlocked, as rain pellets, driven by powerful gusts, crashed against the window.

By 3:30 a.m., the hurricane reached its peak. Few in the hotel didn't feel the building shake, and even fewer were asleep. A loud crash of thunder awakened Sarah. Instinctively, she pushed closer to Mikey, who stirred. He opened his eyes and pulled Sarah's face to his own. After their lips met, he French-kissed his startled sister-in-law, first softly and then more intensely. Sarah initially resisted, but Mikey pressed forward. Before long, the woman responded in kind. The frenzied lovemaking in room 614 nearly matched the pyrotechnics display on the outside.

Mikey pulled down Sarah's underwear and pushed his hardened member against her slit. She turned the tables on him and took control of the approaching intercourse. Olivia had always complained about their sessions together because the young man didn't last long. In less than a minute, he spurted inside Sarah as the sex partners continued French kissing with abandon. Mikey panted as she groaned, and love emanated from both pairs of their eyes. Mikey embraced her for more than ten minutes. Sarah then squeezed him so hard that he squealed and cried.

"I'm sorry, sweetheart. I didn't mean to hurt you," she said.

Mikey then shocked her with a confession she didn't think possible.

"Sarah, I am a woman. I am trapped in a man's body. I've known this for years. I need to become a real woman, or I may harm myself. Please help me, Sarah. I'm not the man I seem," he said, sobbing.

Sarah rubbed his head and encircled him with her limbs. She rocked him back and forth.

"Sweetheart, your sexy talk is different than any I've experienced or heard about. But it is so sweet and creative. It shows how much you feel as one with your sex partner."

Mikey didn't push his confession any further. He sang *Sara Smiles.*

Sarah wiped tears from her face. "I am married to your brother. I love you dearly, but I am spoken for. You and I took things too far. I've been delinquent in regularly taking my birth control pills. I'm terrified, Mikey. I will be on pins and needles for the rest of this trip. And when we get back to New Jersey, I will privately come clean to Adam. How can I hide what happened?"

Mikey cried again. He wrapped his arms around Sarah. After five minutes, the young man, partially responsible for the adulterous act, whispered, "Sarah, I feel confident all will be fine. You will get your period, and we can put this event in the rearview mirror."

"Oh, Mikey, I just told you I've been sporadic taking my pills. How can you be so confident?"

"Just a good vibe, Sarah. "Still, I violated you and my brother. I couldn't help myself. I'm not feeling good right now."

"You know the old expression, it takes two to tango. I forced myself on Adam, and the result was Saoirse. Please, dear one, do not think about what happened. We have eight more days in Aruba," said Sarah, reversing her initial consternation. "We must enjoy ourselves."

"I love you, Sarah. I love you more than any person on this planet and beyond. I've always loved you. I loved you when you exposed me for my lies about Adam. But I guess that's my problem. You and Adam were meant for each other. You and he have three beautiful daughters. I'm an intruder who needs to know his place. Maybe if I didn't always see you, I wouldn't obsess over you every waking minute."

"Aww, sweetie. As I told you, I am not surprised at how everything played out on this trip so far. One day, I'll explain why. But I am deeply moved by what you said. I love you from the deepest recesses of my heart."

"Sarah, I hope we get the power back soon. It's tough without air conditioning and fans."

"You said it, sweetie," answered Sarah, pulling off the sheet and blanket that had covered them.

170

CHAPTER 21

Exploring the Island

"Sarah, how about if we explore the island? I saw a car rental place across the main road from the hotel. Now that the storm has passed, we should have beautiful weather all day."

"Aruba tends to have high humidity, according to some people I know who have been here," said Sarah. "After the deluge, I'm sure it will be oppressive. But the steady wind may help us."

"Maybe we should ask Bram for some advice," said Mikey. "I'm sure he knows every nook and cranny on this island."

"Sweetie, I agree. And his shift started at noon, so he's down there now."

"I'll take a quick shower. We missed breakfast, but we weren't the only ones."

"No, the hurricane stopped everyone in their tracks," said Sarah. "Without power, there was no service. The only food was what people had in their rooms. We can get a snack before we leave the hotel."

***

"Hey Bram!" exclaimed Mikey, holding Sarah's hand as they en-

171

tered the bar.

"How did you two make out last night? Come on, sit at this table by the window. Drinks are on me," said the amiable proprietor."

"Oh, we'll pay. I want a Piña Colada. Sarah will take a rum and Coke."

"I insist. I'll inform the bartender. Give me a sec," said Bram, hastening to place the order.

"Mikey, it's only noon," said a smiling, exasperated Sarah.

"Only on the trip, Sarah. None of this will carry over when we return to New Jersey."

"Mikey, my husband, and my dad are alcoholics. I need to be careful."

"Sarah, I agree. That's why I can safely say it is just a vacation indulgence."

"Oh, Mikey," said Sarah, shaking her head.

Just as the previous night was prohibitively bleak and turbulent, the afternoon projected another extreme, but this time one of glorious sunlight and mild wind currents. Surprisingly, the humidity was low.

"We seem to have the ideal day for outdoor activity," said Sarah.

"You know what they say about the calm after the storm," answered Mikey. "But, yes, we couldn't ask for a nicer day."

Bram carried a tray holding three drinks.

"It looks like your favorite drink is the same as Sarah's," said Mikey.

"They may look the same, but it's only Diet Coke. I never drink while I work. But even when I'm free, I rarely consume alcohol. This is my only vice," Bram said, lighting a cigarette.

"Yeah, well, Sarah and I are smokers too."

"Can I offer you one?" said Bram, looking at Sarah. "You, Mikey?"

Mikey shook his head. "I have my own, thank you."

"Thanks, Bram, but I have a pack in my pocketbook," said Sarah, pulling out a cigarette.

Bram flicked his lighter for her.

"I forgot to ask you last night. You guys are on your Honeymoon, right?"

"No, we are not married," said Sarah.

"Engaged, maybe?"

Sarah looked at Mikey uneasily.

"Bram, we are not engaged either. I am married to Mikey's older brother, Adam, with whom I had three daughters."

Bram smiled broadly to mask his thoughts.

She's married to his brother. Wow! All pointers show these two as madly in love. What a strange family dynamic. Oh well, I shouldn't inquire further. I am fond of them. Maybe they needed this time together to find themselves. It's easy to see mutual love on their faces.

"I'm surprised," said Bram. "But how wonderful about your girls. What are their names, if I might ask?"

"Saoirse is the oldest. She's nine. The twins are eight. Their names are Carol and Michele."

Sarah reached for her wallet.

"Here are their most recent photos."

"Mooi," said Bram, using the Dutch word for beautiful.

"Thank you so much. They are all good students, especially Saoirse. The twins have a mischievous streak."

"Normal for that age, I think, no?" asked Bram, exhaling smoke.

"For sure," said Sarah. "Speaking of age, Mikey's birthday is September 2nd."

"Wait, will you still be here that day?" asked Bram.

"Yes, his birthday is on the Thursday before we fly home."

"Excellent! We will celebrate. I will order a cake!"

"That's too kind of you, Bram," said Mikey. "There's no need for it."

"It will happen," said Bram. "The matter is decided."

Sarah blew him a kiss.

"Now, how about some recommendations for our day outdoors?" she asked.

"I recommend you guys drive to the island's far end," said Jansen. "There are some breathtaking views of the ocean from the high cliffs. Don't worry, it will only take about 45 minutes. Aruba is only 19 miles long. My favorite attraction is the Fontein Cave in Arikok National Park. There are drawings of the Arawak Indians on the ceilings. You might even see a few bats."

"As long as we don't get bitten by one. I'm not keen on turning into a vampire."

Jansen guffawed. "I think I know what you will say next," he said.

"You mean that your first name is the same as the author of *Dracula?*" asked Mikey.

"Of course. You are a sharp guy. In my school years, kids used to joke with me about it. I never forgot one who painted a picture of a vampire and inked my name above it. Even the teacher complimented him on his talent."

"I love it," said Mikey, lighting a cigarette. "I have to tell my brother about it when we get back. He's a fanatic for horror films, especially the Count Dracula movies."

"I think Bram is a more popular name in Holland than Germany," said Jansen. "But there is no doubt the most famous Bram in history is Stoker."

Sarah and Mikey nodded smilingly.

"When I was younger, I had nightmares after watching Dracula films," said Mikey. "I was always a woman getting bit in the neck."

Sarah gave Mikey a funny look but then laughed.

"Bram, is there a vehicle you advise us to rent?" asked Sarah.

"Yes, rent the Jeep. It has a four-wheel drive and is affordable."

"Thanks, our great friend," said Mikey. "We'll report back to you tonight."

"And I'll need my rum and Coke fix," said Sarah.

"Of course. Enjoy, my friends."

***

Mikey booked a three-day rental of a red, soft-top Jeep. However, Sarah rebuffed his attempt to pay, arguing that the cost was well within the trip's budget. After Mikey signed the lease and Sarah paid in American dollars, the excursionists pulled out of the lot. They immediately crossed over Main Street, a half-mile-long array of international and local shops, snack bars, art galleries, and department stores.

"Sweetie, we need to do some shopping there," said Sarah, pointing to the disappearing palm tree-lined steaming thoroughfare, where an overflowing antique streetcar followed a track. "I must buy souvenirs for every person in our family. It will be enjoyable to pick out items for the girls."

"That will be loads of fun," said Mikey as he coaxed his sister-in-law to snuggle against him. "I love visiting the women's clothes stores. I sometimes write to the lady who worked in cosmetics and lingerie at Bamberger's. We are good friends."

Sarah thought:

I'm flabbergasted. Mikey enjoys visiting women's clothing stores. I've never heard this before.

As Mikey drove with his left arm, he draped his right around Sarah. With the windows opened wide and the back windshield down, the travelers enjoyed the breeze generated by the moving vehicle.

"Sweetie, I love the breeze and know you are an excellent driver, but be careful with your speed. I understand some drivers

175

are pulled over and ticketed for going only a few miles over the limit," said Sarah.

"My love, traffic rules are enforced everywhere," answered Mikey.

"I have faith in you, sweetie. You're a great driver. You make me feel safe."

Mikey leaned over and kissed Sarah. "I love you so much."

Sarah didn't verbally respond, but her eyes said it all. She was smitten with her brother-in-law.

Armed with a roadmap and some notes they had written on a pad, they passed through the island's capital and the rural towns surrounding it as they headed north along the western coastline. As Oranjestad was located slightly north of the island's center, Mikey thought it best to check out the Divi and Eagle beaches before veering northeast to the Alto Vista Chapel, a small Catholic place of worship. The yellow-painted structure stood on the hills above the north shore of the sea, near the town of Noord, where they planned on briefly visiting its famous California Lighthouse.

Mikey suddenly pulled over to a small rest area at the side of the road. There weren't any other vehicles parked.

"What's the matter, sweetie? Is everything okay?" asked Sarah.

Mikey didn't answer. He leaned over and pecked Sarah on the lips. Sarah responded immediately, and they engaged in a long French kiss.

"Please hold me in your arms and take charge, Sarah. Please make me your girl," he said.

Sarah complied and became the aggressor. As she kissed and embraced him, Mikey moaned.

"I need to be your real girl," said Mikey. "Do you love me, Sarah?"

"I do, sweetheart. I was meant to adore you. I knew this years ago. And I have no intention of stopping what was meant to be."

Sarah mauled him.

A car passed slowly. When the driver saw what was happening, he honked and laughingly yelled, "Get a room!"

Mikey slid onto the back seat floor, encouraging Sarah to lie beside him. She wrapped her arm around his head and frantically resumed the kissing.

When she stopped for breath, Mikey repeated some of his prior admissions.

"Sarah, please help me. Please. I am madly in love with you and will always be. But I am not a man, Sarah. I am a woman trapped in a man's body. I need someone to help me become a woman. If nobody helps me, I am going to harm myself."

"Shh, sweetheart," she said, forcing her hand into his pants, where she worked on his member. "This proves you are a man."

"Stop, Sarah, please don't make me cum. I want to do my best for you, beautiful girl."

Sarah stopped, enabling them to resume kissing, with Sarah remaining the aggressor. After they mutually agreed to get back on the road, Sarah rested her head against him as he drove."

"I love you, Sarah. You are my soulmate."

On only the second day of the trip, Sarah Furano knew she was in love with two people.

When they returned to the hotel, they took a nap. Mikey pleaded with her to aggressively hold him in her arms, facing him.

"Please tell me I am your pretty girl, Sarah."

"I love you, pretty girl," said Sarah. "You are all mine, sweetheart."

Sarah and Mikey engaged in a passionate affair for the remainder of the trip. There were only a few waking minutes when they weren't in each other's arms, and Sarah wrapped her limbs around him every night. Mikey continued to tell Sarah he was a woman trapped in a man's body and that he needed someone to help him become female.

They held hands everywhere and had intercourse in a dark cubicle of the Huliba Cave.

"Sweetheart, I will take you in this cave. You don't have to move, only stand. I will make it happen, my pretty girl," she said.

Sarah's words were music to his ears. Typically, Mikey didn't last long, less than a minute. As they left the heart-shaped entrance, Mikey asked Sarah why the cave was unique to her.

"Mikaela, the alternate name for this cave is the Tunnel of Love."

Mikey would have pressed her on the meaning of the alternate name, but he was far more astonished and thrilled that Sarah addressed him with a female revision of his name.

"I love the name, Mikaela. Will you always use it for me?"

"Of course, my pretty girl," said Sarah.

They watched a horror movie, *Ghost Story,* in Oranjestad and had dessert in a café called Murphy's.

The Dutch proprietor was an urbane conversationalist. When Sarah and Mikey left, he told them that something about his café would later impact their lives. On the way out, Sarah said:

"Mikaela, since we visited a cave named the Tunnel of Love, I am convinced more than ever that things were meant to happen. The name 'Murphy' might mean something, too. Let's see how things play out."

"We do have a Murphy living with us," said Mikey. "I'm more than intrigued."

The lovebirds had intercourse a third time on the final night. Sarah didn't even consider the consequences because she was now madly in love.

On the plane back, Mikey slept on Sarah's lap. She caressed him, whispering feminine endearments in his ear.

CHAPTER 22

Arrival in Newark

Joseph pulled up behind two airport taxis on Terminal B's departure deck. Carol was on the passenger side and viewed the two returning vacationers.

"Mikey is so affectionate," said Carol. "His promised protection of Sarah includes him holding hands with her. Our family members are so loving towards each other."

"Carol, we've seen the other side of the coin with Mikey. You have a short memory."

"No, I don't, Joe. But Mikey has changed so much. He isn't the same person he was back then."

Sarah's defense of Mikey was cut short when she saw her son and Sarah engage in a prolonged French kiss at the curb. She immediately understood what had happened on the trip.

What have I done? They have fallen in love. Mikey always thought the world of Sarah, but I never surmised that he harbored much deeper feelings. Neither did I get the slightest hint that Sarah's passionate regard for Adam and their marriage could ever be compromised. I once saw Mikey romantically dance with Sarah

179

at Alejandro's wedding. I dismissed it as normal behavior at a significant event. It is clear she loves Mikey as much as he loves her. Luckily, Joseph can't see their open show of affection. But it will only be a matter of time. He will consider it scandalous. The unthinkable has happened because I intervened in clearing the way for Mikey to go on this trip.

Sarah and Mikey broke their lip lock briefly before Joseph Furano eyed his son and daughter-in-law. He noticed they were holding hands but saw nothing unusual about it and was inclined to concur with his wife's sentiments. After pulling up to the curb and shifting the gear into park, the Furano family patriarch exited the car, opened the trunk, and helped with the luggage. Within seconds, the vacationers entered the vehicle.

After seeing a policeman in his rearview mirror, Joseph sped off.

"Wow, they are on top of you right away," said Sarah.

Mikey was more cynical.

"I think they have a ticket quota to fill," he said.

Joseph, as always, defended the men in blue.

'If they aren't strict, the log jam would be excruciating. I wouldn't want their job, that's for sure."

"So, how was the trip?" Carol asked. "I'm going to guess you both had a fabulous time."

Mikey signaled to Sarah to rest her head against his torso, after which he wrapped his left arm around her.

"I had the best time ever," said Mikey.

"I'll remember this trip for the rest of my life," added Sarah. "After the first night and part of the next day, we had to deal with the hurricane."

"We got the reports, Sarah. Everyone was thinking about both of you."

During the trip home, they encountered terrible traffic.

180

Sarah swung Mikey's head on his bosom, kissing and caressing him. When Carol turned around to see if her husband could switch lanes, she saw another profound expression of love, dreading the ramifications.

CHAPTER 23

Family Explosion

Carol, Joseph, Jay, Jennifer, and Jimbo sat around the kitchen table, awaiting Sarah. When the mother of three arrived, she walked in with Mikey. Both of them took up chairs set apart from the table.

"Adam already knows the information I will be telling you all, so I advised him to stay in our room and do some reading," said Sarah. "The girls are downstairs in their rooms."

"Sarah, I hope this will be a good report," said Carol. "These kinds of family announcements are too often made to convey some sad news."

"I will let you all decide, but I think it is wonderful news," said Sarah. "There may be another issue, so I should come clean immediately. I saw my obstetrician two days ago. He confirmed that I am pregnant with twin boys."

Everyone yelped and cheered in unison.

"Another set of twins! I can't believe it!" shouted Jennifer.

"There is only one complication to add," said Sarah. "I know for sure Mikey is the father."

The festive mood quickly turned to looks of disbelief, then ferocious anger.

"Let me at him!" exclaimed Jay. "I'll cut his dick off and feed it to the German Shepherd next door! You are a disgusting piece of shit. This is how you pay Sarah back for her invitation? You destroyed this family!"

Jennifer approached Mikey and slapped him.

He burst out crying.

"Mikey Furano, you are a disgrace to this family," said Jennifer. "You have no shame and deserve to be thrown out of this house. The embarrassment to Mom and Dad is unthinkable."

Mikey cried harder.

"Listen to him," said Jay. "He's a sissy. He's no man. I've known this about him for years. He was covering up since the Wildwood trip and probably before that. He's a girly boy. Mikey covered for years by attacking others because he wanted to be like them!"

"Please help me, please," cried Mikey. "Somebody, please!"

"Help you?" added Jennifer. "When did you ever help anyone? All you did was insult people, bark out orders, and issue threats. You are a filthy, sex-crazed creep. I hate your fucking guts!"

Mikey bawled convulsively.

"Maybe I should tell everyone about the Wildwood trip from years back," Jay said. "It seems like this macho man has always been a girl at heart. I caught him looking at women's underwear and smelling and holding them with serious interest. I covered for you, but I've known for years who you are, pervert. You hid these feelings and have continued to hide them, but you are fooling no one, sissy. Maybe Jennifer needs to offer you some of her clothes? Am I right, girly boy? Do you want to become a real girl?"

Mikey sprawled out on the floor, sobbing loudly.

Jay took a few steps, kicked him in the ribs, and unleashed a series of stiff punches on Mickey's lower back, then yanked at his trousers. "I guarantee he is wearing lady's underwear right now."

"Jay, no, leave him alone!" screamed Sarah. "Don't go near him!"

By then, Mikey's ruffled red panties were entirely in view.

"There you go," said Jay, mockingly. "Just as I thought, this phony self-proclaimed stud is nothing more than a pretty boy. Down in Aruba, he tried to pass himself off as some Casanova, but he's really some transvestite."

Mikey's hands began to shake violently.

"Stop, Jay, stop, now!" Sarah ordered. "Leave him alone!"

Jennifer knelt and yanked hard on Mikey's hair. "Look at me now!" she ordered.

Mikey turned, continuing to sob.

"You better never again tell me or anyone else what to do. Because if you try, I will kill you with my bare hands, sissy boy. From now on, I am the head of this family. You got that? I will make all the important decisions. You have nothing to say anymore. You better hope I don't put you out of this house. I am this far from doing that!"

Jennifer held her forefinger and thumb almost together.

"Please, Jen, I'm sorry, I'm sorry, please," he said in a crying voice.

"Sex fiends and girly boys have nothing to say in this house," she said.

"I didn't mean, I didn't mean, I, I, I," stammered Mikey.

Jennifer slapped him again. Mikey squealed loudly.

"He squeals like a little girl. What a sickening hypocrite he is," said Jay. "Pansy!"

"Stop!" screamed Sarah.

Adam entered and knelt next to Mikey.

"Enough!" yelled Adam. "No more! If you keep this up, I will fuck somebody up!" He hugged his brother and positioned his body as a shield against further physical aggression. "Don't cry anymore, Mikey. I can't understand this fucking family. You all should all be celebrating the coming birth of Sarah's twin boys. Everybody is making such a big fucking deal out of a small matter. Who gives a shit who the father is? I couldn't be happier for Sarah and Mikey."

Everyone in the room looked at Adam as if he had five heads.

"I better not say what I think," said Joseph, who, until then, with Carol, refrained from uttering a single word during this ugliest of confrontations.

"Adam, I'm sorry. Adam, I'm so sorry," blubbered Mikey.

"You think apologizing for the horrible thing you did will make everything well?" barked Jennifer. "In a few days, I will decide whether or not you will be allowed to live in this house anymore. You hear me?"

"I hear you, Jen," said Mikey, his voice trembling.

"This sad affair has shown everyone what a sissy Mikey is. He was finally exposed. He played the tough guy role, but in truth, he is just the opposite," continued Jennifer. "The audacity of him to torture Adam and Alejandro for years! This is a classic example of using aggression for concealment. And look how macho Adam turned out to be!"

"Please, I need to go to the bathroom. Please," begged Mikey. "Please, I'm sorry."

"Let the sissy go," said Jennifer.

"C'mon Carol, I can't take much of this anymore," said Joseph. "Let's go back to our bedroom."

***

Joseph removed his right shoe and flung it against the bureau mirror. Miraculously, it didn't shatter.

"Let me guess, Carol. You arranged to have Mikey go on this trip so he and Sarah would fall in love. Am I not right? To you, the

186

latent sissy could do no wrong."

"Joe, how dare you talk like that! That's grounds for divorce! Don't you dare!" Carol screamed. "Why would I want the wife of my son to get impregnated by my other son? How is that possible?"

"You mean, you never suspected that Mikey might have romantic feelings for Sarah?"

"None!" exclaimed Carol. "Not even the tiniest clue."

"The entire town will look at us as white trash!" exclaimed Joseph. "We will get mocked and laughed at. I am ashamed to go back to work. It will only be a matter of time before everyone knows about this scandal! I can't take the stress anymore. I'm sure I'll die of a heart attack soon. My youngest son is a disgusting sissy and a sex fiend. My genes didn't bring these out."

"Oh, so here we go again—the gene pool argument. My family is responsible. What a deluded man you are, Joe."

"Jennifer is way more masculine than that fruitcake and deserves to be the head of this family. Mikey fooled us for years. Of course, Jay is a source of special pride to me. I wish I had officially adopted him instead of just granting him residence and following the name change he desired and engineered."

"Why are you calling Mikey a fruitcake? Because he wears lingerie? Maybe he has a strong feminine side. Is that such a bad thing?"

"It's not normal, Sarah. And he cries like a little girl. You heard what Jay said about what he knew about him and kept quiet for years. No wonder Mikey abused Adam. If he tried that again, Adam would bury him. But now, the worst marital infidelity known to man has happened under this roof."

"No, Joe, it didn't happen under this roof. It happened in Aruba."

"Carol, it isn't even funny. I am exceedingly fond of my daughter-in-law, but what was her role?"

"Joe, she is obviously in love with both our sons."

"Ah, so how should we work this out then? Maybe Sarah can alternate who she sleeps with. One day with Adam, the next with Mikey, and so on. Or maybe she's at heart one of those liberal free spirits. If so, all three of them can sleep in the same bed and have sex together. I forget what the word is. It's a three-part French term. When my brothers find out, my name will be mud."

"Is that all you are worried about, Joe? *Your* reputation? How selfish can you be? Our children will get through this. Adam is right about one thing. Having two more grandchildren is something to celebrate."

"Don't make me laugh! Adam also said that what happened in Aruba is a small matter. Excuse my French, but how fucked up is that? He calls his brother screwing his wife and getting her pregnant a *small* matter? How many families have such a thing happen? The few that have probably lived in the mountains of West Virginia."

"You better not say that to Adam's face," said Carol. "His muscles are starting to show."

"So he'll kill me. He may as well do it right away, as I am better off dead anyway."

Carol shook her head in resignation.

"And I must also point the finger at Sarah," Joseph added. "How could she have let it happen? It's mighty clear from how she acted tonight that she romanced Mikey for the entire trip. Maybe he initiated it, but she didn't resist it. I know she adores Adam, but now she has two people in her love nest. Do you think this is normal, Carol? Having sexual relations with your husband and your husband's brother at the same time? And which brother does she love more? Will we ever know? Do we even need to?"

"Sarah's relationship with Adam is rock-solid and as loving as any marriage can ever be," answered Carol. "Adam is happiest when other people are happy."

"Right," said Joseph. "Carol. I wouldn't be surprised if Adam encouraged Jay to have sex with Sarah too and maybe even get her pregnant."

"Enough now, Joe. You sound perverted."

"Carol, I am not the perverted one. Our family will soon be the laughingstock of Fairview."

Suddenly, their conversation was interrupted by a blood-curdling scream.

CHAPTER 24

Bathroom Horror

Sarah had opened the door to the bathroom and discovered that Mikey had slit both his wrists with a razor. There was blood all over the white tiles.

Joseph and Carol rushed to the scene.

"Oh my God, Carol, call the ambulance, please, fast, call for an ambulance," screamed Sarah. "Oh God, my love, please stay with us, sweetheart," the hysterical woman exclaimed as she held a wrapped towel around his right arm and quickly moved to attend to the left one. But she went berserk when other family members tried to enter the bathroom.

"All of you get away from him! If anyone touches him, I will take him, Adam, and our children and leave this house forever! Mikey belongs to me now!" she yelled, using the possessive eminent domain-type expression she once used for Adam. "He is the father of my boys. Anyone who says one more bad thing about him, you'll have to deal with me!" She screamed for an ambulance again.

Carol wept.

Adam yelled in the hallway outside the bathroom. "Call the ambulance now, or I'm going to get violent!"

The rest of the family rubbed their eyes, all sporting guilty expressions.

Jay whispered to Jennifer: "I think it is best we back off now. Adam is furious. Sarah is deeply in love with Mikey. It appears there is so much about that Aruba trip that we don't know. But I know you were waiting to end his reign of terror in this house. I am sure he'll be fine. I think Sarah reacted to seeing his blood. But he's done with his leadership role in this house and is deathly afraid of you. Ah, well, we have a girly boy in this family. I kept quiet for years."

Ambulance director Joseph Olivelli and his wife Rosemary entered the house, lugging a sizeable medical box. He worked fast on Milkey and assured the family that everything would be fine. He explained to Sarah that Mikey made the two slits on his wrists horizontally.

"Had he done them vertically, he would have caused much more damage and could have been in danger."

Sarah showed visible relief.

"Who do you want to ride with you to Holy Name Hospital?" Rosemary Olivelli asked Mikey.

"Sarah!" yelled Mikey. "I want my Sarah," he repeated, sobbing.

Carol looked stone-faced, underlining her disappointment in her son's clear shift of allegiance. But she understood he was deeply in love with Sarah. Even a mother can't compete with that kind of romantic passion.

***

The ambulance raced onto Bergen Boulevard, Route 5, and then Route 46. With the sirens blaring, the vehicle rushed up Teaneck Road to the Emergency entrance off Cedar Lane. Doctors readily confirmed the cuts were minor. They checked the young man's vitals, dressed his wounds, and repeated what Olivelli said about vertical cuts being far more dangerous.

"What a lovely young man," said the head nurse in the emergency unit. "He's so sweet. Is he your husband?"

"Not quite," answered Sarah.

"Your boyfriend?"

Sarah smiled and nodded.

The attending physician handed Sarah an admission form for a psychological evaluation that Mikey was ordered to complete within a week. On a night when the unit was busy, they returned to Adam's Mustang. Sarah had asked her husband to follow the ambulance to the hospital.

***

The family were all nervously seated in the living room. Sarah slowly led Mikey up the stairs. Carol pointed to the loveseat and told Sarah there was some hearty chicken soup in a pot on the stove. After Sarah guided Mikey to the two-seater, she rushed to get a blanket from her bedroom. She returned to cover him and filled a bowl with the chicken soup. Everyone watched Sarah as she spoon-fed him the contents, not wanting him to use his bandaged arms.

"Is it good, my sweet Mikaela?" she asked.

Mikey nodded.

Jennifer snickered.

When she finished, she returned the bowl to the kitchen, leaving it in the sink.

"What would you like to drink, sweetie?

"Just some water, Sarah."

Sarah brought back a bottle of Poland spring water, poured it into a cup, and held it to Mikey's lips. He drank about half and motioned he had enough.

Sarah then snuggled up to Mikey and repeatedly administered

peck kisses on his lips.

"I love you so much, Sarah," he cried.

"I love you even more," Sarah answered, her voice breaking.

Adam rose and walked over. He kissed Mikey on the cheek.

Shortly afterward, Sarah helped Mikey to rise. He glanced at everyone with teary eyes and then strode down the hall, holding her hand. A minute later, Sarah reappeared and sat back down on the loveseat. Adam sat next to her and rested his head on her bosom.

***

"Did you hear his voice?" asked Jennifer, speaking to Jay in his garage room.

"Yeah, said Jay. "Unreal."

"He sounds like a woman. Did it change overnight?"

"No, Jen. It has been changing for months now. I have noticed it, and so has Mom. It seems he wants to sound feminine."

"After he recovers, I am going to beat the living daylights out of that faggot."

"I hear you, Jen. He deserves it."

CHAPTER 25

Professor Clarke Assesses the Situation

Mikey found a space in front of Susan Clarke's Palisades Park apartment. The young man insisted on driving Sarah's Challenger, and after he parked, he rushed around the car and opened the door for his sister-in-law and soon-to-be mother of his twin sons. Sarah interlocked her right hand with his left one as they entered the vestibule, where Sarah rang the bell. Less than thirty seconds later, a buzzer let them in. Sarah led Mikey to Apartment 3, on the ground floor, where the smiling academic waited in front of the open door. Susan led them into her immaculately maintained living room and urged them to sit on a purple loveseat on a white oak floor. Mikey asked for permission to smoke.

"Honey, we all have this same addiction," Susan answered. "You never need to ask. An ashtray is on the end table to your left."

Mikey nervously lit up a cigarette but handed it to Sarah, then flicked a lighter on another.

"Mikey, can I interest you in a bottle of Bud? Sarah doesn't touch alcohol, so I'll bring her a soda."

"Thank you so much, Professor," Mikey answered. "I won't go

195

with more than one as I am the one driving."

"Susan, I'm sure you will be quite surprised to hear this," Sarah said. "I've liked rum and Coke lately."

"Well, I'll be," Susan responded, with an incredulous look on her face. "Did you pick up this new vice on your Aruba trip?"

"Yes, I did. And since that time, I've had at least one glass a day. My father was delighted to hear this, but my mom was angry. She hasn't stopped reminding me how I have gone off at my father for my entire life about his drinking. And my father-in-law is visibly displeased."

"What did Adam say?"

"You know him. He thinks it's wonderful if I'm enjoying it."

"Of course," Susan said, smiling. "Nothing is ever seen as wrong with him. Anyway, you know about my history of abusing the bottle, so I should be the last one to judge."

She returned from the kitchen with a tray holding a tumbler glass of Sarah's liquor, Mikey's ale, a glass of red wine for herself, and a plastic bowl of potato chips.

"Well, I can't tell you how thrilled I am to see you again. Five months was a long time to be away, but as I explained, completing all that estate business took a while. Unfortunately, I had to go on sabbatical this semester, but I'm good to return for the spring semester."

Sarah crushed her cigarette and took her first swig from the glass while Mikey held the beer bottle to his lips.

After she completed her host duties, Susan spoke with marked solemnity.

"I've tried to stay calm, but I'm fearful you might have some distressing news. Please say something positive to dispel this. You have me so worried, and that's an understatement."

Mikey breathed heavily and nearly cried, but he held on. Sarah noticed and moved closer to him, draping her right arm over his shoulder.

"Susan, there is plenty to discuss, but I first wanted to come right out and say it. I am pregnant with twin boys."

Susan flashed a broad smile and exclaimed, "Praise to the Lord. What a happy day this is. And a second twin pregnancy!"

But then, it hit her like a ton of bricks. She understood why Mikey was there and glared at him accusingly.

Mikey lowered his head and sobbed. "I want to die. I don't want to live anymore. Please let me die. I don't deserve to live. Please help me."

Sarah couldn't handle Mikey's emotional meltdown and cried, too. She wrapped both her arms around him.

"Please, sweetheart, no more. I will love you forever. You will always make us laugh and feel good about ourselves. Please, honey, no more crying, my beloved."

Sarah's deeply affectionate words for Mikey clarified everything to the school official, a woman whose minor was in psychology but whose experience extended to therapy and guidance. She knew Sarah would stand by Mikey through thick and thin, familial scandal and embarrassment, and this most shocking brand of marital infidelity. The intuitive educator quickly scrutinized the situation, immediately setting out to vocalize a long-term prognosis. But she waited for the emotional outburst to subside.

"I don't feel well. Can I lay down somewhere?" Mikey asked.

"Of course," said Susan. "Please feel free to lay on my bed."

After Sarah helped Mikey to his feet, she led the whimpering young man to Susan's bedroom, urging him to lie on the bed. She closed the door.

"Sarah, you were in Aruba for nine days. What day do you think you were impregnated, assuming, of course, that you and Mikey only had intercourse once?"

"No, three times. Mikey initiated the first liaison on the first day there during the hurricane. I made it happen the second time in a cave, and the third on the final night was by mutual consent."

"Sarah, I am thunderstruck. This romance started on the trip, correct? Nothing at home prior?"

"Yes, Susan."

"I understand. Ah well. You were just as much in the heat of passion as he was. Based on what you have always told me about your sex drive and how you never think of the ramifications of your episodes, you never had a chance here. I love you, Sarah, and you've become my best girlfriend, but your weakness is that you rarely consider the consequences of your actions. You follow the flow and always think the best of any circumstance."

Sarah bowed slightly, then looked up to Susan with teary eyes. "Susan, I have fallen in love with him."

"I am not surprised," said Susan.

"Why do you say that?"

"Things you said about him, dating back to the night of the terrible event in the living room. Riding around in the car, you defended him and told me he was a very good person and a cherished brother-in-law who was good-hearted and the pillar of the Furano family. After all the monstrous lies he promulgated against your husband, you stood by him. You seemed far more interested in talking about what you loved about him than holding him accountable for the heinous acts that nearly broke your family apart. That he is so easy on the eyes – frankly, he's gorgeous – and that he possesses such a dynamic personality is part of your overall, shall we say, *appreciation* of him. You allowed the sex acts in Aruba to go down without much of a fight and even initiated one. I believe that subconsciously, you knew this was wrong, but you didn't possess the emotional or physical capacity to stop it from happening. He also won points because he is your

198

beloved husband's brother."

Sarah rubbed her eyes.

Susan rose, sat beside her friend, and draped her left arm around her.

"Oh no, please don't, Sarah," Suan continued. "You will survive this difficult event. Being in love with Mikey doesn't remotely diminish your bond with Adam. He might be more than a little rough around the edges, to say the least, but he's still your husband and soulmate, and as you once told me, he is your Heathcliffe. Somehow, you will get through this."

"How, Susan? I see scandal and infidelity and unspeakable embarrassment for my family and my in-laws. My father-in-law is enraged, and some old marital problems with Carol have resurfaced. The family hates Mikey, and he is getting abused terribly. The traumatic event has made him submissive and emotionally unhinged. He cries all the time now. My sister-in-law has jumped at the chance to get revenge on him for all his controlling actions toward her for years. She is deriving glorious satisfaction from witnessing his meltdowns. I was shocked to see her use her hands on him."

"Sarah, what has Adam said about this sad affair? Has he vocalized his position?"

"He said we are overrating the situation, which he voiced was no big deal. He said everyone should celebrate the birth of twin boys and not find ways to take issue with it. He said shit happens, and this matter is quite minor."

Susan guffawed.

"Of course," she finally uttered after gathering herself. "I needn't have even asked. I have no words for his response, but however seemingly insane his outlook is, we greatly need positive energy and a rosy outlook. As I said before, Adam is different, mainly for the worse. But he has apparently retained his capacity for tolerance. Mind you, I do not mean to remotely suggest or predict that your future with Mikey will include weekly sexual intercourse, but let's be serious. You will show him the same lovemaking intimacy you have enjoyed with Adam. He is, after all – and this will unquestionably be the deal breaker for you – the future father of your twin sons. This reality won him a place in your heart forever. I know the way you think, Sarah. I know abortion would be a monstrous, impossible option, and putting them up for adoption would be unconscionable. Mikey is their father, and he will help you to raise them. You will maintain an intimate relationship with him while continuing the deepest emotional and sexual bond with your Adam. Your life just got more complicated tenfold."

"Adam is my world, Susan."

"Yes, he is, Sarah. But your world has just doubled. You have other options, but they don't appear realistic."

"Can you explain them, please?" asked Sarah.

"Well, you can hide the fact that Mikey is the dad of your kids and make it seem that Adam, your husband, is the one who impregnated you. They are brothers, after all."

"Susan, you know that such a ruse would be impossible and, at that, most undesirable. For one, Adam would never agree to it – he would oppose it with every fiber of his being – as he would think it would be stealing the boys' birth father and depriving the children of their biological parent. I realize Adam's behavior is much more devious now, but I think he would understand the truth would come out sooner or later."

"Quite right, honey. The way your life is set up in that house, everything is staged in a fish tank. As to the second option, what if either Mikey or you and Adam were to move away, perhaps even out of Fairview? This could lessen the attention paid to your family. So many scandals like this one result in the guilty parties flying the coop. But I also know you need assistance from the Furano family to help raise your five children. While I don't expect you'll live with your in-laws forever, this unexpected development ensures you will remain there for quite a while longer. Mikey could hardly move away, what with his two boys living there and you granting him the blessing to fulfill his fraternal obligations."

"My father-in-law thinks we should be put into the Guinness World Book of Records."

Susan laughed.

Sarah lit a cigarette, inhaled, and took a sip from her drink as she exhaled.

"I'm so terrified, Susan."

"Sarah, could I ask how your parents reacted to this news?"

"My mom cried, and my dad initially said some very hateful things to me. He loves Adam dearly and accused me of cheating on my husband. But he eventually calmed down, and after meeting Mikey at my parent's home, his anger subsided. Believe it or not, he was quite taken with Mikey, though this wasn't the first time he met him. My father is a strange one, however. He seemed happiest to learn I started drinking."

Susan snickered.

"I see. Sarah, I know the answer, but I'll ask you a few questions anyway. Before intercourse, were you and Mikey engaged in some measure of romantic intimacy? Embracing? Snuggling? Kissing?"

Sarah nodded guiltily.

"Mikey initiated all the intimacy, right?"

"Only in the beginning. After a few days, I initiated it just as much. Susan, I must tell you that for the entire trip, Mikey showed me a side of him I'd never seen. He was always funny and generous but was all about love in Aruba. He seemed to worship me. I witnessed charm overload. I couldn't help being won over."

"Sarah, if we were talking about the old Mikey from when he tormented Adam, I'd say he romanced you because your dad is wealthy. I am now convinced this is not the case. I believe Mikey is genuinely in love with you. This was perhaps the downside to you all living in the same house. He sees you every day. If you had stayed in that apartment on the other side of town, none of this would have ever materialized. Mikey saw the loving relationship between you, Adam, and your daughters and no doubt fantasized about being in the same position. I am reminded of a Western classic movie called *The Searchers.*"

"Mikey also mentioned that seeing me daily generated romantic thoughts within him. Adam loves *The Searchers.* He has talked about it often over the years, but I haven't seen it."

"John Wayne plays a character named Ethan Edwards in his most famous role," said Susan. "From the opening scenes, he is madly in love with his brother Aaron's wife. Her name is Martha. After most of Aaron's family is wiped out after an Indian attack, Ethan arrives to search through the burned wooden cabin, yelling Martha's name. Although Martha dearly loved Aaron, she also had the deepest affection for Ethan. I see much of the same now with you, Adam, and Mikey. The way I read the film, Ethan and Martha were in love but could never act on it. The screenplay practically infers they may have had an affair, however short. What's more, some scholarly studies on the film have suggested that the child who survives – her name is Debbie – is the daughter of Ethan, who, according to the theory, had sexual intercourse with Martha."

"My situation isn't quite that way," answered Sarah.

"Of course. But there are some striking similarities," said Susan.

Sarah shuddered, then diverted.

"Susan, Mikey's personality has changed. He is a far cry from what he always was."

"Sarah, I'd venture to guess he is probably insecure and paranoid. And I wonder if that macho exterior wasn't just a front."

"It's funny you say that, Susan. Jay and Jennifer called him a sissy because he cried so much, and Jay brought up some incidents from the past that suggested his macho behavior was always just a show."

Sarah finally decided to drop the bomb. She told Susan all about Mikey's belief that he is a woman living in a man's body and that he needs someone to help him become a woman.

Susan's eyes widened.

"This is stunning, Sarah. Now, everything makes sense. I feel so sorry for that tortured young man sleeping inside. From hatred, I now can tell you I love him. Oh, that poor boy. I am so frightened for him."

"What is the girl's name you use for him?"

"Mikaela."

"What a lovely name. A psychiatrist would have a field day with Mikaela. Sometimes, a person's real personality or essence takes a major traumatic event to come into view. You said other family members are cruel to him, correct?"

"Jennifer slammed her foot on the floor as she passed him yesterday in the hallway to gain his attention so she could stare him down. Mikey cried and rushed to his room. I heard him sobbing through the wall. Because he is so guilt-ridden, he can't engage in conversation anymore. What you saw of him today is the best he's been since the evening we appeared before the rest of the family to announce my pregnancy."

"Sarah, is there anything else I need to know?"

"Yes, Susan, I thought I would hold this until the end of our talk. Mikey cut himself in multiple places with a razor. There was blood all over the tiles in the bathroom. An ambulance rushed him to Englewood Hospital. I can't handle talking about the emotional scene in the house that followed this act."

Susan covered her eyes with her hands, fighting back tears, but quickly rallied.

"This was probably not a serious suicide attempt, but it is close enough to suggest the level of shame he is feeling. He knows what he did was unacceptable and unforgivable. Those two words are not remotely strong enough, and he might be willing to pay the ultimate price. I'm very sorry this happened to him, but the incident raises my overall opinion of him. He is willing to accept any punishment."

Sarah nodded sadly.

"What about Carol and Joseph?" Susan asked.

"Neither one has engaged with Mikey since they discovered everything. I know Carol still adores him deep down, and he'll be her favorite till her last breath, but I'm sure it will be a while before she will again show him any measure of endearment. Carol blames herself for suggesting that Mikey accompany me on the trip. She says it was the worst mistake she made in her entire life. Far worse, she says, than when she recommended that Adam stay another night at my home. I became pregnant that night. Right now, Joe wants nothing to do with Mikey. He says Mikey ruined his life and the reputation of his family. As I said, Jennifer torments Mikey every chance she gets and relishes the opportunity to gain revenge on him after the years he bossed her around. Jay despises him."

"So, only you, Adam, and your three girls are showing him attention and affection. So ironic, considering who he harmed the most."

"Saoirse is one of the brightest nine-year-olds. I did my best to explain what happened. I refused to hide anything from her. I told her I was pregnant with twin boys and that Mikey was the father. I also explained to her that I didn't want or expect any more children. But I left it at that."

"I can never respect you enough, Sarah. Few would have the courage or desire to convey the truth about this event to their off-spring. I am assuming you did the same with the twins?"

"No, I have not yet had the same talk with the twins. I delegated Saoirse to explain to them all I told her. Carol and Michele didn't appear to grasp the significance of Mikey being the father but were thrilled they'd soon have two baby brothers."

"The vast majority of children that age would respond the same way. Saoirse, of course, was always a deep thinker," said Susan.

"Susan, all three of my children are intelligent, but the twins tend to be more flippant. They react impulsively and don't always think of the consequences. I guess in the latter sense, they are like me."

Susan puckered her lips.

"Has there been an official reaction from Jimbo?"

"Saoirse explained it all to him. She told me that he covered his face with his hands and shook his head repeatedly but didn't say anything. As you know, he is extremely introverted."

"Sarah, the talk among people behind your back will be brutal. Few will understand, and sympathy will be scarce. I am sure you know this well. There will be mockery and dark sex jokes, with some aimed at you, hinting at promiscuity. Your determination to have the twins and declare who the father is right from the start sends a message that you were probably on board. The cruelest ones might say something about Jay having *his* turn."

Sarah dropped her head and rubbed her eyes. "I found out my father-in-law said the same thing about Jay."

"I'm so sorry, love," said Susan as she rose to wrap her arms around her best friend. "I wasn't being nice at all. But please don't distress yourself anymore. I know there'll be much happiness at the end of the tunnel. You have to deal with the curve thrown your way."

"But this is more than a curve, is it not, Susan?"

"Yes, quite a bit more, to put it mildly, but after your children are born, I believe the focus will shift from their unconscionable conception to the joy of their existence. It is just getting to that point that will be challenging. Your father-in-law will no doubt feel the family will be disgraced beyond repair by the birth of illegitimate children, even if such occurrences are more and more common these days."

"I hear Mikey crying again," said Sarah.

"I hear him, too. If this continues in your home, I hope you will employ the method you used on Adam," responded Susan devilishly. "Wouldn't that be poetic justice having this formerly macho man emasculated and brought down to the level he once mocked another for?"

"It would be, Susan. But I love him too much to even think of that."

"Of course, Sarah. Once again, I spoke badly. It appears Mikey is already emasculated. I don't believe he will ever again be the kind of self-assured, cocky person he was since you met him. Time might heal, but you will see a different person moving forward. If his statement about himself is true, we might see an outright gender change."

"Susan, thank you for everything. Your advice and ability to peel off the gauze – I remember you once used that analogy – of this awful situation and insistence that there is plenty of hope are deeply appreciated. I don't know what I would do without you."

"I'm always here for you, love," responded the academic. "Oh, I never asked. Did you choose names for the twins? Or is it too early?"

"Mikey and I agreed they should be named after our fathers. So, Joseph and Stephen."

"Sarah, you are so noble. First, your twin girls were named after your mom and mother-in-law, and now the men get their chance. It will take time for the fathers to appreciate it, but I'm sure they will lovingly."

While holding Mikey's hand, Sarah kissed Susan before they departed.

CHAPTER 26

Mikey Served an Eviction Notice; Sarah Intervenes

Jennifer approached her parents in their bedroom.

"Mom and Dad, I want to let you know that I have decided to inform Mikey that he must leave this house within three weeks. Given what happened in Aruba, I don't think it's proper for him to live here anymore. I am being more than fair by giving him the three weeks, as what he did warrants immediate eviction."

Carol sobbed but didn't challenge her daughter's decision.

"Jennifer, are you sure this is the right action?" Joseph asked. "Do you think Sarah would approve?"

"Dad, I love Sarah, but she is not the head of this family. I am. Just because she is willing to set aside this monstrous act doesn't mean we must go along. Sarah will register a mild protest and then back off."

"Jennifer, I don't know about that," said Carol. "Sarah deeply loves Mikey and always wants him close to her."

Carol couldn't reconcile herself that her favorite child would be forced to leave the home he had lived in since he was born. Because Mikey finally acknowledged his gender confusion, the

209

young man needed support and affection more than ever.

"Mom, if Sarah chooses to condone this girly boy rapist's actions, that's her business. But there is no reason for all of us to accept it. I think we have a moral obligation to act. I know how much you have always loved him, but you can't allow yourself to weaken. Mikey isn't guilty of jaywalking or littering; he is guilty of something impossible to imagine. He cannot live under our roof anymore!"

"I think Jennifer makes much sense," answered Joseph. "Mikey needs to go."

"I think he is getting away easy if you want to know the truth. Sarah knows this, even if she chooses to dismiss the matter. I think all of us will rest easy when we rid this house of that monster," said Jennifer.

Carol dabbed tears from her eyes with a tissue.

"Where will he go? What will he do? Jennifer, I am so afraid for him."

"Mom, we need to be strong. Part of me also feels sorry for him. But he brought this on. For years, he abused Adam and me. And what he did to Dad was unforgivable. Now we all know he's a sissy girl and a crybaby. Maybe a guy will take care of him."

"Jennifer, he is not gay."

"Yeah, he doesn't seem to be, but he has surprised us before, right? Anyway, my decision is firm, and I will let him know this afternoon. If he has difficulty finding a place, I might extend him one extra week."

"Jennifer, we will abide by your decision," said Joseph.

Carol rubbed her eyes.

***

The old Mikey would have laughed at what Jennifer ordered him to do. Or worse yet, he would have threatened her. Either way, his younger sibling's injunction would have been denied. But

210

since Aruba and the highly contentious aftermath, Mikey was different. He was guilt-ridden and afraid of his sister, a young woman once perceived as the Switzerland of the family but more recently a strong-willed person determined to do what she believed was right.

Jennifer barged into Mikey's bedroom without knocking.

"Mikey, you have three weeks to find another place to live. I recommend you start looking as soon as possible, as this short window will expire fast. Mom and Dad agreed with my decision."

Mikey teared up and rubbed his eyes.

"Jen, I don't know where to go."

"This is not our problem. After what you did, there can be no turning back for anyone. It would be best if you started looking tomorrow."

Mikey buried his face in a pillow.

Briefly, Jennifer displayed a sympathetic look, but then she turned and left.

A short while later, Sarah knocked on Mikey's door after hearing his wailing through the wall.

"Come in," Mikey answered.

"Why are you crying, my love?" asked Sarah as she sat on the bed and reached over to encircle Mikey with her arms.

"Jen told me I must leave this house for good in three weeks. I don't know where to go."

"Nothing like that will ever happen, sweetheart. Not in a million years. If your family insists you leave, I will take you, Adam, and our daughters to my parents' home. We will live there until I find an apartment in this area. And we would never come back here ever again."

***

Sarah waited until the evening to confront Jennifer, who, as was her ritual, sat with her parents for coffee after dinner. After

211

attending to the girls playing the Parker Brothers game Sorry in Saoirse's room with Jimbo, the woman instructed Mikey and Adam to follow her into the kitchen, where they sat at the table.

"Sarah, would you like a cup?" Carol asked. "Mikey and Adam, maybe?"

"Maybe later," answered Sarah. "Right now, I have an urgent matter to discuss."

Jennifer's expression turned pensive. She looked reproachfully at Mikey, who noticed and quickly put his head down. Sarah continued, bringing on the heaviest artillery.

"Early today, Mikey was told to leave this house within three weeks. He was distraught and told me he had nowhere to go. I must tell you all that while I respect Jennifer's authority on almost everything, this order is unacceptable. I dearly love Mikey and can never live apart from him, now or ever. If you refuse to change your position and insist that he must leave this house, you leave me with no choice but to take him, Adam, and my three girls and move out as soon as possible. I would take both men and my daughters to live with my parents until I find an apartment. I can guarantee you will never see us again."

Adam echoed his wife's request.

"If Mikey must leave, I will go too. Without my brother, I won't fucking live here anymore!"

Adam stood up, walked behind Mikey, leaned over, and draped his arms over his brother's shoulders, glaring at Jennifer. The teary-eyed Mikey grabbed hold of Adam's arms.

Before Carol and Joseph could respond – their head-shaking made it clear they could never accept their beloved family members moving out and never returning – Jennifer immediately backpedaled.

"Sarah, I understand. Let's leave everything the way it is." Jennifer thought:

I shouldn't have wasted my time. Mom warned me. This tells me there is no way Mikey could ever be forced to leave. But the sissy rapist better stay clear of me. I will cripple him if he gives me a reason. I can't believe the people he harmed the most are fiercely standing by him.

"Thank you, Jen," Sarah answered. "Right now, my sweetheart needs so much support and affection. For nine days on the plane and in Aruba, I saw a beautiful, loving, sweet, creative, and passionate young man. My Adam always told me this about him, but I had to witness it. Mikey treated me to some of the best days of my life."

Jennifer thought again:

Yeah, he's sweet, all right. Perfect for the girly image he wants to project now. He was such a tough guy in high school, but now we all see who he is. I can't wait to see him wearing a pair of hoop earrings in a skirt and heels, with a pocketbook over his arm and hair flowing down his back.

The group stayed a while to smoke and drink coffee, though Joseph hightailed it to his bedroom, where there wasn't any air pollution to navigate.

Later that night, Mikey and Jennifer passed each other in the hall, going and coming back from the bathroom. Jennifer stopped and pushed Mikey against the wall, holding his neck against it with her right hand.

"You need to stay clear of me; do you hear me, little girl? One more wrong thing done by you, and I will smash that pretty face of yours into jelly, do you understand?"

After Aruba and the revelations about Mikey's gender confusion out in the open, the young man was no longer able or willing to fight back against anyone. He knew his place and understood that Jennifer, as the family's leader, was the last person to cross.

213

"I understand, Jen," he said sheepishly.

After that night, Jennifer turned Mikey into the family gopher. He was sometimes dispatched to Hiza's for bread, milk, and cold cuts and to the borough hall Sweet Shoppe for cigarettes, cans of soda, and newspapers. Every Sunday morning, he was ordered to buy section bread at Scala's Bakery or alligator loaves at Pedoto's. Mikey performed these duties without complaint.

Sarah wasn't happy about Mikey's new duties. They mired him deeper into his self-perceived role of servility and made him even more docile. But she understood she needed to meet her sister-in-law halfway. She was more concerned about the young man's continued residency at 76 Grant Street than the humiliating compromises required to ensure it.

But Jennifer's tactics became oppressive. Seemingly goaded on by the young woman's desire for revenge over the years Mikey dominated her, she restricted him in other ways. She even invaded his privacy.

One night, she knocked on Mikey's door. The young man rose to open it.

"Mikey, why was your door locked? You can never be trusted ever again. Tomorrow, I am calling Parent's Hardware in Cliffside Park to remove the lock. The only door you can lock in this house is the one to the bathroom when doing business, fixing your hair, or applying your lipstick."

Mikey cried over another of Jennifer's decrees, and Sarah thought the girl had overstepped her bounds. Still, she felt it best to remain silent for the time being.

Jennifer upped the ante a few weeks ago when she saw Mikey's door closed. She opened it to see him applying makeup in front of the mirror. She laughed derisively.

"Why is your door closed? Tomorrow, I am going to have it taken off entirely. You must live in a room without a door."

"Why, Jennifer, why?"

"Because I felt like it, sissy girl. Do you have a problem with it?"

"No," said Mikey in tears.

"I thought so."

The next day, his privacy was taken away from him. Carol thought her daughter had gone too far after Mikey sobbed in her arms later that night.

"Sugar, I'll talk to Jennifer. Don't cry."

A week later, the door was retrieved from a basement closet.

A few hours later, Jennifer barged in and held Mikey by the neck. After she verbally abused him, he said:

"I'm going to kill myself. You won't have to worry about me anymore. I'm going to die."

Jennifer knew she had gone too far.

"Oh no, pretty girl. I'm so sorry. I love you," she said, rocking him.

CHAPTER 27

Meeting with Dr. Levine

Sarah and Carol sat in the waiting room of Dr. Sheila Levine's Dean Street practice in Englewood. An attractive blonde in her early forties, the perky psychiatrist came highly recommended by Susan Clarke, who related to the women numerous success stories connected with Levine's intervention. The Furano family matriarch and her daughter-in-law browsed through copies of *Women's Daily* and *Cosmopolitan* in the upscale third-floor antechamber. Fifteen minutes later, an attendant announced their last name. The women were led into an ornate office featuring burnt sienna furnishings, numerous glass-encased degree certificates, and wall-to-wall bookshelves. Carol and Sarah were invited to sit on red cushion chairs and were told Dr. Levine would be in to see them shortly. She was prompt and entered the room five minutes later.

"Hello, ladies. I'm so honored to meet you both. I've heard so much about you and your family and am mighty impressed. I'd do anything to have friends like you." Levine shook both their hands. "I gave up smoking eight months ago, but if you feel you need to indulge, feel free. I always extend this courtesy. Mikey took full advantage of it, and I barely resisted joining him. I have a feeling it will be only a matter of time before I take it up again."

"We are so pleased to meet you," responded Sarah. "Thank you. We do smoke, but we will wait until the session is over. "

"There's a water cooler in the corner, and I have a coffee machine behind me. By all means, avail yourself. A bowl of Reese's candies is also on the desk to your right."

"We might later, thanks so much," said Carol.

"Well, now, shall we get to our talk? I will tell you upfront that I adore Mikey. What a personable, dynamic young man. I learned so much from our six sessions; he made a positive impression. I am still deciding if I might try to steal him from both of you. I am happy you allowed him to unwind with me all this time before asking for this meeting. It has been over six months now since the family explosion."

Carol and Sarah smiled and nodded.

"Carol and I concluded it was best to wait."

Levine smiled approvingly. "The incident in the bathroom wasn't a serious suicide attempt, as I'm sure you both know well. You saw blood, but he did not wish to die. Mikey loves life. The cuts by design were minor. But after your entire family attacked him in your kitchen, he lost control. Eventually, after many tears, he did his best to recall the ugly event. I understand he was physically assaulted by two family members, one of whom revealed some previously secretive information about him. When I asked him if he would ever seriously consider offing himself in the future, he readily answered, *No. Never!* When I asked him what he loved most about his life, he spoke only one word. *Sarah.* He repeated her name five times."

Sarah rubbed the back of her hand over her eyes.

"I have ordered Mikey to return in a few months for a follow-up appointment. Anyway, let me say right at the outset that the young man is not homosexual. He loves women, and there is one he adores specifically. Not that being homosexual is problematic, mind you – some of my best friends are gay – but I know it might complicate your lives rather adversely."

"Dr. Levine, could you share the answers Mikey may have given you when you asked him why he wanted to appear and act feminine, assuming you questioned him?" asked Sarah.

"I did indeed ask him," said Levine. "Mikey identified several reasons. He said he wanted to be treated as a female. That desire is manifest in his desired feminine role in sex. He said he wanted the freedom to express emotions that women can, but men are always looked down on for displaying. He also said he greatly admired females and wanted to emulate them. Can we speak freely on all matters connected to my study of Mikey?"

"Of course," the two women said simultaneously.

"Carol, Mikey is your favorite child, right?"

"My mother-in-law loves all her children, so she hates answering that question, but yes, Mikey has been her favorite for a long time."

"Of course," said Levine. "After spending so much time with him, I see why he would be favored. He is a remarkable young man, if a bit rough around the edges, with some past infractions that startled me, including the matter in Aruba. But when you talk to him, he makes you think everything about him is fully justified. That said, I believe his dominant feminine side is priceless."

"I agree," said Sarah. "That quality makes you love him even more."

"Absolutely," said Levine.

"Dr. Levine, can you tell me the general percentage of patients undergoing this therapy who transition?"

"I don't have exact figures, but I'd venture to say around 25 percent. Sarah or Carol, have you noticed anything about Mikey that has noticeably changed aside from the cosmetic alterations?"

"Yes," answered Sarah. "His voice has changed. There is a feminine lilt to his speech."

Carol nodded.

"Nothing there is startling or abnormal," answered Levine. "When his feminine side finally broke through, he assisted the new self-perception. He's far more comfortable sounding girly."

"So a person can change their voice themselves?" asked Sarah.

"Technically, no. Transgender people need a voice coach and plenty of help to alter their voice's pitch, volume, and shape. Some opt for surgery to modify the vocal cord structure. Mikey emulates how a female speaks as best as he can replicate. He can do wonders with the tone of his voice."

"Oh, we have already accepted it and are fine with it," said Sarah. "I like it more than his fake old macho delivery, and I know Carol feels the same way."

"One aspect of his behavior that will also be permanent is his submissive sexuality. When he is having sex, he considers himself to be a girl. He expects his sexual partner to be the aggressor at all times, and he is most blissful when a woman holds him in her arms. From speaking to Mikey, I only know of his sexual experiences with a girl named Olivia Torricelli and, of course, you, Sarah. Can you confirm what I just said based on your experiences with him?"

"Yes, I can, Dr. Levine. It seemed to change during the Aruba trip. On the very first day, he implicitly asked me to take charge. I theorized it was probably experimental, but now I know it was real."

"Yes, Sarah, it was always part of him, but he aggressively suppressed it. It reached a point where the yearning was so strong that he couldn't hold back anymore. Can I ask what feminine name you use for Mikey?"

"Yes, I call him Mikaela."

"Oh, what a sweet name. I love it. Anyway, there is absolutely nothing wrong with his sexual behavior. He will always be tame, and he brings a refreshing angle to sex by the role reversal. Your son and husband – and yes, Sarah, I must call him your husband at this point – derives the greatest pleasure when a woman makes love to him. It is a wonderful quality, I think."

"I agree," said Sarah.

"Sadly, when Mikey tried to deny his essence, he abused others who were like him. He took refuge in attacking them, specifically Adam and the young Polish-Hispanic man, Alejandro. When Mikey told me about the bad things he did to them and the instance when he hit his father and caused the man to have a heart attack, he cried his eyes out. Was he always this sensitive?"

"No, he was not," said Carol firmly. "To be truthful, he was as hard as nails. He held his emotions in check, didn't cry, and acted as if nothing bothered him until he returned from the Aruba trip."

"Well, he cried a lot during the Aruba trip. I witnessed the moment of the change, or when he could no longer hold back his feelings."

"He is so sweet and affectionate," Levine continued. "It is important for you to be affectionate to him in return. We don't want a recurrence of that terrible act in the bathroom. I'm so sorry to bring that up, Sarah. But we all need to approach this matter with awareness and caution."

"Yes, you are right, Dr. Levine," Sarah said.

"I think Mikey is surrounded by so much love. Carol, I know that you have been unwavering. Sarah, though not technically married to him, is his companion and practical spouse. Sarah, can I ask you this? On a scale of 1 to 20—with 20 being the highest—how much do you love Mikey?"

Sarah looked at Carol and hesitated but then answered 21.

"I thought so. And I know the same 21 for Adam, right?"

Sarah nodded.

"So, you see where you are now? You are passionately attached to brothers but have juggled extraordinarily well. The love has returned to you comprehensively. Carol, can you confirm your son Mikey's love for Sarah?"

"Yes, I can. It is beyond anything I have ever witnessed. He worships the ground beneath Sarah's feet. I only questioned him once and never again after his reaction."

"What did you say to him?" asked Levine.

"I asked him if he loved her sister-in-law so much because Sarah's parents were wealthy. It was a terrible, terrible thing for me to say."

"With all due respect, Carol, it was indeed awful. How did he respond?"

"He screamed and sobbed. He said he would love Sarah till the world ended or something like that. The next day, when he saw me in the kitchen, he cried again. Oh, it was one of the worst times of my life. I can never forgive myself."

"Did he ever say anything else?"

"He told me he was changing all his paperwork to show his next of kin would be Sarah. When I told him that he was slighting me, his mother, in favor of his sister-in-law, he angrily told me that Sarah was not his sister-in-law but his wife. He said he loved her more than anyone or anything in the world, and everything he owned would go to her. He told me that Sarah would be given the authority to make all decisions about him."

Tears flowed down Sarah's face.

"I am so sorry, Sarah," Carol added. "You know how much I love you. You are more than special to have won the hearts of both my sons."

CHAPTER 28

The Birth of Mikaela

"Changing the subject, Sarah, can you be specific and tell me about the times in Aruba when Mikey behaved in a feminine manner?"

"He pleaded with me to hold him in my arms in our hotel room, he nestled his head under my chin in a movie theater, did the same when we rode across the island in a Jeep – as he insisted I drive – and his physical mannerisms, some body movements, and voice began to change."

"What else?" asked Levine.

"Far more importantly, he told me numerous times when we cuddled in bed that he needed to become a woman," said Sarah. "He repeatedly said he was a girl trapped in the body of a man. He told me he was a woman when we rode in the jeep. I lost count of the times he told me, *Sarah, please help me. I need to be female. I am living a lie. I am going to hurt myself. I need to be a complete woman. I am not a man.*"

Levine's eyes opened wide. She stopped speaking and scribbled on her notepad.

"Sarah, I am shocked. What you revealed to me will greatly impact my conclusion. Mikey deliberately held things back from me, but I could understand why. He was nervous and embarrassed."

"What is your conclusion, Dr. Levine?" asked Sarah.

"Sarah and Carol, I need to retreat to my other office to review some recordings I made of my meeting with Mikey. This will take me about an hour. Can you both take a break and return at 2 o'clock? I want to be sure before I render my final recommendation. I may have downplayed some comments he made to me."

"Absolutely," said Sarah. "Mom and I will catch a snack in the diner across the street. We'll see you at two."

"They have the best Reuben sandwiches there," said Levine, in sponsorship of the Englewood Diner's version of the deli favorite made with thinly-cut corned beef, Swiss cheese, and sauerkraut on rye bread slathered with Russian dressing.

"Thanks so much," said Carol. "We are sold on it."

Sheila Levine thought she had successfully diagnosed Mikey's condition. But Sarah's bombshell admission made a full review urgent. One question and answer made her pause the recording and rub her forehead.

"Mikey, does the idea of becoming a woman repulse you?"

"No, Dr. Levine, it does not. I need to become a woman."

How did I miss that? I blundered. I am ashamed of myself, thought Levine.

Levine found a few other instances where Mikey's answers could have been taken two ways. She went through the tape again. Sarah and Carol were waiting when she arrived at her office 20 minutes late.

"I'm so sorry, ladies. I wanted to be sure, so I listened to the recording twice. I found a few instances that needed definitive clarification," she said, putting a positive spin on the fact that she messed up.

"Dr. Levine, Mom and I understand. Reaching a conclusion on Mikey is probably not possible."

"On the contrary, Sarah, I have reached a definitive conclusion. Mikey has a classic case of gender identity disorder."

"Can you explain what that term means?" asked Carol.

"Carol, your son is suffering distress that will never go away. It is usually caused by genetic, biological, environmental, and cultural factors. Mikey is not comfortable being male. He desires to be female, and in all likelihood, this feeling will get stronger and stronger. When he told Sarah he needed to be female, he pleaded for professional intervention. I believe him, and based on the whole picture with the recordings, we should encourage him to express his feminine side until it eventually takes over completely."

"So, my son is a woman?" asked Carol.

"He can never become a biological female. He has a Y and an X chromosome. Females have two X chromosomes. But with body modifications, surgeries, hormones, breast augmentation, voice coaching, and other procedures, he can assume a female identity and appearance. He will be able to function as one sexually. Some men who transition become more feminine than many biological women."

"Mom, whether Mikey is female or male, we adore him. We can't mourn over what we expect him to be. He has no control over any of this. We must show him unconditional love and support," Sarah said, wrapping her arms around her mother-in-law."

Levine nodded.

"Mikey is a gorgeous young man. But he doesn't identify as one and needs his body to match his mind. In other words, Mikey needs to present as a girl."

"I understand," Carol said, rallying. "So where do we go from here?"

"Look, Carol and Sarah, there isn't any rush to take drastic action. Eventually, that will surely need to happen, but it's best to show him as much love as possible."

"So we don't have to make a major concession now?" Sarah asked.

"I feel it best that you make one and enact it immediately. It will show him you are fully behind him, and it will, for the time being, set aside any possibility of a dangerous act he might initiate."

"What would the concession be?" Sarah asked nervously.

"You must forever retire her first name and will always use female pronouns to greet or identify her. The name you mentioned earlier in this talk, Mikaela, is perfect since it's a female adaptation of Mikey. It would be best to inform all your family members and friends that her name is Mikaela and that they must address her that way. Furthermore, you must change the name on her driver's license, social security card, paychecks, and every means of identification. Please never call her Mikey again. This is vital. Mikaela's identity takes precedence over everything. Mikaela is a *she* and *her.* All male references must end."

"After this name matter is instituted, we will wait. The next step could come shortly after that, perhaps not for a while. The pace all depends on Mikaela's behavior. She will determine the brevity of our next response."

Carol and Sarah nodded. "Dr. Levine, will her physical strength help to dim her femininity?" asked Carol.

"No. Her physical strength is a thing of the past. She sees it as a danger to her female essence. If and when she begins hormone therapy, her strength will diminish further."

Carol, who was always proud of Mikaela's brawn, sadly shook her head and said, "Another Alejandro."

"Carol, I know all about the former Andrzej," said Levine. "He, too, sounds like a beautiful young man. Mikey told me he reached a point when he would never fight back because of a family tragedy he experienced as a young boy. But I am afraid for him. I understand his wife has a volcanic temper and might harm him."

"Yes, we fear for him as well," said Carol.

"Dr. Levine, you just called my lover Mikey."

Levine laughed aloud. "The person who made the rules is the first to violate them. Isn't that the way it always is? I assure you there will be no other mistakes. Are there any other instances regarding Mikaela you want to share with me?"

"Dr. Levine, my brother-in-law Jay confided in me sometime last year while chatting about Mikaela," said Sarah. "Jay said that during our Wildwood trip in 1974, he and Mikaela were checking out all the shops on the boardwalk. Jay told Mikaela he needed to go to the bathroom and would be back soon. When Jay returned, he saw Mikaela handling and looking through panties and bikinis in a women's shop. At the time, he did not think much of it, and if he did, he might be inclined to conclude that Mikaela was looking to buy something for her mother or sister. A few days later, Mikaela was fascinated with lipstick at a storefront and told Jay she loved the burgundy color. Again, Jay thought nothing of it, thinking Mikaela would love it if her future girlfriend wore that color."

"Thank you for sharing that," Levine said, her eyes widening.

"Dr. Levine, do you think it possible that if Mikaela advances toward womanhood, she would be attracted to men?" asked Sarah. "I know you said she is entirely heterosexual at present."

"Not only is it possible, but it is probable. She may love you and live with you, but she may favor men in her life for her sexual needs. When that time arrives, and it may be sooner than you think, you will need to allow her to do that and understand it is normal for a woman to want sexual relations with a man."

"Of course, Dr. Levine, I understand, said Sarah. "Mikaela's need to be held by me in our sessions explains so much."

"Yes, Sarah, that alone signals she needs to be in a man's arms. She may still like to do it with you but may also need a male. Still, I would risk my home to wager that she will never leave you. I know the extent of love she feels for you. Before we conclude, I want to emphasize how important it is for you to regularly compliment Mikaela on her appearance. I will write to her for an appointment to see me in three months. One last question. Does Adam still exhibit the tendencies Mikaela has told me he once did during our talk?"

"No, Dr. Levine. Adam has been moving in the other direction and speedily, too. He is a macho man. He works out at a gym, lifts weights, and does aerobics. He has a terrible temper. Swear words have become part of his everyday vocabulary, and he is quite strong now."

"Oh boy. I know exactly what is happening there. He is violently rejecting his feminine side. I am inclined to believe he never wanted it and will eventually lay the blame on others."

"Our friend Susan said the same thing," said Sarah.

Levine slowly nodded.

"Thank you, Carol and Sarah. I would appreciate being informed when your twins are born. I see you are getting close. I wish you the absolute best."

Sarah blew Dr. Levine a kiss.

CHAPTER 29

Twin Boys Enter the World;
Reception Desk Intimidation

On a Sunday afternoon the day before Sarah's expected delivery, and after the family's ravioli and meatball dinner cooked by Carol and Grandma Delaney, Monopoly was played in the living room. Adam, Sarah, Mikaela, Saoirse, and the twin girls made the game a six-person affair. After a two-hour marathon, young Michele outlasted everyone to claim victory, fueled by her ownership of the high-priced dark green properties, Pennsylvania Avenue, North Carolina Avenue, and Pacific Avenue, that were getting landed on regularly. Michele's holdings also included the much lower-priced dark purple properties, Virginia Avenue, States Avenue, and St. Charles Place. Still, on a day when the dice were on her side, her opponents were bankrupted one by one. Never one to pass up a chance to rub it in, the boisterous Michele jumped up and down after her last challenger, Saoirse, was eliminated.

"You were so lucky," said Michele's twin, young Carol.

"It has nothing to do with luck," said the victor. "It has only to

229

do with skill and intelligent business decisions."

"What business decisions?" asked Saoirse.

"I traded New York Avenue to Dad for St. Charles Place," Michele responded.

"Yeah, and it only worked because everybody kept landing on the purples. Dad's oranges were slightly more valuable," Saoirse said. "Next time, we will play Risk. Let us see how your luck holds up."

"Hey, make sure you let me know when you play Risk!" exclaimed Adam. "That game is my absolute favorite."

"What about Stratego?" asked Saoirse.

"That's my second favorite," said Adam. "And I know your favorite. How could it not be? You are the best speller in the world!"

"Thanks, Dad. Yes, Scrabble is my Number 1."

"There go the Furanos again. Always rating things," said Sarah, laughingly.

"Mom, do you think the new baby boys will be the same way?" asked Saoirse.

The Furano family had gotten over the scandalous conception that would soon lead to baby boys, and everyone was increasingly excited as Sarah's due date inched closer.

"Of course they will," answered Sarah. "That's a no-brainer."

***

"Stevie and Joey," said Mikaela cryingly into the receiver. "They are fraternal, weighing 5.8 pounds, a little more than the average for twins. Sarah is doing great. I cannot tell who they look like; they are beautiful. I can't talk anymore, Mom. I am crying."

"Oh, Mikaela, sweetie, there is so much joy in this house today. Your Dad and I will be leaving in about 15 minutes. We'll pick up some balloons and flowers in the gift shop. Adam, Jay, and Jen will be there soon after that. Saoirse and the twins are begging to go, but we told them the hospital does not want too many in the room. Jimbo and Rob are playing games with them. I understand your in-laws are on the way, too."

"Thanks, Mom. I love you."

Carol Furano dabbed her eyes and hastened to prepare for the joyous ride to Hackensack Hospital.

Carrying balloons, the Furanos caught an elevator to the maternity ward on the third floor.

When Adam, Jay, and Jennifer checked in at the desk, the woman assigning the passes experienced a contentious episode.

"I'm sorry, Mr. Furano. I understand your wife had twins, but by your admission, you are not the father. The two siblings with you are not immediate either, so you must all wait."

"How about if I tell you that I won't wait? How does that sound?" said Adam, moving his hand into the pocket of his leather jacket. "Now, you are going to give me passes for the three of us so we can visit my wife, aren't you?"

The young woman stared at Adam and pondered what she should do. She could easily reach for the walkie-talkie and call for security, but this goateed muscleman frightened her, and thoughts flashed before her that he might have a gun. She froze momentarily and then wrote out three passes.

"Sir, please take the first set of elevators at the end of the hall. When you reach the third floor, the patient names will be displayed on a wall chart."

Jay and Jennifer eyed Adam disbelievingly but followed him to the elevator. The desk receptionist was traumatized by the unexpected encounter and opted not to mention it to anyone.

The Burkes and Furanos teared up, gazing at Mikaela and Sarah, each holding one of the twins. "I love you so much, Sarah," said Mikaela.

"I love you more," said Sarah. "This might sound corny, but

you're the peanut butter to my jelly and the crayons to my coloring book, sweetie."

"Aww," said Michele Burke. "I bet Mikaela could think of something even more profound."

"Sarah, my heart aches for you. I yearn for you every minute of every day. You're my dream person, now and forever."

Sarah wiped tears while everyone in the room clapped.

Adam didn't feel the least bit threatened or slighted. He sang lyrics:

How deep is your love? How deep is your love?

"Oh, Adam, you are so creative," said Sarah. "And you loved the Bee Gees before Iron Maiden won your heart."

"Now, everyone knows Sarah and Mikaela's love is unmatched, and I am the happiest person in the world for them, but we are not here to confirm what we all know already; we are here to lay out a welcome mat for two infants, Stevie and Joey," said Adam.

"Adam, I'm glad you said it!" said Joseph.

Family members took turns delicately handling the twins, with everyone noting features on both resembling either parent. Stevie appeared to have blue eyes and Joey brown, but everyone knew eye color often changes.

***

For the first three months, Sarah and Mikaela slept in a bed next to the infants, who were given separate cribs. Sarah and Adam got together once a week, an occasion that left Mikaela to sleep with the toddlers.

Because Mikaela was such an efficient worker and a young father, managers at the A&P pretended not to notice the feminine touches to her appearance and name change.

"Leave him alone. He can't help who he is," said a sympathetic cash register woman.

"You mean who *she* is. Her name is Mikaela. She is becoming a woman," answered a male checker. "Her voice is completely feminine."

"I understand he is becoming a woman," said the female. "That isn't news. But he's an exceptional worker and a loving family person. That's what counts."

"I can't understand the wife or the lover, whatever. She must be a..... Oh well, I should mind my own business," said the man.

"That's the best thing I've heard you say in months," she said.

Mikaela's fatherly obsession with her twins delighted the family. When she wasn't working, she attended to their every need, and once they started to crawl, she spent hours physically interacting with them.

"I've never seen anyone kiss their children like she does," said Carol to Jay, sitting in the living room. "The kids love it when she holds her lips on their faces and tickles them with her tongue."

"But if one of them cries over the silliest thing, Mikaela loses it," answered Jay. "My God, how much she loves them. She insists on feeding them, holding the bottles in their mouths, and changing their diapers."

"So, you are saying her love is more motherly than fatherly?" asked Carol.

"Mom, I don't know. Her love seems to be a combination. She has changed so much. Maybe she was always that way but needed to find her way through misery."

"Well said, Jay. The opposite happened with Adam, though he is still good but extremely rough-edged."

Jay puckered his lips and nodded.

***

A few months later, Stevie, the more outgoing of the two toddlers, crawled into the living room one night and pulled himself onto the couch where Rob slept. The boy lay down against the man and fell asleep. Rob was charmed, and after Stevie repeated the practice several more nights, he looked forward to having his mate with him. Sarah and Mikaela smiled.

"Looks like Stevie has a new friend," said Sarah.

"I think it is so wonderful," answered Mikaela.

"I agree, sweetie. This is precisely what Rob needed. "Their bonding is a beautiful thing."

Stevie became Rob's world. The man loved little Joey, too, but Stevie was developing a dynamic personality. After work, Rob's sole focus was the child, though he was vigilant not to deprive the boy of his parents, who were smitten with him. Rob loved it when Sarah told either of the twins they needed their Uncle Rob's permission to do something they desired. In a life seemingly headed for bachelordom, Stevie's role in his life was the great equalizer.

CHAPTER 30

Flight from Italy

Dina and her daughter, Maria, boarded a taxi at 7 a.m. outside their picturesque villa in Frascati, twelve miles southeast of Rome, on the Alban Hills, a dormant volcanic complex. Two years prior, they had moved to the historical conurbation at the behest of Dina's wealthy brother, who had given them and his mother an apartment next to his own, free of charge. Mario Petrigliano and his sister grew up in Bari, a southern port city on the Adriatic Sea, where the young man attended the University of Bari Aldo Moro, studying English and economics. After he graduated, he opted to take a position in tourism, a career that took him all over Italy. Though he dearly loved his only sibling, his influence diminished because of his absence, leaving Dina to pack up and move to America. Assunta, Dina's mom, was heartbroken by her daughter's departure but understood Dina had trouble holding an Italian boyfriend, mainly because she wasn't anything to look at. Not happy that his widowed *madre* would be alone, Mario offered his sister a sizable sum to stay a little longer and try harder to find a mate, but Dina resolved to leave.

After the violent death of Jimbo Gorman Sr., Dina and her daughter Maria, returned to Bari in late 1971. Her 19 years in the United States were anything but happy. Though she and her daughter spoke English fluently and enjoyed Fairview's Italian-American population, the annual feasts, bazaars, parades, and the abundance of belvederes and bread stores, she was part of a loveless marriage marked by physical abuse and the juvenile delinquency of her son. Maria begged her mom to stay in America, suggesting she move to another New Jersey town, but Dina insisted on a clean break and wanted to move as far away from her son as possible. While the males in her family were monstrous, she was proud of her daughter, a good-natured and supportive girl whose existence was the silver lining of a bad marriage. Like her mom, Maria wasn't blessed with good looks and always had trouble losing weight, two physical handicaps that didn't portend well for the girl's future wedding prospects, especially in Italy. Several dates led nowhere, leaving Maria to settle in with her mom and grandma and hope for a lucky break. The girl was fluent in two languages and possessed a kind heart, but turning 27 the month after the return trip to the States to see Jimbo and the Furano family, she had all but given up hope.

"Maria, when we left it thirteen years ago, you wanted to stay in America badly. Would you still want to live there if you had the chance?" Dina asked her daughter as they sat inside Terminal A's coffee shop at Rome's Leonardo Da Vinci-Fiumicino Airport.

"No, Mom, it's too late for that. I'm used to Italy now. We have a great home. I am attached to you and Grandma, and Uncle Mario is very good to us. Italy is far more beautiful than America. I'm surprised that you ever left it."

"Maria, you know well why I left. And if I didn't leave, you wouldn't be here."

"Yeah, you got me there, Mom. I won't deny that I loved many things about Fairview, even with the bad home life I suffered. Dad was a terrible man, but he was still my father."

"Honey, please don't bring him up. You know how I feel. Yes, he was your father, but I couldn't have chosen a worse man to marry."

"I miss my brother too," said Maria.

"Maria, I'd be lying if I said I didn't miss him, even with all the bad memories. He's still my son. I think about him almost every day. I'm happy things have been good for him with his new family. And I can't wait to see my granddaughter. This is the most exciting moment of my life."

"And I'm just as thrilled to meet my niece, though she is neither a granddaughter nor a niece. Her love for Jimbo allows us to get around that."

Mother and daughter lit cigarettes and sipped espressos. Twenty minutes later, they heard their flight number, and *Volo 24* announced on an intercom, instructing them to walk down the long passageway to the gate they would soon use to board their plane. An airport attendant signaled to take seats in the waiting area until they were called to stand in line.

Heavy turbulence maligned the eight-hour, forty-five-minute flight to John F. Kennedy International Airport. The excessive seat belt strain doomed their hopes of catching some shut-eye, though the trip's excitement would have kept them awake anyway. The flight arrived fifteen minutes early, but Dina and Maria took nearly an hour to clear customs. Shortly after they emerged through the double glass doors in the International Arrivals Building, they spotted a short, older man wearing a jacket and tie, standing behind a rope holding a sign that read Gorman. Dina hand-signaled the driver, who worked for Air Brook Limousine, a service based in Rochelle Park, New Jersey.

"Hello, ladies. Please let me take your luggage," he said, grabbing both large suitcases by the straps and wheeling them. "But by the way, my name is Josh. Josh Krueger. How was your flight?"

"Josh, you don't want to ask," said Maria. "We often thought the plane would crash, but somehow we made it."

"Oh, one of those, eh? I'm sorry you had to go through it, especially on such a long flight," said Josh. "Turbulence isn't fun, but it seldom results in serious problems. Is this your first time flying?"

"No," said Dina. "We flew from the States to Italy 13 years ago, but we've also flown to England, Spain, and inside Italy a few times. We're airplane veterans."

"Nice. I've only traveled twice by plane to Washington, D.C., each time a forty-minute flight," Josh answered, leading the women down an escalator to a lower-level parking lot, where his black sedan was parked close to the exit gate. After placing the luggage in the oversized trunk, the driver opened the doors for his passengers, sat behind the wheel, and headed off, using the Van Wyck Expressway service road to beat congestion.

"Josh, do you mind if I smoke?" asked Maria.

"Not at all, go right ahead. I'm not a smoker, but my passengers are free to indulge. If you could crack your window, I'd appreciate it."

On an unseasonably warm November day, Maria used the automatic latch to lower the window on the passenger side of her back seat four inches. She flicked her lighter.

"I set a bad example for my daughter," said Dina. "She ended up a heavier smoker than me."

"One thing I do not miss about living here is the snow," said Maria.

"I've lived here my entire life and never liked the snow," said Josh. "It's bad for my business if you know what I mean."

"Of course," said Maria, exhaling smoke. "I remember the plows on the dead-end section of Hamilton Avenue and how some people had to work for hours shoveling out their cars."

"You're lucky you don't have to deal with it anymore. I bet the weather in Rome is glorious."

"We don't live in Rome, but we are only a half-hour's drive away," said Dina. "Snow is rare, and temperatures dip into the high 30s at worst. We only moved close to Rome two years ago. Before then, we lived in Bari on the Adriatic Coast for many years."

"Bari? That's way warmer than Rome," said Josh. "I doubt the people there have ever seen a snowflake."

"It has snowed, but when it does, it is considered – what's that word? – a phenomenon," Maria said.

"I'll take the weather in Bari daily," Josh answered.

Dina and Maria smiled and nodded.

After exiting the Van Wyck service road, the limousine traveled on a primarily open road.

"Wow, Mom, there's the Unisphere!" exclaimed Maria, pointing to the most famous symbol of the 1964 World's Fair, a short distance from Shea Stadium in Flushing.

"Maria, I never forgot the Belgian Waffles and Turkish coffee. You were only six, so I doubt you'd remember much. Jimbo was five years older, so he'd remember much more."

"Mom, I remember the Monorail and the Disney boat ride, 'It's a Small World.'

"Fantastica mia figlio (Fantastic, my daughter!)" exclaimed Dina. I do remember how much she enjoyed the boat ride.

Forty-five minutes later, Josh pulled up in front of the Furano house. Dina tipped him generously.

239

CHAPTER 31

Arrival on Grant Street

"Is Adam home?"

Jennifer pointed at her brother, who was smoking marijuana, as he leaned on the alley fence.

"Adam tends to be a little forward these days," she snickered.

Maria and Dina strode over to where Adam stood. His back was turned.

"*Ciao*, Adam!" said Maria.

Adam turned and smiled broadly.

"*Caio,* Maria, and Signora Gorman!" he exclaimed, kissing each on both cheeks per European custom. He brazenly held out his joint, offering them a toke.

"No, Grazie, Mom and I never touch that stuff. Does Jimbo indulge?"

"No, he never does. I tried to interest him, but he always refused. He's no fun."

As Dina asked about Sarah, Maria thought:

He's a druggie and doesn't try to hide it. Dad was right about him, after all. He was high as a kite that night in our house. I'm so

241

proud of Jimbo for refusing to join him. Sarah must be so embarrassed. He's a disgraceful father and husband. We need to wash our faces after those disgusting kisses. What school would hire such a person to teach kids? He looks so much different than when I saw him last. He's much broader and muscled, and he likes tattoos. He probably works out. I'm sure he physically abuses his wife. He broke the law in front of his family. What a low life he turned out to be.

"Sarah's doing great," said Adam. "We'll head up soon," he added, dragging on his joint.

Dina had a difficult time hiding her disgust. She turned to address Jennifer.

"How is your dad?"

"Dad is fine. Jimbo thinks the world of him."

"I'm so happy to hear that. What about your younger brother? I recall his name is Mikey. He was young when we left."

"Mikey is now known as Mikaela," Jennifer said. "She is transitioning."

"Mikey is becoming a girl? Wow," said Dina. "We know some trannies in Bari. One of them, Asunta, is one of Maria's best friends. We barely knew Mikey when we left. We must say hello to her. Did you say her new name was Mikaela?"

"Yes."

"Is she going all the way?" asked Maria.

"I'm sure. There isn't much male left anymore," Jennifer said.

"Good for her!" exclaimed Maria. "She needs to be true to herself. So, your family is made up of two girls and a boy. Adam is the only male, right?"

"Yes, but we also have an adopted brother, Jay. He's my favorite sibling."

"It's great when you have such a close relationship with a brother or sister," said Dina, beaming.

Mainly since the other siblings include a drug addict and a trannie, thought Maria.

"Let's head upstairs," said Jennifer. "I know there are two people you can't wait any longer to see."

"I've seen my son before," said Dina laughingly. "But not my granddaughter. I can't wait to wrap my arms around them."

When they reached the top of the stairs, Mikaela rose from the loveseat. Her pink blouse, black pants, facial cosmetics, jewelry, streaked hair, high-pitched voice, and body movements screamed femininity.

"Hi, all," she said. "I am so thrilled to meet you."

"Ciao, Mikaela, sei cosi carina (Hello, Mikaela, you are so pretty.)" said Dina.

"Grazie," said Mikaela, embracing the women in turn. "That means so much to me."

"Your perfume smells wonderful," said Maria. "I remember you from when you were male but forgot your face. I love your streaked hair."

Mikaela smiled appreciatively.

Stevie, who heard the last part of the conversation, rushed in. The toddler wrapped his arms around Mikaela's legs. "I love my Dad. She's my hero."

"Ah, Mikaela is your Dad. Who is your Mom?"

Mikaela answered.

"His mom is Sarah. She had twins. Our other son, Joey, is around here somewhere."

Dina thought:

So, Mikaela wanted to have children before becoming a woman. That makes sense. Asunta did the same thing. And this little boy fully approves that his dad is a woman. But is it possible that Sarah had children with two brothers? What kind of family is this? Molto disfunzionale (So dysfunctional)

243

Carol and Sarah arrived to greet the Gormans.

"Hello, Dina and Maria! We've been looking forward to this day for a long time," said Sarah.

The four women took turns hugging each other and then settled into chairs.

"I'll have some fresh coffee ready in a jiffy," said Carol.

Sarah opened the fridge, took out the Italian pastries bought earlier at Rispoli's, and placed them on the table.

"Later, we will have lasagna, sausage, and meatballs," she said. "Husband, would you do the honors and summon Jimbo and Saoirse? I'll fetch Dad and Grandma Delaney."

The Furanos deliberately delayed the showcase reunion between mother, daughter, and son until everyone was present.

Adam excused himself to rush downstairs to alert Jimbo and Saoirse. When they returned, the tears flowed with abandon. Dina sobbed on Jimbo's shoulder as the young man cryingly embraced his mom. Maria moved in, simultaneously embracing them both. Saoirse edged her way in, stretching her arms around Jimbo's waist.

"So we finally meet the beautiful Saoirse. We've heard so much about you, young lady."

"I love you, Grandma and Aunt Maria," said Saoirse.

The Furanos and Gormans spoke for hours, playing catch-up on community events and some businesses the Gormans patronized that still operated. Dina mentioned numerous times how much she missed Fairview but just as readily acknowledged their home and town in Italy were more beautiful, and life was enjoyed at a more leisurely pace. She added that the terrible memories surrounding her departure would never be forgotten, but she realized the blame rested with her deceased husband, not her son.

After the late night, a car took them to their hotel, but not before they cried as they embraced their son and Saoirse. They promised to return as quickly as possible.

***

"When we return, I'll plead with Mario to pay for Saoirse to visit us during the summer. She'll love Italy. She'll learn to speak fluent Italian. I must convince her over the phone to come over this summer. I will work hard to make it happen. You know how obsessed I can be when I want something badly."

"So, the plan is to have her live with us every June to August? When she gets older, she'll date, and this routine will die out," said Maria, lighting a cigarette.

"She could meet someone over here during one of her summer trips. We could help make that happen and get a nice man to ask her on a date, maybe when she's 16 or 17. If she falls in love, we'll have her forever. We'll get her a beautiful place to live, and she could raise her family here."

"Mom, you are devious. I'd love her over here, too, but it won't happen. Sure, she loves Jimbo. But she also loves her family, including the drug-addict dad. I think it is more realistic for us to travel to New Jersey more often."

"I can dream, can't I?" asked Dina as they prepared to board the plane back to Italy.

CHAPTER 32

Adam's Growing Cynicism; Jimbo at Our Lady of Grace

"Adam, your dad can hear your heavy metal music from his bedroom," Sarah said. "He says he hates it."

"Fuck, Sarah! I'm not listening to it to gain his approval," said Adam, scowling. "I guess I'll have to lower it. Dad acts like I'm a teenager, for fuck's sake."

"But sweetie, you love your dad."

"Yeah, I guess I do."

"What's the name of the song?" asked Sarah.

"Am I Going Insane (Radio)," Adam answered. "The album is called *Sabotage*, and the group is Black Sabbath."

"I see the cassette," Sarah said, smiling. "This is music I need to get used to."

"It is best when you're high."

Sarah grimaced.

"How about watching a movie in the living room on VHS, sweetie? Of course, you make the choice."

"I'm in the mood for *Angels with Dirty Faces,"* said Adam, light-

247

ing a cigarette. "Why don't you ask Mikaela if she's interested? I don't know if she's ever seen it."

Adam had championed Betamax since he purchased his first machine in 1978. Experts said the smaller tape format yielded a more precise image. Adam preferred better quality to the eco0-nomic appeal of more hours on the larger VHS cassettes. Around the time Adam started working out, he lost interest in taping television shows and movies but still bought the occasional pre-recorded movie. He had seen the James Cagney crime drama several times on television but hadn't watched the tape he bought a few months prior.

Adam inserted the cassette and perched on the loveseat, yielding the couch to Sarah and her soulmate.

"I never saw *Angels with Dirty Faces*," said Mikaela.

"Sister, I'm not sure this kind of movie is your thing, but it's a classic. Shit, the last line is one of the most famous in movie history."

"Adam, I'm intrigued," said Mikaela. "I loved Cagney in *Yankee Doodle Dandy.* He won an Oscar for it!"

"Mikaela, as you know, I used to worship the Oscars. I could not have been happier when *Ordinary People* and *Chariots of Fire* won Best Picture. But over the last year, I've concluded that the whole awards process is nonsense. I read that many of the voters never even see the films. I was a cultist when I cared about who won. Those assholes never gave an Oscar to Edward G. Robinson, Cary Grant, or Alfred Hitchcock. And how fucked up that Cagney only won a single time!"

"Dear brother, you once told me that Robert Donat and Maggie Smith deserved their Oscars for playing inspiring schoolteachers."

"Yep, I did. Those were among my two favorite wins. But you have to question their worth when they give the Oscar to John

Wayne for *True Grit* over those two fantastic actors in *Midnight Cowboy*. I like John Wayne, but he should have won for *The Searchers,* not *True Grit.* Anyway, I will tell you this. The ending of *Angels with Dirty Faces* is electrifying. And I use that word in two senses. You'll have to wait to see what I mean. I'm going to show this film to my students next month. I'll be using this same VHS tape."

"Adam, what size is your television?" asked Mikaela.

"27 inches. It's a Sony. Bergen Tech has a decent audio-visual department."

After the Warner Brothers logo appeared and the opening credits rolled, the three viewers watched two teenage boys attempt a train robbery.

Mikaela rested her head on Sarah's torso, where they kissed and caressed.

Adam noticed, shook his head, and thought:

Fuck, they sleep together and have sex every night. I'm sure it won't be too much longer before their activities will officially be lesbian sex. I'm the odd man in this three-way relationship, but so be it. Mikaela is Sarah's true love, dating back a long time, no matter what she told me. They'll be together over 90% of the time. Yes, I'm legally married to her, but it's a farce. Still, I'm good as long as she cares for me when I'm in the mood. I can never begrudge them the profound love they share. I'm content with being Sarah's Number 2.

Sarah and Mikaela emerged from their lovemaking to watch the last half hour of the 1937 classic. They understood the dual meaning of electrifying. Both women sniffled when James Cagney's Rocky Sullivan cried as he was forced to the electric chair in a faked cowardly reaction aimed at ending the adoration the kids had for the murdering gangster.

***

As the members of the Furano family aged, their weekly attendance at Our Lady of Grace grew spotty. Saoirse still attended weekly, not wanting to disappoint Jimbo, whose religion and Bible reading were as devoted as ever. The two faithfully appeared at the 10:15 mass, where Father Peter Sticco officiated. On a snowy Sunday in early December, the venerated pastor spoke to Jimbo at the doors as he and Saoirse left the church.

"Hi, Jimbo, Hello Saoirse!" Father Sticco greeted the pair.

"Hi, Father Peter," said Saoirse.

Jimbo shook Father Peter's hand.

"I'm always honored, Father."

"Jimbo, we have an opening for an usher. For years, you have shown yourself to be a devout Catholic. I don't know if you'd be interested, but if so, we would love to have you. As always, you and your fellow ushers would ensure the service is welcoming and comfortable. You would be advised to shake hands, circulate bulletins to parishioners, and help facilitate seating. You would be called on twice during the mass to pass around the collection baskets in coordination with your colleagues. The opening is for the 10:15 mass, so you won't need to change your routine."

"Father, I'd be honored. I've considered being an usher, but I wasn't sure if you would want me. My past isn't something to be proud of. I don't know if the Lord has forgiven me. I don't think I can ever be forgiven."

Father Peter rested his arm over Jimbo's shoulder.

"Young man, you are the Lord's disciple. You are not to blame in any way for your difficult childhood. Not only are you fully forgiven in the eyes of the law, but the church has long accepted you as a model person to spread the word. I am proud of you. Father McTague is proud of you. Our Lady of Grace Church is grateful for you. Since you moved here from St. John's, I don't think you've missed mass once."

"Father, I had the flu twice, but I still attended. I could have passed the germs to others. I sat alone in the back row on the right side in front of the confessional, but I didn't know if anyone was infected."

Sticco smiled. "Once again, you prove how much you care about others. I'd be hard-pressed to find someone as worthy as you for this position. Saoirse, are we proud of him?"

"I couldn't be prouder, Father Peter. I love him so much. From when I was a young child, he was there for me. We never fell out of favor with each other, even once. I have two fathers in my life. I adore them both, but Jimbo is by far the more spiritual of the two. I think God is smiling today."

Jimbo wiped tears from his eyes while hugging Saoirse.

"Young girl, you are so gifted. You speak as insightfully and eloquently as a grown woman," said Sticco. "I know how much you mean to Jimbo. I am happy you share so much quality time in our church."

"Father, I would be honored to serve as an usher. Thank you for making today one of the greatest days in my life."

Though Jimbo had been exceedingly introverted since moving into the Furano home, he spoke more often after he became an usher. His conversations always veered off into religion and the need for everyone to accept the Lord. When he wasn't working or interacting with Saoirse, his waking hours were spent reading the Good Book.

***

On a Saturday afternoon, he saw Adam smoking a cigarette in the alley.

"Adam, we must do more to bring the Lord directly into our lives."

"Jimbo, I accepted the Lord a long time ago. However, I have zero interest in reading the Bible and only attend mass occas-

251

ionally. You know what I think of you, but I'm not the Holy Roller you are. It isn't my thing anymore."

"But Adam, when you were young, Father McTague was your idol. And then you said the same thing about Father Peter. The church was a big part of your life, dear friend."

"Jimbo, people change. I'm not the same person. There was no one happier than me when you found God. I'll die a Catholic, and I love Father Peter, but I've become a cynical guy. I'm a lot like you were as we grew up," he said, crushing his cigarette on the ground.

Jimbo rubbed the back of Adam's head.

"I'll never give up on you, Adam."

CHAPTER 33

Accident in Pop's Park

On a warm Saturday morning in March, Mikaela spoke to Sarah at breakfast.

"Sarah, I'd like to take the boys to Pop's Park. Do you think the girls might want to join us?" The temperature is supposed to reach the mid-70s, which is highly unusual for early March."

"Sweetie, I agreed to take the twins to Valley Fair for clothes shopping. I will also pick up my mom, but maybe Saoirse will accompany you. She loves spending time with her brothers."

Sarah headed downstairs. Saoirse played Parchesi with Jimbo, who had an hour to kill before his Saturday shift at Palermo's.

"Don't worry, you know how long your aunt takes to get ready," said Sarah, referring to Mikaela's newfound obsession with her hair and how she looked before leaving the house. "Finish your game with Jimbo. Figure at least 30 minutes more before they leave. Jimbo, I forgot about you working today."

"Sarah, I work every third Saturday. Three of us rotate."

"Oh, I know, honey. I didn't remember this was your week. Rob is also working today. He has a weekend shift with Dad."

253

Mikaela, the twins, and Saoirse went to Pop's Park on foot. They waved at Martha Chiappetta, the assistant librarian who inspired many residents as the woman left her Lincoln Street home.

"Such beautiful kids," said Chiappetta. "Soon, the boys will be old enough to get their library cards."

"Not too much longer," said Mikaela, beaming, though realistically, they were still a few years away.

"If they wind up with just half the aptitude of Saoirse, they'll make the honor roll."

"Thank you, kind lady," said Stevie, as Joey smiled appreciatively.

The sky turned cloudy as they passed Kennedy Drive and the court, where teenagers played games under all four baskets.

"Stevie and Joey, this is where you will learn to play basketball," said Mikaela.

"Aunt Mikaela, my dad took me here many times. Maybe I should have taken our ball today."

"Honey, we'll certainly do that on another day," said Mikaela. "I was only thinking of the playground. I have a feeling we won't be here too long. The sky is getting darker. Nobody checked the forecast."

The weather called for heavy rain until after midnight, though the starting time for the precipitation was unclear.

"Daddy, you know my favorite ride, right?" asked Stevie.

"Yes, precious," said Mikaela. "But how about if we save that for last? We have swings, the handlebars, and the merry-go-round. I know you and Joey love those, too."

Mikaela knew that once Stevie experienced the sliding pond, he wouldn't want to go on another ride. The young dad mused.

Stevie is so obsessive. He's a typical Furano, following in his father and uncle's footsteps. As he grows up, I bet he'll play the same

254

record 50 times a day, read the same book repeatedly before tackling a different one, and probably fall in love with one type of food at the expense of diversity. The best way to combat single-mindedness is to offer variety. The jury is still out for Joey, but I sense he is different from his twin brother.

Saoirse sat between her brothers, arms wrapped around each other. Mikaela stood close to the ride and intermittently pushed it whenever the circular movement abated. After the ride spun over thirty times, Joey exclaimed, "Dad, I'm getting dizzy!"

"Of course, honey pie," said Mikaela, grabbing hold of the safety bar to help the Merry-Go-Round grind to a halt. When Saoirse and Stevie rose, they staggered. Mikaela smiled.

"Looks like we have three disoriented people," she said.

"What does disoriented mean?" asked Stevie.

"Precious, when you get older, you'll know it. I don't want you to think about such a state of mind right now."

"I think it means dizzy," Stevie said.

Mikaela nodded.

"I'm always sad when I think about Palisades Amusement Park," she said. "All of you missed out on it, as it closed in 1971."

"Aunt Mikaela, it closed the year before I was born. My mom and dad were so young. Dad was only 18."

"Sweetie, that is correct," said Mikaela as the group headed over to the swings, located just inside the fence bordering the sidewalk of Sixth Street. The aunt and niece conversed as Mikaela pushed Stevie and Saoirse pushed Joey. Mikaela wasn't remotely prepared for the next question.

"Aunt Mikaela, did Jimbo try to kill my dad in Palisades Amusement Park?"

Mikaela's eyes widened.

"Sweetie, whatever gave you such an idea?"

"Aunt Mikaela, I love Jimbo. I've loved him since I was only a few years old. But I would appreciate it if you were honest with me. A girl in my class at Lincoln School told me this six years ago. She said her parents found out. Did Jimbo hate my dad so much that he wanted him to die?"

Mikaela was floored. She tried to figure out what to say, but the shock of her niece's question temporarily froze her. Stevie asked her for another push. But Mikaela understood that continued silence in this instance meant she was confirming Jimbo's guilt.

"Saoirse, Jimbo has always loved your dad. I don't think there is anyone else he loves as much other than you."

"Then why did he want him dead?" asked Saoirse.

"Oh, sweetie, you are making things so difficult for me. Jimbo and your dad had a complex friendship. Jimbo was a troubled young man in the late 1960s and early 1970s. Some of Jimbo's issues were the same as my own. He had a difficult childhood. His dad was a heavy drinker and was abusive to his entire family."

"Aunt Mikaela, I know that."

"Jimbo saw your dad as growing up in the ideal family," said Mikaela. "He wished he had such an upbringing. It was natural for him to become jealous of his friend. I was envious of your dad, too."

"Aunt Mikaela, I can't believe you could ever be jealous of anybody. You have everything. You are the most intelligent person I've ever known."

"Thank you, sweetheart. But you overrate me. Your dad is exceptional, and your mom is a living saint."

"You are too modest," said Saoirse, smiling. "You are everybody's favorite person."

Mikaela kissed her niece.

"Your dad's influence is immeasurable."

"So, what made Jimbo snap?"

"Sweetie, you used the right word. There is no reason for me to lie or sugarcoat anything. For one split second, Jimbo was determined to harm your dad."

"He unbuckled my dad's safety strap?"

"Yes, sweetie."

"Dad always loved life. He would never commit suicide."

"Exactly, sweet one," answered Mikaela, whom the twins implored to keep pushing their swings. "Please don't torture yourself about the past. At the time, everyone wanted Jimbo banished from our world, but your dad stood by him, fought for him, and, with the help of a famous priest, forced your grandparents to take him in. The rest is history."

"I heard about Father McTague," said Saoirse.

"Jimbo suffered for years after what happened. But after he found God, his outlook on life changed. You have been the major force in bringing out the goodness in him that had been suppressed while he suffered through his terrible home life. Your dad has always loved him and saved his life. If Jimbo were not brought into our home, he probably would have perished on the streets. Now, he is a responsible man and has maintained a decent job a short way from home."

Saoirse sniffled.

"Aunt Mikaela, do you think he will ever get married?"

"Sweetie, that's a good question. He has always been timid with women; as far as I know, he has never dated even once. After finding our family, especially you, he didn't even try to meet anyone. We are his world, and I'd venture to say he has never been happier. I predict he'll never leave."

"I thought the same," said Saoirse, pushing harder on Joey's swing.

Mikaela smiled and nodded.

"Honey, I need to smoke," she said. "Can you take the boys to the sliding pond? It is safest to stand at the bottom and catch them before they hit the ground. I'll be watching from the other side of the fence on the Sixth Street sidewalk."

"I'd love to!" exclaimed Saoirse.

Two teenage girls walked past Mikaela as she watched her boys run up steel stairs to the top of the standard tower slide, sit down, and slide down the chute.

One giggled as she whispered to her friend.

"That man looks like a woman."

"I wouldn't go that far," said the other. "He's just a feminine man. He likes to wear earrings and lipstick and style his hair. We see more and more men like that."

Stevie, an inveterate show-off, stood at the top of the slide and announced loudly, "Saoirse, I am going to slide down backward."

"No!" shouted Mikaela. "That's too dangerous! Stevie, slide down the regular way!"

"Dad, you're no fun," said Stevie.

As the boy turned to slide conventionally, he lost his footing and fell. The back of his head hit a support near the bottom.

Mikaela's scream attracted the basketball players and others in the park. Several rushed to lend assistance as the young father reached her son. Kneeling beside her injured brother, Saoirse was too overcome to help.

"Saoirse, please keep watch on Joey! I must carry him to the doctor's office!"

Mikaela held Stevie with one arm as the other was pressed against the bleeding cut. She sprinted faster than ever, reaching the intersection of Sixth Street and Kennedy Drive in less than ten seconds. A minute later, she opened the door to the medical practice of Dr. Robert Osder and Dr. Howard Stricker, partners working out of a square, one-story building on the corner of Kennedy Drive and Anderson Avenue.

"Please help my son! He fell off the sliding pond in the park! He has a big cut on the back of his head! He lost a lot of blood! Please!"

A receptionist dashed through a door behind her tiny office and alerted Dr. Stricker. Stevie was crying hysterically, and Mikaela wasn't in a state of mind to exert a calming influence. Stricker took a cursory look at the boy's cut and heaved a sigh of relief.

"Sir, your son needs stitches. I'm confident he'll be fine. Please try and control yourself. The boy is partially reacting to your behavior," said the doctor, opting to address the parent as male.

"I can't help it! I see blood oozing out of my son's head. Please help him!" Mikaela yelled.

"Your boy will be fine, I assure you," said the head nurse, directing Mikaela to sit in the waiting room.

"Thank you, but no!" Mikaela exclaimed. "I want to be next to my son for any procedure."

"I don't think this is necessary," she responded coldly.

"I must insist!" yelled Mikaela.

The nurse knew that unless she called the police, Mikaela would not be dissuaded.

"Follow me."

After they entered a narrow hallway, Mikaela was led to a small room where Dr. Stricker was preparing stitches.

"Dr. Stricker, this parent insists on being with the patient."

"That's fine," said Stricker. "Sit in this chair, please."

Mikaela held Stevie's hand as Stricker cleaned the wound with mild soap and water. He administered a local anesthetic to numb the cut and the surrounding area. The nurse used her hand to hold the wound closed, lining up the edges of the wound precisely. Stricker gently lifted the exposed skin with forceps and pierced it about 4 millimeters from the wound's edge. Stevie and his dad both sobbed. At the end of the first stitch, the nurse tied a knot at the end of the suture line.

Stevie needed twelve stitches. The nurse covered the area with a bandage.

"As your son heals, there will probably be some swelling or redness, though you won't see this because of the bandage. I will fill out a prescription for a painkiller. You can pick it up at Safe-Drug on Nungesser's Corner. The boy will need to take one dose every morning as long as there is pain. I don't think he will feel discomfort after two to three days."

"Thank you, nurse."

Mikaela apologized for her unhinged conduct. She carried Stevie to Grant Street, where she expected to see Joey and Saoirse. When Rob, who had returned home an hour before, learned what had happened, he was inconsolable. Crying his eyes out, he sat next to the boy on the couch, where Mikaela held and rocked Stevie.

"Feel free to hold him," said Mikaela, sharing her son with the man whose life had centered around the child for some time. Rob delicately placed Stevie on his lap sideways, where he gently petted him, offering verbal assurances that all would be well.

Another round of intemperate bawling commenced after Sarah and the twin girls arrived.

"Oh, my baby!" screamed Sarah.

"Stevie will be okay," said Rob. "Mikaela will explain what happened."

Jennifer diverted.

"I forgot the name of the movie with Dustin Hoffman. He played a father in a divorce case. It came out a few years ago and won many awards."

"*Kramer vs. Kramer*," said Adam.

"Yeah, that's it. I remember the child falling off the handlebars in the park. His face hit the ground. There was a lot of blood. Hoffman picked him up and ran several blocks to the hospital. He was hysterical. As it turned out, the boy got a bunch of stitches."

"Yes, ten," said Adam. "And the doctors let the father stay next to the boy as they administered them. Ted felt the same pain Billy did when the needle punctured the boy's skin."

"Adam, you are amazing," said Jennifer. "You remember all the names and every detail."

"Fucking A!" exclaimed Adam.

CHAPTER 34

Aerial Calamity

November 10, 1985

Mikaela Furano was approved for membership as a firefighter in the Grandview Firehouse five months before the most consequential disaster in the Borough of Fairview's history. The unit's fire officials ignored the cosmetic appearance of the new applicant and her first name, concluding she was still a man regardless of how she chose to present herself. A few other members sported unusual appearances. One had more earrings protruding from his eyebrows and ears, and another had tattoos on most of his skin. The department insisted she be called Mikey until or when she underwent gender reassignment surgery. Mikaela's desire to become a firefighter was her final backpedal on her budding new identity.

"What was that?" exclaimed a visibly terrified Sarah after a booming sound as dusk had just overtaken the area on a chilly Sunday.

"Maybe we experienced a mild earthquake," opined Rob, encircling Stevie.

"I am certain the crashing sound came from above," declared Mikaela before she rushed down the stairs and out the door. She got outside just in time to see some objects falling near the ground over an area only a short distance northeast of where she stood. Sarah and Rob soon joined her, each holding one of the twins.

"Oh, Mikaela, how terrible. Lives were probably lost. I hope the pieces of the plane didn't harm anyone on the ground," said Sarah in a strained voice.

The rest of the family appeared as the siren atop the Grandview Firehouse thundered.

"I have to go!" shouted Mikaela.

She jogged down Grant Street. A driver slammed on his brakes as she raced across Garfield Street and slid under the vertical door set in motion by the only firefighter arriving before her, Captain Craig Peterson, who lived on Anderson Avenue a short distance from Grandview. As other firemen answered the call, policemen dashed to squad cars and headed north on Anderson, roof lights flashing and sirens blaring.

Mikaela and her fellow smoke eaters changed into their firefighter garb in minutes. The urgency was stressed over a police two-way radio.

"We have a major plane crash," announced Peterson. "Falling sections of the planes hit several houses in Fairview and Cliffside Park."

"Planes?" asked former Fire Chief Craig Krivda.

"The word is that two planes crashed in mid-air," answered Peterson as he, Krivda, and a dozen other firefighters sped off on the company's hook and ladder truck. Krivda spoke on a two-way radio with the town's Fire Chief, John Mesisca, whose company on Walker Street was only two blocks from the calamity.

Two private airplanes—a Dassault Falcon 50 executive jet belonging to Nabisco Brands and a Piper Cherokee—collided at 1,500 feet over Teterboro Airport as the latter aircraft approached for landing. The two jets fell several miles east in the residential areas of Cliffside Park and Fairview, communities across from Manhattan's Upper West Side. Witnesses later likened the crash to a torrent of explosions and fireballs that led to an on-ground inferno. Still, during the madness that directly followed the catastrophic event, uniform chaos temporarily derailed the police and fire departments from maintaining order. Residents were outside screaming.

When Grandview's Hook and Ladder made its way through just-erected barriers, Mikey jumped off the truck, hoping to help anyone possibly injured.

"Someone is dead on the ground," shouted Fireman Pat Buglione, referring to what appeared to be a pedestrian under part of the plane who happened to be in the wrong place at the wrong time.

The Fairview and Cliffside Park police departments cordoned off a four-mile area from Gorge Road to Bergen Boulevard and north of Edgewater Road to Fairview police headquarters on Anderson Avenue. Many residents fled their homes and rushed to the crash site on foot.

The wingless Piper Cherokee fell at the intersection of Fifth and Kamena Streets, where the impact set off flames on the porch of a two-story building. One Hispanic-American woman yelled the names of her two children, Ana and Manuel, who were outdoors when the crash occurred.

"Ana, Manuel, where are you?" the frantic woman screamed. She suddenly bolted for the fiery entrance to the building but was restrained by Walker Street Firehouse Captain Paul Mantone.

"I'm sorry, Ma'am. Nobody is allowed near that building."

"But my babies are outside!" she exclaimed.

265

"We will search the area. Don't worry, we'll find them," said Mantone.

The woman's next-door neighbor embraced her and led her to the front steps of her home, directly across from the Our Lady of Grace Church rectory. Pastor Peter Sticco stood outside, telling two special policemen that the church was available for anyone battling fear or stress. Mikaela Furano arrived at the scene.

Mantone instructed Mikaela and another firefighter, Barney Bulay, to inspect the area near the affected two-story home. The two branched off, with Mikaela heading back toward Anderson Avenue and Bulay rushing toward the intersection of Seventh Street and Kamana Street.

As Mikaela dashed toward the apartment building on the west side of the Anderson Avenue and Kamena Street intersection, she saw two young children out of the corner of her eye. Ana and Manuel, the kids of the woman restrained by Captain Mantone, were huddled against a brick wall that served as the border between two yards. Mikaela's eyes widened when she saw the wall collapsing. She leaped through the air, pulling down the children and covering them with her body. The kids screamed as bricks and broken cement fell on their human shield. A heavy chunk of stony material smashed into Mikaela's helmet. Without that protection, the firefighter would have died instantly. Mikaela was in tremendous pain but didn't move. The lives of Ana and Manuel were all that mattered to her.

Anderson Avenue resident Maxine Grgurev, who had recently moved from Weehawken to Fairview, approached the police barrier, speaking to a friend:

"My landlady thought her furnace had exploded. I saw the sky turn orange as my son Michael stood near the dining room window. A minute later, my friend, who lives at the Parker Imperial on the 22nd floor, called me to say she saw the two planes hit and checked to see if we were okay. It was a hot night, so she was on her terrace. Right after that, the phones went down."

"Fireman down," yelled Harold Parker, who didn't immediately notice the two children under Mikaela. After signaling other firefighters and one policeman that the situation was urgent, he approached his fallen colleague to discover what happened.

By that time, Mantone, Fire Chief John Mesisca, and his brother Michael Mesisca, another firefighter from the Walker Street company, were notified by radio. Within minutes, they descended to the scene of the accident. Michael Mesisca rightly surmised the wall was poorly constructed and couldn't withstand the ground rumble caused by the plane hitting less than a hundred yards away.

"He's alive, thank God," said Chief Mesisca, who instructed firefighters Eugene Nappi Jr., and Frank Foglio to extricate the children by removing the bricks and cement and carefully lifting firefighter Furano. Ana and Manuel were sobbing, but a quick inspection revealed no visible harm. Chief Mesisca advised ambulance corps Chief Mark Citakian to rush them and the injured Mikaela to Palisades General Hospital in Edgewater.

Pat Guiliano and Walter Kimball wheeled gurneys to the site, where the three firemen lifted firefighter Furano and guided the kids to the vehicle's back doors. Citakian told Chief Mesisca he saw the midair collision through his living room window. Initially, he saw the planes flying side by side.

"I observed a small flash and then suddenly a large one. The bigger plane was enveloped in flames and broke into pieces as it fell," said Citakian.

The emergency response unit vehicle sped down Kamena Street to Gorge Road, making a right on River Road, where the hospital stood less than two minutes away.

Mantone informed Mrs. Ramirez that her children were well

but needed to be examined at the hospital. The woman screamed in the arms of her husband.

"Por favor, Maria. Dijeron que los ninos estan bien. (Please, Maria. They said the children are fine.)"

The man help his wife up and continued.

"Nosotros iremos al hospital shora. (We will go to the hospital right now.)"

Shortly afterward, Joseph Furano received a call from Police Chief Samuel Linardi, a close friend who ironically resided only a few houses from the Fifth and Kamena Street intersection.

"Joey, they just rushed your son to Palisades General Hospital. He was injured, saving the lives of two children. I've been told his injuries aren't critical, but he's likely to spend some time recovering. Your son is a hero. He risked his life to save the life of those kids. I'm sure what he did will be all over the news."

"Sammy, I don't know what to say," Joseph answered, his voice breaking. "I can't express how proud I am. But what you tell me is terrifying. My family and I will get to the hospital quickly."

"Joey, stay safe. I'm sure your son will be fine," answered Linardi.

"Thank you, dear friend," said Joseph.

Joseph Furano had the unenviable task of informing the family about Mikaela.

Carol covered her face and sobbed, but Sarah screamed and turned hysterical. Adam, Joseph, and Jay tried to calm her, but she broke loose and ran out the door.

"Please run after her," said Joseph. "Remind her that Mikaela will be fine."

Adam and Jay dashed down the stairs and sprinted down Grant Street, where they caught up with the grief-stricken woman near the front of the Grandview Firehouse.

"I'm sorry, Sarah, but I am carrying you home," said Adam. His wife carried on awfully, but Adam emphasized that Mikaela's injuries weren't life-threatening.

"I don't believe what happened to my sweetheart. I want to hold her in my arms right now. Why couldn't I have protected her? I should have delayed her earlier tonight when she rushed off!"

Jay carried Sarah up the stairs and delicately placed her on the couch. Adam encircled her with his arms.

"Sarah, your lover is a heroine," said Adam.

She cried on his shoulder.

"The boys don't know what happened. Can you call my parents, sweetie? They will be devastated when they hear what happened. Can you ask them if they will break the news to the boys? I can't do it. Stevie will go crazy."

"Of course," said Adam, rising. "I'll explain everything to them."

"Don't call them just yet," said Sarah. "I want further confirmation."

Chief Linardi called Joseph again to inform him that the hospital would prefer no visitors for at least one hour until the fallen firefighter underwent tests and X-rays.

A half-hour later, Sarah signaled Adam to call her parents.

The Burkes were deeply upset, but after Adam reassured them that Mikaela wasn't in critical condition, they felt confident enough to inform the twins about what happened to their dad.

"Adam, we listened to the news reports," said Steve. "According to the commentator on ABC, at least five people were known to be dead. Two in each of the planes and one on the ground perished. Eight people were injured, two seriously. I understand they are battling fires in three buildings. They think jet fuel ignited them. People were seen jumping out of buildings, and power was lost to 1,400 homes."

"We still have power in our home, Dad," said Adam. "I guess we are on a separate grid from the ones on Anderson Avenue."

"Adam, we didn't lose power either, but I hear that the southern part of Cliffside Park is out. I also heard firefighters from Edgewater, Fort Lee, Palisades Park, Englewood, Ridgewood, Leonia, and North Bergen respond to fight the blaze. Even helicopters were sent by the New York City Police to help illuminate the area. Wait, Adam, Michele just heard something; hold on!"

"Sarah, Mom, Dad, please put on Channel 7!" Adam exclaimed.

Both the Furano and Burke families heard about Mikaela at the same time.

The newscaster announced:

We just received word that a young Fairview fireman named Mikey Furano was hospitalized after saving the lives of two children who were nearly crushed by a falling brick wall just a hundred yards away from where a piece of one of the planes had fallen. There will be stories of this catastrophe, but none as inspiring as this report of a local hero. Our sources added that Mr. Furano is married to Sarah and is the father of twin boys. A Palisades General Hospital spokesperson said she does not think his injuries are critical, but Mr. Furano is undergoing exhaustive testing.

Tears of pride flowed in the living rooms of both homes. Joseph Furano completely lost it, and Carol cried softly.

"Mikaela is the girl and has always been the girl," said Jay. "Now the country will know the meaning of the word *heroine*. Nobody or no event could make this family prouder."

As the Furanos flipped through the other stations, hoping to hear more reports about Mikaela's heroism, a CBS newscaster quoted Peter Nelson, a spokesperson for the Federal Aviation Administration. Nelson said the French-made Falcon 50 Executive Jet was flying from Morristown Airport to Teterboro, where it was expected to pick up passengers for a northward flight. The plane made its final approach to Teterboro, a general aviation reliever airport twelve miles west of midtown Manhattan. The FAA spokesman added that the Piper Cherokee left an even smaller airport in Caldwell, New Jersey, ten miles north of Morristown. The newscaster said both pilots had contacted the control tower, and radio transcripts confirmed they alerted each other of their presence.

After changing to another station, it was learned that a 39-year-old woman named Josephine Esposito was admitted to Palisades General with a fractured hip. Another resident, Ann Sevenjka, 49, was airlifted to Montefiore Hospital in the Bronx after several of her fingers were severed and required microsurgery.

CHAPTER 35

Mikaela at Palisades General Hospital

After spending ninety minutes in the waiting room, a doctor arrived to speak with the Furanos.

"Who I am speaking to," Dr. Harold Rothstein asked.

"I'm Mikey's mom," said Carol, reverting to Mikaela's previous masculine name.

"Carol, are all in this group family members?" Rothstein asked.

"Yes, this is my husband, Joseph; Mikey's wife, Sarah; my son, Adam; my daughter, Jennifer; and my son Jay. Sarah's parents are sitting in the corner."

"I see. I want to speak to Mikey's wife privately. I will appraise her of your son's condition. We will allow the rest of your group to see Mikey, which is against our normal policy. He is in Room 234."

The Furanos proceeded to the elevator, and Sarah followed Rothstein into a consultation room through a door.

"Sarah, the good news is that your husband didn't sustain any serious injury. His headgear saved his life. He sustained a fractured olecranon, which is part of the elbow. This kind of injury

273

caused considerable pain. We have Mikey on paracetamol. In addition, he suffered three fractured ribs and numerous serious bruises. A rib fracture can take up to twelve weeks to heal."

Sarah put her hands over her face as she sobbed.

"Sarah, your husband is a lucky young man. And I can imagine how proud you are. He saved the lives of two children," said Rothstein. "I know you can't wait to see him, but can you fill out a few forms before you do?"

"Of course, doctor," said Sarah, following him to a small room, where a nurse handed her a clipboard and a pen."

***

The Furano group was startled to see two uniformed firemen standing sentry-like on both sides of the door to Mikaela's room.

Carol was the first to approach the bed, where Mikaela lay attached to an IV. Her right arm was covered with cast material, and her stomach was wrapped in gauze.

"Mom, I have so much pain."

Carol fought back tears but knew she needed to stay strong.

"Sweetie, I'm sure they have you on painkillers, but they can only administer a few at a time."

Joseph, Jay, Jennifer, Steve, and Michele Burke took turns approaching the injured firefighter.

Adam attempted to talk to her but withdrew after he was overcome by emotion.

"I'm so sorry, sweet sister," said Jennifer. "You'll be as good as new. You are everybody's heroine."

Suddenly, Mikaela yelled, "Where's my Sarah? I want my Sarah!" repeating the refrain several times.

Hearing his daughter's name mentioned so longingly by the bedridden young heroine he had come to adore, Steve Burke retreated to a seat in the back of the room and cried.

A short while later, Sarah entered the room to hear another

round of Mikaela's pleas.

"I'm here, sweetheart!" she exclaimed cryingly. "I spoke to the doctor. You have a few fractured ribs and a fractured elbow, but other than a few serious bruises, you didn't suffer any complications. You'll be perfect in a week or two," she added, pulling a chair next to the rolling table where she poured ice water into a cup. She inserted a straw and held the top end to Mikaela's mouth. After signaling she had enough, Sarah put the cup back on the table, rolling it back. She leaned over and showered Mikaela with kisses as she stroked her hair.

"When the bricks hit me, your face appeared. I knew then that I must survive. It was much too soon for true beauty to disappear. You are the sun, the moon, the stars to me, and every waking moment I see your image, hear your reassuring voice and smell your sweet fragrance," Mikaela declared loudly in a mawkish outburst that still sounded authentic and deeply moved everyone in the room to tears.

Sarah pulled up a chair, gently placed her arm around Mikaela's head, and rested her head against the heroine's face.

"What about the boys?" asked Mikaela.

"I'll bring them here tomorrow, sweetie. My parents told them what had happened and dropped them off with Rob and Jimbo, who were home with the girls and Grandma Delaney. Stevie lost it when he heard. Rob is administering affection overload, of course. Brian took a cab to the house. He is going to stay with us over the next week."

"I love that kid," said Joseph. "Yet another boarder in our house, even if he's only part-time."

"All the kids love him too," said Carol. "Saoirse is wild for him."

"Sarah, when you return tomorrow with the boys, could you bring me vanilla ice cream?" asked Mikaela.

"What do you mean when I return, my beloved? I will not leave

275

your side for a second. I will stay overnight and wait for you to be discharged. If it takes five days or a week, so be it. Rob will bring the boys and the ice cream tomorrow."

"And I'll take the girls," said Adam.

Sarah again snuggled her face against Mikaela's. She caressed and kissed her.

"You are a heroine, sweetheart. Mikaela Furano will soon be a household name."

"I am still known as Mikey by the press," Mikaela said. "They think I am a boy."

Everyone laughed.

Adam, Jennifer, and Jay left the room to smoke outside. They saw NBC News and other outlet vehicles lined up along the curb.

"Wow, the television stations are arriving. Mikaela's heroism has spread all over," said Jennifer.

"Well, we did see the reports when we were home," answered Jay. "I think they want to find out if Mikaela will be okay. I doubt the doctors will let them get anywhere near her room, but they probably will share some information about her condition."

Adam lit a cigarette. As he exhaled, he exclaimed, "Fuck, I could have sworn I just saw Tom Brokaw walk into the hospital."

"I don't think it was him," said Jennifer. "He's almost always in the studio. Others bring reports to him."

"I could be wrong. Maybe the excitement of seeing an NBC news truck made me think of the main anchor."

"Adam, you never know. It could be him. This crash didn't just produce a hero. Six people died," said Jay, referring to the tragic loss of five people on the two planes and one person in a home. "I'm sure this disaster will receive full coverage."

After the three of them finished their nicotine fixes, they returned to Mikaela's room. Within minutes, the door opened. A Hispanic-American couple and their two children entered.

The woman, Maria Ramirez, spoke fluent English. She declared, "Mr. Mikey, you saved our children's lives. I brought them here to thank you in person."

The Ramirez family were already at the hospital. Doctors administered tests on Ana and Manuel, who were released later. The timid children approached Mikaela's bed. Sarah cupped her hand over her mouth.

"Mr. fireman," said Ana, "we owe our lives to you."

Mikaela hand-signaled them to come closer. Sarah helped them draw within Mikaela's arm's length. She clasped their hands and burst out crying. Though everyone in the room had already exhausted their tear ducts, their canaliculi worked in overdrive after the latest visit.

***

"I have the best dad in the whole world. You mean everything to me," said Joey, approaching his father's bed the next day.

"What about Mom, Adam, Rob, and the rest of the family," answered Mikaela. "They mean just as much, beautiful boy. Perhaps even more."

"Daddy, none of them are lying in a bed with broken ribs," said little Joey.

Mikaela and the others guffawed. The humor initially helped the emotional Stevie, who approached his dad's bed tentatively after hysterics in the car and the moment he entered the hospital.

CHAPTER 36

Mikey Honored at Borough Hall

January 14, 1986

Television crews crowded into the street-level staircase corridor, anticipating Mikaela Furano's arrival. A three-pronged stairwell led to the second-story council chambers, a sizable space occupied by long benches with wooden backs divided by an aisle leading up to a two-step stage where the mayor and six councilpersons sat behind their respective nameplates. Fairview Democratic Mayor Mario "Billy Schettino," an insurance agent and former councilman, was sworn in as the Borough's top elected official in early January 1979 after his election in November of the previous year. Schettino sat in the middle chair on the platform, to the right of attorney James J. Deer, a former mayor. Fairview's political alignment in 1986 comprised three Democrats and three Republicans. When voting was negotiated along party lines, the mayor would break the tie. Republicans James Cigolini, Eugene Fagnano, and Bart Talamini filled out the right flank, while Democrats Nancy Sarube, John Rossi, and John Mountain were seated on the left. Mountain, a history teacher at Lincoln School, was the current council president. Police Chief Samuel Linardi stood in full uniform to the right of Cigolini, with Fire Chief John Mesisca, also dressed in his department's attire, beside him.

When Mikaela and the Furano family entered, they were inundated with newspersons holding microphones and the photographer's light bulbs flashing. An ABC reporter tried to solicit a comment from the besieged hero, but with the wall of people pushing forward, the attempt failed. Special police lined up inside the entrance to the chambers to prevent residents and the press from entering. Once the Furanos arrived, they dispersed, allowing the multitude to rush for the available seating. All seating was taken within two minutes, leaving all the others occupying the limited space between the last bench and the wall with windows facing Garfield Street.

Mikaela's Grandview Fire Department and the town's ambulance corps operated under the chambers, connected by a hall corridor to offices atop the Fairview Police Department at 59 Anderson Avenue. The door to the passageway remained open to accommodate a few more people for an event where every nook and cranny was utilized. However, with fire department members from Cliffside Park, other Bergen and Hudson County companies, and hundreds of citizens hoping to witness the event, not even a room five times the size could have accommodated the crowd. Police Chief Linardi ordered Garfield Street from Anderson Avenue to Grant Street closed off for traffic, allowing the overflow of people to mill around outside. Temperatures on the winter evening hovered around 40 degrees, so hanging around was comfortable enough for those wearing coats or jackets. Veteran Grandview firefighters and Department of Public Works supervisor Mario Saracino, who owned the gray stucco house on the north corner of Garfield and Anderson, welcomed friends to sit around the two barbeque grills he lit for outside heat.

About ten minutes before the special meeting began, Adam rose from his seat. He approached Borough Clerk John Tomaras, a civically active Greek-American seated at a desk before the public officials' platform. With the volume in the room deafening, Adam whispered into the clerk's ear. Tomaras smiled, nodded, and shook the young man's hand.

"Will Mikey Furano and his wife, Sarah, please come to the front?" Tomaras said into a microphone.

Sarah looked at Adam lovingly, realizing what he had told the Borough Clerk earlier. But she was deeply moved and considered herself the wife of two brothers, so any reference claiming she was married to either was proper to her.

Already tearing up, Joseph, Carol, and Sarah's parents beamed from the front row.

Thanks to her mom's efforts, Mikaela dressed in her uniform and was dolled up in feminine finery. Her long blond hair was dyed and red-streaked; she wore a shade of pink, almost indecipherable lipstick, and sported flat red earrings. The pink-toned LOVE tattoo on her neck was visible. But she decided against any makeup or nail polish. She knew the general sentiments on girly men and thought the fire department was one of the last institutions for a member to exhibit such proclivities. But her appearance was still markedly feminine, especially since she was instructed not to wear a helmet.

Mayor Schettino spoke after Mikaela and Sarah stood at the front next to Tomaras.

"I understand the Furanos have five children. Will they please join their parents up here?"

Saoirse picked up Stevie and pulled along Joey. The twin girls followed.

Though Schettino and many in the town knew two men fathered the five children, they had long since thought the Furano love triangle was acceptable and the entire family was good people. Of course, some secretly scorned the family dynamic.

"Please, Mayor, can my brother Adam join us?" asked Mikaela, unexpectantly.

"Of course," answered Schettino. "Adam Furano, please come forward."

The muscled, tattooed Adam sheepishly strode to the front, carefully positioning himself on the outskirts of where Mikaela and Sarah stood.

Schettino signaled to a policeman standing in the back to escort the eight-year-old girl and six-year-old boy whose lives were saved by Mikaela Furano. When they approached Mikaela, the firefighter cried. Several women in the audience wept. Sarah pulled out tissues and dabbed the tears off Mikaela's face. After she kissed the heroine, the room exploded in applause.

"Mr. Fireman, thank you for saving our lives," said Ana Ramirez.

"Gracias," said her brother, Manuel.

The audience was wholly charmed.

"Such a feminine young man; he's so emotional," said an elderly woman seated near the back. "And he's so sweet."

"So you think men never cry," said her husband. "I know he's pretty feminine. His appearance and movements make that obvious, but I'd own a desert island now if I were given a quarter for every time I cried."

The children's parents soon joined them and hugged Sarah and the blubbering heroine.

Schettino spoke again. His slight Italian accent enhanced his homey tone.

"We in Fairview have never been as proud of one of our residents as we are tonight. Mikey Furano is being hailed all over New Jersey as a hero. And we are so pleased to say that he is *our* hero. He risked his life to save two children during his call of duty. People lost their lives during the plane crash over our town and neighboring Cliffside Park, but it could have been much worse. Mikey used his body as a shield to save a boy and a girl from being crushed by a collapsing wall. We know now that Mikey's helmet saved his life, but his body mass prevented the exploding debris from reaching Ana and Manuel. What Mikey did was offer his own life to ensure the children would survive."

Schettino was interrupted by boisterous applause. When it subsided, he continued.

"Mikey comes from one of the best families in Fairview. First and foremost, his lovely wife Sarah is the dutiful mother of their five beautiful children. His father, Joe, has been a good friend of mine for many years. He runs a successful security firm in Clifton. Joe's wife, Carol, is a gem. She is one of the kindest people I've ever known. Will Joe and Carol please stand?" the mayor asked.

Joseph and Carol sheepishly stood for a rousing ovation.

"Mikey's brother Adam was the young man everyone knows survived a terrible accident in Palisades Amusement Park," said Schettino. "He's a fantastic teacher and has inspired many. Joe and Carol are the parents of Jennifer, an attractive young woman with a winning personality. Please stand, Jen. And then there's Jay, their other son. I know he is hard-working and devoted. Please rise, Jay."

Again, the chambers exploded in vigorous clapping.

"If you ask me, that guy is a woman," whispered an older resident to his wife. "What is our country becoming? How revolting!"

"Oh, shush, Jimmy. He can't help the way he is," she whispered back. "Besides, he's a loving husband."

"Yeah, a girly husband," Jimmy snapped back. "Mikey should

have worn a dress and heels. But I'm sure it will only be a matter of time before he does."

The wife shook her head. "I understand he's the best father you'll find anywhere."

"Or a second mother," the man answered.

"You're impossible. I should have left you years ago."

Mayor Schettino spoke again. "I know Councilman Talamini would like to speak."

"Thank you, Mayor Schettino. I am proud to say I have known Mikey Furano for almost 11 years. He was one of our best students in high school and had one of the most dynamic personalities of any young man I've ever known. Mikey and I had a few long talks in my office as Vice-Principal. I learned so much about him and his family. He was athletic back in those years, quite a bit different than he is now, but I always loved his refreshing honesty about everything. I'm happy he's found his real self. I'll never forget when he was called to my office by my secretary, who used the name 'Michael.' He was fit to be tied. He angrily lectured her about using his real name, Mikey. I always knew he was unique, just like his brother Adam, and I am hardly surprised that he turned out to be a hero. That he was willing to sacrifice his life to save others tells us all we need to know about this remarkable young man. His wife Sarah attended high school with me, too, and she was a great student and one of the loveliest girls I've ever met. Joseph and Carol, you parented a fearless son. Mikey's sister Jennifer was a joy when she attended our school. She was super friendly and good-hearted. The Borough of Fairview can go on for 500 more years, and what young Mikey Furano did during our darkest hour will never be equaled. Mikey, you are our champion, and I am deeply honored to pay tribute to you."

The packed audience erupted as Mikaela cried again, leaning

onto Sarah's bosom.

Fire Chief Mesisca read the lengthy inscription on a gold-plated plaque the department had ordered for the occasion. Again, Mikaela was lauded as a courageous firefighter who put the lives of others above her own and that Fairview's fire department had experienced its finest hour."

"Didn't Churchill say something like that?" asked an auxiliary fireman to his colleague as they stood against a side wall.

"Which one do you mean? What Councilman Talamini said or what Chief Mesisca said?"

"Both."

"Well, I think you nailed it."

The beaming, mustached fire chief instructed Mikaela to hold the brown and gold tablet before her chest as Sarah cuddled the heroine. Mesisca stood on the other side as reporters, photographers, and residents took pictures. A short while later, the entire family positioned themselves for a photo.

The audience clapped, with the most vociferous applause coming from Rob Murphy, Susan Clarke, and Cindy McNally, seated in the second row on the left side.

After a burst of flashes, the microphone was passed to Mikaela, who tried to say a few words.

"I want to thank you all so much," she said but couldn't continue.

Sarah quickly grabbed the microphone. She decided to conform with the fire department's gender preference for Mikaela.

"As you all know, my husband is a highly emotional person. We love that part of him so much. All of us in the Furano and Burke families are prouder today than we have ever been in our lives. On behalf of Mikey, our children, his parents, and siblings, I want to express heartfelt thanks to the mayor and council, the Fairview Fire Department, the Fairview Police Department, the ambulance corps, firefighters from neighboring towns, and our beloved friends and residents who showed up tonight to attend the ceremony. We send our love and kisses to the Ramirez family. And to our dear friends, Rob Murphy, Susan Clarke, and Brian Fischer, we sincerely thank them for their love and passionate support. Remembering one of my husband's favorite movies, a 1937 romance starring Janet Gaynor, I will say now how proud I am to identify myself tonight as Mrs. Mikey Furano."

The audience wildly applauded.

Unnoticed by anyone, Mikaela's former girlfriend, Olivia Torricelli, standing in the mass of people behind the seats, wiped tears from her eyes as she pondered the past and present.

I kept his secret all the time we were dating. I'm happy he won't be tortured by it anymore. I thought it was a fetish he would outgrow, but I see it is part of him. All he ever did when we were intimate was cry. He had people fooled by his macho appearance and behavior, but he was far more emotionally frail than his transformed brother ever was. I used my fists on him many times. Well, he finally looks the way he should. I am so proud of him tonight. If things were different, I'd hold him in my arms tightly, the way he always wanted me to. He is such a girl. But I loved him. I still do. He's so gorgeous. Now, Sarah owns him. She's quite a woman. She has two men (or one man and one woman) and five children. I'm sorry I roughed her up. At the time, I thought she deserved it. She spoke against Mikey, and now she's his lover and mothered his twin boys. I suspect she now loves Mikey more than she loves Adam, and undoubtedly, she is more sexually attracted to Mikey. But I'm sure she'll never admit it since she's legally married to Adam. Now Mikey and his boys are as financially set as Adam and his girls are. Good for them.

Olivia squeezed through the crowd and approached her former boyfriend, who was accepting handshakes from all who managed to navigate the hoards.

"Hi, sweet one," she said, kissing Mikaela.

When the young heroine recognized Olivia, she cried and embraced her.

"It's been so long, Olivia. Thank you so much for coming!"

"I'm so proud of you. I think of you often and wish you and Sarah the best in your lives together. I love your new look! It's about time! And wow, your voice changed so much!"

Olivia hugged Sarah and kneeled to embrace and kiss little Stevie and Joey.

"Thank you, Olivia. Everyone misses you. How wonderful that you came here tonight. We must all meet up for dinner soon," said Sarah.

"I'd love that! Now, let me say hello to Carol and Joe."

Carol smiled when Olivia approached her. The women hugged and rocked each other.

"I'm sorry about what happened in your home that night," Olivia said. "The fault was all mine."

"Olivia, that's a long time ago. It's water under the bridge. I think everyone bears part of the blame. Your appearance tonight goes a long way in erasing that ugly business. Do you have a steady?"

"Yes, Carol. Erik is the exact opposite of Mikey. He's a macho truck driver who sometimes disappears for a few weeks doing cross-country runs. He drinks too much and got in trouble once for stealing, but he's good-hearted. Maybe one day we can get together. Mikey's not his type, but he gets along with everybody."

Olivia returned to Sarah.

"I have a new phone number. Please call me. I would love for us to keep in touch," said Olivia, writing several numerals on a small piece of paper.

"Of course," said Sarah. "I will do that. And you know ours too.

It never changed."

"It's still 945-4592," right?" asked Olivia.

"One day, we need to get a different number," said Carol. "The Furanos have had the same one for almost 30 years."

Laughter ensued.

Mayor Schettino asked for everyone's attention.

"All residents are welcome to enjoy catered Italian food from DePalma's Pizzeria and an open bar at the American Legion on Anderson Avenue across McKinley Street. The organization's commander instructed volunteers to set up chairs and tables in the large hall upstairs, but the downstairs bar is also available to all. We also have a Sabrett hot dog cart and an ice cream stand at the back of the hall. My brother John donated chop meat for the hamburgers that American Legion members will cook. The pastor of the Greek church said we are free to use their lot for parking. Thanks to everyone who showed up tonight to honor our hero."

A woman approached Mikaela and Sarah after edging her way through the crowd.

"Hello, my sweet girl, long time no see," she said.

Temporarily stumped, Mikaela solved the identity of the attractive brunette wearing a red and white floral dress. All the memories and images of October 1974 and the subsequent intimate letters flooded her consciousness. She hugged the woman and sobbed loudly. They rocked each other for five minutes.

"Cindy, I missed you so much. Over all these years, there hasn't been a single week when I didn't think of you. You've meant so much to me, even from so far away, more than you'll ever know."

Sarah knew about Cindy's long-distance relationship with Mikaela from conversations about the letters but only discovered the depth of their bond this evening. Never one to entertain or exhibit pangs of jealousy, Sarah was deeply moved that the relationship survived 12 years and 800 miles.

"Sweetie, you're so pretty, and I love your voice. You were always a heroine to me, but now the world sees you as a woman of courage, a champion in every sense. Now, where are those two beautiful twins?"

"Adam was entertaining them. Let me get them," said Sarah. "I think they found their way to the back."

"Honey, I have so much to tell you. I think you will be shocked and saddened to hear what happened in my life, but I also have some news that I think will make you happy," said Cindy. "Maybe we can talk on the phone."

"Dearest Cindy, tonight's event is far from over. Everyone is heading over to the American Legion Hall for refreshments. It is less than two blocks away. Will you walk over there with us? You are part of my family."

Cindy kissed Mikaela on the cheek. "Of course, sweetie. There is nowhere in the world I'd want to be other than with you and your family. I'd be honored."

"Cindy, here are the boys," said Sarah.

"Oh, my. They are the spitting image of their dad. Such cuties. Oh my God," said Cindy, beaming,

Sarah whispered into Mikaela's ear.

"Stevie and Joey, say hello to Mrs. McNally," said Mikaela.

"No, Mikaela, not Mrs. McNally. Cindy to everyone, including the boys."

"Hi Cindy," said Stevie, always the more spontaneous and forward of the twins. "I'm pleased to meet you."

"Oh, how cute," said Cindy. "Can I pick him up?" she asked Sarah.

"Of course."

Cindy whisked Stevie up, held the child over her head, and twirled him around.

Stevie laughed, immensely enjoying the ride.

Joey was next, and he, too, was exhilarated.

"You two must be so proud. What gorgeous and personable children you have!"

"Oh, we are, Cindy, we are," said Sarah. "Thank you!"

Applause and more picture-taking followed. Mikaela, Sarah, and the Furano family were the last to exit, though reporters continued approaching them as they descended the stairs. One journalist from the *Bergen Record* followed the family as they walked up Anderson Avenue, peppering Mikaela with questions.

When the Furanos entered, people at the packed bar applauded. Susan got first dibs and embraced the blubbering heroine, rocking and kissing her cheeks.

"I'm so proud of you, sweetie pie!" Susan exclaimed.

But many other town residents edged in to bolster their chances to administer physical felicitations. Mikaela didn't recognize most of the wall-to-wall crowd, though some familiar faces were conspicuous. Hanging high on the wall to the left of the bar were framed monochrome photos of every American Legion commander since the organization was founded until the present day. Mikaela recognized Al Contessa's picture. She knew the community activist was the father of her fifth-grade teacher, Ann Marie Kradenski. Mikaela also recognized the glabrous Otto Bonin from the wall of portraits. Bonin represented the Veteran's Post at numerous community events, including those involving the Fairview Little League.

The malty smell permeating the space triggered Mikaela's craving for a beer, but she knew she'd get all she wanted upstairs, where she could also smoke. After an inevitable long delay caused by everyone wishing to share a few words with the celebrity, she ascended the stairs with Sarah holding her hand. When they reached the top, more frenzied applause ensued.

CHAPTER 37

Celebration at the American Legion

The American Legion Hall was adorned with flags, streamers, and enlarged photos of Mikaela. Eighth-grade art class students created rectangular signs honoring the firefighter's heroism. "Fairview's Finest," "Hometown Hero," "The Pride of Bergen," "Brave Blondie," and other catchphrases were neatly etched on the white background with colored markers. The overflowing crowd clapped and cheered as soon as Mikaela, Sarah, and the Furano family reached the top of the staircase and were visible at the open double doorway. Firefighters from all over East Bergen, public officeholders, school officials, the clergy, educators from Fairview and Cliffside Park, relatives, friends, and the press turned the modest-sized space into wall-to-wall humanity. No chairs were available at the tables, and the stage was utilized for more seating. Father McTague and Pastor Sticco were escorted to the hall by a patrol car driven by Patrolman George Muller. The two clergymen sat on either side of a postern. Sticco was assigned the invocation. Other priests and ministers from the Trinity Lutheran Church, the Greek Church of the Ascension, and St. John the Bap-

291

tist were seated on the stage. McTague's request to speak about Adam, Mikaela, Jimbo, and the Furano family was granted weeks in advance, though he promised to keep his talk short.

"Hey, Adam, it's been a long time," said Bill Peters, seated at a table on the ground floor enjoying a beer. "Man, have you changed! You're as solid as any of my fellow servicemen during my two tours of duty in Nam."

"Well, I wouldn't go that far, Bill. But I've been bodybuilding for a few years now. I felt I needed to make a statement. Anyway, as I recall, you are the third generation of the Tiger Hose Fire Company. So today's event must make you proud."

"I couldn't be prouder," said Bill. "Whether his or her name is Mikey or Mikaela, he or she has put our town on the map. Risking your life to save children was the ultimate sacrifice, and tonight's tribute was well-earned."

"Hearing Mayor Schettino speak earlier made me think of you. Didn't you once tell me you were elected Mayor for a Day at Lincoln School?"

"Yes, Adam. I beat none other than the esteemed Joe Olivelli. I was the 2nd Mayor for a Day."

"You had to be popular to prevail!"

"I'd like to believe that. But Mikey or Mikaela is in the Fairview record book for incomparable greatness. Our fire department has achieved so much over the years, and what happened after the plane crash was an act of incalculable heroism. I've seen courage overseas, and your sibling's bravery is comparable."

"Bill, those are beautiful words. I will convey them to Mikaela tonight if you don't speak to her."

"Adam, I heard you are quite a teacher. Looking at you, I'm sure you have well-behaved kids. I can't see one challenging you now."

"Thanks," said Adam, chuckling. "Well, all but Brian Fischer. I'll stay clear of getting him mad at me. But he's such a great kid. He's here circulating somewhere."

"It figures you have kids idolizing you. Good luck, friend. I'm going upstairs to enjoy the festivities."

Adam ran into other longtime friends, some of whom engaged with him at length.

"If it isn't Patrick O'Brien! How the hell are you?" asked Adam.

"Great to see you again, Adam! It's been way too long."

"You moved to Lodi in 1976, right?

"One year earlier than that, Adam. I got married in 1975 and moved out immediately. But as you know, my parents still live at 412 Ninth Street."

"You still have the machine shop at 201 Anderson?" asked Adam.

"Oh yes! It is still in operation."

"My wife and I miss St. John's," said Adam. "You and your family attended there for years. After Father McTague left, we switched to Our Lady of Grace."

"My family still attends St. John's," answered O'Brien.

"I remember you served on the First Parish Council. And, of course, you work in management at Lowe Paper in Ridgefield," said Adam.

"You still have that great memory, my friend," said O'Brien. "I was told you have become a great teacher at Bergen Tech. I love your new physique and appearance and pity anyone tangling with you. I'm so proud of Mikaela. Your family was blessed when she was born. My parents called to tell me about tonight's event. I felt I needed to attend."

"Pat, I am so thrilled you came. We are deeply honored," said Adam.

EMT member Troy Burton greeted Adam with a vigorous handshake.

"Hey Adam, wow, you have changed! I don't mean to bring up

bad memories, but I never forgot that terrible incident behind the A&P. Not only did you recover in flying colors, but you have transformed yourself into some badass dude. How did you do it?"

"Shit, Troy, I've been working my butt off at a gym for a few years now. Weightlifting and aerobics did wonders."

"If I could ask, how many nights a week did you work out?"

"Depending on the week, four or five," said Adam. "Some sessions lasted two hours. I am still working out and haven't any plans to stop."

"Adam, I've seen other friends transform, but I must tell you none quite as extreme as what you achieved. They should write an article about you in the Hudson Dispatch!"

"Thanks for those glowing sentiments, Troy. I was on a mission to undo a great fucking wrong that was committed against me. For too long a time, I was perceived as a wimp. As far as newspapers are concerned, my sister Mikaela deserves all the press she can get."

"I agree with you on Mikaela. She'll be inducted into Fairview's Hall of Fame. Heck, New Jersey's Hall of Fame! But I hear you on the matter of perception. Your family is unique. If you know what I mean, what you perceive seems the opposite of what is real. I love the new you, my friend!"

"Oh, our family is unique, all right," said Adam laughingly. "But I couldn't be happier for Mikaela for embracing her correct gender. Give my regards to Angelo!"

"Will do, Adam."

A bunch of Adam's lifelong friends approached him to shake hands. These included Tony Lucibello, Pete Ciufitelli, Joseph Boylan, Danny Gaito, Russell Martin, Joe Courtsales, and Frank Scerbo.

"Adam, you had so many friends growing up," said Lucibello. "So many have showed up tonight. Isn't it odd that Mikaela, who is so beloved and is the subject of this event, didn't develop many friendships growing up?"

"You are right, Tony. She was a phenomenal student and a far better person than I ever was, but she was a homebody. Mikaela had this image as a bully, so many stayed clear. The only relationship she ever had was with Olivia."

"But Olivia was abusive."

"Yes, she treated Mikaela terribly. But she showed up at Borough Hall, and she's standing in the back."

Tony turned around. "Wow, so she is!"

Bill Peters spoke into the microphone and introduced "Mikey" Furano to loud applause.

"The American Legion is proud to be given the chance to honor the Fairview Fire Department's finest, a person who will live in the annals of greatness for now and for all time. I am proud of my long-time relationship with the Furano family and join them in paying homage to Mikey. His courageous heroism was the one silver lining behind this terrible disaster."

When Mikaela appeared, everyone called her by her new feminine name. Tears rolled down her face.

Fairview's officials would be seriously challenged to identify a more moving or celebratory event in the town's nearly nine-decade history.

***

Late that night in bed, Sarah mauled Mikaela in frenzied lovemaking that ended with intercourse but was preceded by declarations of love matching any spoken between Shakespeare's lead characters in *Romeo and Juliet.*

***

The following month, Sarah missed her period. She was shocked to learn during her fifth-month ultrasound that she was again carrying twins, and once again, both were boys. If the pregnancy

295

and delivery went well, Mikaela Furano would have fathered four of Sarah's seven children and all her males.

CHAPTER 38

The Tunnel of Love in Palisades Amusement Park

July 25, 1964

"Dad, look at that sign," said eleven-year-old Sarah Burke, excitedly pointing upward at a billboard over the main doors to the restroom building near Kiddie Land. "It says the second season of *The Outer Limits* starts on September 19!"

"So it does," answered Steve, the 42-year-old Burke family patriarch. He was at Palisades Amusement Park with his wife Michele and only child. The Burkes lived in Cliffside Park. Steve was an enormously successful Wall Street trader who allowed his spouse to serve as a housewife. Sarah's favorite pastime was visiting the famous 38-acre pleasure ground, and since she was six, her parents made at least four excursions there every summer.

As The Four Seasons's *Rag Doll* played loudly through a speaker attached to the basketball chance stand, Sarah indulged in her cocoon-shaped pink cotton candy but stayed the course in discussing her favorite television show. The one-hour science-fiction program ran on ABC at 7:30 p.m. on Mondays.

"The name of the first show is *Soldier*," Sarah exclaimed. "I can't wait!"

"Honey, let me guess your favorite episode. Was it the one with David McCallum playing the alien whose head expands as he advances to the future in a time machine?"

"Dad, that one was called *The Sixth Finger*, and I loved it. But the one I liked most was *The Zanti Misfits*. The aliens attacked men in the army and looked like ants."

"I know you loved it, honey, but it gave you nightmares. I like *The Outer Limits* too, but I prefer *The Twilight Zone*.

"I love both," said Sarah.

"Of course you do," said Steve as he crushed his cigarette in a park receptacle.

"Thanks for keeping the park clean," said a casually dressed, medium-height man around 70.

"You are most welcome, sir," said Steve. "I'm honored to meet you, Mr. Rosenthal," he added, shaking the hand of Palisades Amusement Park's owner.

Rosenthal registered a broad smile as he headed to Kiddie Land.

"Who was that, Dad?"

"Honey, his name is Irving Rosenthal. He's the owner of the park. Well, one of the owners. His brother Jack is the other one."

"Wow, Dad. We should have gotten his autograph."

Steve guffawed. "Honey, he's always walking around the park. He wants to be seen as a regular guy, not a celebrity. Sometimes, he's seen with a broom."

"He's the owner, and he sweeps?" Sarah whispered to her dad.

Steve nodded. "Honey, that's a hands-on way to run a business."

Near the entrance, Rosenthal caught one of his ride managers, Angelo D'Arminio Jr., tossing a cigarette butt to the ground.

"Hey Angelo, do you think mine park should look like Coney Island?" the owner exclaimed in a distinct Jewish cadence and with an amusing grammatical error.

"I'm so sorry, boss," said Angelo as he picked up the butt and rushed it over to a nearby garbage can.

"Dad, one boy in my class said that almost all of Palisades Amusement Park is in our town. He said only a tiny part is in Fort Lee."

"Honey, I'm afraid he's wrong. Palisades Amusement Park is half in Cliffside Park and half in Fort Lee."

"Are you sure, Dad?"

"Yes, honey. The matter came up once at a town council meeting. Mayor Calabrese told a person in the audience that the borderline ran through the center. By the way, honey, Mr. Rosenthal's wife is a celebrity."

"Wow, Dad! Is she a movie star?"

Steve laughed. "Not quite. But she wrote the Palisades Amusement Park song you always hear on the radio and television. Her name is Gladys Shelley."

"His wife wrote that song? Really? The name of it is *Come On Over*," said Sarah, singing a few lyrics:

Palisades has the rides; Palisades has the fun. Come on over. Shows and dancing are free and the parking's so cheap. Come on over. Palisades from coast to coast, where a dime buys the most. Palisades Amusement Park. Swings all day and after dark.

"Honey, you have a great voice. You have to join the choir in high school."

"I'm not *that* good, Dad."

"Don't sell yourself short. And honey, there is a much more famous song about this place. You own the record."

Sarah smiled. "Of course, Dad! *Palisades* Park by Freddie Cannon made it to Number 3. I even know the singer's real name is

299

Frederick Picariello."

"Honey, you are a fountain of knowledge. Most of my Italian friends from this area are proud of him."

"Dad, I'd like to meet nobody more than Cousin Brucie. I'd love to see the face behind all those ABC song countdowns!"

"Honey, you have my word. I will make it happen. Cousin Brucie is here at the park quite often!"

Sarah kissed her dad.

"Steve, let's visit the Penny Arcade," said Michele. "Sarah loves Skee-Ball and trying the crane game with the stuffed animals, and you love playing Fascination. Maybe we can spend an hour there and then take her on some rides."

"Mom, you promised I would be allowed to ride the Arabian Nights Tunnel of Love this year. I'm tall enough."

"Honey, you were tall enough last year, too, but I thought you were too young for a ride with such a mature theme," said Michele. "That ride is mainly for dating couples."

"Mom, maybe I'll meet my future husband on it."

"Oh, tush, Sarah. You have many years to go before you date. But I like the fact that you are romantic. How about we do what I suggested and then go to the back of the park so you can go on the Whip and the race cars? We'll save the Tunnel of Love for last."

"Sounds great, Mom!" exclaimed Sarah as the family headed to the Penny Arcade.

"Sarah, I'm intrigued. When your time does come to date, what kind of man would you prefer?"

"Mom, I've dreamed of marrying a muscleman with a goatee who rides motorcycles. I want to ride behind him, holding my hands around his waist."

"Uh-oh," said Michele. "I think we have a wild one here."

"I hope he has tattoos all over his body," said Sarah.

The Burkes guffawed.

Michele knew that her husband's Fascination addiction would ensure an extended stay in the game room. After Steve sat down on a stool chair and started rolling rubber balls towards 25 holes barely wider than the circumference of the balls, he beamed when the light on the backboard lit up after the corresponding number on the hole matched up with the backboard numeral. The ball then rolled back to the player on a slanted wooden incline. The goal was to light five rows across the matrix, in a vertical column or on a diagonal like Bingo, another game with a free space in the middle. A glass plate, installed on the end of the table closest to the player, aimed to deter those reaching too far over the table to improve their aim.

Like many gamblers addicted to the action more than winning or losing, Steve was in it for the thrill. After placing a quarter down on the glass in front of him, he waited for a worker to collect it and an announcer sitting on an elevated platform to signal the start of the game. As the balls rolled back and forth, the player who lit the lights first would win and be given coupons. The many gifts showcased on shelves and walls in the arcade required sizable numbers of coupons. A wealthy man, Steve couldn't care less about prizes but still wanted his daughter to be happy.

No sooner did the Burkes enter the arcade than Sarah, armed with a pocketful of nickels, dashed to the Skee-Ball machines. After she inserted a nickel, a queue of nine Masonite balls about three inches in diameter lined up on her right. In Skee-Ball, the player rolls the balls over a ski-styled hump, where they will land into white bullseye rings of various values. The most challenging ring is the one furthest away that awarded 50 points.

Sarah used all the nickels in her pocket in a half-hour session that netted her 240 tickets. She spotted her dad at the Fascination table and crowed over her winnings.

"Wow, honey, you did so well!" the Burke family patriarch exclaimed. "I'm afraid I'm not doing nearly as good. I only won a single time," he added, referring to the sole instance he beat out his fellow challengers. There were 20 Fascination tables, but there weren't more than twelve participants for most games.

"Daddy, the tickets I won are enough for a pink and blue marbles bag."

"Nice, Sarah. Bring your tickets to the prize counter. I will play one last game, and then we'll head off for the rides," Burke said, parroting an addicted player who always says, *Just one more.*

After Sarah claimed her prize, Michele pestered Steve to end his marathon game session. They headed to the pleasure ground's southeast section, where Sarah immediately voiced her preference.

"Mom and Dad, please let me go on the Rocketship."

"Of course, honey, we knew that would be your first choice."

While a step above its Kiddie Land equivalent, Palisades Amusement Park's Rocketship was tamer than most rides categorized as adult attractions; children were allowed on as long as they passed the minimum requirement on the height gauge.

All three went on the Whip, with Sarah wedging between her parents. The ride consisted of two circular wheel-like turntable platforms on opposite sides of a rectangular configuration. The cars accommodated three riders and were equipped with a safety bar. They followed the track until they reached the platform corner, at which point it would accelerate. The cars "whipped" around the corner, providing riders with the attraction's unique thrills.

"That was great, Dad," said Sarah. "Let's go on it again!"

"Honey, don't you want to go on the Tunnel of Love?" said Michele. "And maybe some other rides?"

"You're right, Mom. Let's go to the Tunnel of Love!"

The Arabian Nights Tunnel of Love was situated across from

the Carousel and the ticket booth for the Cyclone.

Sarah boarded the platform, followed by a skinny black-haired ten-year-old boy holding the hand of his blond-headed four-year-old brother.

"Sir, my brother is too short and young to go on this ride, but I'll hold him tight. My mom and dad are talking to a friend they met over by the information booth," said Adam Sean Furano.

"I'm sorry, young man, but I can't break the rules. I'll lose my job. You'll have to leave your brother with your parents before I can let you on the ride."

"I'm sorry, Mikey, but you can't go on this ride. You are too small," Adam said to his younger sibling.

Suddenly, Mikey sobbed so pitifully that the ride operator was moved to take a risk.

"This is my last summer working here, so what the heck. How about we seat him between you and this young girl?" he asked, pointing a finger at Sarah.

Sarah registered a wide smile as her parents looked on.

"Hi, boys. My name is Sarah. What are yours?"

"Hi Sally," said Adam, mistaking the girl's pronunciation. Sarah let it slide.

"My name is Adam, and this is my brother Mikey."

"Adam and Mikey. I love both names."

The operator asked the children to hasten to an open boat. Once the three children sat and the seat belts tightened, the boat soon disappeared into darkness. Frightened, Mikey rested his head on Sarah's chest, embracing her with his right arm.

"I love you, Mikey," said Sarah. "And I love you too, Adam."

"I adore you, Sally," responded Adam.

"I love Sally," said Mikey, snuggling closely to Sarah, who draped an arm around the shaking child.

Floating along dark passages, the ride was more of a haunted attraction than a make-out rendezvous, though older passengers with raging hormones weren't the least bit fazed by the spooky ambiance. As the boat hit the wooden sides of the guided waterway, the loud banging induced Mikey to cry loudly. Adam and Sarah squeezed him tight as the former repeatedly kissed the boy's face.

"Don't cry, cutie. Sally will protect you," said Sarah, embracing the incorrect name the boys had previously used to address her. For the remainder of the ride, Mikey kept his eyes closed and his head nestled against Sarah's bosom.

The exit doors opened as the boat crawled to the platform, where passengers would claim it and start the ride all over again.

"I'll never forget you, Sally," said Adam. "And I'll always treasure our first ride through the Tunnel of Love." Sarah hugged Adam and reflected.

Such a sweet boy. I'll probably never see him or his brother ever again. I'm so sad.

Sarah kissed both brothers on the cheek, dabbed a tear from her eye, and turned away.

Steve and Michele Burke met their daughter as she walked down the exit ramp.

"Did you fall in love, honey?" said Steve. "Now remember, you are only eleven. You have many years before such thoughts can cross your mind."

"Steve, time is flying by. Before you know it, she'll have a steady boyfriend," answered Michele. "Maybe it was best she got an innocent taste of what romance might be like one day."

"Michele, I think you are right," said Steve. "It's just that Sarah is our only child, and I'd like to hold on to her as long as possible. I know this is selfish, but I think my feelings are natural."

"Yes, they are, Steve. I feel the same way."

Sarah embraced her parents and quickly turned to deliver a

final wave to the Furano boys, who had just reconnected with Joseph and Carol. The latter was pushing a carriage, where Jennifer was playing with a stuffed animal dangling from a horizontal string.

"Now, if my little boy weren't part of the decision, I'd be tempted to turn in the ride proprietor for allowing a four-year-old on a ride that should only be offered to teenagers," said Joseph.

"Oh Joe, don't be such a tough cookie," said Carol. "These kids are too young to understand romance. To them, this ride was more of a haunted house experience. I'm sure they thought it was spooky. The young girl looked like a sweetheart, though."

"How about we take them to the Funhouse?" asked Joseph. "It would be a first for Adam."

"Joe, the Funhouse is located in the northwest section of the park. It's a bit of a walk. Adam will be allowed on the ride, but Mikey is far too small and young. No proprietor wanting to keep their job would dare let a kid not much more than a toddler pass through the gate. A child could get injured in the tilted room or the spinning barrel. They will never risk a lawsuit."

"Sounds like you are a big fan of that ride," said Joseph. "We've been married long enough for me to have known."

"Joe, you are an airhead sometimes."

"Talk about calling the kettle black," Joseph answered.

Carol gently punched her husband's arm as they headed to one of Palisades Amusement Park's most popular attractions.

"Mom, could I go on the Wild Mouse?" asked Adam, pointing to a roller coaster to the immediate right of the Funhouse and across the road from the famous saltwater pool.

"Sugar, look at the way those carts turn on the tracks. I was on that ride once and don't remember if I was ever more terrified. You feel as if the cart will fall off the tracks."

"Why, Mommy?"

"Adam, the people who designed the ride did that deliberately," said Joseph. "The ride is so scary because you think you will fall off."

"I take back what I said. I don't think I'd like to ride it," said Adam.

"Everybody says the Cyclone is much scarier because it's so much bigger and has steep hills and dips, but the Wild Mouse is more nerve-wracking," said Carol.

Adam Sean Furano and the Wild Mouse would meet up with fate seven years later in September of 1971.

CHAPTER 39

Susan Talks with Stevie; Mikaela Registers for College; Twins Born

June 2, 1986

"Do you mind, Dad?" Mikaela asked if she could take a cigarette from his father-in-law's pack.

"Go right ahead, Mikaela. You never need to ask."

"Mikaela Furano, don't you dare!" Sarah exclaimed. She clenched her fist and punched Mikaela. Because she caught her just right, blood flowed from her victim's nostrils. Michele hastened to pour water over a paper towel and held it tight over Mikaela's nose.

"Sarah!" exclaimed Steve Burke.

"Dad, I love you, but please don't interfere. Mikaela defied my orders."

"I understand, Sarah, but you know how hard it is to quit smoking. Just because you haven't smoked in four or five months, it doesn't mean others will be able to do the same."

Susan took over from Michele and held the damp towel as the

bleeding slowed. "Shh, sweetie pie. Sarah loves you. She is just concerned about your health," said the professor.

"But Adam smokes plenty more than I do. Sarah never tried to get him to stop. She loves me much less than she loves Adam, so he can do what he wants. Of course, I understand that. Adam is her husband."

"Did you ever think I might love you *more* than I love him*?*" Sarah asked. "Did you ever think of that possibility? Maybe *your* health is the most important thing to me."

Susan smiled approvingly as the Burkes nodded.

Sarah cried as she sat next to Mikaela, embracing her.

"I am sorry, sweetheart. I know how hard it is to quit; you are still young. Maybe we'll try again for a few years down the road. Adam is a hardcore smoker. He will never surrender that. If I suggested it, he would assault me."

"Adam loves smoking some other things, too," said Michele, snickering.

"He's an addict," said Susan. "Adam is a poor example for you to use, Mikaela."

"But he's a great teacher," Mikaela answered.

"There are many great teachers who have substance abuse problems. I know a few at my college. Adam has been successful in keeping his profession and private life apart. I hope that never changes."

"I'm sure I'd be wasting my time if I tried to tell Jay, Jennifer, and Rob to quit," said Sarah. "The only person in the house with willpower is Jimbo. He hasn't touched a cigarette or a drop of liquor in over two years. Saoirse helped, but his religion mellowed him. Remember when everyone said Jimbo was a bad influence on my husband? Now, it's the other way around. I give him all the credit in the world for turning down Adam when he was asked to share a joint. My father-in-law is even proud of

Jimbo."

Susan and Michele nodded.

Not only did Sarah end her crusade to get Mikaela to stop smoking, but she resumed the habit after five months without a cigarette. She grabbed two cigarettes from her dad's pack, handed one to Mikaela, and flicked a lighter on both.

"I have to admit, I missed it. Susan?" asked Sarah.

"No, I'm good for now. Welcome back to the wonderful world of nicotine addiction," Susan answered. "You did well to last five months."

"I'll try again, hopefully, sooner than later," Sarah said.

"Hey, sweetie," Susan said, diverting to Mikaela. "I have a beautiful pair of purple earrings that would look fantastic on you. I'll bring them over this week. I also have some attractive nail polish you can use."

"Thanks so much, Professor Clarke. I'd appreciate it," said Mikaela, taking a drag on her cigarette.

"Susan. Always call me Susan, cutie pie. You are looking more and more beautiful every time I see you."

Blushing, Mikaela answered, "Thanks, Susan. That means a lot to me."

"So, when will you be registering at my college? I heard so much about you. I understand you are practically a Rhodes schoolar."

"Well, I wouldn't quite go that far, Susan. Adam is much smarter than me."

Sarah pounced like a lioness protecting her cubs. "No, he is not, sweetheart! It isn't even close, and you know it! You are exceptionally gifted. If you decide to teach, you'll be the best educator in the system where you work. Adam is bright, but you are a genius."

"Thanks, Sarah. I haven't decided, but I am leaning toward that profession. I might want to teach English at the high school level. I would enjoy using many novels, plays, and poems I love."

"You are brave," said Susan. "To succeed, you must be an excellent disciplinarian. Do you feel you can handle behavioral problems? We first saw what happened with your brother at Bergen Tech."

"But he only had problems at the very beginning. He is a fantastic disciplinarian now."

"Yes, that's true," said Susan. "He and I fought over his strategy, but he proved me wrong. He has serious issues in his personal life, but he is loved at his high school. His method is the most unorthodox I've ever encountered."

"Isn't it ironic the way we switched places? He is the way I was as a teenager, and I, as an adult, became what he was as a child and teen," said Mikaela.

"Ironic isn't the word," said Susan. "But he's worse now than you were then. He flies off the handle too much."

"Sweetie, you know how much I adore you. But honey, please don't take this the wrong way, but..."

"I know Susan. But I'm proud of who I am, and while I prefer to present femininely, I also know I must tone down my physical appearance in a classroom if or when I fully transition."

"Yes, sweetie pie. Your hair's streaks and color will be fine, and you can wear earrings and keep your nose and naval rings. You can probably keep your pink love tattoo. But you can't use lipstick, makeup or nail polish and must wear men's clothes. You can't help your feminine voice and body movements. You are who you are. When you are not working, you can dress as you like."

"I still think Adam is a great disciplinarian. He's a macho man. I don't have that quality."

"That's for sure," Susan smiled. "But I think you will uniquely reach students."

"I love you, Susan."

"Aww," Susan said, pulling Mikaela's head to her chest. One day, I will steal you from Sarah."

"As long as you return her the day after, Susan," answered Sarah. "I can't survive more than a day without my sweetheart."

"What do you think?" Susan asked, looking at the Burkes. "Is Sarah right?"

"I'm afraid so," said Michele. "I think it's more like five or six hours, tops, the most she could go without Mikaela."

Sarah snuggled against Mikaela on her other side.

Susan smiled broadly. "Let me see what the boys are doing," she said, heading to the extra bedroom the Burkes had designed for their grandchildren.

Joey and Stevie were playing Operation, but when the latter saw Susan, he instructed his brother to finish the world map crossword puzzle they were both working on before diverting to the Milton Bradley skill game that tested the players' hand-eye coordination and fine motor skills. He signaled Susan to follow him to a corner of the room.

"Aunt Susan, can I ask you a question?"

"What is it, honey?"

"When will my daddy become a complete woman?"

Startled at such a question, the academic hesitated and stared at the child but then rallied.

"Honey, I'm not sure."

"Aunt Susan, my dad looks like a girl, just like my mom. She wears lipstick, makeup, and earrings and dyes her hair. She has a girl's voice, even more girlish than Mom's."

Susan ruminated.

This kid is so intelligent and observant. I think it's beautiful that he accepts his dad for who she is and even prefers her to continue presently that way. For a boy at this age to be able to rightly say his dad is more feminine than his mom is incredible. This boy couldn't have a better role model than his feminized dad.

Susan smiled. "Do you love your dad?"

"I love her so much. She's everything to me. I have the best daddy."

"Yes, you do, sweetie," said Susan. "There isn't a better father anywhere. I love her dearly."

She picked up Stevie and kissed him repeatedly.

"Aunt Susan, my daddy loves my mommy a real lot."

"Honey, I have never seen anyone love another person like that. You know what the word *worship* means, right Stevie?"

"You mean like worshipping God?"

"Yes, sweetie, something like that. When you get older, you'll understand the concept more."

"But my mom is married to my Uncle Adam. He loves her a real lot, too."

"Yes, he does," Susan said, dreading what Stevie might ask next.

"Aunt Susan, who does my mom love more, my dad or Uncle Adam?"

"Your mom loves them both very much."

"I know she loves them both, but I think she loves my dad more. I hope she does."

"Sweetie, she might, she just might. Your dad is the easiest person to love, and your mom is wild about her. But sweetie, it is always best not to compare. Your mom adores your dad *and* your Uncle Adam. Your dad and uncle are both fathers in your family."

"Aunt Susan, is Uncle Adam a drug addict?"

"Why would you think that, Stevie?"

"I've heard things. When Saoirse's grandma and aunt from Italy were here, they said things to each other."

"I see," said Susan.

"I'm sorry about Uncle Adam," said Stevie. "Is he an alcoholic?"

"Your uncle likes to drink, Stevie. But don't worry about him. He'll be just fine."

"Well, Uncle Adam is Saoirse's dad, and Saoirse says Mom should be married to my Dad. Uncle Rob feels the same way. And I think my sister's real dad might be Jimbo. My mom won't admit it, of course."

Susan barely maintained her composure.

"Sweetie, I heard Saoirse say that, but your mom is in love with two brothers. It doesn't matter who she is married to. She loves them the same. Saoirse's *real* dad is your Uncle Adam. But yes, your sister also loves Jimbo."

"Aunt Susan, I *know* Jimbo is Saoirse's real dad. My mom never denied it."

Susan didn't answer the child. Instead, she lifted him and petted his hair.

This most unusual family dynamic was something young children couldn't understand. Still, it was inevitable at some point to raise the questions and observations Stevie was now posing to Susan. There was part of Susan who was honored to be asked such intimate questions about a family the woman adored. Still, the downside was having to give potentially disconcerting answers. She decided not to challenge the boy anymore. Years later, he would learn the truth, though Jimbo being posed as Saoirse's dad was the height of absurdity.

"Aunt Susan, I love my dad so much. Please tell me who you love more, my dad or Uncle Adam."

Susan was mortified but felt compelled to answer the boy.

"I love them both."

"Please be honest with me, Aunt Susan. Please. Please tell me who you love more."

"I love your dad more," said the smiling professor, telling the boy what he wanted to hear and expressing her honest feelings.

"Quite a bit more."

"Thank you, Aunt Susan. I figured you did."

Stevie was a male version of his half-sister Saoirse. Inquisitive, insightful, and incorrigible, he always kept his listeners on their toes, but it didn't take long before people found him wholly irresistible. However, his cute round face, jet black hair, and blue eyes prejudiced adults before they engaged with him.

***

Susan returned to the yard.

"Sarah, that's your third rum and Coke," exclaimed Michele. "You criticized your dad for years, and now you are just like him."

"Oh, leave her be," said Steve. "She finally learned how to have a good time; I'm proud of her."

"Mom, I never thought I'd say this, but Dad was right. I'm sorry I gave him a hard time."

Steve beamed, but Michele scowled.

***

"Susan, my family is planning a coming-out party for me next month," said Mikaela in Susan's Palisades Park apartment.

"That's such wonderful news, Mikaela. I recommend you only wear female clothes. To dress as a male for the first month of your classes would be absurd. It would be best if you put your male life behind you. You are a woman now and must present that way from the start. I'd be interested in joining you and Sarah when you shop. I'd like to have some input!"

"Sarah is seven months pregnant, but she gets around like she's not carrying anything at all," said Mikaela. "I'd love you to help me build my new wardrobe."

"Isn't that consistent with her other pregnancies?" asked Susan.

"Yes, she never had a single complication. Doctors were always amazed."

"Sarah eats very well, though she smokes and drinks. I still need to get my head around the idea that she will soon be the mother of seven children. My only wish is that you two be legally married. She loves you far more than the person she's married to, and you know that well, Mikaela. He is standing in the way of a classic romantic relationship."

"Yes, Susan, Sarah is my soulmate. But you are kidding yourself if you believe she doesn't still adore Adam. I know how difficult he is and how abusive he can be, but she'll stand beside him and will do everything he wishes. Besides, we would have to get married right away. Same-sex marriages aren't legal."

"I know, sweetie. I'm only dreaming. I'm content with the knowledge that she loves you more than him. For so many reasons, how could she not?"

Mikaela smiled broadly and held Susan's hand.

"Do you think I can pass as female, Susan?" said Mikaela, lighting a cigarette.

"Mikaela, I have to be honest with you. It would be best if you started taking female hormones soon. You look great as you present now, but the hormones will erase any doubt. Still, by dressing completely feminine and having your hair styled, you are telling everyone that you are transitioning. So you don't have to pass completely. You only need to serve notice. As the months go by – and with the help of what I recommend – you will be seen and appreciated as a complete woman."

"Thank you, Susan," said Mikaela, leaning over to kiss the professor.

Susan beamed.

"You, Sarah, and young Stevie are my most treasured people worldwide."

"Susan, you are turning into a Furano with the rankings," said Mikaela.

The professor chuckled.

"Mikaela, I made out your schedule. I hope you won't get mad that I signed you up for the classes I want you to take. I made the schedule as if the classes were for me."

"Susan, you are entirely in charge. You make all the decisions regarding classes and times. My only role in this is to attend and do the work."

"My sweet girl, I have you down for Women in Literature, Women's Gender Studies, Feminism in Philosophy, The Bronte Sisters, Shakespeare's Comedies, and Women and War in the 20th Century. Six classes, each 50 minutes, the same length as the classes your brother teaches in his high school. All will meet three times a week. I have you off on Friday. Each class is worth three credits, so your load for the first semester is 18 credits. I know three professors well and consider them among the best at the college. All six are women. Will you continue to work on the weekends?"

"Susan, some of the workers at the A&P won't even look at me anymore. They know I am changing gender and find it deplorable. One gave me the finger last week when I passed him in an aisle. The store manager and his assistant are still very nice to me, mainly because of what I did after the plane crash. They address me as Mikaela now. Sarah said she doesn't want me working while I attend college, but how much can we lean on her dad."

"What does Steve say?" asked Susan.

"He says that money is no object. He's unbelievable."

"Your father-in-law will do anything for you. There are no limits."

"I hate to take advantage, Susan."

"You have the best partner anywhere and soon will have four beautiful boys. They should be your focus. Steve has the funds to support you. He will care for his daughter, daughter-in-law, son-in-law, and grandchildren. It would be best if you spent your weekends reading and studying."

"I guess you are right, Susan," said Mikaela, resting her head on the professor's bosom.

"I love how long your hair is growing. I hope you will let it grow much longer. Girl, you'd be a knockout if it reached halfway down your back. Wait till you start taking hormones. It will grow faster, thicken, and turn luxuriant. You're a natural blonde."

"I plan on letting it grow down my back. I love long hair and have dreamed of having my own for years. I want long nails, too."

Susan smiled broadly.

"One more thing. I gave you the earliest class to start your days for selfish reasons. I, Professor Clarke, will pick you up in front of your home every morning. Well, four mornings, anyway. And I am confident my girl will wait one hour after her classes end to ride home with me. Can I expect you to do this? You can accomplish quite a bit in the library during that hour."

"I'm in!" said Mikaela. I'd love to start and end my days with you!"

***

The birth certificates of Sarah's new fraternal twins revealed that Mikey Furano weighed 5 pounds, 1 ounce, and Adam Furano weighed 4 pounds, 14 ounces.

"So, the baby-making machine has done it again!" Jay said in the living room. "And typically, the offspring are in perfect health. How wonderful that Mikaela's old name has been resurrected, though she hates it because it reminds her of who she once was."

"I think it's awesome that Adam was honored, too," said Jennifer. "As the father of three daughters, he never had an opportunity. I understand Sarah and Mikaela enthusiastically endorsed both names despite what Jay said. Let's get ready to head out there!"

"Seven children. Now Sarah knows how the Von Trapps felt in *The Sound of Music,*" said Carol.

The birth of little Adam and little Mikey further complicated Mikaela's life. Her weekends were a veritable juggling of feeding the infants, changing their diapers, cleaning, and completing her reading assignments. On the weekday evenings, they encompassed the same tasks, albeit in a shorter time frame.

"Carol, isn't it amazing that my name will be passed down by my four grandsons, fathered by our daughter, and that our son only had daughters?"

"Joseph, is there anything conventional about our family?"

They held hands, sitting at the kitchen table, and chuckled.

CHAPTER 40

Mikaela's Coming Out Party

After sustained encouragement from Sarah and Susan and the belief that her children wanted her to be true to herself, "Mikaela" Furano finally came out to her family on a Sunday evening.

"The tortured girl living inside you for so long has finally emerged. I love you, Mikaela," said Carol, wrapping her arms around her new daughter as they sat on the living room couch.

"I am the luckiest of men," proclaimed Joseph Furano. "I have two beautiful girls. This one just took her time arriving. But now that she's here for good, I am proud to be her father."

He hugged Mikaela.

"When you were my big brother, I loathed you. Yet, I knew you weren't the bully you pretended to be. Now that you are my big sister, I will help you be the prettiest girl. I love you, Mikaela!" exclaimed Jennifer.

Though Jennifer abused Mikaela relentlessly – exclusively to gain revenge for the way she was treated by her former brother – the youngest child of Carol and Joseph Furano was progressive-minded and accepting of Mikaela's new gender. She was satisfied that Mikaela had paid her penance and believed her longtime tormentor was always a girl inside and needed to transition.

The emotional Jay was in tears when he approached his former brother. "You are finally who you were meant to be. You are so beautiful. You, the woman!" he added, gender-revisioning the term he always used when Mikaela was male. Jay blubbered as he embraced and rocked the subject of his endearments.

"It's about time!" said Rob, hugging Mikaela.

No other person in Mikaela's sphere was happier than little Stevie. He had always wanted his beloved dad to dress as a female. From his earliest remembrances, "Mikaela" was always presented as a feminine male, and he felt his dad would never be happy unless he officially changed gender. Besides, the youngster thought his dad would be a false person as a man.

"I am so proud of you, Dad. You finally did it!" exclaimed the boy. "Now get rid of all those boy clothes, and don't you pretend to be a man ever again!"

"Dad, I love you and am so happy you will become a woman," said Joey.

"Don't forget your other boys," said Sarah. "And your three girls!"

Saoirse approached Mikaela after she kissed her twin stepdaughters and the toddlers, Adam and Mikey, in their bassinettes.

"I love you, Aunt Mikaela," said Saoirse.

***

Susan, Cindy, Brian, Sheila Levine, and a few firemen who were close to the former Mikey were invited. Mikaela insisted that Sarah invite Olivia. Adam, in a request that surprised everyone, asked Sarah if she would invite Sandra, the woman who attended the card games. There wasn't a person in the house who would refuse Adam on any request. In the past, they deferred to his resilience, but presently, they were terrified of him. Jennifer still led the household because of Adam's indifference to the position.

Sarah held back on the surprise guests. After the two children whose lives Adam saved appeared with their parents, a tear fest was initiated.

"You are my heroine," said Ana.

"Thank you, kind lady," added Manuel.

Their parents took turns hugging Mikaela.

The house was adorned with balloons, banners, and signs Saoirse fashioned. "Welcome, Aunt Mikaela," "Gorgeous Girl," and "Being Herself" hung on the kitchen walls, and pictures of Mikaela from her youth as a boy were displayed in the living room.

Sandra always honored invitations from the Furanos and looked forward to seeing Carol and her family, but she purposely wasn't told anything about the event. When she arrived, Adam approached her.

"Hi, Sandra. Can I speak to you privately?"

The woman looked fearful but followed Adam to his bedroom. After she entered, he closed and locked the door.

***

"You fucking cunt, you think I forgot about you! I don't raise my fists to women, but I will make an exception with you!"

"Please, Adam! I was so wrong about you! I deserved to be punished!"

"I had you invited so that I could beat the shit out of you! You will bleed way more than I did!"

"Please! Oh God, please, I'll do anything for you. It was the worst thing I ever did in my life. But I was asked to join in! Please!"

"Sure. You're a fucking coward, too. Do you think I don't remember how that attack played out, you fucking bitch?"

Sandra was terrified, but Adam's vulgar language was a turn-on. She was used to such verbal treatment from her husband and liked when men swore and talked dirty. She resorted to flattery.

"I had no idea your brother became a woman. I wish her the best. As a man, he was a hunk, but as a woman, she is gorgeous. Adam, you look fantastic! I love those muscles, your new physique, and your goatee!"

"You always called me a sissy!"

"You are anything but that now! I adore your new look and personality! You are my kind of man!"

"I'm fucking happy to hear it! Maybe I won't hurt you. I have always been the forgiving type."

"Thank you, Adam! You are the best!"

"Now you go back inside and tell Mikaela she is the most beautiful woman you've ever seen. If you dare say anything to make her feel bad, I'll chop your fucking head off and throw it in the trash heap."

Again, Sandra was aroused by Adam's graphic threats.

"Of course, Adam, I promise."

"But before you do that, how about if you and I get high?" asked Adam as he pulled a joint from his pocket.

Sandra's eyes widened. She smiled broadly.

"Wow, Adam, I'd love to!"

Adam lit the joint, took a deep drag, and handed it to Sandra. They passed it back and forth. They both laughed during the time it took to finish it. Adam extinguished it in the ashtray and lit a cigarette.

"Adam, my husband would love to meet you. He needs a friend like you. Would you be willing to visit us?"

"I just might, Sandra," Adam answered in a newly acquired infatuation with perversity.

"I'll contact Carol. You turned out fantastic! I'm honored to consider you my friend! Please hang around with us."

Adam smiled as Sandra left and closed the door. He collapsed on the bed and lay on his back, finishing his cigarette.

After Adam left the room, he fetched a can of Bud from the fridge. Sandra observed him admiringly as he took his first swig. She approached Mikaela.

"Mikaela, you are a thousand times better as a woman than you were as a man! You are stunningly beautiful!"

"Thanks so much, Sandra; your words mean the world to me," he said in a voice that startled Sandra.

The longtime card player, feeling the effects of the marijuana after smoking her first joint in over a month, later told Carol that she thought Adam was a "total masculine dream."

"Yes, he certainly is, Sandra. Who would have thought? Life throws us so many curve balls. But this is one I welcome with open arms! He's amazing! And he's become the most popular teacher in his high school! He's rough around the edges if you know what I mean."

"I love that part of him the best! God, I need him in my life!" said Sandra.

Carol smiled broadly. "Sandra, I'm sure he'll fit you in. I love him, but he has developed a scary temper. Sarah used to wear the pants for years after their marriage, but all that changed. I can't believe how physically strong he has become. He went from one extreme to the other."

"Really?" asked Sandra, becoming even more excited. "I love everything about him. Does he work out a lot?"

"Several nights a week for a few years. He was wildly committed to bodybuilding, aerobics, and weightlifting, and he took testosterone supplements. He purposely drank more protein drinks than prescribed to help him put on weight. A trainer said Adam's extreme physical transformation was rare, but he knew others who pulled it off. He said the key was mental application. I never would have believed Adam had such discipline. In many other ways, he is reckless and undisciplined. He has some terrible habits."

Sandra beamed. For the rest of the night, Sandra found ways to observe him without being noticed. Smoking a joint with him was one of the highlights of the last year for her. She yearned for an encore.

Sheila Levine couldn't complement Mikaela enough.

"Young lady, you progressed quicker than I expected. I'm sure I'm not the first to mention how gorgeous you have become."

"Doctor, my dad is the most beautiful woman in Fairview, probably in the world," said little Stevie.

That statement by the former Mikey's young son confirmed what she suspected. The family was supportive of her patient's gender change. Levine speculated that no matter how far the transformation went, Mikaela and Sarah would never separate.

"I have no doubt she is, young man. I have always thought that!" said Levine, leaning down to kiss the boy. "You are such a cutie. I bet you are the apple of your daddy's eye."

Stevie smiled. "Thank you, kindly, sweet lady."

"My mind is made up. He's coming home with me!" she exclaimed.

"Rob won't let you!" said Sarah.

"Oh, I heard so many good things about Rob. I must meet him."

"He's here. You'll see him soon," answered Sarah.

"So, is this the extent of the transformation," Levine asked, directing her question to Sarah, Carol, and Mikaela.

"What do you mean, Dr. Levine?" asked Sarah.

"Sheila. Always call me Sheila. I mean, will you take the logical next step?"

"What would the next step be?" asked Carol.

"Mikaela is becoming a woman. From what I can see today, she and her family are supportive. She needs to feel like a woman, think like a woman, and undergo physical changes that will permanently erase her masculine appearance and personality. I will ask her directly. Mikaela, do you want to become a complete woman?"

Mikaela hesitated.

"Please don't be afraid to tell me the truth, sweetie. Your coming-out party speaks volumes. Since you are not legally married, I assume there are a few obstacles, but your children love you as a woman, and your voice is already there."

Her confidence bolstered, Mikaela answered, "Yes, Sheila, I want to be a complete woman."

"I am thrilled to hear it. It would be best if you start taking female hormones immediately. I see no reason for you to wait," said Levine, concerned about previous revelations from Sarah about Mikaela threatening to harm herself. "They will change your male body to a female one. You will grow breasts; Your hips will widen. Your waist will narrow. Your skin will soften. Your hair will thicken. I'm happy to see you have grown it long. Your male personality will fade away. Your thoughts will become feminine."

"I'm afraid to do that," Mikaela answered.

"Why, Mikaela?"

"I'm not sure," she answered, her voice quivering.

"Sarah and Carol, are you in favor of Mikaela taking female hormones and testosterone blockers?"

After a pause, both nodded.

"Excellent. But the final decision rests with Mikaela. Girl, are you willing to start?"

"Yes, Sheila," she said tearfully.

"Oh, don't cry, honey. You will be happy with the results. I am licensed to write out a prescription and will state you have been under my care for several years and are transgendered. Please visit my office tomorrow. We can handle the financial business at a later date. Starting tomorrow, you must take two pills a day. One is the female hormone estrogen, and the other is the testosterone blocker, spironolactone, which blocks the masculinizing effects of the male hormone. After two weeks, I will send you to a gender specialist who will start you on monthly injections. They are powerful and will speed up the process. You should start seeing results in five or six months."

After no one asked a question, Sheila got even bolder.

"Everyone is different, but I'd say six months after that, you will be ready for the full sex reassignment surgery. You would get a vaginoplasty, which would invert your penis and give you a functioning vagina, facial feminization, and a shaved Adam's apple. More work on your voice would be advised, though you have come a long way on your own. You don't sound anything like a man anymore."

"I can't do all that. I'm mortified," said Mikaela.

"Are you saying you would like to go all the way but are afraid?"

"Yes. I want to go all the way, but the process is alarming."

"I assure you that after 18 months of aggressive hormone therapy, you will be begging to get the date for your surgery."

"Sarah, can I be personal?" said Levine.

"You've already been as personal as anyone could ever be, but by all means, continue."

"Touche, Sarah! Once Mikaela has the operation, you won't be able to have the same kind of sex anymore. Will this realization make this a deal breaker?"

"Sheila, Mikaela has been a pretend man since we first got intimate in Aruba. I love her more than any other person, though I will remain married to Adam till I die. Mikaela and I had four children together. As a mother of seven overall, I have zero desire to assume another pregnancy. I am done with having children! I don't need Mikaela's sperm, nor Adam's, for that matter. I hate having sex with Adam, as he is far too aggressive and strong for me in bed, but when he demands it, I have no choice. He doesn't ask often. So if you are asking if I will miss Mikaela's penis, the answer is no. My lovemaking with her will continue in full force, though I'd be entering a same-sex relationship. Mikaela got me pregnant twice, and she barely ejaculated. She was never a man sexually. Her first girlfriend said the same thing."

Mikaela whimpered.

"Oh, sweetie, you were and will always be the best sex partner for me. It was never about your penis. It was about kissing and feeling you. We can still arouse each as women."

CHAPTER 41

A Secret Revealed

"The time has come for me to tell you about something that happened over twenty years ago. I was tempted to tell you many times but held back, waiting for the right time. Because I have openly professed my undying love for both of you, I want you to finally understand what I meant when I said our love triangle was preordained."

"Sarah, I was only a child two decades ago," said Mikaela. "What year did this event happen?"

"Nineteen-sixty-four. And I was only eleven."

"I was ten that year," said Adam.

"Where did this event occur?" asked Mikaela.

"It happened on the Tunnel of Love at Palisades Amusement Park. Do you remember the girl, Sally?"

"I remember Sally!" exclaimed Adam. "Was she a friend of yours?"

"No, she was not. I am Sally. Sally was *me.* When I told you my name was Sarah, you misunderstood me. You called me Sally. I felt bad about correcting you, so I let you continue to call me Sally."

Adam's eyes widened.

"Unfuckingreal!" he exclaimed.

"I don't remember any girl named Sally," said Mikaela. "And I can't remember very much about Palisades Amusement Park. I was too young."

"Yes, Mikaela. You were only four years old. You have a fantastic memory for most things, but this asks you to go back too far. Adam remembers, though, don't you, sweetie?"

"I remember everything. I should have figured this out years ago, but there wasn't any reason to remember an encounter with a girl named Sally. So it was you, Sarah. And what happened was meant to happen. I also believe that."

"Maybe I should call you Sally from now on," said Mikaela.

"No, Mikaela, my name is Sarah," she said laughingly.

"What else do you remember about the Tunnel of Love?" asked Mikaela.

"I remember it being too dark to see anything," said Sarah. "I recall some shadows and outlines, but there was no chance for visibility since we were pulled along a narrow, covered passageway."

"I remember reading a book about amusement parks in the library," said Mikaela. "It mentioned the Tunnel of Love. I think it said there were over 700 around the country in the 1950s, but there have been fewer in recent years."

"Shit, I bet there were many relationships that started on that ride," said Adam.

"I wouldn't say there were many. Far more had to be couples who went on the ride to make love in the dark," said Sarah. "Of course, as I already said, I am a strong believer in fate. We three were meant to be together."

"But it didn't play out conventionally," said Adam.

"What is so unconventional about a woman in love with her

husband and brother-in-law?" asked Sarah laughingly. "We are a rare breed."

"Dad suggested we are not fucking normal," said Adam, lighting a cigarette.

"He said far more," said Mikaela. "But after all the pain and embarrassment he said we caused him, he has become a proud father and grandfather."

"Your dad loves you both more than he can express in words," said Sarah. "He was always so much bluster, but he's one of the most loving people I've ever known. How many fathers would allow strangers to move into their homes? By my count, three took up permanent residence, and another sleeps over sometimes."

"There can't be another," said Mikaela. "My dad is unique. What did I do to show him appreciation? I caused him to have a heart attack." She dabbed her eye.

"Oh, sweetie, that event happened long ago, " Sarah said. "Your dad forgave you, and you expressed remorse many times over. You are his heroine. He brags about you regularly. Don't bring up the past. You are a completely different person now."

"You are the eternal pride of our family," said Adam.

Mikaela shook his head, pointing at Adam.

"No, you are, brother. From when we were both young, I knew how special you were. I think God wanted you to be battle-tested. You can't be outstanding until you experience some corruption. You couldn't be more perfect now, Mikaela. You are the family's superstar and the smartest person I have ever known."

"I love how you hold the torch for each other," said Sarah.

"Shit, I have always missed Palisades Amusement Park," said Adam. "After today's revelation, I would say that no setting in my lifetime has mattered nearly as much. I nearly fucking died there and now realize that meeting Sarah was predetermined by a childhood event near the park's center. God was watching over me, over *us*, in a place that will live forever in the recesses of my mind."

"Though I could not possibly remember the Tunnel of Love in 1964, I recall other visits to the park," said Mikaela. "I miss the pool. And in the few years before it closed, I fell in love with the Cyclone. Mrs. DePhillips once asked us to write a composition on the scariest episode of our life. I chose to describe my fear of riding that giant coaster. The scariest part was how the ride started. Our row of cars was pulled up a steep incline. The clicking and clacking sounds served as a fearful reminder that we were inching close to the hump. As we reached the top, everyone raised their arms in the air. The girls screamed, and the boys pulled their dates closer. The fall was simultaneously exhilarating and terrifying. You can say we felt like we were on top of the world. The breeze rushed through our hair, our hearts beat faster, and the blood rushed through our veins. The adrenaline rush produced a euphoric feeling as we reached the bottom, but lest we become too comfortable, the car chain rushed up and made its way to a second, less steep hill that helped us feel like our hearts were in our throats. As the cars screeched, our encore produced dizziness sustained to our exit when we nearly stumbled as we traversed the wooden exit ramp."

Sarah and Adam were awestruck.

"You are fucking incredible," said Adam. "You will write a best-selling novel one day."

Sarah nodded.

"I've loved you for twenty-two years, Mikaela, sometimes consciously, sometimes unconsciously. Other times, I forgot about you, as one would never think an innocent encounter had any reason to be remembered as anything special. But shortly after I met your brother, my recall of the Tunnel of Love was vivid well before we were married. And then I knew what fate had in store for me, for all of us. Our sacred threesome will last as long as we breathe but even well beyond. I'll hold your hands as we pass through the pearly gates."

CHAPTER 42

Dual Tribute Monologues

"Mikaela's crying again," said Adam. "She claims she is happy but continues to be emotionally unhinged."

"Adam, I'll bring her back here," said Sarah.

Sarah held Mikaela's hand and guided her to the married couple's bedroom.

Mikaela sat at the end of the bed but then rose to leave.

"Mikaela, don't leave. Let's talk," said Sarah.

"I'm sorry, Sarah, but I must," said Mikaela.

Adam, with lightning speed, extended his muscled right arm and arrested Mikaela in a vice-like headlock while simultaneously pressing his knee hard on her chest. Adam gritted his teeth and squeezed as hard as he could. Mikaela couldn't breathe and choked.

Adam squeezed harder.

"Stop, Adam! You are hurting her!"

Mikaela tried to break the hold, but the muscular Adam overwhelmed his transitioning sister.

Mikaela gave up and lay prone on the bed.

"I'm sorry, Mikaela. I needed to do what I did," said Adam. "But don't you ever fucking defy me again. I love you, but I won't hesitate to hurt you. This is payback time, little sister. You treated me like shit for years and had this coming. I never forgot your role in the bedroom assault."

Mikaela whimpered. "I'm sorry, Adam. I was a terrible person back then. Please forgive me. I love you, brother."

Smiling, Sarah leaned over, kissed Mikaela on the cheek, and repeated the same gesture on Adam.

"Don't cry, sweetheart. Adam will never hurt you again; he loves you too much."

"Sarah, I *will* hurt him again, and far worse than I just did, if he crosses me."

Sarah grimaced.

"Sarah, I have decided you belong with Adam," Mikaela said. "I deserve eternal damnation for what I did to my brother. I destroyed the perfect marriage because I was selfish. I had no right to force myself on you in Aruba, and everything snowballed after that. Adam is your husband; I am a shameless intruder and a fraud. It would be best if you never had a choice. Sarah, I love you more than life itself, every person in the world combined, or any tangible object; I love you more than the very concept of love. Beyond that, only *you* matter. All else is insignificant. But I haven't earned you. Sarah, you have always belonged to Adam."

"No, Mikaela," said Adam. "You are the one who should be with Sarah. You are a much better person than me. I can never match your capacity for love; your passion for Sarah is unlike any man has ever shown for a woman. *Au contraire*, (On the contrary) dear sister, it is you who has earned her. You are far more intelligent than me and possess a dynamic personality. Maybe you did play me fucking dirty at the start, but what you did after that with Sarah, your kids, and your heroism have made you far more worthy than I ever was. The lights around the world would go out permanently if you ever left. You are the best father and husband on the planet. And yes, you are a husband. You don't have to be legal. You and Sarah are a classic couple. It would be fucking criminal if you two weren't together. You fathered most of Sarah's children. Your love has always been more focused than mine. Sarah is yours, dear sister. She'd be insane not to choose you. Everyone in our family favors you, and I discovered that even my daughter Saoirse feels you should be married to Sarah. I also know that Susan has said you two need to be together. Susan loves you way more than she loved me. I said the meanest words to her. I'm a fucking alcoholic, and I always use foul language. Sarah and I need to divorce quietly, and maybe you will pick me as your best man. It would be the biggest honor of my life."

"Adam," said Mikaela through her sobs. "You are far stronger than me now. You shared Saoirse with Jimbo; you brought Jay into the house, and he got a job with Dad because of you; you lied about what happened at Palisades Amusement Park to protect Jimbo. You risked so much to put a roof over his head. You brought Rob into the house, where he has remained for several years. He will never leave because of his bond with Stevie. Rob is one of the child's two dads. You did so much for Brian Fischer, who sometimes lives with us. You forgave me instantly for all the terrible things I did to you. I was jealous of your gender projection. You encouraged Sarah to let me go on the Aruba trip. You applauded the pregnancy, and months afterward, you urged her to spend time with me and even to be intimate. When I was honored in the council chambers, you instructed Mayor Schettino to announce Sarah as my wife, and all the other town officials followed suit. That alone was an act that should have you canonized. You doubled down that night and ordered Sarah to spend the next week with me. Of course, we all know what it led to. You paved the way for this love triangle, didn't you, Adam? You wanted to share Sarah's love with me. Dad is right. What you did is not normal, older brother. Some people think it is sick or deranged. But I'm your sibling. I have always known you are a saint. Some have described you as a modern-day Jesus. Your example taught me how to be loving and generous. Your influence changed my life. If it is true that my love for Sarah can't be equaled, it is only because you taught me about love through your example in living your life. If I have changed, you can take full credit for it, dearest brother. Nobody knows the concept of forgiveness like you do because only you employ it regularly in your everyday life. Would Sarah want to toss aside her marriage to a living saint because Mikaela Furano fathered four of her seven children and can't bear losing a woman who is his whole world? *"No estoy de acuerdo,* (I disagree)" Adam, if she left you, it would be more shameful than a wife who leaves her husband after she finds out he's terminally ill. You taught me about love, Adam. And you continue to teach it to everyone who crosses your path. I always think of Professor Fowler, the aging literature instructor in that *Twilight Zone* episode, *The Changing of the Guard*, and everything he taught his students at that Vermont prep school for boys. I've learned so much from you, brother. I love you so much. I know you have changed a lot, but I prefer to believe you are now who you were always meant to be."

Profoundly moved, Adam wiped the tears flowing down his face, but Sarah erupted.

"Please, no more! Nobody better say another word! I have no tears left! I adore you equally! I will be married to you both for the rest of my life! I would die in a heartbeat for either one of you! I will remain legally married to Adam, but Mikaela is my lover and soulmate. You mentioned a love triangle. Well, this is the purest example of it. From this day on, please consider all the children as your mutual possessions, though, of course, the kids understand who their birth fathers are. Your faces will always be in front of me. First, they will be clear as they are now, and then slowly, they will blend. Oh God, how much I love you both. Adam, you are right, though, when you admit you are an alcoholic, and you talk like a truck driver."

The trio guffawed.

CHAPTER 43

Adam Wrestles Rob

"You think you can handle me, tough guy?" asked Rob Murphy, greeting Adam, who returned from his gym session. "Your arms are more prominent, but I'm inclined to think you're still a wimp."

Sarah heard the challenge, knowing her husband had grown stronger from his bodybuilding and weightlifting.

"I'll give you the same answer Tybalt gave to Mercutio in Act 3, Scene 1 of *Romeo and Juliet:* I'm for you. We haven't swords, of course, but let's wrestle," said Adam, pushing a couch to the wall and moving two end tables to provide sufficient space.

After the initial hammerlock position, Adam immediately locked Rob in a cradle by grabbing his neck with one arm and wrapping the elbow of the other arm behind his knee. Rob struggled to escape, but Adam increased the pressure. After Rob persisted, Adam angrily used all his strength and head-locked his opponent.

"Adam, you're strangling him. Stop! You are going to hurt him seriously!"

"That's the point, Sarah. He acted like a fucking wiseass, and now I'm going to punish him."

Adam exercised his leg strength and rose with Rob's body draped over his shoulder.

Joseph and Carol heard a commotion and saw Adam twirling Rob.

"Please, Adam, please let him go," said Carol.

"Oh, I'll let him go all right," said Adam, dropping his body hard on the floor. Rob's head hit the rug with a thud. In severe pain, he held an arm behind his head and sobbed loudly.

"You hurt him!" exclaimed Sarah.

Adam wasn't in a generous mood.

"You're the fucking wimp. I've known that for a few years. The next time you challenge me, I'll break your neck. I owe you from college, football man. You always thought you were high and mighty."

Adam kicked him in the ribs and stormed out of the house.

Sarah, Carol, and Joseph attended to Rob. They helped him reach his feet and sat him on the pull-out couch.

Sarah wiped his tears and draped her arm over his shoulder.

"I asked for it. He's much stronger than me. I goaded him."

"He spoke to you badly. I never thought he could be so mean," said Carol.

Joseph shook his head in disgust. He had grown to love Rob and couldn't believe Adam was so insensitive and brutal.

***

The next day, Adam approached the dispirited Rob.

"I'm sorry, Rob. I got carried away. I didn't mean to hurt you."

"I understand, Adam. You were right when you called me a wimp. I had no business challenging somebody who could mop the floor with me. I'm going through so much depression. I need to get my act together. I apologize for starting this shit."

"Rob, let's get a shake."

Adam drove to the Ridgefield Dairy Queen, where he bought a strawberry and a vanilla shake. He handed the latter to Rob, who never deviated from the same flavor.

As Rob drank his shake through a straw, he struggled not to cry.

"Adam, I have a serious problem."

"Ah, man, I'm sure you'll be fine. Your health is good, and you've lost some weight."

"The problem is psychological. It had a lot to do with why Maureen left me. I've been unhappy ever since."

"Rob, you told me that Maureen left you because she fell in love with that other guy."

"Yeah, she fell in love with Delfin. I wasn't lying. But she would not have allowed herself to fall in love with him if she didn't give up on me."

"Well, why did she give up on you?"

"I wasn't manly enough for Maureen. She wasn't willing to wait until I got my act together. I've tried to hide my failure to live up to my male role in the relationship."

"Oh boy, Rob. Are you saying that you are another Mikaela?"

"No, Adam. Nothing close to that. I'm happy to be a male, though I greatly admire Mikaela for being true to herself. And she is something I'll never be. She's a father. Still, I have failed Maureen."

"Can you give me a clue?" said Adam, lighting Rob's cigarette and then his own.

"I couldn't meet her needs. I have erectile dysfunction. Maureen told me more than once that I wasn't the kind of man she wished to marry. She had no desire to be the dominant sexual partner as she always was."

"Rob, I know the feeling. I've been through that phase!"

"I know you went through it, Adam. But you turned the corner.

343

Look at you now! I envy you. You are a macho man who controls your marriage. You were right to call me a wimp. I'll never be anything else. I have considered suicide several times. I love Stevie as much as if he were my biological child, and my loving relationship with him has kept me afloat, though barely. I desperately want my own child, even if I could never love him or her more than Stevie. But I feel I am a failure unless I am a biological parent. What girl would want a compromised man such as me? My parents hate me, and my dad won't even see me anymore. I am a loser."

"Fuck, man, you are not anywhere close to a loser. You've been a second father to Stevie, and everyone loves you. Don't you dare think about ending your life! I understand your desire to have a biological child, but you are young. Who's to say your time won't come?"

"Adam, I appreciate the positive energy. But I missed my chance. I wish Maureen the best. She is happily married and deeply in love with her husband. I found out they have a beautiful boy, Delfin Jr."

"Rob, something will click when you least expect it."

"Adam, how in tarnation did you get so strong? Remember what you were like when we first met at Bergen Community College? And do you remember what I called you?"

"I do, buddy, I do. I have worked myself to the bone to get to where I am now. You know what an obsessed person I am, and I channeled that obsession into bodybuilding. I added weightlifting and aerobics and maintained a protein shake regimen. When I first saw muscles appear, I wanted them bigger. I made it happen with uncompromised determination. I am still working out hard, as I want to get even stronger."

"I have to hand it to you. You've astounded many people. But physically, there was no reason why you couldn't do it. When one is set on doing something, it happens. I may soon be in the same position but for a different reason. Maureen knew this, got scared, and flew."

Adam grimaced, rubbed the back of Rob's neck, and pulled out of the lot.

CHAPTER 44

Amazing News

Sarah opened a letter to Mikaela after noticing the return address read *The Phil Donahue Show.* She read a few lines and yelped as she rushed down the hall to notify the heroine. Sarah called Steve and Michele Burke and ordered them to drive to Fairview quickly. She instructed Saoirse to tell her grandparents and great-grandmother to convene in the living room for an announcement. Sarah alerted Adam and dispatched him to inform Jay and Jennifer.

"Jay, I believe Rob is in the backyard with Jimbo. Can you summon them?"

"Of course, Sarah."

When everyone was seated or stood around the fringes of the house's most spacious room, Sarah joined Mikaela on the loveseat, draping her right arm around her.

"Please give my mom and dad just a few minutes to get here," she said. On cue, the doorbell rang four minutes later. Saoirse ran downstairs to greet her grandparents.

"In the past, I've made family announcements that conveyed bad news," said Sarah. "And we've had to endure reports of violence against our loved ones. But a few times, we shared happy news. Tonight, I will make an announcement that will amaze you. I only wish Susan, Cindy, and Brian were here. I'll call them later." Looking at Mikaela, she added, "Sweetheart, you are a celebrity! You have been invited to appear on *The Phil Donahue Show!*"

The room erupted.

"I don't believe it!" exclaimed Carol.

"I am still trying to come to terms with it," answered Sarah. "No doubt her heroism is why she was invited, but the letter also said they learned about our unique family dynamic and Mikaela's transformation."

"I hope they won't say anything negative about us," said Carol.

"Mom, I'm sure they intend to honor Mikaela. Phil Donahue has a great sense of humor, so there might be a few barbs, but good-natured ones."

Carol approached Mikaela and kissed her.

"You never stop making me proud of you," she said, tearing up over the latest honor bestowed on her favorite child.

"Are you excited, young lady?" asked Steve Burke. "All of *us* are."

"I still don't believe it," said Mikaela. "I have stage fright. I don't know if I can do this."

Stevie and Joey snuggled up to her.

"Mikaela, not only can you do this, but you *will* do it, sweetest," said Sarah. "Adam and I will be sitting on both sides of you."

Mikaela uttered a high-pitched squeal and shook her head in disbelief.

Everyone lined up before her to express their excitement over this surprising development.

"I have the best daddy in the world!" exclaimed little Stevie. "She's my hero!"

"Sweetie, she's a hero to so many," gushed Sarah. "And millions will find out about her on television."

Everyone hung around for two hours discussing old Mikaela stories and speculating what Phil Donahue might ask her. A beaming Sarah wedged between Mikaela and the older twins, wrapping her arms around the Furano family's most celebrated member.

"I love you, Sarah," Mikaela whispered.

"Not as much as I love you, sweetest."

***

Sarah was delighted when a spokesperson for *The Phil Donahue Show* informed her over the phone that the Furano family would be given many tickets for the show. The primary participants—Sarah, Mikaela, and Adam—would be joined by the four grandparents and five children, as well as Jennifer, Jay, Jimbo, Rob, Susan Clarke, Brian Fischer, Cindy McNally, and Tony Lucibello. Grandma Delaney wasn't physically able to attend.

"We are so lucky the show will be filmed in New York City," said Sarah. "Phil moved it here just two years ago."

"Sarah, where was it filmed before Gotham?" asked Mikaela.

"I understand it started in Dayton, Ohio, and then was moved to Chicago."

"I am sad to admit I never watched it," said Adam.

"Neither did I," said Mikaela. "But all of us were occupied by our many other interests to pay much attention to it."

***

Carol cooked everyone an early breakfast on the big day.

"Shit, in all our excitement, I don't think anyone even asked where the show is being staged," said Adam.

"30 Rockefeller Plaza. It's a famous office building between West 49th and 50th Street," said Sarah.

"It's probably a skyscraper, right?" asked Carol.

"Yes, it is," answered Sarah. "I found out it has 70 floors."

"I'm so terrified of heights," said Mikaela. "I hope there are no windows in the hall."

"Sweetie, according to the woman I spoke to, the place is on the ground level. No worries."

The contingent walked down to Nungesser's Corner, where they caught a bus to the Port of Authority, the famous terminal occupying the blocks between Eighth and Ninth Avenues and 40th and 42nd Streets in the heart of Manhattan.

"Uncle Rob, what building is taller, the Empire State Building or the World Trade Center Towers," asked Stevie, sitting on the man's lap as the bus headed south on Boulevard East. "They look the same."

"Good observation, Stevie. The World Trade Center is a tiny bit taller. If I am right, the North World Trade Center is 110 floors, and the Empire State Building is 102."

"So that means the North Tower is the tallest building in the world," answered Stevie.

"No, Stevie. There is one even taller, although just slightly. It is known as the Sears Tower. Some call it Willis Tower. It is located in Chicago."

"I want to see the Sears Tower!" exclaimed Stevie.

"You will, little guy," answered Steve Burke, sitting in the row behind. "If I have to drive you there, so be it," he added, beaming at his favorite grandchild and the bearer of his name.

Before they made the sharp right that would lead to the final stretch near the viaduct into the Lincoln Tunnel, Mikaela pointed to a plaque set against stone atop a manicured section of the cliff.

"Look!" she exclaimed. "That's where Aaron Burr dueled Alexander Hamilton. There's a bronze statue."

"I don't see anything," said Stevie.

"Sweetie, you can't see it from here," said Mikaela. "It is located at the bottom of the cliff near the river. But I pointed out the approximate location from where we are now. The statue of Hamilton is part of what is known as Hamilton Park."

"And there is a boulder that Hamilton rested on before the duel, according to folklore," said Adam. "You can't see it because it is behind the statue."

"Well, we can't see anything anymore," said Sarah, noting that the bus was well past the subject of the conversation.

"Duh," said Mikaela.

Stevie laughed.

"What town are we in now?" asked Brian.

"This is Weehawken."

"I noticed this area has many towns with Indian names," said Brian. "My high school is in Hackensack. I also know Mahwah, Ho-Ho-Kus, and Paramus."

"Great observation, Brian. You were one of my best students," said Adam. "We also have Hopatcong and Passaic. But of course, all these names were Dutch interpretations of the Indian names. The Lenapes had no written language."

"Uncle Adam, who are the Lenapes?" asked Stevie.

"An Indian tribe from our area, Stevie," said Adam. "Their real name was the Lenni Leape," he added, lighting a cigarette.

"Oh, Adam, do you have to smoke everywhere? Can't you follow the rules? The sign says no smoking."

"I'm sorry, Sarah, but I don't believe in rules, and I enjoy smoking. Besides, I opened the top part of the window."

"I'm just kidding, my love," said Sarah. "If you're happy, I'm happy."

Joseph Furano shook his head.

"You guys are forgetting another town with an Indian name very close to where we are now," said Joseph. "Secaucus. From what I remember, the name means where snakes live or hide. A few friends of mine know a few politicians from Secaucus. They claim the name is appropriate," he added derisively.

Adam guffawed.

Before much longer, the sunlight disappeared, yielding to the darkness inside the Lincoln Tunnel. Stevie wrapped his arms around his Uncle Rob, and Little Joey snuggled up to his Dad.

"Don't worry, little guy," said Rob. "The tunnel is safe."

"Is the Lincoln Tunnel the longest of the three Hudson River crossings?" asked Saoirse, seated on the wide seat behind the aisle at the back of the bus.

"Honey, the Holland Tunnel, built in the late 1920s, is the longest of the three," said Steve. "But further up the Hudson, we have the Tappan Zee Bridge, which is even longer."

"Thanks, Grandpa. I hope to cross it one day."

"Steve, I'm sure you know why they decided to construct the Tappan Zee Bridge across the widest spot of the Hudson River, right?" asked Joseph.

Steve laughed. "Yes, I certainly do, Joe. Let's say that certain politicians benefited from that decision. I know and respect that your family is Democrat, but for me, the politicians who run things in our region are corrupt."

Joe smiled, mired in thought.

I think Steve is one of the finest men I've ever known. He has a heart of gold. But I can't say I'm surprised he is a Republican. He is, after all, a prominent Wall Street trader, and the big-money people always get substantial tax breaks. But at least he has the common sense to stay close to Gerry Calabrese and the Cliffside Park Democrats. Gerry and his friends only care about the local and county elections. Anyway, we are in the Ronald Reagan era. Conservatism is wildly popular, as are taxes and government spending cuts. Some positives exist, but I wouldn't dare say that to my wife and children. They are black Democrats. All except Adam and Sarah, that is. They are with Steve now.

"Steve, I hear you. One day, you and I will discuss the political situation locally and nationally. You'll be surprised where I stand on certain issues. At least we can agree that dynamic mayors lead our towns. Mario Schettino and Gerry Calabrese are all for the people."

"You got that right, Joe," Steve said.

The bus emerged from the tunnel and accessed a circular ramp that emptied onto a platform. The Furano entourage followed the other passengers to an escalator that transported them to the sprawling main concourse, where food, clothing, and accessory stands were abundant. Some people spoke into microphones and promoted various causes. Rob held Stevie over his shoulders as they passed a table under a broad umbrella where two women sold toys and stuffed animals.

With lust in their eyes, several men stared at Mikaela, whose sublime green dress, sequined heels, and long flowing blond hair drew looks from near and far.

Always observant, little Stevie said to Rob, "My Dad is the most gorgeous woman anywhere."

"Yes, she is, Stevie. She's a knockout!"

"Do you think she'll find a boyfriend?"

"Stevie, I don't know; she might," said Rob, quickly changing the subject. "Look at that mechanical soldier, little guy!"

"Wow, I love it, Uncle Rob."

"How much for this?" Rob asked one of the sellers.

"Twenty."

"I'll take it," answered Rob, pulling a wad of bills from his front pocket and handing over a Jackson.

Steve Burke saw the exchange and told Rob, "I'll pay for that."

"No, you will not, sir. This is mine."

When it came to Stevie, Rob would do anything.

"Fine, Rob. I'll find another way," said Steve, smiling widely.

After passing through rotating glass doors, the group crossed 8th Avenue and turned right onto 42nd Street. The smokers lit up.

"Adam Sean, do you remember your first time on 42nd Street?"

"Fuck, Sarah, I never forgot. In the Sixties and Seventies, most theaters on this stretch showed adult films. I didn't care to watch such films, but I did see *Midnight Cowboy*, which at that time was rated X. Because it won the Oscar for Best Picture, I needed to see it. I remember sitting on the balcony."

"You must have seen it around when we met," said Sarah.

"A short time before," said Adam as he and the party entered a pizza emporium after Steve hand-signaled them.

"We're lucky this place has so many booths," said Mikaela.

Steve ordered five pies with various toppings but specified one with extra cheese and pepperoni, little Stevie's favorite.

Sarah heard her dad place the order.

"Dad, Stevie, and Joey can each eat only one slice with toppings. There wasn't a need to get a whole pie. But thanks, I love you."

"Maybe some of the others can help. It's a popular combination," said Burke.

"The only problem is that we won't be able to bring home any leftovers," said Michele.

"Honey, I wanted to make sure I ordered enough."

"Steve, you are incurable," Michele answered, wrapping her arms around his waist.

Cindy approached Mikaela. "Hey, pretty girl, let me fix your lipstick. Your pizza messed it up."

As Adam ate his mushroom slice, Tony Lucibello sat on the stool beside him. "Where's the White Castle when we need it?"

"Fuck, Tony, those burgers were your sole sustenance when you worked that security guard gig across the street. You'd get four, one order of fries, and an orange crush, right?"

"Sometimes five. But I rarely got an orange crush. My drink was always a medium coffee, dark with three sugars."

"Yes, of course, Tony. My memory failed me."

As Michele predicted, they left behind a bunch of slices and headed north on 42nd Street until they reached Sixth Avenue, also known as Avenue of the Americas, and turned left.

"Adam, did you ever see any movies in the Radio City Music Hall?" asked Rob, referring to the New York City landmark they had observed as they neared their destination.

"Only one," answered Adam. Sarah and I saw *1776*. It was quite an experience."

"I'll second that," said Sarah. "Adam couldn't stop singing *Is Anybody There?* for months."

"I also liked *Molasses to Rum*," said Adam. "And *He Plays the Violin*, *The Lees of Old Virginia* and *Yours, Yours, Yours*. Heck, I've always loved the entire score."

"Did you see the stage version?" asked Rob.

"I missed it. I saw some other famous musicals, but not that one. But most fans say the film is at least as great as the original play."

"I saw both," said Sarah. "I liked the film more. As always, Adam has the best taste. His favorite songs are my favorites. I'd add *Momma Look Sharp* and *Sit Down, John*. William Daniels is one of my favorite actors. And for once, Howard da Silva's scene-stealing corniness was effective."

"I read somewhere that the reviews were mixed at the release time," said Tony. "But since then, opinions have gotten better. Adam, do you remember what Rex Reed said about the film?"

"I do," said Adam. "I sometimes agree with Reed, but not with that movie. Saying that it was a history lesson for the mentally retarded was so fucked up."

"As always, you say things uniquely," said Tony, referring to Adam's regular use of foul language.

"I'd say it was downright deplorable. Reed can be so nasty, and he attacks some actors for their looks or appearance," said Sarah. "I won't even repeat what he said about Barbara Streisand."

"I read what he said about her. His comments were shameful," said Adam.

CHAPTER 45

The Phil Donahue Show

The group entered 30 Rockefeller Plaza. The doorman led everyone down a walkway. A big sign advertising *The Phil Donahue Show* informed them to enter a studio auditorium a short distance from where they were standing. An usher led all but three of them to sit in the front rows while another representative said:

"Mikaela, Sarah, and Adam, please follow me."

The Furano trio followed him through a side door. After they met Phil Donahue, he instructed them to sit at a table where refreshments were offered.

"Thank you, Mr. Donahue, but we just left a pizza parlor."

"Which one?" asked the suited, bespeckled, white-haired talk show host.

"It is called Ray's," said Sarah.

"It's the best place," said Donahue. "Maybe you'd like soft drinks. Thank you for arriving early. I want to explain the strategy I will be using for this taped session. Depending on how the show proceeds, I might do some roasting. Do you know what that word means?"

357

"I believe it is good-natured ridicule," answered Mikaela.

"Yes, a roast is a form of comedy when the subject or subjects are joked about at their own expense. Insults are common, but only to get laughs."

"I should introduce myself. My name is Mikaela Furano."

"I've heard so much about you, Mikaela. You are a stunningly beautiful young lady."

"Thank you, sir. I am deeply honored."

Donahue asked his three guests some pointed questions about their past lives, education, and employment and specifically questioned Mikaela about the fire department.

"I didn't realize you resigned your position as a firefighter," said Donahue.

"I handed in my resignation the day after I took my first dose of hormones. I didn't want to put them on the spot. It isn't a female institution, at least not yet."

"Of course," said Donahue.

Before long, the talk show's announcer intoned the program's title into a microphone, the curtains opened, and Donahue appeared on the stage. The audience clapped wildly.

"Thank you, all! Ladies and Gentlemen, today, we are honored to present some of the most unusual guests ever to have appeared on the show. Please let me introduce three members of the Furano family: two women and one man: Mikaela, Sarah, and Adam."

The audience stood and applauded. A few in the Furano contingent whistled. Susan and Cindy blew kisses.

"Mikaela Furano is a beautiful young woman and former firefighter from Fairview, New Jersey, who risked her life to save two children after a plane crash this past November."

Before the host could continue, the audience erupted in tumultuous applause. Donahue let it go on for almost three minutes before finally interrupting.

"Mikaela's heroism has been documented in the newspapers. Before the show, I changed my mind and decided not to ask her to describe events that would cause her renewed grief and the terrible memories of her hospital stay. Suffice it to say there is mass veneration when her name is mentioned. Mikaela's brother, Adam Sean, and her sister-in-law, Sarah, make a startling family dynamic. Sarah is legally married to Adam but is also in love with Mikaela. Is that right, Sarah?"

"Yes, that is correct, Phil. I love them equally. I met them at the Tunnel of Love in Palisades Amusement Park when Adam was ten and Mikaela was four. They thought my name was Sally, and over many years, I never told them the truth about this meeting. We rode on the ride together."

"Sarah, who was in the middle? You? And how old were you?"

"No, Mikaela was in the middle. She was only four and afraid of the dark. I was eleven."

"Of course. So you felt you made an immediate connection, and years later, when you met Adam, you recalled the amusement park occurrence."

"I only came clean to them recently," said Sarah. "I kept this under wraps because something told me to wait until it coincided with a major change in my life."

"And the change was the realization that you were fated to love two people, the siblings sitting with you on this stage."

"Yes."

"You are a thoughtful and brave woman, Sarah. But before discussing the heroism in your family, I want to discuss Adam a bit. Adam Sean, can you explain what happened when you were 17?"

"Phil, I fell off the Wild Mouse roller coaster at Palisades Amusement Park. I accidentally disengaged my safety strap, and when the car I was riding in took a sharp turn, I found myself hurtling through the air."

Sarah looked into Adam's eyes, recognizing his distortion of what happened. Still, she quickly looked to the side, knowing her husband had told his classes about what Jimbo had done. *Adam could be such a hypocrite. He didn't want to be truthful on national television,* she thought.

From his seat, the man who committed the terrible act that nearly cost Adam his life looked sullen until Saoirse, sitting in the next seat, reassured him with a kiss.

"Adam, I remember from the reports that you went into a coma but recovered days later," said Donahue. "I don't wish to bring up such a terrible time, but I wanted everyone to know you were surely a favorite of God and were meant to live a long, loving, and successful life."

Many in the audience cheered.

"Thank you, Phil," said Adam, lighting a cigarette.

"Mikaela, I understand you are becoming a woman. You have a long way to go, but you look fabulous already," said Donahue, referring to the heroine's stunning green dress, gold hoop earrings, light brown pantyhose, sequined black stiletto heels, longish green painted nails, ultra-long wavy blond, pink-streaked hair reaching the middle of her back, ruby red lips, a gold bracelet, a floral tattoo, femininely crossed legs, feminine arm movements, a white pocketbook over her shoulder, and a lyrical high-pitched voice no man could ever own. "You are positively gorgeous!"

The women in the audience clapped vociferously.

"Thank you," said Mikaela, blowing the host a kiss.

"Can I ask how old you were when you realized you were a girl?"

"I was in my early teens when I started acting on it, but I have known it since I was four."

"How long have you been taking female hormones?

"16 months."

"Just pills?"

"No, I also get two injections every month."

"Would you say you feel and think like a woman?"

"Yes, I rarely think and feel like a male anymore. My thoughts, feelings, and emotions are largely feminine now."

The audience applauded.

"Mikaela, have you had any modest procedures done yet? If so, did you experience any pain?"

"Phil, I did during my electrolysis sessions. So far, that's the only physical procedure I've had done to this point."

"Can you explain, Mikaela?"

"Each hair follicle on my face and body was permanently destroyed. I experienced sharp, burning sensations. It didn't last long, but as it happened, it was excruciating."

"I'm so sorry to hear that, Mikaela. To change the subject from that awful business, how about the expense for your full transition? I know insurance won't pay a penny, is that right?"

"I am sure it will cost at least $85,000. And yes, insurance won't cover any of it," Mikaela said.

"This must have been a financial hardship for you. You were barely an adult when you began this process."

"Sarah's father and the grandfather of my four children paid everything. His name is Steve Burke."

"Is Steve Burke in the audience? If he is, will he please stand?" asked Donahue.

Sitting in the second-row middle, Burke stood.

"Steve, was she worth it?

"I love her. I'd die for her in an instant."

Mikaela covered her face and sobbed. Many in the audience wept happy tears.

Sarah comforted Mikaela and yelled from the stage, "I love you, Dad!"

"What a lovely family," said Donahue. "They are so emotional, and in the best sense."

"My dad also paid for my husband's college tuition and is now paying Mikaela's full tuition," said Sarah.

"There will be more!" shouted Michele in the audience. "Tune in to the end of the show!"

"Mikaela, when will you have the sex reassignment surgery?"

"In just six weeks."

"I bet you can't wait!"

Mikaela nodded but inwardly felt a tinge of sadness and uncertainty.

"Yes, Phil."

"Wow, Mikaela," added Donahue. "You are almost across the finish line! Congratulations!

"Thanks so much, Phil."

"Mikaela, can you explain the other procedures you will have done on the same day as your reassignment surgery? Perhaps they will be done the day after or before the gender-changing operation?

"Phil, I chose to spend a week at Johns Hopkins so that the procedures will be performed over several days. I will have facial fem-inization, and my Adam's apple will be shaved. I will also have most of my lower ribs removed to narrow my waistline, liposuction to remove excess fat, a tummy tuck to tighten the abdominal muscles and remove loose skin, and a Brazilian butt lift to create shapely buttocks."

"Amazing! How many ribs will be removed?" asked Donahue.

"Three. The rib numbers are 10, 11, and 12, and the prime benefit is that once they are removed, there will be no physical impediment to developing an hourglass figure."

"Incredible. Some of these procedures are newly developed, right?"

"I was told a few have only been performed in the last two years."

"Mikaela, your lips look fantastic already, but I suspect you will have more done."

"Correct, Phil. The planned surgery will shorten the strip of skin between the upper lip and nose. Other facial feminization procedures I have signed for include a rhinoplasty, which will reduce the width of the nose and lift its tip. The team will also reshape my forehead, brows, cheeks, and jaws. I also opted to do something usually reserved for older patients. I will have my eyelids lifted to achieve a more feminine look. I'm not sure if I mentioned it before, but I will also have breast augmentation."

"I am so amazed, Mikaela. They can do so much these days, but I'm sure when the week is over and you've recovered, there won't be a single person able to distinguish you from a biological woman, other than perhaps a gynecologist."

"Thank you so much, Phil. I hope what you say comes to pass."

"On another matter, will you have any procedure done on your bone structure?

"Yes, Phil, on a follow-up visit, I will have clavicle shortening surgery, which will substantially reduce my shoulder width. The doctors will remove some small bones. I was told this and removing the ribs would favorably impact my weight loss."

"Mikaela, I told you I would ask some personal questions initially. I know your relationship with Sarah is strong, but now that you are becoming a woman, can I assume you will date and be intimate with men shortly?"

Mikaela blushed. "You might be right, Phil."

The audience cheered. Some men whistled.

"Is this a problem for you, Sarah?"

"Not one bit. I'll bless her if she finds a boyfriend."

"Mikaela, I understand that when you were a boy, you finished Number 6 in your senior year at Cliffside Park High School. Not only are you a gorgeous and personable lady, but you are also a scholar."

The audience cheered.

"I don't think I am anything like that," said Mikaela, blushing.

"My sister is modest," said Adam. "She's brilliant. Her knowledge of literature and history is unsurpassed. She's also a film and music expert."

"I'm not surprised, Adam. I can see she is gifted. I've been told you recently began attending college, Mikaela. What are you majoring in? After you graduate, what profession do you plan to enter," asked Donahue.

"My major is English. I want to teach."

"At what level?

"Maybe high school, but eventually in a college."

"The forms say Adam is a highly regarded teacher," said Donahue.

"I'll let my brother tell you about his position, but all his students idolize him. He is sensational. When we were young, I never could have predicted we would both be English majors. But Adam exerted a formidable influence. Adam may be the most unconventional teacher in our region, but he gets results."

"I am happy my students like me, but my sister is many times more intelligent and knowledgeable," said Adam. "I would bet the farm she becomes a college professor."

In the audience, Susan and Cindy clapped.

"Mikaela, aside from the interests your brother just noted, what are your current hobbies and interests?" asked Donahue.

"I love clothes shopping, spending time behind the mirror fixing my hair and applying my lipstick and makeup, collecting jewelry and fashion magazines, and having my nails done. Recently, I have been learning how to cook."

"Your nails are stunning."

"Thanks so much, Phil."

"I hope you don't have bad habits," said Donahue.

"Yes, I'm an everyday smoker, and I like mixed drinks. I used to drink beer when I was male."

"We can forgive those vices for a beautiful, feminine woman like you. What do you say, audience?"

Loud applause was heard.

"Don't ask me the same question," interrupted Adam, a heavy smoker, drinker, and dabbler in substance abuse.

"Adam, I will keep it a secret," said Donahue, laughingly. "Sarah, do you remember any other interesting things about Mikaela?"

"Mikaela used to be a bully when she was younger," Sarah said.

"Who or what did she bully? A litter of kittens, maybe?" asked Donahue.

Most of the audience laughed, but Cindy and Susan gritted their teeth.

Mikaela fought back tears.

Donahue realized instantly that he needed to abandon the roast aspect of the show, even though it barely got started. His subject was too easily frazzled.

"Sarah, can you compare Mikaela to anyone else, or even to a fictional character, like you did with Adam Sean?"

Sarah broke into a wide smile.

"Mikaela is a female version of Jean Valjean."

"Oh, you mean the hero of *Les Misérables?* The Frenchman who was transformed from a thief into a model citizen of society? Even if Mikaela is a hint of Valjean, she'd be an amazing woman."

"Phil, my beloved Mikaela is the whole deal. She's an incomparable father, a brilliant intellectual, and a generous and loving woman, but she went through a terrible time as a teenager. She embraced goodness after experiencing the other extreme. But even then, I loved her and knew we were destined to be together, as I explained earlier about meeting up at the Tunnel of Love."

"So, Mikaela underwent a metamorphosis in becoming a modern-day female Valjean?" asked Donahue.

"Yes, Phil. Mikaela was deeply flawed when she mocked and abused Adam. But even then, she'd give you the shirt off her back and loved her family. She was tough with her dad, but now she adores him."

"What about her mom?" asked Donahue.

"Mikaela has been Carol's favorite child for many years. She has always loved all her children, but she never hid that Mikaela was her Number 1. I think she loves her even more today."

Carol nodded and dabbed a tear from her eye.

"So I understand you are the mother of seven children. Adam Sean fathered your three girls and Mikaela, two sets of twin boys. It is obvious that when you get pregnant, there is a likelihood of twins."

"Yes, Phil. I did have one single birth, but we can eliminate coincidence since I had three sets of twins. I don't know the specifics. I don't even think the doctor does."

"Sarah, when do you plan to have Number 8? You're still a young woman."

"Bite your tongue, Phil. I'm done. In the beginning, I envisioned two children the most. It is still surreal to me that I have seven. In case you ask, I love them all equally. Saoirse has made her mark with her personality, and my son Stevie from the older set of twins – Mikaela is his dad – was sent to us from heaven," said Sarah. "My Stevie," she added, sniffling.

Rob Murphy rose from his first-row seat, holding Stevie over his head. The audience applauded. Steve Burke's pride in his favorite grandchild precipitated another emotional outburst from the Furano family's benefactor.

"My other adored children are Joey, Adam, Mikey, Saoirse, Michele, and Carol."

"Will a few family members bring up the Furano children?"

As the audience applauded, Rob carried the boys, Jimbo escorted Saoirse and her sisters to the stage, and Jennifer and Jay carried Mikey and Adam.

"Please stand together and face the audience," Donahue said.

Saoirse stood at the center, her sisters to her right and her half-brothers to her left. The host asked them to hold hands and signaled the audience to welcome them. The auditorium responded with vigorous applause.

"And now, it is my turn to announce a surprise," said Donahue. "Will the parents of Ana and Manuel Ramirez please bring their children up here?"

There was a short silence as the children's identity temporarily stumped the audience. But Mikey, Sarah, and Adam knew what was coming and fought back tears.

When the four Hispanic-Americans reached the stage, Donahue unveiled their identity.

"I would like to introduce Ana and Manuel, the two children whose lives were saved by Mikaela Furano. She risked her life to ensure their survival."

As the children reached Mikaela, the heroine embraced them.

The audience's response was thunderous. Donahue had planned the defining emotional moment to close his show.

"Does the audience have any questions for Mikaela and her family?"

An elderly woman raised her hand.

"How tall is Mikaela, and how much does she weigh? I pose the same question to Adam and Sarah."

"Are you willing to answer?" asked Donahue.

Adam spoke first.

"I am five-foot-eight, and I weigh 194. Years ago, before I built up my body, I weighed 125."

"Adam, you are so exact."

"Shit, Phil, what do you expect? I work out almost every night, and when I am finished, I hit the scale."

"You got me there, Adam. How did you gain 79 pounds?"

"I drank three protein shakes a day. It was only advised I drink one. I also ate foods like pizza and cheeseburgers. I took plenty of vitamins."

"Your height didn't change as your weight increased?"

"Nope. My height stayed the same," said Adam, lighting a cigarette.

"Well, Adam Sean, you are a guy I wouldn't want to meet in a dark alley. So much of your weight is in that amazing muscle mass on your upper arms and calves."

"Adam scares me," said Sarah.

"Sarah, you have my sympathies. Can you give us your personal information?"

"Phil, I am five-foot-seven and weigh 165."

"Perfect, Sarah. Those are excellent numbers for you."

"How about you, Mikaela?"

"I am five-foot-eight like my brother, and I weigh 135. I once weighed 196."

"You are such a delicate flower, Mikaela."

"Thanks, handsome," she said.

The audience laughed and applauded.

"How about the man with the red shirt in the sixth row on the right? What is your question?" asked Donahue.

"I know I'm being a bit risqué, but what movie star would you want to be intimate with over all others?"

"I like that question," said Donahue. "What do you think, Adam? A strong, macho man like you must fantasize about somebody."

"It is a tie between Sharon Stone and Kim Basinger," said Adam.

The men in the audience whistled.

"I love your taste, Adam. Something tells me you and I would get along marvelously well, though I quit smoking years ago."

Adam exhaled and grinned.

"Sarah?"

"Mel Gibson would be my choice."

Female audience members clapped.

"Popular pick, Sarah. Now, how about you, Mikaela? Who do you dream of being intimate with?"

"Robert Redford," she said.

The audience cheered, especially the women.

"You have great taste in men, Mikaela. Mr. Redford is an icon."

"I wouldn't throw Paul Newman or Ryan O'Neal out of my bedroom, either!" she added.

The statement received a standing ovation. Sarah smiled broadly, and Susan and Cindy whispered to each other.

"Our girl has come of age," Susan said proudly.

"I love her so much," answered Cindy. "I consider her my soulmate."

"Cindy, you and I both. My affection for Mikaela is more bottomless than the Challenger's Deep. She is a superstar. And her son, Stevie? I have no words. For me, they were life-changing."

"Susan, she's our best girlfriend. I can't wait for all the times we go out together."

"Yes, Cindy. For sure, until a man steals her from us."

Cindy nodded sadly. "She adores Sarah, but I fear her hormones will eventually lead her into a man's arms. But I could be wrong."

"If so, she deserves a man who will undyingly protect and care for her. Like Phil said, she is so delicate. But I've been wrong about her before. I can also see her never leaving Sarah under any circumstances. Maybe she'll have a few boyfriends, but nothing serious."

"The big day is approaching. I'm happy she is using Johns Hopkins. We can go over there by car. Would you like to ride with me? I can pick you up?"

"You know what, Cindy? That would be awesome! I'd love to go with you. The conversation would be divine. I'd love to hear about Mikaela's visit to your store and whatever parts of her communications you want to share."

An announcer mentioned Steve Burke's name, asking him to stand.

"Mr. Burke, we were told you wanted us to acknowledge you."

Burke stood up and signaled for an usher to take a folded paper from him to Donahue.

"Ladies and Gentlemen," said Donahue. "Mr. Burke has purchased a home on Grant Street, Fairview, New Jersey. He indicates it is next door to the Furano family's house. The address is 74. The two-family house was put up for sale six months ago by the resident owners, who are planning a move to Florida. Mr. Burke wrote the deed to Sarah, Mikaela, and Adam Furano, though by extension, the home will one day be passed down to his seven grandchildren, who are expected to live in the house for many years. Sarah, your dad has bought you, Mikaela, and Adam a new home. I wish I had a dad like that."

The audience exploded in applause. In disbelief, Sarah held her hand over her mouth and dashed to hug Mikaela. After a long embrace, she hugged a gobsmacked Adam, who whispered to Sarah that her dad had done a fantastic job keeping his plan a secret.

Sarah dashed off the stage and down her father's row to embrace him and her mom.

"Everyone, I don't have much more to say. Many of you know what happened in Fairview and Cliffside Park, New Jersey's skies, on that fateful late November day last year. Mikaela Furano's heroism was rightfully plastered all over the news. I won't review the particulars, as doing so might cheapen what happened. Many of us will count her courage as an inspiration throughout the rest of our lives. Thank you, Furano family. You've helped make one of the most memorable shows we've ever filmed. Oh, before I forget. We have a prize for Mikaela, Sarah, and Adam – a paid one-week vacation in Aruba."

After the applause died down and the curtain closed, Sarah whispered to Mikaela: "Our old stomping ground, sweetheart. Now, you will go as a woman."

Sarah approached Adam. "I think this was meant to be, sweetie. You missed our last trip down there. Now, you can finally enjoy that fantastic island."

"Shit, Sarah. It's a good thing I missed the last time. We'd have no Stevie or Joey or the other twins."

Sarah grinned and kissed her husband.

Two rows from the back of the auditorium sat Justin Wetterling, a bearded, overweight man with a beard mired in thought.

I had no idea the hero of the show was a transgendered woman. I despise those people. They are destroying our culture and our country. They are disgusting. I have a job to do, but I'll bide my time. Mikaela Furano, enjoy your life while you can. Your day will come. Fairview, New Jersey, is across the river from my Bronx, New York City home.

***

Olivia Torricelli took a day off from work to watch the show. Her father was also home and joined her at their Cliffside Park residence.

"Olivia, you were planning to marry that sissy?"

"Dad, I went out with her for a few years. We never reached that point. I would never have married a woman."

"I always knew there was something off about her."

"Can we at least admire her as the heroine she is?

"You are right about that, honey."

"I am so proud of her," she said, rubbing her eyes. "I abused her terribly and did some mean things to her family. I once beat up Sarah and made her cry. I was so terrible to their friend Alejandro."

"Sarah is Adam's wife, no?"

"Yes, Dad, but in reality, Sarah has two lovers. She's a lucky woman. Mikaela is lucky, too. I destroyed my relationship with her. I wish I could go back in time."

James Torricelli looked up at his daughter, shaking his head. "But you have a boyfriend. Why would you want a girlfriend? You're not a lesbian."

"Dad, I wish I could have spent more time with her when she was a boy. Of course, I would have had to break up after she announced the transition plans. Mikaela had to understand how it felt to be a macho male before becoming the prissy girl she is now. Her brother Adam, on the other hand, needed to experience being a sissy girl before becoming the macho male he is today."

"That is one fucked up family," said James. "Especially Mikaela."

"They are a beautiful family. I understand them. They are unique. Dad, you have no idea how hard I will work to make Mikaela my best girlfriend. I need her in my life forever."

"Honey, if you love her that much, make it happen," said James.

***

372

Three days after his appearance on *The Phil Donahue Show,* Mikaela walked down the block to get the belongings in his locker at the Grandview Firehouse that he had long avoided claiming. The young men smiled when they saw him enter, and one whispered to the other.

Mikaela nodded and ambled over to the cluster of lockers. A colorful sign covered her own. Emblazed on the white sign were red and blue letters that read *Congratulations, Mikaela. We'll love you forever.*

Mikaela's first feeling was profound embarrassment. Craig Krivda and the other firefighter, Dennis Licamelli, rushed over after they noticed Mikaela looked like she was about to break down.

"Buddy, we all love you. You're a superstar!" Craig exclaimed as he and John guided the heroine to a lounge chair outside the entrance to the kitchen.

"Mikaela, we are so proud of you!" exclaimed Fireman Buglione.

"Thanks, Craig! Thanks, Pat! Thank you, everybody! Your love and support could not move me more deeply."

Other firefighters entered and greeted Mikaela as the celebrity she was. They brought her a super-sized sandwich, a beer mug, and a bowl of chips. After receiving a call from Krivda, Fireman Mario Schettino Jr. entered with a flower piece he picked up at Pangione's Florist on Fairview Avenue, across from the entrance of the Fairview Cemetery. Mikaela couldn't thank her friends enough, and when she returned home later that night, she cried in Sarah's arms.

CHAPTER 46

Carol Confesses to Mikaela

"I adore you, Mom. Your full acceptance of me is from the deepest recesses of your heart," said Mikaela as she snuggled against her mom on the loveseat, nestling her head under her mom's chin.

"My beautiful girl, I have a confession to make. When you were born, I was greatly disappointed. After Adam, I had my heart set on a girl. All my girlfriends told me that the baby's position in my lower stomach strongly indicated that I would be having a girl. Even your dad predicted you'd be a girl. When you were born - and I am ashamed of myself for feeling that way – I didn't even want to hold you. I purposely let Dad and other family members spend most of their time with you. I let you remain in the bassinet. I refused to breastfeed you and let the nurses bottle-feed you. I never forgot one older woman who asked me if I was unhappy with you. I told her the truth. I said you were supposed to be a girl, but that nature played a trick on me. She sympathized with me and said she'd probably feel the same if she had similar expectations. As I didn't know if I would have a third child since your dad was militantly against me having more than two, I considered your birth an abomination."

Mikaela whimpered.

375

"Shh, Mikaela," Carol said, rocking her daughter. "It is best you know the truth. We both know there was a happy ending."

Carol showered her daughter with kisses and continued.

"I was supposed to name you Michael. But I developed a hatred for the name because it meant I surrendered. I insisted you be called Mikey on your birth certificate because the 'y' at the end made the name sound more feminine. I know Mikey is short for Michael, but since it is rarely used as a first name, I would be making a statement. I'm sorry, Mikaela. I don't mean to break your heart, but I didn't name you Mikey because it was unique or made you stand out; I named you Mikey for purely selfish reasons."

Mikaela bawled.

Sarah heard the emotional meltdown and rushed into the living room.

"Mom, please stop torturing her! Don't you think she's been through enough? Do you want her to have a nervous breakdown?"

Sarah pulled Mikaela off the furniture and onto the floor and wrapped the sobbing woman with her arms and legs.

"I'm so sorry, Sarah. What I said to her was out of unconditional love."

"I know, Mom. But you know she is physically and emotionally frail. She is self-conscious about her figure and eats like a bird, living mostly on salad and blueberries. Her body has been assaulted with hormones, some by injections, and she's had painful electrolysis done. She'll be on the hormones for the rest of her life, and she has major operations awaiting her," said Sarah as she rocked Mikaela back and forth. "I love you, Mom, but I won't allow anyone to distress my lover, soulmate, and parent of my children. I'd rather die. Mikaela is mine."

"I understand, Sarah. She's yours, indeed. I might be her mom, but you are the most important person in her life. In the future, I will confer with you first. I'll only say that God watched over us when Mikaela finally assumed the gender she was meant to be. She was confused and depressed for much too long."

"Mom, I couldn't agree with you more," said Sarah, guiding Mikaela to their bedroom. "Just two more days, sweetheart, and your male equipment will be gone," said Sarah. "It was only useful for two brief instances in your life as a boy. I need not remind you what I am referring to."

Mikaela cried but was quickly comforted.

Though most families in the 1980s would have been mortified at the prospect of their son or daughter changing genders, the Furano family stood by Mikaela, a heroine her mother thought was always there but delayed from making her debut because of a biological error.

CHAPTER 47

Sex Reassignment and All Sex Change Procedures Canceled

Two vehicles left the front of 76 Grant Street at 5:00 a.m. on the big day. The Johns Hopkins Medical Center at 1800 Orleans Street in Baltimore was nearly a three-and-a-half-hour drive from Fairview, though traffic could alter the estimate. In the car driven by Joseph, his wife sat in the front seat, and Sarah and Mikaela in the back. From the instant they sat, Mikaela rested her head on Sarah's torso and cried softly.

"Don't cry, my beloved. By this afternoon, it will be all over. I'll be next to you in your room every minute for the five days you will be in the hospital. I will get you through this, sweetheart. You will be the happiest woman in Fairview when you return. But I think you'll be the most blissful girl in Baltimore when you awaken from the anesthesia."

"I love you, Sarah. I love you. I love you," Mikaela repeated over and over. "Your face is all I want to see for the rest of my life."

Carol turned around, smiling soulfully, to behold the lovers embracing.

***

Adam drove Sarah's Challenger. Jay sat in the passenger's seat, and Jennifer sat next to Steve and Michele Burke in the back.

"Fucking shit," Adam screamed out his half-open window, giving the finger and honking at a car that cut him off in the middle lane. "The dickhead thinks he owns the road because he drives a fucking Mercedes."

Jennifer and the Burkes glanced at each other, but like Jay, they didn't dare contest their driver's latest temper tantrum.

"Adam, how are you making out on the bike front?" said Steve Burke, diverting.

"Dad, I have my eyes on a few. With everything going on, I haven't had a chance to move forward."

"When you make your decision, come and visit me. I'll write you a blank check."

"I can't do that, Dad. You've given all of us our lives."

"Yes, you can, and you will," said Steve. "Take your time in picking the right one."

Adam shook his head.

***

"Cindy, I envy you for knowing her longer than I have. And I'm also jealous you loved her when you first saw her and continued that classic epistolary relationship. I am ashamed to say my initial opinion of her was negative. I blame myself for making summary judgments without proper information or evidence. Looking back, I find it impossible to believe I preferred Adam. He's vile, vulgar, and a sickening male chauvinist. He's a right-wing Republican, and I don't even want to discuss his substance abuse," said Susan from the passenger seat in Cindy's red Oldsmobile as they headed south on the New Jersey Turnpike. "I dislike him intensely."

"Susan, I always felt privileged. When Mikaela presented as a boy, I thought she was a girl, but I wasn't sure how long it would take her to transition. After my conversations with you and her mom, it appears she needed to resolve her gender by first trying to be a macho male. I have since learned she was abusive to her brother because she was jealous he was pushing the buttons she couldn't. By the way, Susan, I am also a Republican. My husband was active on the local political scene when we lived in Bergen County."

"Ah, Cindy, my apologies. Sometimes, I am too outspoken for my own good. Adam was right about that. I'm a liberal Democrat, but I have some other friends who are like you, including a few at the college. Mind you, I don't always agree with some of my party's positions."

"Same here, Susan. I know some of the more extreme right-wingers would shun what is happening today with our beautiful girl. They think it is abnormal and morally wrong."

"Cindy, the same people are opposed to gay relationships as well."

"Yes, some are," said Cindy. "Anyway, Mikaela is a card-carrying Democrat."

"Yes, she is," said Susan, smiling. "But she's afraid of Adam, so she doesn't talk politics when he's present. Sarah sticks with Adam. She says she must support her husband in politics, yet we both know she loves Mikaela more. Ah, well."

"What about Sarah's parents?" asked Cindy.

"They are staunch Republicans," answered Susan. "Steve was a Wall Street trader."

"I wish everyone could just get along. Politics isn't worth fighting over."

"Aye, Cindy. I fall into the trap much too often. Adam is such an extremist."

"Does Adam have any good qualities?" asked Cindy.

"He is a terrific teacher. He talks to his students like they are his peers. He uses vulgarity and makes them laugh. He has turned many into readers, students who previously hated reading. He got involved in his student's personal lives. One of the kids, Brian Fischer, has lived in the Furano home several times. Brian adores Adam like many others in his classes do."

"That's quite a bit of praise," said Cindy, passing the sign for Exit 9, New Brunswick.

"Yes, no doubt. But if you take his teaching out of the equation, he's a creep. He's a nasty piece of work, one of the most detestable people I've ever known. He had me and others fooled for years."

"But Sarah loves him," said Cindy. "She may not love him as much as Mikaela, but she still loves him."

"Yes indeed, Cindy. And that's what matters. What I say or think is meaningless."

"I'll try and stay clear of him," said Cindy. "The last thing I need is more negative energy in my life. He's scary looking. On another matter, I regret not explaining to Mikaela what happened in my personal life. Frankly, I didn't want to spoil the celebration on her big night at the American Legion. I told her I had some good and bad news."

"Cindy, I hope everything will work out for you. I'm sure you'll win an audience with our girl soon. If you care to share the good news, I'm all ears."

"Susan, I'll share both—first, the bad. My husband and I have separated and have filed for divorce. We never got along, and things reached a head about six months ago. My children chose to live with him for financial reasons. I have long been devastated, especially since I am extremely close to my son, but I understand they were being practical. The good news is that I live in Teaneck at my parents' old house. I'll see my girl and all of you much more often now."

"Cindy, I am so sorry. I didn't mean to pry and wasn't expecting to hear anything but heartening news."

"That's fine, Susan. You weren't prying. I volunteered. Life is too often difficult to navigate. I saw this coming but never found an answer. Hopefully, we can get together from time to time."

"Of course. I greatly enjoy your company."

Cindy smiled broadly.

"I bet our girl is beside herself now. One could say they are ready, but it must be terrifying on the day or days of the surgery," said Susan, lighting a cigarette.

"These are complex procedures, and she will probably experience much pain afterward. The thought of that makes me want to cry," said Cindy. "She'll be under the knife for three days."

"You and me both, honey," said Susan. "What was your fondest memory of first meeting Mikaela?"

"I remember rescuing her from my co-worker. The woman made her admit the items she planned to buy were not for her mom."

"Sounds insensitive."

"No doubt, Susan."

***

Two minutes after Mikaela was wheeled into the operating theatre, she exclaimed:

"No. I have changed my mind. I don't want this operation or any of the other procedures planned for my stay done at this time. I can't say if I will ever have any of them done. I've been at war with myself for months. I have a few private reasons which I will discuss with my lover. I'm sorry for putting you all through this."

The leader of the team was shocked.

"You have every right to halt all the procedures, but I don't understand why you waited till the very last possible moment," said Dr. James Curry, the head surgeon.

"I'm sorry, Dr. Curry. I consider myself a woman, but the idea of finality and the point of no return has always freaked me out. Until this morning, I set aside my issues and continued to delay until the final moment because I wasn't sure until now."

"I understand, Mikaela. Some of your scheduled procedures would be difficult to reverse, but not impossible. But today's vaginoplasty would have been irreversible. There would be no going back for obvious reasons. I am frankly surprised you preferred to have the most extensive surgery done first. Most patients save it for last. Anyway, I'm sure you'll understand you will partly be responsible for the financial agreement. But I'll leave that for your follow-up meeting with the professionals. I'm unsure of how that will work."

"I fully understand, Dr. Curry. I apologize for the last-minute decision. It wasn't fair for me to wait this long."

A team member signaled two nurses to wheel the patient to the recovery room. Sarah and the Furano group were startled to learn of Mikaela's change of heart, but Sarah assured her soulmate that she stood by the unexpected decision.

"Sweetie, I am not surprised," she whispered into Mikaela's ear. "I saw this coming. Your facial expressions since *The Phil Donahue Show* told me so much. Still, I am astounded you waited till the very last moment."

Mikaela whispered back.

"Most of it has to do with you. I don't think it is fair to expect you to continue a passionate relationship with a transitioned woman. I know you said my penis and testicles never mattered, but I would rather keep them. I don't need to make the ultimate statement. I don't want Mikey to be eliminated. Mikey is the one you fell in love with during our time in Aruba, and a considerable part of him must always be there. I'll identify as female, but I'm not actually female without the sex change operation. Heck, I know I can never be technically a female anyway. My chromosomes already spoke for that. If you want Mikey, you'll get him. If you prefer Mikaela, you'll get her. So much is symbolic, but as long as I keep my male parts down there, I don't think anyone will ever be able to say that I forced you into a lesbian relationship. Although I don't see myself as anyone other than a woman, life is unpredictable. Look what happened with Adam. I can never be sure of anything. It's less critical, but it's worth mentioning that I fear being cut down there. I regret not being truthful to Dr. Levine, Cindy, Susan, and others."

Sarah spoke aloud as the other Furano family members and friends arrived in the room.

"My love for you is so complete that I never wanted to lose the slightest bit of you for any reason. Sweetie, I applaud you for thinking everything through. Oh, how much I love you," she said, bursting into tears.

After everyone was informed of the cancellation, Joseph Furano, who could never come to terms with sex change surgery as the father of a son ready to have it performed, looked happy and relieved despite his past celebratory comments about welcoming his new daughter. His thoughts focused on the future.

Maybe my daughter has realized she would rather stay as my son. It took her a long time to decide, but she made it just under the gun.

"I think Mikey made the best decision," he said, suddenly reviving the male name for his biological son.

Mikaela read her father's thoughts and smiled.

Outside, Susan spoke with Cindy.

"I don't think this is unusual at all," said the professor. "This is a major decision, one that requires exhaustive consideration. Our girl may yet have it done, but it is best to let her move forward at her own pace."

"Yet, there would seem to be an equal chance she will never have it done," said Cindy. "Enough doubt has been registered."

"You are right, my friend," answered Susan as the women headed back on the road. "Still, I believe she will have it done within the next few years."

"You would like to see her have it done?" asked Cindy.

"The decision rests with her, but she wants to be fulfilled. I think she needs to have it done, and until it is all over, she will continue to have bouts of depression. I will continue to encourage her to do it. Mikaela is a woman, Cindy. Reminders of her male self will be more destructive than helpful. Already, we saw Joseph wavering. His hidden bias against transgendered people surfaced."

"Of course, Susan. I will do my share to convince her to reschedule all the procedures. We need to go out with Sarah and argue our case. If we can convince her that the transition needs to be complete, I think it will happen even sooner than we hope."

"I'm happy we agree," Susan said.

"But if Mikaela remains opposed, her wishes are first and foremost. In that case, we must permanently back off."

Susan slowly nodded.

CHAPTER 48

Return Trip to Aruba

Joseph Furano hugged Mikaela in the kitchen on the morning of the plane flight to Aruba.

"My beautiful girl, I will be depressed for the twelve days you are gone. You are the brightest star in my life. I think you always were, but I was too stupid to realize it," said Joseph Furano. "I wish I were on the plane," he added, squeezing Mikaela harder.

"Dad, you're hurting me!" exclaimed Mikaela, wincing.

"Oh, I'm sorry, sweetie. I let myself get carried away," said Joseph, releasing his daughter and former son, who once physically assaulted the Furano patriarch, causing the man to suffer a heart attack.

"Joe, she'll be back in no time," said Carol.

Steve Burke embraced his daughter and Mikaela in turn.

"I love you, Dad," said Mikaela. "I owe you the blood in my veins. But truthfully, I owe you far more." Burke, who drove down from Cliffside Park with his wife Michele to see the trio off, rocked Mikaela.

Everyone shook hands, smoked cigarettes, and chatted with

Jay and Rob in the living room.

"Adam, your arms keep getting bigger and bigger," said Steve. "This is the first time I saw your tattoos. They are awesome. I am especially partial to the black and green inked alligator, but the skull and crossbones grab your attention. These two ladies have nothing to worry about with you next to them, that's for sure."

Adam smiled appreciably as he dragged on his Marlboro.

"I bet your students love them!" added Burke.

"Shit, I am tired of receiving their compliments," Adam said, scowling. Then he smiled. "But yeah, they are crazy for them, and a few boys want to get the same ones. One is a big motorcycle guy."

"What about the teachers?" asked Burke.

"That's tough shit what they think," said Adam, crushing out his cigarette in the kitchen table ashtray. "I will soon be getting some on my legs."

Everyone guffawed, hiding their fear of Adam.

"You could say that again," said Rob, who thought Adam's physical transformation was miraculous and admired his friend's defiant manner.

Jay made his rounds and held back his emotions until he approached Mikaela with misty eyes.

"I love you all, but Mikaela," he said, covering his eyes.

Laughs followed until young Stevie entered. He screamed bloody murder, grabbing Sarah and Mikaela's legs and pleading with them to stay. The scene resembled how young Ricky Schroeder carried on after Jon Voight died in *The Champ*.

Steve Burke addressed his crying grandson.

"My sweet boy, the time you spend with Michele and me will be the finest in our lives. Your beloved brother and you will make us feel like we are in heaven. Don't worry; your parents will be home sooner than you think."

The final goodbyes were interrupted by the honking of an Air Brook Limousine sedan in front of the house. After the driver loaded the trunk with the luggage and carry-ons, he opened the back door for Sarah and Mikaela, saying, "Hello, ladies." Adam sat in the front seat, and within 15 minutes, they were rolling down the New Jersey Turnpike.

Sarah pulled Mikaela against her torso.

"Sweetie, I love that your hair is so long, but we need to schedule an appointment at the salon so they can trim the ends and style it. We'll be sure to keep the pink streaks."

Sarah kissed her lover, petting the side of Mikaela's face.

The driver, who had turned briefly to ensure he could negotiate a lane change as the side mirror clouded up from the freezing rain, pondered.

Lesbians. I haven't seen any as of late. The guy next to me must control them. Maybe he's their pimp. The blond is gorgeous. I'd do her in an instant. But this guy's a bodybuilder and looks like a serial killer. I better be as friendly as possible to survive this trip.

Without asking if he could smoke, Adam lit a cigarette. He quickly backpedaled after he exhaled through his cracked window. "You don't mind, do you?"

"Not at all; go right ahead, sir," said the balding, middle-aged, uniformed chauffeur. "I'm a smoker, too."

Adam smiled. Sarah accelerated her lovemaking after she had lifted Mikaela on her lap.

"Just cigarettes?" asked Adam.

"Oh, well, I don't know, I think so, maybe."

The line of questioning frightened the driver.

Is this guy trying to set me up? Maybe it would be best if I didn't say anything else.

"Shit, you're no fun," said Adam. "Be cool, buddy. I won't turn you in," Adam added, reading the vibe. "Hey, where's that fucking smelly landfill? I smell rotten eggs." Adam tossed his butt out the window in an act he once admonished Jimbo for doing when they were teenagers.

"Sir, the landfill is about half a mile to your left. The smell is even worse by Elizabeth, where the smokestacks pollute that entire area."

"Ah, I know that spot well. When I was a kid, my family passed by it going to and from the seashore," said Adam, lighting another cigarette.

A short while later, the driver pulled up to the departure deck at Terminal C. Adam handed him the fare plus a generous $25 tip.

"This is for you for putting up with all my fucking bullshit."

"Thanks so much. That's so kind of you. You didn't have to give me that much."

"I don't think I gave you enough. We loved your company."

A bellhop checked the bags curbside. The three travelers headed to the waiting area with Adam leading the way. Sarah clasped Mikaela's hand protectively until they sat, though Mikaela immediately leaned her head on Sarah's torso.

"I love you, sweetie," said Sarah.

The flight to Aruba took 4 hours and 25 minutes. Astonishingly, they were lodged at the same hotel Sarah and former Mikey had used years before. The same manager, Bram, greeted them and immediately remembered Sarah.

"My good friend, this is my husband, Adam."

"Pleased to meet you, Adam. And who is this beautiful young lady?" asked Bram.

Sarah didn't see a reason to be coy.

"I want you to meet Mikaela. You remembered her as Mikey."

Bram looked as if he had seen a ghost.

"Sarah, I'm confused."

"Bram, she finally identifies in the gender she feels most comfortable with."

Nervous and embarrassed, Mikaela avoided Bram's eyes.

"Well, what do you know?" exclaimed Bram, a progressive guy. "She makes a far better woman than a man. She is stunning! I'm thrilled to see you again and see you as the person you should always have been."

"She has had the operation, I assume," said Bram.

"No, she has not," said Sarah. "She may never go to that length."

"I see," said Bram.

"I'm so pleased to see you again," said Mikaela. "I'll never forget our fabulous talks and your valued assistance."

Wow! She sounds more feminine than any born woman I know. What a dream girl! When she was a man, she was exceptionally handsome. As a woman, she is breathtaking! I'll be sure to hang around!

Bram kissed Mikaela on both cheeks. The fragrance of her perfume intoxicated him.

"I'm glad you found yourself. Thanks for remembering me. You'll want to check out your rooms and set up. Dinner will be served in an hour. We have a fabulous buffet. I recommend the veal scampi and the seafood casserole, but you can't go wrong with the salmon and the eggplant parmigiana. There are many soups, salads, and desserts. Does all of that make you hungry, Mikaela?"

"Years ago, it would have, but I am trying hard to get my weight down."

"But you are on vacation, right?"

"We'll see, Bram. I'll sample the salads."

"Bram, does this hotel have a gym and a weight room?" asked Adam, lighting a cigarette.

"It sure does, Adam! It's the best of its type on the island. Your physique shows me you are committed. How much do you press?"

"I'm around 190, and I press 250."

"I'm impressed, Adam."

"Thanks, Bram. I also do bodybuilding and aerobics and over-indulge in protein shakes."

"You must have a physically active job, right?"

"Not really," said Adam. "I teach in a high school."

"Awesome! We'll have plenty of days to discuss!"

"Are you working, Mikaela?"

"I am a college student. I hope to finish two years from now."

"Fantastic," said Bram. "What is your major?"

"English, just like my brother Adam."

"Incredible!" exclaimed Bram. "And Sarah works in a school, too, as I recall!"

"Right now, I am not working," said Sarah. "I must raise my large family. I'll discuss my brood with you during this trip."

"I'm using your time," said Bram. "As I said, do what you need to do. The dinner is from 6:00 to 8:30."

"Thank you," said Mikaela.

The 8th-floor accommodation was spacious and luxuriant.

"Sarah, I'll sleep alone in here. You and your favorite lover have the king-sized canopy bed, which is ideal for two women."

"So you don't think a man is appropriate for a canopy bed?" asked Sarah.

After Adam evinced a crooked smile, Sarah hugged him and said, "You know I'm only kidding, sweetie. It *is* ideal for two women."

CHAPTER 49

Meeting Mark

Mikaela wouldn't eat anything except a small green olive salad and a mixed cup of blueberries and strawberries. Adam consumed two large pieces of chicken parmigiana and some spaghetti. Sarah opted for the eggplant parmigiana and tortellini salad. They all praised the food.

Adam and Sarah visited the bar to order beer, rum and Coke, and a wine cooler for Mikaela.

They chatted at their table until after 9 p.m. when Adam saw a man at the bar complete a transaction with a guy who had just entered the resort. He was sure he knew what had happened, so when the person who forked over some cash departed, he quickly approached the other man and spoke softly. The man enthusiastically nodded. Adam pulled out a large bill from his pocket and received a plastic bag with six fatties in return.

"How often do you come around here?" Adam asked the supplier.

"I'm here around about 9 o'clock every other night. So I'll be back Tuesday."

"Cool, man," said Adam. "I'll buy more weed. Do you also sell blow?"

"Sometimes. Just ask me."

"Cool, I'll see you soon," said Adam.

Adam looked out the window and noticed an unpopulated garden area. He returned to the table.

"I would like you two ladies to accompany me outside immediately."

"Why Adam?" asked Sarah.

"Don't ask questions, just do it," said Adam.

Rather than risk a public disagreement, Sarah grimaced and arose, signaling Mikaela to do the same. They followed Adam to a patio bordered by flowerpots and darkened by an overhang. Adam opened his supply bag and pulled out a joint. He lit up and took a deep toke, holding the smoke in his lungs, before exhaling. Sarah was revulsed.

"Adam, we are going back inside right now!" she exclaimed.

"No, you are not!" he exclaimed, clasping the top of her blouse. And neither is Mikaela! You are both going to get high with me."

"No way, Adam," said Sarah.

Adam gritted his teeth and answered, "Don't make me physically force you. Since this is your first time, you will probably cough a little. But stay with it. It's like smoking a cigarette, except you need to hold the smoke down longer."

Sarah nearly cried. "Adam, it is unfair that you are forcing us to do this."

Mikaela nodded.

"It *is* fair, Sarah, now do it!"

Sarah held up the joint and looked at it uncertainly but did what Adam ordered. For the first time, she did astoundingly well. As a longtime cigarette smoker, the general similarity made the task less complicated. She coughed when she finally exhaled. She handed the joint to Mikaela, who also performed well. After they passed it back a few more times, Sarah and Mikaela, like Adam, were buzzed.

"Oh, Adam, I am seeing brighter colors. The sounds from inside are amplified," she said, laughing.

"Wow, this is awesome," said Mikaela. "Everything looks distorted! I feel a bit dizzy, but I like the feeling."

"Yeah, man, this is fucking great! "said Adam. "I love the hallucinatory high."

After the joint was finished, Sarah had to hold Mikaela, who looked ready to collapse.

"I'm so dizzy," said Mikaela.

"See, girls! I know how to have fun."

"I don't know about you," said Sarah, smiling.

Adam advised them to sit at the table for a while. "Mikaela has less body mass than us. The effect on her will be more acute, though some people say there is no truth in that."

"I'm hungry again," said Sarah.

"It is normal to get the munchies," said Adam. "Let me fetch you some snacks."

Adam returned with bags of pretzels, chips, and two protein bars.

"I want to hang at the bar a little bit. I'll be back soon," he said.

Adam knew the type immediately. A young, good-looking man about 5 feet, 10 inches tall was flirting with women at the bar. He handed a young woman a piece of paper with his hotel phone number and instructions for when to call him. Adam approached him.

"Listen, buddy. My wife and sister are at the table in the back to the right. My sister is shy, but she's gorgeous. One look and you'll have the sexpot you are looking for. Please take a look at the table and wink at her. She's wearing a turquoise dress."

Mightily intrigued, the man stared at Adam's table and finally caught Mikaela's attention. He winked.

"However, before you go any further, I need to know if you like special girls, " Adam asked.

"What do you mean special?" asked Mark.

Adam spoke softly, explaining to Mark that Mikaela was transitioning.

"I can't believe it!" exclaimed Mark. "She looks like a biological woman, and extremely so."

"She takes female hormones. She's an amazing girly girl."

"Did she have the actual sex change surgery?"

"No, she has not. I suspect she won't ever have it. Does it matter to you? If so, we'll call everything off. I can completely understand you or any other man being turned off by such females."

"I've never had a special girl, but I've long been intrigued. I'm excited! Count me in!"

"If you play your cards right, she'll sleep with you for as long as you want. I'm sure she'll do anything you want her to do," said Adam. "I would only ask that you treat her like a woman who needs it. Don't wear kid gloves. Ignore her when she cries, which she does a lot. You can't go all the way with her for the reason you already know, but you can have all the foreplay you want. She can please you as well."

"I'm thunderstruck! What's your name?"

"I'm Adam."

"I'm Mark. Pleased to meet you, Adam."

"Mark, I will approach my wife and tell her I want to speak with her privately. After we are gone, go over to Mikaela. Work your charm on her. I suspect you'll have her in your room within an hour if you are good. You better not physically hurt her. She's rather delicate. If you do, I'll forget we're friends. Please walk her back to our room when your time with her has ended. Here's my room number." Adam handed Mark a card.

"Adam, you just made my week!"

"Good luck, Mark."

Walking down a long hall with Sarah, Adam explained the situation.

"Are you insane, Adam?" But Sarah was under the influence. "You might be right. She needs a man to make love to her. Do you trust him?"

"Of course. He's a regular here. I'm sure he's had many conquests. Let's go up to our room. I'm in the mood to have sex with you."

"You're too rough, Adam."

"That's too bad."

***

"Hi, is your name Mikaela?"

Nervous and taken aback, the girl didn't answer right away.

"I'm Mikaela," she finally said softly.

"Mikaela, you are a beautiful woman. Would you like to get to know me better?"

She smiled.

After going back and forth for 15 minutes, when fear, uncertainty, and shyness initially held the meeting at a standstill, Mikaela finally relaxed. An expert at small talk and flattery, Mark was impressed to find out the girl attended college. Mark lit her cigarette, then his own, and after he was sure he had won her confidence, he resituated to the booth side of the table, where she sat. He slid against her and draped his arm over her shoulder. Mikaela shuddered, but soon after, she liked how it felt.

After more flattery about her lovely figure, gorgeous eyes and lips, intoxicating perfume, and the sexiest voice he ever heard, Mark got bolder. He pecked her lips a few times. He looked funny at the waiter, who interrupted him to ask if they wanted drinks.

397

The server, a dark-skinned islander, realized his intrusion wasn't appreciated.

"I'm very sorry, Mark, but I wanted to be sure you were good with the drinks," he said in a rich, colorful voice that made it clear English wasn't his first language. Mikaela surprised Mark by telling the waiter she wanted a Malibu Bay Breeze.

"You have creative taste in drinks, my beautiful girl. That's a real ladies' drink – coconut rum with cranberry and pineapple juice. Waiter, you can also get me a scotch. I like your English. Your first language, Papiamento, has a distinct sound."

"Thank you, sir," said the waiter. "And thank you for your order, lovely lady. We'll make you the best Malibu Bay Breeze you've ever had."

"Now, remember, she's all mine!" exclaimed Mark.

The men enjoyed a hearty laugh. Mikaela blushed.

After they finished their drinks, Mark graduated from pecking to French kissing. Mikaela didn't fight it, but she wasn't answering in kind. She interrupted Mark when she said she would like another drink.

Mikaela's body finally responded after a third round of drinks for both. Mark was ecstatic. He pulled her closer, groped her breasts, and French kissed her more aggressively.

"Those two need to go to their room," said a guy at the bar to his girlfriend. "Geez, they are shameless."

"I'll say," said the woman.

After Mikaela, who by then was inebriated, stroked Mark's bulge, the man knew, happily, that it was time to relocate.

Mark held her hand until they got to his room. He instructed her to sit on the couch and locked the door in two spots. The last action scared Mikaela, but she didn't let on. Mark took off his jacket and turned on the television.

He lit Mikaela's cigarette and used his remote to turn on a channel about Aruba, underscored by classical music.

"Do you love classical, pretty girl?"

"I adore it," she said.

"Perfect."

He wrapped his arm around her and pulled her as close as possible. He turned to look at her and pressed his lips against hers. He instructed her to remove her clothes and then to disrobe him. He picked her up, carried her to his bed, and wrapped his limbs around her. As the lovemaking became more intense, Mikaela cried. Mark knew he needed to ignore it.

"Please, Mark, no more!" she exclaimed.

"Sorry, Mikaela, you can cry and complain all you want, but I will not stop," he said, continuing to maul her. Eventually, her cries turned to whimpers. Mark knew he had her.

"Mikaela, now make Mark happy and use that gorgeous mouth. No teeth, please, or I will turn angry."

Mikaela proved surprisingly proficient. Mark was hard as a rock before long. He held on for a long time, but before he exploded, he pulled the girl off him and ordered her to lie on her chest.

"No, Mark, no! I won't!"

"Yes, you will, Mikaela!" said Mark, moving her into position. "Don't make me hurt you."

He pinned her with his knees and penetrated her. As she screamed, he thrust harder and harder. Mikaela was in severe pain. After he exploded, filling her with his seed, he stayed inside her for a few more minutes.

"You're so sexy!"

"Thanks, Mark. I love you!"

Her words led to an encore of passionate kissing, though to Mikaela's delight, the aggression was gone.

"I'm in love with you, Mikaela. I never said such words to any other woman. Can we see each other several more times during your trip? Heck, more than several!"

"Mark, there's nothing I'd like more."

"Will you sleep with me tonight?"

Mikaela thought of Sarah and Adam but needed to be with Mark.

She smiled. They fell asleep in each other's arms.

For most women, it would take much more than calculated flattery and one night in the hay to commit themselves to a lover, but Mikaela's first time with a man influenced her judgment.

CHAPTER 50

Adam and Sarah's Spousal Dynamic

"Adam, you are hurting me. Please stop," exclaimed Sarah.

Adam ignored his wife's plea and continued his rough lovemaking.

Sarah couldn't suppress her anger.

"In the years after we met, you were a wimp. Did you forget, sissy boy? Do you think because you are a macho ruffian now, your past can be forgotten?"

Adam exploded.

"You fucking bitch!" he shouted, punching Sarah hard in the face. "Don't you ever mention the years I want to be erased from memory in my life! I was manipulated, encouraged, and degraded. I was forced to drink milk from baby bottles when I was 20. You poked my eyes on the day we first met when I was taken for a ride by those sadistic bitches. One day I'm going to visit that cunt Ann Teresi in the salon. I'll be arrested for murder! You made me wear lipstick and makeup, worked at trying to make my voice more feminine, and had my nose cut for a ring, Sarah! I was the victim of a conspiracy aimed at complete emasculation. You took advantage of my prolonged physical growth and bragged to people that you were ten times stronger than me. Guess who's ten times stronger now, you miserable cunt!"

Sarah sobbed.

His anger unabated, Adam opened his hand and slapped her across her mouth.

"That's the first time you ever hit me, Adam. And you hit me twice. Why? I love you so much! Why, Adam? Why, Adam? Why, Adam?" she cried.

"I'm sorry, Sarah. I'm so sorry, Sarah," he said, crying hysterically.

"You are right, sweetie," said Sarah. "What was done to you was unforgivable. Several people need to be held accountable, and I'm one of them."

They cried in each other's arms until they fell asleep.

When they awoke at 6 o'clock, Adam looked into Sarah's eyes and exclaimed, "I can't believe what I did! You are everything to me, Sarah. I deserve to die. I used my hands on you. Oh, God."

They hugged each other as Adam continued his sobbing contrition.

"That's okay, sweetie. I forgive you. I'd forgive you if you did a lot worse. I do take responsibility for what happened to you. I was the main culprit. You can't even blame Ann, though the nose ring was her idea. She did it without my permission. Sweetie, I agree that the way you presented yourself in those years was not you. It was temporary confusion you needed to sort out."

"I know you love me, and I love you more than anyone else, but I am no longer your soulmate. Isn't that right?

Sarah's face flushed. "No, Adam, you are not my soulmate. Mikaela is my soulmate. I thought you were for a long time, and I remember once, on a stormy night, thinking you were my Heathcliffe. But honey, so much in life doesn't last. I can't try to hide the depth of my relationship with her."

"Sarah, I accept that. So much has changed. But I have to be honest with you. I love the way I am now. The old Adam was a buffoon. I curse my teenage years. The reason I was always so depressed was that I hated myself. Anyway, if Mikaela was finally allowed to become the woman she always was – and that was certainly the right way to go – do you think it's fair that I not be myself, warts and all?"

"Adam, you are so right. I will have to deal with your ferocious temper, macho personality, use of vulgarity, and some other dark activities you dabble in. They are part of your nature. But please, sweetie, be careful with the loansharking and the drugs. I don't consider marijuana a drug, as so many do it. But cocaine and other substances are another matter. Adam, you have an addiction. You chain smoke cigarettes and drink beer daily. You may get away with these habits if you are lucky, but expanding your horizons to serious drugs is beyond risky. Please be careful. I wouldn't want to live anymore if anything ever happened to you. You are so gifted and intelligent and idolized at your school."

"Sarah, I blamed you and everyone else for trying to emasculate me, but I, too, was complicit. My body was so slow to mature, and in my teens, I liked films, music, and literature associated with feminine tastes. I once even sang *I Am Woman* in the car with Jay on a rainy night. That was the height of my female immersion."

"Sweetie, I heard all about that," Sarah said, smiling. "But don't bother torturing yourself. Everyone has seen who the real Adam Furano is in the last few years. I'd still love to hear you sing that Helen Reddy song," she joked, trying hard for humor to put some distance between their current exchanges and the ugliest time of their marriage.

"I'll think about it," said Adam. "Sarah, I am also thinking of how you tossed me over your back and carried me around as my arms swung back and forth, made me dress in pajamas and carry a rattle, and controlled every aspect of my life, including what I wore, what I ate, and where I went."

"Sweetheart, how would anyone know you weren't authentic? The Adam back then was an overload of love, a young man devoid of anger and resentment and unwilling to say anything negative about anyone. And yet, I prefer the new Adam, who is world-wise and hardened. I want a real man as my husband, not a fairy tale character. The new muscular, tattooed Adam might have a ferocious temper, a vulgar vocabulary, and a cynical slant – not to mention he's a scary guy – but he's refreshingly blunt and masculine. There is no comparison, sweetie. I loved some things about the former Adam but couldn't be happier that he was gone. I'd rather be punched in the face repeatedly than suffer through all those gooey platitudes and obnoxious patronizing. Toward the end of the old Adam's life, I realized he was a fraud."

Adam rested his head on Sarah's bosom. "In all the years we've been in love, you've never said anything so penetratingly brilliant, Sarah."

"You will never lose your endless capacity to love, but you are unwilling to let it surface too often," said Sarah. "I like it better that way. You make it earned."

"Sarah, I'm sorry you must live with my dark side. It isn't going anywhere and might surface later today, tomorrow, or any time soon. My cynicism is based on my disgust with how my body refused to catch up with my age. But here's one that will make you laugh. I have concluded that my previously beloved *MacArthur Park* is one of the goofiest songs I've ever heard. And as you know, I've listened to it hundreds of times. I prefer Iron Maiden, Def Leppard, and Guns N' Roses. Led Zeppelin and Black Sabbath are also among my favorites."

"Honey, I think I'll always love *MacArthur Park.* You made me love it; now, it means so much to me. Is heavy metal your absolute favorite type of music now?"

"Sarah, I still like some of the music I liked as a teen – though I don't care for most of it – but heavy metal is my current favorite. I spend plenty of time listening to the cassettes in my car with Dave. Many of my students are wild about it, and we discuss it often. They're thrilled I'm a big fan."

"There is probably no hobby or interest in a person's life that changes as much as music. Some go from pop to hard rock, to opera and classical. You did it in reverse, sweetie. But your favored music matches your personality."

Adam gave Sarah a thumbs-up.

"One more thing, sweetie," Sarah added. "Now that you want to buy a motorcycle, I want to tell you how I answered my parents in Palisades Amusement Park on the day we met. I told them I wanted to marry a muscular motorcycle guy with a goatee and loads of tattoos. After years of being fooled, I got what I wanted."

Adam grinned.

"Oh my God, we forgot about Mikaela," he exclaimed.

"I am so happy for her," Sarah said. "It looks like Mark officially made her a real woman. I doubt you and I will see much of her this trip."

"I guess you are stuck with me," said Adam.

"You haven't been this emotional in a long time, sweetie. You keep torturing yourself. Look, honey, you are seriously flawed. But you have always demonstrated a capacity for good. Between all the chaos, I'm sure you and I still have many priceless moments to share."

Adam took a final drag on his cigarette, crushed it, and wrapped his arms around his wife.

"I'm hard to deal with. But I'll do all I can never again to violate you the way I did last night," he said.

"Don't torture yourself, sweetie. I'd die for you."

Adam kissed her before heading for breakfast. He held Sarah's hand as Brad approached.

"Mark called me. He wanted me to tell you that he took Mikaela to the best breakfast place on the island. It's about a 40-minute drive from here."

"Wow, he is smitten with her," said Adam.

"Adam and Sarah, I want you to know that I never told and never will tell him about Mikaela. He might not even care, but I would not want to risk compromising their love. They should enjoy themselves since he may never see her again after you leave."

"Bram, Mark already knows about Mikaela. I told him at the beginning. He was fine with it and even said he was excited."

"Well, I'll be," said Mark. "I think this is wonderful."

"Fucking A," said Adam.

Sarah smiled and gave Adam that 'You are hopeless' look. She didn't admit during her long talk with Adam the previous night that his vulgar language and macho personality were starting to impact her appealingly. A voice within her wanted him to take charge. She opened the door for her capitulation when she told Adam at breakfast that she would order what he ordered. Adam was delighted, and later that night, when Sarah expressed interest in smoking another joint, he was thrilled.

Sitting at a booth beside each other, Adam and Sarah shared their most profound thoughts again.

"Listen, my love. I'd repeat this till I'm blue in the face. You love Mikaela more than you love me. When she was Mikey, you loved him more as well. That she is your soulmate puts the question to rest. When Mikaela and I bared our souls in those long back-and-forth tributes to each other, you said you loved us equally. I appreciated that. But I knew you weren't being honest. Who could have possibly loved me more unless the person was mentally retarded?"

"Adam, you are incorrigible. You are a teacher. It would be best if you never used such words."

"Your intimacy with Mikaela is as vital to your emotional well-being as it is to her own. She needs you, and she will never want to leave you. Her love for you was hatched in Cupid's bow. I've never seen love like that between two people. She fathered the favorite of your seven children, a boy who I suspect will become a superstar in his own right. Am I right, Sarah?"

"Why do you always have to make me cry? Yes, you are right, Adam. She invented the word *love.* She brings passion to the highest level of expression."

"Mikaela might find favor with a few men for meaningless brief relationships. But you will always be her prime sexual partner. You and she can kiss for all eternity, and I'd sit back, smile, and wish you the best."

"Adam Sean Furano, I will fucking love you until the universe ceases to exist," whispered Sarah, burying her head under his neck.

Despite Adam's increasing ability to keep his emotions in check as part of his macho overhaul, he cried harder than he had the previous night, more than he had in years. He vice-gripped Sarah, and they slowly rocked each other.

When the blissfulness subsided, Sarah said:

"Sweetie, I love all my children equally."

"Sarah, Mom said the same thing, didn't she?"

Sarah knew she was beaten and didn't respond.

Mark wanted to spend time with Mikaela every day. She happily complied, and they slept together for the remainder of the trip, performing the same sexual activities every evening. However, Mark got creative by incorporating mammary intercourse, a sex act Sigmund Freud thought perfectly normal but, by some others, a perversion. Mikaela barely qualified for the choice since her breasts had barely developed. They held hands everywhere they went, spent time at the tables and the bar, and when Mark was driving, he held Mikaela against him with his right arm. He took her to restaurants. They visited caves, beaches, cliffs, and shops. All men's eyes were always on Mikaela, delighting Mark, who always delighted in the envy of others.

Sarah had a hard time sleeping as Adam's muscular arms sometimes made it difficult to breathe, though she found it increasingly erotic to be in the arms of a strong, macho man. But Adam wanted intercourse. During the day, Adam spent several hours in the weight room and, at other times, got high with Sarah.

Mikaela sobbed on the last day. Mark was nearly as troubled, but he was used to whirlwind romances. He later told people that his previous girlfriend, Mikaela Furano, was the hottest he had ever bedded and that he had never had such fantastic sex. He never told anyone the truth about her. However, weeks after Mikaela left, her memory faded as he planned another conquest at the bar.

When Mikaela remained sad on the plane, Sarah pulled her close.

"Sweetie, I completely understand," she said, comforting her soulmate. "There'll be others; when you're bored, you'll always have me."

Echoing what Adam had movingly said to Grandma Delaney in her hospital room when he quoted a line from Lucy Maud Montgomery's *Anne of Avonlea,* Mikaela said, "My dearest Sarah, I don't want sunbursts or marble halls, I just want you."

Sarah grabbed for her tissues.

Adam, who never forgot when he, too, recited the same line to his beloved grandmother in her hospital bed, dabbed his eye.

When they arrived home, the family treated them like the Second Coming. Little Stevie's happiness rivaled George Bailey's when he reunited with his family at the end of *It's a Wonderful Life.*

Soon, they would move their belongings to the house next door, the gift of anyone's lifetime from Steve Burke.

CHAPTER 51

Moving Day

"Carol, she's gone. Mikaela's gone!" cried Joseph Furano, drinking coffee.

"Joe, you are such a drama queen! Maybe you should consider transitioning, too! She's moving next door! She will be living less than a hundred feet away!"

"That's still too far, Carol! She won't be under my roof. I won't see that beautiful face anymore," said Joseph.

"Except that she will be in and out of our house daily. Her kids will always be here, as will Sarah, Adam, and Rob. I'm so happy they are turning over the basement apartment to Rob. They said they would not let him pay a penny."

"I worry constantly about Adam. He's capable of harming them. He flies off the handle, and every word is a curse. That man has serious issues. All he likes to do is smoke, drink, and get high."

"He's also a committed bodybuilder and weightlifter," said Sarah.

"Oh, that's just great. He's a Hercules who might kill us all."

"Joe, you are being ridiculous. Adam is a successful teacher. So

411

many young people idolize him."

"That's a laugh. They idolize a drug addict. Who will they embrace next, a serial killer? Jay fears him, and Rob always kisses up to him."

"They also love him. Sarah adores him. I agree that he is challenging, and he's certain to cause us more grief, but he's our son, and we need to accept him for who he is. He isn't going to change anymore."

"He treats Sarah like shit. He orders her around, makes all the decisions, and loses his temper if everything isn't as he wants."

"He never hit her, Joe."

"How wonderful, Carol. He specializes in psychological abuse. And don't be so sure he hasn't hit her."

"I'm afraid you are right there, Joe. Sometimes he is heartless. We had a false Adam for years. The old Adam wasn't sustainable. That goody-goody stuff was a development stage. The honest Adam you see now was delayed because of his confusion and stunted growth. He's still our son, our *only* son. I love him. Do you love him, Joe?"

Joe arose and hugged his wife.

"Yes, I love him, Carol. I've always loved him. But I am so afraid for him," Joe said before breaking down in tears. "He's even corrupted Sarah now."

"I know Joe. I know. He's a far cry from the old days. He spoiled us. But as I said, all that was counterfeit. Sarah has changed, too, because of his influence. She's just like many of my card game friends now. They allow their husbands to rule them, and they like it. Because of Adam, Sarah's vocabulary has changed too."

"Carol, I'll try my best. But will you at least admit that you are more than apprehensive about Adam living in a home with two defenseless women and seven children?"

"Yes, I am concerned, Joe."

"They aren't safe when he goes on one of his temper tantrums. There isn't an adult male in that house to cool him down."

"Joe, did you forget Rob will be living there?"

"Carol, did *you* forget Rob lives in the basement apartment with a separate entrance at the back of the house? While living there, he will hear nothing, especially since all the bedrooms are on the top floor, two levels over Rob. The living room is at the front of the house. Rob's three-room apartment doesn't extend that far. The cellar and boiler room take up that space. Technically, Rob lives in the building, but he is completely isolated from Adam's family. Besides, even if Rob heard anything, what could he do? Adam would destroy him."

"You got me on that, Joe. You are so right. I love Rob, too. I am hopeful everything will work out, but like you, I think there is ample reason to be concerned. By the way, we are hosting a card game next week. It's the first I've hosted in a few years. I will be introducing our new daughter to everyone. Many called me after they saw her on *The Phil Donahue Show.* They can't wait to see her in person."

Joseph registered a half-smile.

CHAPTER 52

Fairview Cinema Bombshell

Shortly after Jay Furano arrived home from his security job in Clifton, after he had changed into his shorts and white T-shirt, Jennifer knocked on the garage door.

"Come in," Jay instructed.

Jennifer entered and blew Jay a kiss.

"So, how was your day, big brother?" she asked, lighting a cigarette. "I bet you are relieved. Today is Friday, no?"

"You got that right, Sis! I do love the job, but sometimes it is just so boring. So, what do you have planned for tonight?"

"I'm just hanging, Jay. I may hear from Naomi. She might come up with a good idea."

"There are always girlfriends, girlfriends, girlfriends. You're beyond your mid-twenties, Jen, and you must consider meeting someone and settling down."

"Dearest, you are considerably older, having reached your mid-thirties, and are in danger of being a lifelong bachelor," Jen answered, suddenly sensing her chance.

"Ah, Jen, marriage isn't in the cards for me. I sometimes wish I

415

had a companion."

"Jay, I have met someone and plan to announce him to my family this week."

"Really? I'm so floored, Jen, and so happy for you," Jay exclaimed as he stepped over to embrace her. "Who is the lucky man? Do I know him?"

"Jay, I think you might, but I'd rather discuss everything privately with you later tonight. How about an entertaining diversion? The Fairview Cinema has been showing older movies over the last month. Tonight, they are screening *Atlantic City.* Adam loves it. Burt Lancaster plays the lead."

"Oh, I know Adam loves it. Susan Sarandon is in it, too!" said Jay. "It isn't so old, just a few years."

"How about if we leave here about a quarter to eight? The movie starts fifteen minutes after that. We can talk more at The Point after the movie and get a snack," Jennifer said.

"Sounds like a plan, Sis. Thanks so much for choosing me to learn about this before anyone else in the family."

Smiling wryly, Jennifer crushed her cigarette in an ashtray on the table and responded, "Jay, you know what I think of you. You should be the first to know."

***

Adam was delighted his siblings were interested in seeing *Atlantic City* and happily handed Jay the keys to his Mustang. He told them he would walk to the gym. Jennifer wore some of her best clothes, a floral-patterned blouse and a red skirt with matching shoes. When dressed this way, the long, black-haired, light-skinned Jennifer was undeniably a pretty young woman; though clothed casually, she was still attractive.

Jay paid for the tickets, a large popcorn, and two medium-sized Diet Pepsi containers. Jennifer grabbed the tub, and Jay carried the beverages. The theater's single-screen auditorium was recently divided into two smaller rooms. The siblings entered the door to Theater 1 and surveyed the seating choices.

"Smoking, right Jen?"

"Of course," answered Jennifer, who sat in the last row against the back wall in a section where no other theatergoers were seated. She reached the last seat in the corner, where she could touch the grey wall drapes. Jay sat next to her.

After the Paramount logo appeared, the two munched popcorn.

"Adam used to love opera before he got into heavy metal. He would say this aria is garbage," said Jen, referring to Bellini's *Casta Diva,* playing on the soundtrack in the opening scene.

A half-hour later, Jay couldn't wait any longer.

"So, who is it, Jen? The suspense is killing me," he declared.

Jennifer smiled wide, turned to Jay, and exclaimed, "Why, it's you, silly man. Who did you think it was?"

Jay couldn't quite process what he heard, but Jennifer extended her announcement to physicality. She leaned over and used her right hand to guide Jay's face next to her own and aggressively French-kissed the unsuspecting man. Initially, Jay resisted and attempted to pull away, but the tenacious woman was ready for such a rebuff and doubled up her assault. Finally, Jay succumbed and responded in kind. They went at it for over five minutes. When they stopped to catch their breath, Jay wept.

"Oh, stop now, big, strong man. You can be so emotional sometimes. Didn't you ever catch how much I have always loved you to the moon and back? I never wanted you as my favorite sibling; I wanted you as my husband. I gave you some hints but waited. I remember telling you at Adam's graduation that I would convince my future husband to make you the best man. Even then, I knew you would be the one. And I was confident enough to believe you would want me as well. But I understood I needed to

417

wait for the right time. I decided this week that I could not delay any longer. I want to start a family with you, sweetheart."

Jay's weeping intensified, but he managed to blurt out in a crying voice, "My heart is forever yours, Jennifer. I adore the ground you walk on. I would love to spend the rest of my life with you, but what will Mom and Dad say? We are brother and sister, after all."

Jennifer couldn't resist laughing aloud. A few people turned around from a few rows before the newly minted couple and gave disapproving looks.

"Yes, we are brother and sister, but we don't have the same blood. You lived in our home and decided to change your last name. I am fair game for you, as you are for me."

"Will Dad be angry about this?" Jay asked.

"Sweetie, I am certain he will be thrilled. He loves you. And I can't wait to make this all public. Would you mind if I asked to speak in front of the family tomorrow night?"

Jay was still shell-shocked, but the exhilarating reality was making its way into his consciousness.

"I never thought you felt this way about me," he said. "But of course, I don't mind. It has the potential of being the happiest moment of my life."

"Well, my love, the happiest day will be when we get married a year from now."

"Wow, Jen, you have the date all figured out, too?"

"I haven't figured out the date yet, but I would love it if we could plan for a February wedding. Neither one of us is getting younger."

"We are hardly ancient, Jen, but February would be wonderful."

A middle-aged woman turned around and politely asked the wedding planners to stop talking so she could watch the film.

"Miss, I am very sorry. My fiancé and I are discussing our up-coming wedding," said Jennifer.

The woman smiled. "Honey, that's much more important than this oddball gangster movie. I wish you both the happiest life together."

"Thank you, sweet lady," answered Jennifer.

Jay blew the woman a kiss.

"I am still in disbelief," said Jay. "Please bring me down to earth."

"My love, I will try to get you to stop thinking," said Jennifer as she initiated a French kiss again. This time, Jay matched her feistiness. He twirled his tongue and embraced her tightly.

"Now that's the lover I was waiting for," she said after temp-orarily breaking the canoodle.

Jennifer rested her head on Jay's torso for the rest of the movie. For his part, Jay got friskier – much to Jennifer's delight – and initiated a series of back-and-forth verbal endearments. Jennifer wrapped her arms around him, never wanting to let go, even after the movie ended.

After they both sucked on their soda straws, they deposited the cups and the partially-eaten popcorn tub in the lobby trash receptacle and walked out into the parking lot. Jay lit Jennifer's cigarette, then his own, before they boarded the vehicle and arrived at The Point Diner.

They sat in a booth. A waitress approached and asked if she should bring coffee.

"Yes, absolutely," said Jennifer. "We love our java!"

After the server returned with two cups, a whole pot, and some cream and sugar, she asked, "Are you fine with the cream? Or should I bring milk?"

"Cream is perfect," answered Jennifer, who played footsies under the table. She looked at Jay with love eyes and bluntly said:

"Jay, I can't wait for our tumble in the hay later tonight."

"Tumble in the hay, what, Jen? But how could?…"

"Jay, get real. I'm madly in love with you. From tonight till the end of time, you will never be alone again overnight."

"What will Dad say about this?"

"What will he say? Not a word. We are adults. It's not like we are having intercourse, but we can do everything else. And I mean everything. I will make you very happy, sweetheart."

Jay sniffled and answered:

"I love you so much. I have to think of other words to say to you. I'm not in a league with Mikaela or Adam. But you want to sleep with me?"

"Honey, tonight, tomorrow night, and every night for the rest of our lives, and no more garage for you. My bed is your bed. My pillows are your pillows. My furniture is your furniture. You co-own anything belonging to me except my cosmetics, clothes, and tampons. Mikaela would like to share those with me, but not a real man like you."

"You have the best sense of humor," Jay laughed. "But I always thought you had the best sense of everything."

Jennifer blew an air kiss.

"We'll take two cheeseburgers," she said. "And a large order of fries, which we will share. And some water."

"How did you know I wanted a cheeseburger," asked Jay.

"Sweetie, I know a lot more about you than you think. I've lived with you for 12 years. Would you believe it? 12 years. I know so much about you. I know you are loyal and caring and have a heart of gold. And you are so handsome but always shy about girls. I guess I was lucky for that last observation. Otherwise, someone would have scooped you up a long time ago."

Stirred by Jennifer's words, Jay shed some more happy tears.

The lovebirds nursed their food as they returned affectionate looks.

"I was blown away when I was accepted into this great family," said Jay. "But marrying into the family would be even more awesome."

"Yes, it would be, my beloved. I think we are a great family but not the most typical group of people, and that's an understatement," Jennifer said laughingly.

"Jen, do you know what I loved the most? The day you turned the tables on Mikaela. She used to order you around and bully you; now she is terrified of you."

"I found it satisfying to reverse things. I mean, the event in Aruba destroyed her psychologically. It made her so docile and eventually more girly. She has always had a difficult time looking me in the eye. It is satisfying to be able to control an older sibling, especially one who abused me for years, but since I'm much stronger than her, it was easy."

"I guess Olivia always knew, right?" asked Jay.

"She said Mikaela had trouble getting it up, cried far too much for her taste when they had sex, and told her he preferred that she be on top. She's been fighting these feelings for years. Sarah told me she thought she was experimenting with her feminine side in Aruba. It seems she always wanted to be on the bottom."

Jay paid the check. Jennifer wanted to smoke again, so Jay flicked his lighter as they headed into the Mustang. In less than two minutes, they were home. By then, it was nearly 11:30, so the house was asleep. They sat in the car and chatted until Jennifer finished her cigarette. Jennifer led Jay into the house, where they entered the garage apartment.

Jennifer sat on the recliner and chatted some more.

"Jay, you know how all of us Furanos are drama queens. I want to make the announcement tomorrow night in the living room. I will inform Mom in the morning. I'll say I have something vital to tell the family. I'm sure she'll think I will unveil an affair I am having. It would be best if you didn't come upstairs until someone heads downstairs to alert you to come up. When you get there, sit far away from where I am standing. I will confirm Mom's suspicions when I tell the group I'm engaged. Mom and Dad will flip out and ask why I waited so long and complain that I never introduced the man to them. I think you will love how I answer them."

"Jen, I love the way you handle things. I loved it when you replaced Mikaela as the head of the family, and I never doubted you would be the best for that role."

"Now let's stop talking and catch some shut-eye," Jen answered as she removed every last stitch of clothes from her body. Jay was open-mouthed but followed suit. The two embraced and snuggled as they lay on the sheet. The kissing began and continued for over a half hour. Jennifer used her mouth to relieve Jay after the heated session, and they fell asleep in each other's arms.

Jay Furano was a new man.

***

"Mom, I have something essential to announce to the family tonight at 7 o'clock. Can you relay this to Dad? I see he is not home right now."

"Sure, Jen," said Carol. "Sounds like something inspiring."

"It might be," said Jennifer, coyly. "Is Mikaela here?"

"Yes. She's in her room."

Jennifer opened Mikaela's bedroom door without knocking and beheld her, fidgeting with her hair in front of the bureau mirror.

"Mikaela, I want you in the living room tonight at 7 o'clock for an important announcement."

"Sure, Jen. Of course," she said sheepishly.

"Please don't be late," added Jennifer.

"I won't, I promise," Mikaela assured her.

"Sister, I love the new color you chose for your streaks," Jennifer said, referring to the purple hair dye that replaced the red. "Your salon does excellent work. You might want to try that color on your nails."

"You like it, Jen? Thanks so much!" Mikaela responded.

Jennifer winked and nodded, then walked down the hall to ask Grandma Delaney to be present. Finally, she spoke to her sister-in-law, who registered a wide smile. She also asked Sarah to convince Adam to attend.

She met someone, Sarah thought.

***

A few minutes after the planned time, the entire family assembled in the dining room.

"Thanks to everyone for responding to my request. I love you all and wanted to share some important news in my personal life."

Carol smiled, knowing where it was going.

Jay looked up, simultaneously thrilled and frightened.

"I will come right out and say that I am engaged to be married as of yesterday. I will soon make plans to tie the knot in one year. So, we are looking at a winter wedding."

"Engaged?" asked Joseph Furano. "None of us have ever met this person, and now you suddenly tell us you will soon be married. Jen, I'm so disappointed and surprised at you. How can you do this to us? You never acted so impulsively before."

Carol and Grandma Delaney nodded in agreement.

"Dad, you have met this person many, many times."

"Jennifer, there is no reason to make a joke of this. You know I haven't met him even once. You never mentioned any boyfriend to any of us."

Jennifer made her way around the table and stood behind Jay. She leaned over and kissed him squarely on the lips.

423

"I love him dearly and have for many years. We will be together till death do us part."

"Jennifer, you are quite the jokester tonight, aren't you," said Joseph.

But everyone knew she was telling the truth when Jay cried and held his right hand over his face.

"Oh my Lord!" exclaimed Sarah. "How could none of us have seen this coming? They have long enjoyed a special relationship. And this union is perfectly proper. I am so happy. I love you both so much."

Joseph's eyes widened before he lost his composure.

After the Furano patriarch gathered himself, he spoke:

"None of us had any idea. Not even a clue. Everyone knows how much I love Jay. He is the finest man anywhere for my daughter. He will protect her and love her like no other. And we all know what kind of a father he will be. Today is one of the happiest days of my life. Only the day of the wedding will top it. And I will do my best to ensure the wedding is paid for. No Italian father can fail to gift his daughter with this gesture of love."

Jennifer finally cried and hugged her father. Jay left the table, sat on the couch, and covered his face but was soon approached by the rest of the family. Adam kissed him, but Mikaela outdistanced her brother by showering her future brother-in-law with wet ones all over his face.

"Slow down, Mikaela," said Jay. "Now I have experienced what Sarah has regularly. I love you, girl."

Grandma Delaney proclaimed, *"Praise the Lord! What a happy day this be!"* Carol kept clearing her face with tissues. Joseph spoke again.

"Jay, I want to offer you some advice. The confusion with last names will be difficult. A Furano marrying another Furano is tough to explain and justify. I was deeply honored when you changed your last name and joined our family. But now, everything has changed. When you have children, I think you need to honor your biological father's legacy and not deprive him of what he deserves. You will decide, but you should change your name to Morris."

Jay pondered, then nodded.

"Dad, that is so noble of you. I think you made much sense."

"We loved you as our adopted son but will love you even more as our son-in-law," said Joseph.

"I can't wait for my name to be Jennifer Morris," declared the betrothed. "Dad, you need not worry about us breaking the cardinal sin of marriage. It will never happen. But as of tonight, and forever after, Jay will be sleeping with me in my room, now *our* room."

Though Jennifer had long since assumed control of the family, she respected her father's feelings enough to assure him.

Joseph grimaced but slowly nodded.

"You mean as of last night," interjected Carol. "Now I know why you didn't sleep in your room. You were spending some time in the garage, eh? Maybe to feed the cats?"

Everyone laughed.

"Jen is the first girlfriend I had in my entire life," Jay said.

"And she will be the last!" Jennifer exclaimed.

Again, the happy crowd chuckled.

"This family gave me everything," said Jay. "First, Adam arranged to put a roof over my head. Despite all the terrible things I did to him, he stayed with me. He is truly a disciple of the Lord. His goodness spreads to everyone. I'm afraid to look at him the wrong way, but I've always loved him. Joseph gave me a lifetime job and residence in his home, and he is the father I look up to. Carol gave me a mother's love. Mikaela was the rough-and-tumble brother I so wanted. She's not rough-and-tumble anymore and will never be again, but this sensitive and loving young woman is a superstar to me and everyone else. Jennifer was a sister I loved, and now she will be the best wife ever." He approached Jennifer and gave her a deep soul kiss.

All and sundry clapped until their hands ached.

CHAPTER 53

Loansharking

"Sarah, I have just one question for you," said Susan Clarke into the receiver. "Was it worth losing your total freedom to keep Adam?"

"Yes, Susan, I have seen the light. I'd do it a thousand times over. Shit, the women at the card games were right."

"Sarah, you are a far better woman than me."

"Susan, Adam treats me as a woman should be treated. He is my husband and the center of everything. We have a wonderful marriage."

She drank Kool-Aid. I always thought she was more intelligent. I honestly believe she is sexually aroused by being wholly controlled. It's such a sad situation. She won't admit it, but I'd wager my life that Adam physically abuses her. There is no possible way his ferocious temper hasn't resulted in domestic violence, Susan thought.

"But you love Mikaela more, right?"

'Yes, Susan, Mikaela is my soulmate. I love her more than any other person in my life. When the three of us are gone, we will all

427

be buried in the same plot. I will tell my children I want Mikaela on the bottom and me on top of her. And then Adam on the top."

"What a morbid thought. You are a young woman. Your life hasn't even started."

"You love Adam, too, right Susan?"

"Sarah, I like him. I don't love him. Mikaela, on the other hand, is someone I adore. Even that word does not express my love for that delicate flower, a heroine for our time."

"Please call me tomorrow, Susan. I have to cook supper for Adam. He's calling me. I love you!"

"Will talk soon, bestie!" answered Susan.

I was being far too generous by telling her I liked Adam. At best, I find that revolting chauvinist barely tolerable, and only because we shared a beautiful past. But at worst, I despise him. Sarah has a complicated life ahead of her, but this is what she wants, Susan thought.

***

"Jay, we haven't connected in a while. I'd love to spend some time with you, brother. Would you take a ride with me," asked Adam after dinner on a Saturday evening. "We'll be back well before the 9 o'clock card game."

"Perfect. Jen will be at The Point with her girlfriends so I can do it."

"Jay, I can't believe it. Do you need to get permission from your future wife? It would be best if you grew a pair. You don't have a chain around your ankles."

Jay laughed uneasily, knowing the alfa Jennifer would call the shots in their marriage.

"I know, brother; I idolize you, man!"

"Don't idolize me, Jay. Just follow my advice!"

Jay snickered.

"You run a tight ship, brother. Where are we going, Adam?"

"That's a secret," Adam said laughingly.

"Uh-oh," said Jay, privately nervous, knowing some of Adam's interests. "Well, let's roll."

Adam drove the Challenger south on Anderson Avenue.

"Adam, your arms got even more prominent. Are you taking steroids or something?"

"Fuck, no! What do you think I am, a Russian weightlifter?" exclaimed Adam, lighting a cigarette. "Help yourself, brother," he added, laying down the pack.

"Rob must have been impressed," said Jay, lighting up.

"He was, but he made the mistake of challenging me to a wrestling match on the living room floor. I annihilated him. After I held him in a headlock, he cried."

"Rob's a cool guy, but lately, he's always crying. Something is eating at him. Mom and Dad are concerned. But yeah, he's no match for you. He never exercises anymore, has a sit-down job, and has a few health issues, including diabetes. I can't believe how much weight he lost. Mom says he sometimes skips meals. The poor guy is a shell of what he once was."

"So true, brother," said Adam, dragging on his cigarette.

After they cut through Hudson County Park, they headed south on Park Avenue.

"Adam, I know you don't appreciate when people talk about Alejandro, and if I am violating your wishes, please forgive me. But since we are almost in West New York, I thought about him living here. I wanted to ask what you thought about him and his parents moving back to Poland."

"Jay, I heard the news from Sarah. His father, Jakob, called Sarah to say goodbye. Yolanda and her brother Alfredo used him as a fucking punching bag. Jakob said that Alfredo didn't want him to get too close to the kids Alejandro fathered. I understand he had a son and a daughter, born in consecutive years. They named the daughter after that bitch Rosa. Alfredo fucked him up so badly that his face was unrecognizable. He needed plastic surgery and barely survived the attack. Jakob also said that the West New York Police believed Alfredo when he told him that Alejandro had struck his kids. Yolanda told the police that her husband was always abusive. A friend of Yolanda's who knew the truth, and felt the need to pass it on, got word to Jakob and his wife that the fucking scum bag Alfredo was lying and that Alejandro adored his kids. A county judge with no conclusive evidence released Alejandro with a fine. The Wisniewskis and Alejandro packed up and moved back to Krakow. Jakob told Sarah they moved to America so their son could begin a new life, but instead, he was beaten and abused. I understand Alejandro cried hysterically for months, realizing he'd never see his kids again."

"That's one of the most tragic stories I've ever heard. And not because he was beaten to a pulp, but because he will never see his children ever again. The one child had his dead brother's name. I feel like I am going to cry, Adam. You loved him, didn't you?"

"Jay, I feel sorry for him, and what was done to him was a human catastrophe. I remember some beautiful times with him over several years. He was innocent and harmless, but by marrying Yolanda, he invited disaster. Still – and you might think I am cynical – I thought Alejandro was a user. Anyone who takes orders from their wife is an asshole. He needed to be the one in charge. He didn't think enough of us, even to make contact. And when he decided to forget English and embrace Spanish, he showed himself to be a reactionary, though, in his defense, he was desperate to find happiness after a life of tragedy. When he lost his brother in the boating accident, he was much too challenged to find happiness. Sometimes he was laughable, and I don't mean his use of broken English," said Adam, tossing his cigarette butt out the window and pulling into a parking space on 51st Street.

"You have me enthralled, Adam. So why do you say he was sometimes laughable?"

"When we met in Wildwood, and for at least two years afterward, he kept calling me Irish Jesus and thought God sent me down. What a crock of bullshit! I'm Catholic, too, but some of those Polish people have cult-like beliefs. I'm about as much of an Irish Jesus as Hitler was a German John the Baptist."

"Oh, Adam, you are too much. You've changed a lot, but you *were* an Irish Jesus and still *are* an Irish Jesus. You're just not a guy many people will want to tangle with."

"Jay, Irish Satan would be more accurate. And I resent being called Irish. Yes, I'm half-Irish, but my last name is Furano. I've become much prouder of my Italian side in the last few years. I was such a sickening momma's boy."

"Adam, as you should be. That jet-black straggly hair and cool dark goatee scream Italian, and everyone says you look more and more like Dad as you age. Your sisters are different. Mikaela looks all Irish, and Jennifer is an even blend. You hold the torch for Italy in your family."

"What does Dad say about that?" asked Adam, exhaling.

"I heard him tell Mom he is proud you look like him, but he is terrified of you, as you know."

"Jay, I would never lay a hand on him. I love my dad."

"Maybe we should go, Adam?"

"Yes, we need to. Oh, I forgot to show you this," said Adam, letting his cigarette dangle from his mouth and exposing his shin under his pants on his left side.

"Wow, Adam! That body art is cool!" exclaimed Jay, admiring a jumbo *Vive Italia* tattoo featuring the red, white, and green Italian flag.

"You like it?" asked Adam.

"It's awesome!" exclaimed Jay. "I am going to ask Jen if I can get a tattoo. I have a few in mind."

"If you weren't my brother, I'd put your lights out for saying that!" exclaimed Adam.

"Be cool, man. I didn't mean anything by it," answered Jay demurely.

After Adam impressed Jay with another tattoo he had engraved on his other leg – a horned Satan's head, with a cigarette dangling from its mouth – they disembarked and walked up the street to a six-floor building with a 677 address.

Adam rang the bell for apartment 506. In five seconds, the buzzer sounded, admitting them into the lobby.

"What are we here for, Adam? I never asked you."

"Brother, I need to pick up some cash. Somebody welched on a bet. A friend of Dave's thought I'd be a good choice to collect it."

Jay was mortified.

"Geez, Adam, You think we'll make it out alive?"

"Fuck, Jay, grow a pair! Please leave it to me. Just stand and watch!"

"Your wish is my command," said Jay.

They boarded an elevator to the fifth floor. Adam pushed the doorbell to 506, further identified by a white rectangular nametag that read, 'Eduardo Rivera.'

A bespeckled middle-aged man with salt and pepper hair, dressed in a plaid button-up shirt and blue dungarees, partially opened the door, which was flimsily secured with a chain. Adam spoke.

"I'm here to collect the two thousand dollars you owe."

"I don't have it," Rivera answered in clear English. "Go away!"

"Open the door, or I'll break your fucking legs!" yelled Adam.

Jay looked at his brother disbelievingly as his heart raced.

"Please, good man, I'm sorry, I'll get the money soon. Come back next week."

"I'll ask you again, but this will be the last time. Open the fucking door!" Adam exclaimed.

The terrified man disengaged the chain lock, his hands trembling. Adam pushed the door open and entered with Jay in tow.

"Please don't hurt me," Rivera pleaded cryingly.

"Why shouldn't I fucking hurt you? You were given four weeks to come up with the cash. You expect to get paid on the spot when you win, right?"

"The Cowboys scored in the last minute!" Rivera explained. "I should have won the bet!"

"I was told you lost a parlay. So you lost both ends of the bet, not just the one involving the Cowboys."

"Please," said Rivera, looking at Adam's muscled arms. "I send money to my parents in Cuba. My sister is there too, and she's been sick. I don't have any money, but I will borrow some this week."

"You won't borrow shit!" exclaimed Adam. "You're a degenerate gambler. Don't you think I know that? Stop telling me fucking lies!"

"I'm telling you the truth," said Rivera.

"Look, I don't have time for this fucking shit. I'll give you one minute, and then I'm going to break all your fingers, one by one," Adam announced, flexing his hand aggressively.

Rivera broke down hysterically and pleaded. "Please don't hurt me. I beg you."

Jay stared at Adam and thought how inconceivable it was that such a non-violent, timid boy who loved everyone growing up could threaten such grisly violence against another person and ignore the man's plea for clemency.

"I'm a Catholic. I go to mass at St. Joseph's Church a few blocks away."

"I know that church well," said Adam, remembering that Yolanda and Alejandro married there. Rivera had finally reached Adam's heart.

"How much do you have?" asked Adam.

"I'll give you one thousand. I'll have the other thousand next week."

Adam nodded. Rivera reached into his pocket, pulled out ten Franklins, and handed them to Adam.

"Come back next week, and I'll have the rest," Rivera added.

Adam considered shaking the man's hand but decided against it, thinking it showed weakness. Compulsive gamblers didn't deserve friendly gestures. He turned and left, followed by Jay.

When they got to the car, Adam flicked a lighter on Jay's Marlboro, then his own. He didn't immediately engage the ignition.

"Adam, I just can't believe what I just witnessed, man." When Adam didn't respond, he turned to see tears streaming down his brother's face.

Adam leaned over and rested his head on Jay's chest. Jay petted his brother's hair.

"Jay, I was going to hurt that guy seriously. What have I become, brother?"

"Brother, you are just as great a person as you always were. I think you proved tonight that compassion has to be earned. I love you, brother," said Jay, kissing Adam's cheek.

"But if you do plan on killing someone, please don't give me a thought. Remember, I saved you from drowning in the lake and baking in the clothes dryer during those long-ago days when I was stronger than you."

Both brothers broke out into hysterical laughter. Adam pulled away, driving west to Bergenline Avenue, where he made a right.

"Next stop is Garfield," said Adam. "I promised Brian I would

434

pick him up. He's sleeping by us tonight. He told me he has an announcement to make."

"Sounds exciting," said Jay. "Did he get someone pregnant?"

"No way," said Adam. "Since the living room is no longer occupied, I thought I'd have him sleep there. We haven't set up the extra room yet. Since we'll already be there for the game – and it will last till after midnight – it makes sense for him to go there. Otherwise, he won't see us. The couch at 76 Grant is softer. He could stay by us, but I will recommend he sleep by you for this one time."

"Nice, Adam. Brian's a fantastic teenager. All the kids adore him. Mom and Dad love him too, though Dad puckers his lips at his smoking."

"Yeah, that's Dad. He broke my balls for two years after I started, but I ignored him," said Adam, tossing his butt out the window.

CHAPTER 54

Picking Up Brian

Minutes later, they arrived at the Outwater Lane residence.

"Hey, man!" said Jay. "Where the hell have you been?"

"Oh, Jay, there's always something going on around here, and it's not all that good," the teen said, lighting a cigarette.

"Did anyone touch you," asked Adam.

"No, Adam. Even if he did, I wouldn't tell you anymore. It would be best if you didn't lose your job over me. Fuck, man, you'd be arrested for murder. And Bergen Tech would lose the best teacher they've ever had."

"You got that right, Brian!" said Adam. "I would be arrested for murder. As far as me being the best teacher, that's nonsense."

"My stepdad is bipolar. I am getting tired of always seeing him ordering my mom around."

"Brian, I despised your stepdad when I found out he abused you. But I don't blame him for being a proper husband. He's supposed to give orders to his wife, and your mom needs to honor them. If it weren't for him abusing you, I'd say his mind is in the right place."

437

Brian and Jay squinted at each other, shaking their heads.

"Brian, aside from the home problems, do you like Garfield?" asked Jay.

"Jay, to be honest, I hate it. It's only good if you like banquet halls and train tracks. The people who live here are so fucking stupid."

One day, you'll have to give me a tour," said Jay. "You should still give the wedding couples a break."

Brian scowled.

As they rode up Bergenline Avenue, Jay noticed political signs in what seemed to be every other storefront window.

"Boy, in this town, they play politics all year round. I thought everything was supposed to end in November. Now, they have some primary elections.

"Our town is mostly Democratic," said Brian. "But I always hear people arguing in the eating places."

"We're Democratic too," said Jay.

"Speak for yourself, Jay," said Adam.

"You were always Democratic as far as I remember, but then again, you and I hardly ever talked politics."

"Mom and Dad are Democrats, and I used to be, but now I'm a staunch Republican. I'll never vote for a Democrat ever again. That party is a bunch of snowflakes. Ronald Reagan is the best thing that ever happened to this country," said Adam.

"What does Sarah say? I thought she was this big liberal Democrat."

"Not anymore, Jay. She's like me now. She votes Republican, and she's become a conservative. She's the first district Republican county committeewoman in town. She had a meeting with other committee people at the home of a man named Eugene Fagnano on Park Avenue. Sarah said he's one of the nicest guys she's ever met and once served as a councilman."

438

"You twisted her arm!" said Jay laughingly. "Jennifer and Mikaela are Democrats. Jen voted for Walter Mondale. That was her first election."

"Yeah, so did Mom and Dad. I tried to convince them to vote for Reagan and nearly did, but no matter. Mondale and Ferraro got crushed," Adam said, clenching his fist and pumping it in the air. "Imagine them running a woman for vice president? And a whacky liberal woman to boot! Women need to know their place. Yeah, I know my sisters are die-hard Democrats. They'll come to their senses one day, like Sarah has. My father-in-law agrees with me. He's a big Republican, like all his Wall Street buddies. Susan gave Sarah a hard time for becoming a Republican, but Sarah held her ground. Susan doesn't care for me anymore, but how about asking me if I give a fuck. I don't care for her, either. She's this big campus liberal activist."

"Do you give a fuck?" asked Jay, laughing.

Adam snickered.

Brian thought.

He's such a male chauvinist pig and a budding misogynist. He's a mirror image of my stepdad. From what I remember about my real dad, he was the same way. I love Adam. He's brilliant and the most important man in my life, but he has the same issues as many guys I know. I haven't seen it, but I'm sure he physically abuses Sarah. He has a ferocious temper. It goes with the turf. All my role models have the same qualities. Adam is more intelligent; that's the only difference. If I see him touch Sarah, I will put his lights out. He's tough, but I'm tougher. I hope it doesn't come to that.

"What about Rob?" asked Jay. "I don't recall discussing politics with him."

"Rob is a wimp. He's not the man I thought he was. He does all the feminine chores around the house. Since I destroyed him in the living room, he has always sounded nervous when talking with me, even though I apologized and we took a ride."

"Yeah, I witnessed that mauling. You made him cry and broke Stevie's heart. But Rob is a sweet guy."

"Jay, I love him, but he needs to be more responsible. He lives with us to serve Mom and Dad. When we first met at Bergen Community College, I thought he was this rugged athlete. I think it was all for the show. After Maureen broke up with him, he never dated again."

"Do you think he is gay?" asked Brian.

"I am not sure, but I don't think so," said Adam. "Something is happening with him, but I try not to pry. Mom says he cries a lot. She often wakes up in the middle of the night to get water, and she hears his sobs. The same happened with Mikaela."

"And someone else I know," said Jay.

Adam shot him an angry look. Jay quickly diverted.

"Adam, speaking of crying, what was the name of that Swedish movie you used to talk about years ago? It was cries and something. It came out in the early 1970s, shortly after you and Sarah married."

Adam smiled. "*Cries and Whispers* by Ingmar Bergman. It is one of the most depressing movies ever made but undeniably brilliant. The use of red in that film made one think they were seeing what the soul looks like, and viewers were treated to four electrifying performances, especially the one by Harriet Anderson as the cancer-stricken Agnes. I'd say it was one of Bergman's most powerful and emotional films, and the use of Bach was sublime."

This is the Adam I love the most. He's a real Jekyll & Hyde. He's articulate, intelligent, and a deep thinker. The other side of him is often cruel, ignorant, and bigoted, and he's an alcoholic and substance abuser. Adam is one of the most complex people, thought Jay.

"Adam, you have no idea how brilliant you are," said Brian. "You are my idol. I love you, man."

Adam stretched his right arm over the front seat, where Brian embraced it. "You know where you stand with me," he said. "There were also specters in the film, which makes me think of Roy Orbison's song, *Crying*, with its ghostly chorus."

"That song is awesome!" exclaimed Brian. "And Don McLean's remake is almost as good."

"Don't get Adam started on Don McLean," said Jay. "*American Pie* and Vincent are still among his favorite songs."

"They are," said Adam. "But I like this much more," he added, pressing the start button on his cassette deck.

Iron Maiden's *Run to the Hills* from the heavy metal band's *The Number of the Beast* album blared through the car's speakers.

"Yeah, man," exclaimed Brian.

Adam raised the volume, lit a cigarette, and sang the lyrics in his gravely baritone.

Jay and Brian moved their hands in a drum-like fashion.

"This group is fucking tremendous!" exclaimed Adam. But his anger management issues intruded on the musical bliss. At a light near Ed Fricke's Seafood Restaurant on the Hendrix Causeway in Ridgefield Park, Adam saw a driver behind him give him the finger for stopping at a yellow signal near train tracks.

"What the fuck!" yelled Adam, jumping out of the Challenger.

He confronted the driver at the other car's window. The man was terrified to see the bodybuilder approaching.

"Get the fuck out of the car right now!" Adam yelled.

"I'm sorry, sir. I didn't mean anything. Please accept my apology."

Adam noticed the driver's wife and young son were crying. He scowled, turned around, and returned to his vehicle.

"C'mon man," said Jay. "This isn't cool, Adam."

441

Adam cocked his arm back and smashed his brother in the nose. Blood flowed over Jay's lips and chin, causing him to cup his hands over his face and sob.

"When I need your fucking advice, I'll ask for it!" exclaimed Adam. "Brian, there is a roll of paper towels under your seat. Please help Jay."

Brian wiped the blood and, with another towel, pressed on Jay's nose.

"Sit up straight," said Brian, a veteran of bloody noses. "Jay, if you don't stop crying, I will give you a real reason to."

Jay softly whimpered.

"Brian, maybe he should tilt his head back," said Adam.

"Adam, that's not a good idea. Blood might run down his throat, which could cause him to swallow it. Then he could vomit."

Brian reached over, pinched the soft part of Jay's nose, and held it shut for the rest of the ride home.

"Don't move," Brian said.

A few times, Jay looked at Adam, teary-eyed and saddened at his brother's misplaced anger and penchant for violence and thought:

After what I did to him when we were teenagers, I deserved it. The shoe is on the other foot now. I bet more will be headed my way. And I better not get Brian mad at me. That strongman is scary.

When they disembarked on Grant Street, Adam apologized. Jay told everyone he had picked his nose too deep.

CHAPTER 55

Card Game

The family convened at 76 Grant Street.

"Hey, Brian," said Sarah. "We always consider it a treat to see you, young man."

"The honor is mine, dear lady," said Brian, kissing his host.

"Mikaela made lasagna. She's never done it, but I think it will be out of this world."

"I used extra ricotta, ample wine, and chunky chopped meat and made the layers firm. I fashioned the sauce from scratch," said Mikaela.

Brian followed the voice to the oven, where Mikaela, clad in an apron, was checking the progress.

"Hi, Mikaela. I haven't seen you in a long time. You are so beautiful," said Brian, embracing the chef. He picked her up a foot off the floor and set her down.

Michaela twinkled. "Young man, I know you love German food, so I will learn to make sauerbraten for you. I have a reliable recipe."

"Wow, Mikaela. I haven't had good sauerbraten in years. You are my Julia Childs."

"Oh Brian, I'm more like the grill girl at the White Manna," re-

443

ferring to the fast-food hamburger joint on Hackensack Avenue about a mile south of Bergen Tech High School.

"I need to see all those adorable kids. Are they where they usually are?"

"The toddlers are with my parents tonight," said Sarah. "But the other five are downstairs. Saoirse is playing Stratego with Jimbo, but I'm sure she and the others will go wild when they see you. They always ask about you. I hope they don't make you prisoner to a Clue marathon."

"I can't wait," said Brian, descending the stairs. "I still can't believe you have seven kids!"

Carol asked Mikaela to hang in her room so that she could introduce her to the women. When her twelve lady friends sat, the Furano matriarch summoned Jennifer to take her place at the table. Jay sat on a couch. Joseph chatted in the kitchen with a progressively frail, practically immobile Grandma Delaney.

"Ladies, I want to introduce my beautiful daughter Mikaela, whom you also know as a heroine and celebrity on a television show," said Carol. "Mikaela canceled her surgeries and isn't sure when she will reschedule them. She made lasagna, a seafood salad, and cold-cut platters for us tonight," she added as Mikaela appeared at the front of the table near the kitchen opening.

Everyone clapped. There were uniform smiles, though most hid their true feelings, including Cheryl:

He's the ultimate sissy and should be in a mental health facility. So what if he's beautiful; he'll never be a real woman. My husband despises trannies, and so do I! He changed himself from a hunk to this revolting creature. I can't even repeat what my husband said about him after the television show. Carol should be ashamed she is the mother of a freak instead of boasting about him. I heard he canceled his operation, but it's only a matter of time before he does it.

"You have two beautiful daughters, Carol," said Joanne.

"Yes, I do," said Carol. "And I am proud of them both."

Mikaela took her place at the table. A few women complimented her on her perfume. Jay, Rob, and Brian sat on the furniture chatting.

"My husband's here!" exclaimed Sarah. All eyes were peeled on the goateed, muscular-armed Adam. Adonis had just entered the room for some, and they each hoped he noticed them. The women were pleased when Sarah forfeited her seat to him because they realized he would be playing. Heading to the refrigerator, Adam nonchalantly announced that Brian would sleep on the couch tonight. When he discovered there wasn't any beer in the fridge, Adam yelled, "Where is the fucking beer?" After he saw his dad scowl, he added:

"Does anyone in the house have a fucking problem with that?" as he smashed his fist through the sheetrock of the wall behind him.

This unexpected but welcome affirmation of male authority captivated the women.

Sarah rushed over to be sure Adam's hand wasn't hurt.

"Let me see your hand, sweetie."

Joseph was shaking. "Nobody has a problem, Adam. We are all happy."

"Fucking A, you better be happy!" Adam exclaimed.

Joseph retreated to his room and convulsed on the bed. Mikaela followed him.

Adam returned empty-handed from the refrigerator and sat, but a minute later, he spoke again.

"Sarah, we need beer!" he exclaimed.

"Don't worry, sweetie. I will rush over to Orlando's to get some six-packs."

"Adam, I will go," said Jay.

"No, Jay, sit down! This is a wife's job. Sarah will get them!"

Again, the women smiled approvingly.

Sarah returned from Orlando's with four six-packs.

"Would any of you lovely ladies be interested in joining me for a brewski?" Adam asked.

Sandra raised her hand immediately, but six others nodded shortly after. The women loved watching Adam chain-smoke and down one can after another. The young man was even more talkative than Mikaela when she attended the games as Mikey.

"Holy shit, Sandy!" you fucking aced it," Adam exclaimed after the woman pulled four aces.

The woman smiled broadly.

***

"Mikaela, I can't take him anymore. I hate him. I never liked him. He's always been as phony as the day is long. Now, we see him for what he is. He's a vulgar creep. If only Father McTague knew what he turned into. He's a terrible husband and father."

"Dad, he's a Republican as well," said Mikaela, wearing a crooked smile. "But you know you love him. He's a fantastic teacher and a good husband."

She sat beside her dad, caressing him.

"Yes, he's a good teacher. His students love him. Dr. Grieco likes him. But he doesn't act like a teacher when he's not in the classroom. He drinks and smokes dope, he's violent, and he treats his wife like shit. He's more vulgar than a truck driver and makes friends with some of his students. I love the kid Brian, but your brother is a bad influence. I suspect Adam's doing other bad things with his friend Dave. He wants to control everything. Jay and Rob are petrified of him."

"Dad, he's your son and my brother. He is who he is, the same way I am who I am. I'll always love him. Sarah loves him."

"Yeah, and Sarah loves you far more than she loves him! Who

wouldn't, honey?"

"Dad, Sarah loves both of us. She'll never abandon Adam."

"Why did he have to punch a hole in the wall? We all know he's strong. Why does he have to show off?"

"Dad, anyone can punch a hole in sheet rock. You don't have to be strong. What he did was an expression of his anger. He'll get it fixed. And as far as showing his strength, who can blame him? He was told he was a wimp endless times growing up. He turned the tables on everyone, and he's boasting."

"He did this in front of everyone. He embarrassed me in front of Brian and all those women."

"Dad, please look at me. He loves you, Dad. He loves you. He has always loved you. He is proud of his black hair and looks like you after years of appearing more like Mom. He had an Italian tattoo etched on his leg and 'I Love Italy' bumper stickers affixed to his car. He loves you, Dad. Did you forget when he slept next to your bed for a week after you had the heart attack that I caused?"

"I know he does; I know he does," said Joseph, his voice breaking. "I didn't forget him sleeping near my bed."

"Dad, Adam told me months ago that he hates shepherd's pie. He said it was a silly adolescent fetish. He says lasagna and chicken parmigiana are his favorite foods. He said zeppole are his favorite desert. Adam is his Italian father's son."

Joseph cried happy tears.

"Mikaela, the only good zeppole are the ones from the feast," he said.

They both chuckled.

***

After a few more hands, the guests were instructed to help themselves with the food on the kitchen table.

The lasagna was a huge hit. A few of the women asked about the recipe.

"You have talent, girl," said Joanne. "I've never had a more delicious example!"

"Everything is awesome," said Shirley. "That was the best seafood salad I ever ate."

Though Adam handled alcohol well after years of drinking, he began to feel the effects of his overindulgence. He summoned Sarah to sit on his lap while he played.

Again, the women were amazed over another macho act that affirmed Adam's controlling nature. When Adam won two hands in a row, Joanne jokingly asked if he had plans for the money.

"I've been looking at bikes. I've had my eye on a Harley," said Adam. "But someone in Cliffside is selling a Blue Softail. I may pull the trigger over the next two weeks. After I get it, would any of you ladies be interested in taking a ride with me?"

The women were turned on by his flirtatious behavior.

"I can see most of you are," he added, taking a drag on his cigarette. "I'll get some phone numbers from my mom."

This guy is a red-blooded dreamboat. Sarah is so fucking lucky. I wish I had sat on his lap. And now we learn he's into bikes. Please let me be one of the ones he calls. I love the way he flaunts those tattoos. The alligator one is so badass! This guy must be a monster in bed. I never catch a break. I love how he orders his wife around and how she happily obeys him, thought Shirley.

Adam rose and winked at Sandra. She followed him to the backyard, where they shared a joint.

"I told my husband about you," Sandra said. "He is begging to meet you."

"We'll get together. I promise," said Adam.

"You and my husband would be a perfect match."

"I'm sure," Adam said. "I'll give you a holler."

The game lasted until 1:30 a.m. By then, Brian was asleep, and Jay had long since retreated to Jennifer's room, where he conked

448

out with his arms around his fiancé. A half-hour before, Sarah and Mikaela carried the kids – except for Saoirse, who slept on the basement couch across from Jimbo's room – from Rob's apartment to their bedrooms in their new house. The soulmates retired to their bedroom, where they made love and shared endearments, telling each other there was no other person they loved more in the world. As agreed, Adam would sleep alone in his bedroom every night, except when he desired to be intimate, roughly around once every ten days. Sarah bestowed her affection for Adam in their living room and when attending to him during the daytime on weekends when they were together.

A drunken Adam kissed every woman as they left before crashing on his bed in his new home, yards away.

Only Jimbo, immersed in his Bible reading, was still awake the night before his off day at work.

CHAPTER 56

Brian's Announcement

"I understand you want to make an announcement, sweetie. Is that right?" asked Carol. "Announcements happen regularly in this household."

"Yes, dear lady," said Brian. "I would appreciate it if everyone heard what I said."

"I fear you will tell us you will be moving out of state," said Carol.

"I may move, but I assure you it won't be out of state."

"Young man, I'm relieved to hear it. All of us have grown fond of you. My husband brings you up a lot," said Carol, placing a dish of pancakes in front of the teen. "Butter and syrup?"

"You know me well, kind lady."

"You still like your coffee dark with sugar?"

"Right again," said Brian, grinning.

Carol poured Tropicana orange juice into a glass, carrying it and the coffee to the table.

"I know you also like grapefruit juice, but this family isn't the biggest fan."

451

"Carol, my mom and stepdad don't like it either. They say it is too bitter."

"Only Adam likes it," said Carol.

Brian smiled. "I'm happy to hear my idol likes something else I do."

"You like my son a lot, don't you?"

"I do. He is far from perfect, but he's impacted my life positively. He's the best teacher ever, and he'd do anything for anybody," Brian said, working on his pancakes.

"Adam was that way his entire life. He's changed, but as far as his kindness, he would never deny anyone, as you say."

"Adam is complex. Over the two years I have known him, I could never predict what he would do next. He's an original."

"Young man, you could not have described him any better. And he became a Republican, too!"

They both guffawed.

"I'm a liberal Democrat," said Brian. "My mom and my stepdad are the same as Adam. But I told him I agreed with him. I love him, but I fear him. He's also afraid of me and is certain if we ever fought, I would crush him."

"All of our family fears him, sweetie. Nobody knows when that terrible temper of his will surface. If only you knew how he was as a teenager. You would insist this had to be two different people."

"Kind lady, I heard all the stories. I do find it unbelievable," Brian said, lighting a cigarette.

"Don't assume your political views won't change, either. One day, you might embrace Adam's positions."

"I think you are right, Carol. I can't be sure."

"Saoirse, sweet girl, would you please go next door and tell your mom to rouse everyone?" asked Carol. "Brian wants to make an announcement and wants the family to hear it."

"I love you, Brian Fischer," said Saoirse.

After the boy kissed her, the girl happily left the house and opened the front door of her new home.

The family gathered around the kitchen table. Brian quickly got to the point.

"I recently told my mom and stepdad I wanted to live independently. I've been out of high school for several years now. I've worked as a busboy at the Cameo banquet hall. I reminded my mom and dad how much I loved them but politely alluded to the problems living in their home. My dad is bipolar, and he drinks heavily. If I stay there, I will put him in the hospital. His abuse is psychological. I haven't found a place to live yet."

The Furanos looked at each other. Their austere expressions turned to smiles. Joseph spoke.

"Young man, welcome to our home. We are all overjoyed. Saoirse's old room downstairs is yours. Sarah, Mikaela, and Adam also have room for you next door, but I will not surrender you. Carol and I want you here. You'll see Adam and all the others every day. But you are sleeping here. You belong to us!"

Many laughs and hugging followed Joseph's touching acceptance of Brian into their home.

"Fuck, Dad, I never knew you were so devious!" exclaimed Adam. "He was *my* student!"

"Maybe so, Adam. But he's *my* son forever!"

Joseph's response to Adam made Carol cry.

Saoirse and the twin girls clapped and jumped up and down. The twin boys hooted.

"Remember, anyone wanting to spend time with him must ask my permission," Saoirse said. "But don't hold your breath. He's too cute for me to give up! And what a hunk!"

Chortling ensued.

CHAPTER 57

Susan Visits New Home

At Sarah's invitation, Susan Clarke first appeared at 74 Grant Street a week after Brian moved into 76 Grant Street. She walked down the hall to the kitchen and noticed Adam drinking a can of beer on the living room couch out of the corner of her eye. She thought.

Today I will confront that piece of shit. I've heard twice from Mikaela that he's used his hands on my beloved Sarah.

"Girl, you are prettier and prettier every time I see you," said Susan, kissing Sarah's soulmate.

"Thank you, Susan," said Mikaela laughingly. "But you see me almost every day. Anyway, I have a long way to go to match your beauty inside and out."

Hearts appeared in Susan's pupils.

Sitting on a chair beside Sarah, Mikaela leaned over and rested her head on her lover's chest.

After coffee and biscuits, Sarah and Mikaela led Susan on a house tour. They sat on lounge chairs in the second-floor extra room.

"You have so much room and two floors! The house is enormous. Bless your dad, Sarah. He's another in your sphere who should be canonized."

"Susan, sometimes, I think my dad's primary role in life was to help those in need. Mom said he saved and made some brilliant investments after they married, but he played it tight to the vest with spending. They both wanted a larger family, but Mom had difficulty conceiving. Dad sees all my children as his own, literally and in terms of financial support. He's paid for so many things and will pay for more, but this house is undoubtedly the gift of gifts."

"He's wild for Mikaela," Susan said.

"You had to be there to see how he acted when she left for the Aruba trip. Both he and my father-in-law acted like she was moving to China. They blubbered endlessly."

"That's my girl," said Susan, beaming. "The biggest sin I ever committed in my life was grossly misreading you back in the day when you disguised yourself as a boy, and a macho one at that. Adam registered for my classes only to establish a friendship that would lead me to you. You'd be the pride of any family, but to the Furanos, you are the eternal beacon of joy."

"Oh, Susan, you overrate me. I am far from perfect, but I am confident I learned from my evil deeds. Thank you for your steadfast kindness and all you've done for me at the school."

"Speaking of school, sweetie, Virginia Vessels told me you are the best student she's ever taught."

"Professor Vessels lectures from bell to bell," said Mikaela. "I'm surprised she acknowledged my contributions."

"She might be referring to your test grades."

"Adam told me he took Age of Chaucer as well."

"And what did he say about her?" asked Susan.

"He said she was a bore, and her class was torturous. But Adam was never a big Chaucer fan. The Bard was always his guy."

"I have very few good things to say about Adam, but at least he has some good taste in literature, his disdain for the Father of English Literature aside."

"Susan, I always find it interesting that Shakespeare and Chaucer used unoriginal stories that often originated in foreign lands, especially Italy and Greece."

"An excellent critical observation, my girl. That was a direct outcome of the Renaissance. Changing the subject, Sarah, I apologize for not asking you sooner. How is your dad's health?"

"Susan, it was a miracle. The prostate cancer never returned."

"Praise the Lord! His goodness was rewarded!"

The three women returned to the kitchen.

"Red or white, Susan?"

"Ah, Sarah, you know my weakness too well. I'll be able to get away with one glass. White, please."

After setting the glass in front of the visitor, Sarah fixed a rum and Coke and a Malibu Bay Breeze.

"My girl has a new favorite drink," said Susan , referring to the latter cocktail favored by Mikaela.

"I developed my love for it in Aruba," said Mikaela, lighting a cigarette.

"I am averse to pineapple juice, but if it's made with coconut, I'm fine with it," said Susan, lighting up.

"Next time, I'll take you to Rob's apartment," said Sarah.

"How is that sweetie doing? He's been through so much."

"He is happy Stevie will spend some nights with him. The boy will keep an eye on Rob."

"Depression is difficult, sometimes impossible to conquer," said Susan.

"You said it perfectly," said Sarah.

"I'd like to speak to Adam briefly. I won't be long," Susan said.

"Of course," said Sarah. "Mikaela baked a carrot cake. It will be ready when you return."

"Fantastic! That's my favorite!"

"Don't you think Mikaela knew that?"

Susan smiled broadly.

***

Susan plopped on the loveseat across from the couch where Adam sat.

"Would it be right to say we don't like each other?" she asked Adam.

"That is correct," answered Adam bluntly. "You are my wife's friend and my sister Mikaela's friend. The less I see you, the better."

"Thanks for being honest," said Susan.

"I don't think I ever liked you. You were too bossy and meddled in business that wasn't yours to meddle in, and I'm not fond of your worldview and politics. Worst of all, you tried to bring out some feminine side of me I wanted erased. You are a devious woman. You thought you knew everything when you tried to interfere with my teaching methods, and I proved you wrong."

"You are a great teacher, Adam Furano. You are an inspiration to your students. Nobody can ever take that away from you. And you did it on your own. Your unorthodox method was a long shot, but you made it work. I could never match your popularity. I admire you for it."

"Fucking A," said Adam.

"But that's the only thing I admire you for. You have plenty of issues as a person. To begin with, you are a male chauvinist pig."

"I am not a male chauvinist. I believe the man is the rightful leader of the family. I am in love with my wife and adore my daughters, mom, and sisters. You are a radical feminist. I think all liberals are delusional," said Adam, taking a deep drag on his cigarette.

"And your wife is deeply in love with you as well," said Susan. "As Lou Gehrig said, you were the luckiest man on the face of the Earth when you married her. Sarah told Mikaela and me that she loves you much more as the person you are now than the way you were. She is the most incredible person I've ever known. She and Mikaela are my two best girlfriends. You don't deserve Sarah. But before I go back inside, I want to tell you one more thing," added Susan, rising from her seat and approaching Adam. "If I hear that you've hit her again, or if you ever touch Mikaela, I will cut your balls off. Did you hear me, Adam Furano?"

Adam looked Susan in the eyes and said, "I heard you, Susan."

Watching him fight back tears, she left triumphantly.

CHAPTER 58

Adam's Castle

Sometime after seven on a Thursday evening in October, Adam was laughing up a storm while smoking and drinking a Bud on the living room couch. WPIX was staging a *Munster's* marathon, the black-and-white sitcom about a family of immigrants from Transylvania who believe they are perfectly normal. At the same time, they think weirdos populate the rest of the world. One of Adam's favorite episodes, *Herman the Rookie*, shows the Frankenstein dad being offered a position on the Dodgers baseball team.

Sarah, who had long since resigned from her position in the Cliffside Park school system to concentrate on being a mother and housewife, was toiling away at the kitchen table smoking and grading nearly 120 vocabulary tests, a task Adam had assigned her at the beginning of the school year. Adam had long considered grading papers a bore, and he happily turned over the answer key to his wife so he could relax and enjoy the time and evenings in the house when he wasn't working out at the gym or hanging out with Dave. Mikaela helped Sarah with cooking, vacuuming, and

461

general maintenance, although she needed time to read for her college classes.

"Adam, sweetie, a girl named Sharon Pizzolo managed to get every answer wrong. As I recall, she got some answers right in previous weeks."

"Sharon has some family issues. Her parents are divorced, and she doesn't like living with her mom. She's a nice girl, but academically, she's dire."

"So sad," said Sarah.

Stevie, an academically gifted first-grader, opened the front door. He was followed by his twin, Joey, a boy who appeared likely to excel in sports. They had just finished having their Chicken Delight dinner with Rob. The man made sure to include mashed potatoes and vegetables with the pail of fried breasts, wings, and legs. Though Joey continued up the stairs to his bedroom, Stevie paused when he heard loud laughter. He sat on the couch and cuddled against his uncle. Adam took a final deep drag on his cigarette, exhaled upward, and extinguished it.

"Uncle Adam, do you know who my favorite character on *The Munsters* is?"

"Here we go again," said Sarah from the kitchen. "The Furanos are eternal rankers."

"Let me guess. Eddie Munster?" asked Adam.

"Uncle Adam, how did you know?"

"Little man, it makes sense. Eddie is the closest to your age, and you see him as someone you would like to be."

"Exactly, Uncle Adam. You are so smart!"

Adam and Sarah laughed simultaneously.

"But Herman isn't chopped liver, right?" asked Adam.

Stevie understood the expression.

"How could I not love Herman and Grandpa? They are icons!"

"Stevie, one day you will sit on top of the world," said Adam, incredulous at the boy's use of such a word.

The affectionate boy leaned over and kissed his uncle. Adam picked up Stevie and cradled him.

"I love Marilyn, too. She's so pretty, but nothing like my dad."

Adam decided it was time to confront Stevie's perception of Mikaela once and for all. Mikaela reasoned the boys would learn the truth in their late teens, but growing up, Adam was repulsed by the idea of children calling a woman their dad. He was progressive on the matter of a man having a sex change, feeling such a person was never a man in the first place. But to call a woman by a masculine title was unacceptable. He thought it would corrupt the mind of a child.

"Steven, is the person you keep calling your dad a man?"

"No, she's a woman."

"Do you think it is right to call a woman your dad?"

"Uncle Adam, since my earliest memories, she has been my dad."

"Stevie, I'm going to ask you the same question again. Is Mikaela a boy?"

"No, she's a girl."

"Yes, she is a girl. Now, what gender are mothers? Male or female?"

"Female."

"And what genders are fathers?"

"Male."

"Is it possible for a woman to be your father?"

"Uncle Adam, it is possible. My dad used to be a boy. He and my mom did it together, so no matter what gender he is now, he was a male nine months before Joey and I were born. He was technically a male when little Mikey and little Adam were conceived. My dad is a happy woman now, but she is still my dad. I am so glad that both my parents are women. My brothers and I are so lucky."

"Stevie, you won't have to learn about the birds and the bees in a few years."

"Uncle Adam, I learned about many of them in science. My favorite bird is the cardinal."

Sarah burst out laughing.

"Stevie, your answer is classic," said Adam. "You have a bright future ahead of you, young man."

"Thanks, Uncle Adam. Can I ask why you are sometimes mean and nasty to people? And why do you always curse and order Mom around?"

"Stevie, it's time for you to go to your room. You have school tomorrow," said Sarah, mortified at the boy's questions.

"No, Sarah. He will stay here. I want to answer his questions. I'll decide when he's ready for bed."

"Of course, sweetie," said Sarah.

"Sarah, I need another beer," said Adam.

Sarah brought her husband a Bud. "Would you like pretzels, sweetie?"

"Not for myself, but maybe for Stevie. He may want a soft drink, too."

"Yes to both," said Stevie.

Sarah brought a glass of lemonade and a bowl of jumbo sourdough pretzels, Stevie's favorite.

Adam pulled the tab off his can, took a swig, and lit a cigarette.

"Stevie, curse words are part of my personality. That's the way I talk. I hope you don't talk that way until you are much older. I'm sorry, but I am nasty and mean sometimes, and that is also part of who I am. I try to tone down those bad qualities, but sometimes I can't help myself. I am who I am, little guy."

"Were you always that way?"

"Stevie, I wasn't always that way. Many told me I used to spread positive energy. I tried to help people and derived pleasure when others were happy. But my eyes were opened when some people in our family, including your mother, tried to force me to become someone I was not. I was weak and couldn't fight back. One day, when you are older, I will tell you about your uncle's teenage years."

"I don't believe you were ever weak. You are the strongest man I have ever seen. You are even stronger than Uncle Rob."

"Yes, I am much stronger than your Uncle Rob. Years ago, I wasn't. He was a star football player when he was young. He's lost so much weight. But I am not the strongest man. Brian is stronger than me. I'm number 2. Now you asked why I give orders. I give them because I am supposed to give them. Your mom, Sarah, is my wife and a woman. Her job is to cook, clean, maintain our home, go shopping, and attend to all of her children. I am the husband and the head of the family. I am the breadwinner. I make all the decisions about our family's welfare. Nothing can be done without my agreement. I love your mom, but she needs to understand, and she does, that the husband orchestrates everything. When you get older, you'll understand, and like so many other men, I think you'll agree with me."

Sitting in the kitchen, Sarah nodded and thought.

I was far too liberal for years. What Adam says is entirely accurate. I used to poke fun at the card players for their subservience to their husbands, but they understood the correct and safest family dynamic. I am not a conservative, but when it comes to this, I am. I belong to my legal husband and must honor my role in this marriage. Some women oppose this concept, but I think it leads to chaos and marital discord.

"I understand, Uncle Adam. You always make so much sense. I think that's the way every family should be. I forgot about Brian. Yes, he is the strongest man I ever met. Uncle Adam, I didn't un-

465

derstand one word. What does breadwinner mean?"

"Of course, Stevie. That's tough for a second-grader, even someone as bright as you. A breadwinner is the person in the family who earns the money."

"But Uncle Adam, Grandpa Steve has way more than us. If you didn't make money, he'd help us. He gave us this house."

"Little guy, you know everything," said Adam, finishing his Bud. "I am the breadwinner in our everyday life, but what I earn doesn't compare to what your Grandpa has amassed. I always wonder if your mom thinks I'm worth putting up with."

Sarah entered the room and snuggled up to Adam. She pulled Stevie onto her lap, looked into her husband's eyes, and blissfully serenaded him with a lyric from a 1956 song by Elvis Presley:

I want you, I need you, I-I love you with all my heart.

CHAPTER 59

Rob Murphy's Suicide Attempt

"Hello, Maureen. This is Sarah Furano. My son told me to get your number at your place of employment. I told the operator it was urgent. She was initially reluctant to give it to me, but after I pleaded, she relented."

"Hi, Sarah, my old friend. I think about you often. I saw you on television, and you looked great," Maureen said into the receiver. "How is Rob these days? Is everything okay?"

"Sarah, Rob is fighting for his life in Holy Name Hospital. He overdosed on sleeping pills."

Sarah heard a screeching wail and muffled sobs.

"Why, Sarah? Why? Word got back to me that he loves your family, especially your son Stevie, who he worships. Why would he want to give that up?" she asked cryingly.

"Maureen, perhaps you know the answer. Yes, he loves my family and considers Stevie, his son. He couldn't possibly love a biological son more. Rob has suffered from depression for a long time. I don't think he has ever recovered from the break up. He has been happy yet sad all this time."

467

"Will he make it, Sarah? Please say yes," she said, again bursting into sobs.

"Today's report indicates he will probably survive. When he was first rushed there after Stevie found him unresponsive on his kitchen floor, paramedics feared the worst would happen."

"Little Stevie found him? Oh, how horrible. That boy will be mentally scarred for life!" Maureen exclaimed.

"He hasn't stopped crying, Maureen. The boy won't leave his hospital room. He sleeps on the floor next to Rob's bed. The nurses were kind enough to provide him with blankets and pillows. It's been pitiful to watch my boy carry on this way."

"Did Rob ever give you people any indication he wanted to end his life?"

"Never, Maureen. We weren't given clues that pointed to anything so extreme. But he lost a lot of weight."

"Is he ill?"

"No, he lost it by dieting. He ate less, skipped some meals, and stayed away from carbohydrates."

"How much did he lose, Sarah?"

"Eighty pounds. He was once 220. Now he's about 140."

"Sarah, I can't even picture him at 140. Does he still have the beard?"

"He got rid of that over a year ago. It's funny, but Adam has a goatee now and gained about 70 pounds. They went in opposite directions. Adam is a weightlifter and bodybuilder and has become a muscular strongman. He destroyed Rob in a wrestling match on our living room rug. My husband hurt Rob's neck and made him cry."

"I can't believe it. Rob was so much stronger than Adam. But I guess people change, and sometimes drastically. Good for Adam. You all have a bodyguard now."

"Maureen, would it be possible for you to meet in person? You might know much more about Rob than you can discuss over the phone. Since the hospital is in Teaneck, perhaps we could catch a sandwich at Noah's Ark on Cedar Lane. It's an excellent Jewish deli restaurant. Adam loves their pastrami. It is located next to the movie theater."

"Sarah, my husband and I go there often. Delfin likes their corned beef. Would 6 p.m. work for you? I want to visit Rob at the hospital, but I'll wait an extra day so you can be sure he'll welcome me. I'd be delighted to meet up with you."

"Thank you, Maureen. I can't wait to see you. There's Bischoff's, the ice cream place across the road, but I think we should spend more time in Noah's Ark."

"Honey, I agree," said Maureen. "I'm unsure if I should notify Rob's parents, assuming they don't already know."

"Maureen, no one has tried to reach them. He's been estranged from them for so long, but it seems wrong not to inform them."

"Sarah, I will explain what happened with Rob's parents. I'll only say that they have no desire to see him again. He has a sister who feels the same way."

"How terrible, Maureen. I'll see you soon."

CHAPTER 60

Meeting at Noah's Ark Jewish Deli in Teaneck

"What can I get you, ladies?" asked a short, stocky waiter wearing a yarmulka.

"I'll have a turkey sandwich on rye and a Diet Coke," said Maureen.

"I'll try the pastrami," said Sarah. "Whatever my husband likes, I like. I'll take a Snapple iced tea."

"Both sandwiches come with pickles and coleslaw. Is that okay, or would you like another side?" the waiter asked.

"The coleslaw and pickles will be fine," said Maureen. "Sarah, I can see you are a loyal husband. Does Adam have anything to do with deciding your meals?"

"He does, Maureen. He makes the menu every week and tells me what to buy at the supermarket on the weekends."

"Wow, he's an old-fashioned husband. I hope your marriage isn't suffocating."

"Maureen, I love my husband. I know my place in the marriage."

"You are remarkable, Sarah. Dutiful wives are rare. However, I never would have figured Adam to be a chauvinist. What did he say when Geraldine Ferraro ran for vice president?"

471

"He said women have no business leading our country. My husband hates the Democrats."

"Wow, well, there we have it," said Maureen.

After the waiter returned, both women squeezed Gold's traditional delicatessen-style spicy brown mustard on their sandwiches.

"Do you know what Adam would say right now?" asked Sarah.

"I haven't the slightest," said Maureen.

"Where the fuck is the Kosciusko mustard?" exclaimed Sarah.

Maureen snickered.

"Getting back to Rob, I will tell you that he couldn't provide for my sexual needs. Whenever we made love, we'd embrace, but he couldn't get aggressive. It always came down to me dominating him. He would try, but he always melted. Once, I got super-aggressive with him."

"Did he cry?"

"He did. For years, I witnessed him struggling with himself. He always told me he hated himself."

"Why did his parents hate him?"

"His dad is a conservative guy. When his wife showed him some magazines Rob had hidden in his drawer, he distanced himself from his son."

"Can I ask what was in those magazines?"

"Photos of men dressed as women. Transvestites."

"So Rob is transgender?"

"No, Sarah, he is not. With Rob, it was a fetish. He could never do what Mikaela did. He could never muster up the courage, but aside from that, he hasn't any interest in changing sex. He likes playing the spectator. I'm sure part of him resented Mikaela's actions, but he has had to deal with other problems. I discussed the situation with his parents, who said I did the right thing when I broke up with him. They didn't show him an ounce of compassion. His dad said he wanted him out of their house and called him a disgusting freak. I cried for him but wasn't willing to continue such a relationship. I understand he had no control over who he was, and my heart broke for him, but I wanted to settle down and raise a family. To me, Rob was compromised."

"Maureen, I suspected his parents hated him for a reason other than that he struck you."

"Sarah, he never struck me. He lied. He was ashamed to reveal the true reason. If he would have touched me, I would have beaten him into a coma."

"But wasn't he this big football star?"

"He lied about that, too. It was all part of his cover. He was on the team, but the coach rarely played him. Some of the other players called him a pussy and said he would be better off being a cheerleader. The only reason why he joined football was to appear macho."

"That's the reason my Mikaela joined the fire department."

"Yes, both used the same front," said Maureen.

"I see. I feel so sad for Rob. I have grown to love him. My Stevie idolizes him."

"Sarah, you are a saint. You dealt with Mikey's issue and bonded with her even more when she became Mikaela. You are an inspiration to all who know you. Before your husband Adam became this extremely macho man, you needed to nurture him when he was perceived the way he was by everyone."

"The difference is that Adam hated appearing feminine," said Sarah. "His inner self was ultra-masculine, and he worked hard to release it. Mikaela is the opposite, of course."

"Rob said it was his dream to have a family with me. We became lovers in jr. high school. He said we were meant for each other. We were both Irish and had similar tastes and habits. It was tragic, but I had to end it. This brings me to the major problem that separated us. Rob has erectile dysfunction. He is unable to stay hard for sexual intercourse. Our sessions always ended with me losing my temper and hitting him. I deeply regret what I did. Rob couldn't do anything about his condition. He was embarrassed and had low self-esteem. Rob made an appointment with a doctor. He was told he had low testosterone levels. They tried to compensate with drugs, but the problem persisted."

"I had no idea, Maureen. How sad and unfair. Poor Rob."

"Though he loved your family and treated Stevie as his son, he must have snapped. Sometimes, it takes a while for people to conclude they are failures. Rob needs love from someone badly. I wish I could furnish it."

"I will show him love, Maureen. I'm sure Mikaela and Adam will permit me to."

"There isn't another person like you, Sarah. You are God's messenger."

Sarah held Maureen's hand.

"So, I recall you have one child. A boy, right?"

"Yes, we have a four-year-old named Delfin Jr. We are trying to have another. Let me show you a picture of my son," said Maureen, opening her wallet.

"He's beautiful. I've never seen your husband, but I think your son looks like him."

"His spitting image. Black hair, brown eyes, skin shade, features, and even mannerisms. He doesn't look Irish, that's for sure!" exclaimed Maureen.

"You can say that again," said Sarah. "You are madly in love with your husband, right?"

"He is everything to me. I can't imagine myself not being attached to him, Sarah. I also have the best relationship imaginable with his parents."

"That's so wonderful, friend. You made the right choice. I wish you and your family the best."

Maureen smiled and squeezed Sarah's hands.

"Let's eat our sandwiches, Maureen. We're lucky they didn't require gravy. They'd be cold by now."

CHAPTER 61

The Return of Mikey; Damnation in Hades

After Rob was released from the hospital three days later, Mikaela and Adam approved Sarah's proposal. Mikaela cried, deeply moved by her soulmate's gesture, while Adam typically was crude and sarcastic.

"Sarah, I've always fantasized about pimping my wife out. I will write a book, *Sharing Sarah,* when I retire from teaching."

"My husband, you have developed the same biting humor as your dad," said Sarah. "But I like it."

Adam chuckled but then displayed a severe look.

"I love my dad, Sarah."

"Sweetheart, you have always loved him. Please show him sometimes. He adores you, but simultaneously, he's terrified of you."

"I want my wife to get me a Bud and sit on my lap," Adam announced, sitting on the couch.

Sarah returned with a Bud and rested her rump on her husband's knees.

"Sarah, you are the *real* saint in this family. Mikaela is a close second, but I was always a fraud. I love how I am now and embrace my cynicism, but sometimes I feel guilty for misleading people," said Adam, flicking his lighter on a Marlboro.

"Sweetie, without you, there would be no Stevie, Joey, or a little Mikey or Adam. You paved the way for and later encouraged my relationship with Mikaela. Without you, Jimbo might be dead or in jail now. You saved and brought meaning to his life and gave your eldest daughter an adored second father. Jay would never have joined our family without you, meaning Jennifer would never have married and had children with him. Without you, Rob might now be deceased, depriving my twins of his unique affection. Without you, Brian would have missed out on a loving family. Without you, hundreds of students would have been deprived of the most inspiring teacher of their lives. Without you, my life would be meaningless directly and by extension. Without you, my nest might have been forever empty."

"I can't live if living is without you; I can't live, I can't give anymore," Adam crooned in his raspy, baritone voice.

"How did I know you would reference that Harry Nilsson song? Until now, I would have said my favorite by him was *Everybody's Talkin'.*"

"And you always accused the Furanos of being eternal rankers."

Adam and Sarah laughed and hugged.

***

"Sarah, I thought long and hard," said Mikaela. "I don't want to take the estrogen or the testosterone blockers any longer. Please dispose of them. I am done ingesting hormones forever. I don't yet know the consequences of taking them for the lengthy period I did, though I'm sure I am already impotent. But heck, does it matter? I could barely get it up when I was completely male. Still, I fathered four children."

"Oh, Mikaela," said Sarah, bursting into tears.

"One more thing, my beloved. Please don't call me Mikaela anymore. My name is Mikey. From now on, I want all my paperwork to reflect this, and all the family should address me with my former and birth name. Soon, I will explain why I have reversed myself. There are several reasons, but a good part is because of you. Nothing about my existence should ever compromise society's perception of *you*. You are the most beautiful human being God has ever created. Being with you is my only meaningful function in this world, and nothing I do or say or how I identify should even remotely compromise how others perceive you. I feel my incomplete transition has drawn attention away from you. Sarah, you are all that matters. I must put on the best face in a relationship I never deserved. I have a strong feminine side that will co-exist with Mikey, but I've determined Mikaela will only lurk from now on."

"Mikey, your name will never matter, only your essence," said Sarah cryingly.

"Nearly as essential for me is how our children perceive me. All of them have supported my change unreservedly. Part of me feels I have betrayed them. They deserve a male as their father. While I applaud men who transition to be true to themselves and don't even remotely feel they are betraying anyone, I can no longer place self-identity over the norm of a conventional family dynamic. I want our four boys to have one male and one female as their parents. I will always be a gender-compromised male, but a male, nonetheless. Sarah, I have finally concluded that I should not put myself over my family. I repeat, I do not nor will I ever condemn those who move forward to the transition, and such people should always be lauded for their courage; still, I speak for myself. Every family and every person involved in similar situations is different. Sarah, I suspect gender change will be all the rage years down the road. Right now, it is frowned upon, and some out there threaten violence against those who present themselves opposite of their biological gender."

Sarah struggled to speak. After "My beloved," she surrendered,

479

weeping.

"Sometime in the next two weeks, I will shop to reinstate my male wardrobe. I would appreciate your help. I will no longer use cosmetics or jewelry and will have my tattoo removed. I will cut my nails and remove my nail polish. I have been a distraction for too long. Our lives must center around you, Sarah. No matter what you say, my saintly sweetheart, Mikey is a better fit for you than Mikaela. While living as her, I learned so much about tolerance and empathy from you and our family, immediate and extended. The best therapy for a troubled Mikey was to live as Mikaela for a time. She'll always be my alter ego, but more importantly, she was the catalyst in defining the true meaning of love for me. I have concluded that I needed to live as Mikaela for a time to be the ideal Mikey and the person who stood the best chance of ensuring our love would be eternal. I want to live the rest of my life as Mikey Furano, a male lover of Sarah and father of her children."

"Oh my God, I love you so much, Mikey. Oh, my God."

She wildly kissed and caressed him.

"I will work hard to return my voice to as close to a tenor as possible," said Mikey. "I will need to have a surgical procedure to eliminate my budding breasts, and I will present myself as a male at the college at the beginning of the week. I will gain weight."

"My beloved, would you do me one favor?"

"Of course," said Mikey. "I'd give you the world if I could."

"Will you always maintain the red streaks in your beautiful blond hair? I would be thrilled and grateful to see that part of your life as Mikaela always honored."

Mikey smiled broadly. "There is nothing I'd like to do more, Sarah. I will always wear my flat red earrings as well." As they snuggled, Mikey whispered. "After I get my hair cut – again within two weeks or so – I would like to return as Mikey in front of the entire family. You know well how wild this family is for dramatic announcements in front of everyone. While all are seated in the living room on a Saturday at noon, I will enter the house and appear with the boy's haircut and all the promised modifications. Aside from the breasts – which will be rectified soon – and the permanently red streaks in my hair, and the earrings, I will appear male. There won't be bracelets or necklaces. The sneakers are unisex. Of course, I will need more time to remove the love tattoo."

"Sweetie, why don't you always keep that tattoo? It is part of you."

"Yes, Sarah. As always, you are right.

"What about your red and pink panties? I think you should continue to wear them every day."

"I do, too, my love. I've grown to love the feeling of them."

"Sweetheart, I will be careful not to give anyone a clue. Everyone will think the announcement is about you changing your mind about the surgeries. I know you will want to do it in your parents' living room next door. I will alert my parents, Susan and Cindy, and make sure every family member and Jimbo are present."

"Thank you, my beloved," said Mikey. "I'd like to rejoin the Grandview Fire Department soon."

"Sweetheart, this has all the makings of a return appearance on *The Phil Donahue Show!*"

They both laughed wildly until their lips met. Sarah locked Mikey with all her limbs. She rocked him to sleep with their corneas practically rubbing against each other. She whispered, "You'll never know how much I love you" into his ear and joined him in slumber.

After they both awoke, Sarah asked Mikey, "What do you think Stevie will say? Joey, too, for that matter, but Stevie was the one most supportive of your identity. I dare say he might be disappointed. The boys never really knew you as a male."

"Sarah, I fear his reaction, but somehow I see this all turning out well."

"You are probably right, sweetheart. One other matter you forgot about, my love," said Sarah. "All your hair follicles have been burned away. Your face and skin will always be smooth, though not as soft as they are now because of the end of the hormones."

"I never cared for hair on my skin, so no loss there. I'll also carry over my newfound love for cooking, tidying the house, and attending to the children."

"And you are a fantastic cook," said Sarah. "It will be interesting to see how the ladies at the card games react after Mom reintroduces you as her returning son, Mikey."

"Oh, boy," said Mikey. "I don't think I can handle that drama again."

***

Down in Hades, an angry Beelzebub interrogated Mephistopheles, asking him how it was possible that repeated adultery by Sarah and the male chauvinism by Adam wasn't enough to break up the Furanos.

"Oh, great master of darkness, I did everything I could. I even made him physically abuse her and got him to do some drugs and shake down gamblers. I gave him a fantastic temper and Herculean strength. Please don't cast me aside. I'll work harder. I got him to renounce that goofy Irish Jesus label the braindead Polish boy gave him and have significantly reduced his appearances in that home-town Catholic church. I made the rest of his family fear him."

"By no effort of your own, Mephistopheles. You didn't know that a woman spent her adolescent years as a man. Now that she finally emerged as her preferred gender, Adam became the male leader of that family. I always told you to stop taking credit for developments you had nothing to do with. You also don't know that she has decided to return to being a male. Do you even try to keep up with the latest developments? You did the same thing with Jimbo. You had no idea he would dislodge that safety belt, yet you acted like a hero when it happened. The condemned sinners down here are well-versed in deviant behavior. They knew what you were up to. Adam's meta-

482

morphosis was genuine. Nobody made it happen. I love his change and hope it gets more severe, but I knew you were busy trying to get wars started and disasters to happen. You never worked hard on the little stuff. And how many times did I tell you that the Polish people are a real problem? Their faith is unwavering. We can't ever make headway in that country. Whenever I think I have someone ready to do my bidding, they end up in a church. It is disheartening. That charlatan John Paul II did so much damage to our cause."

"Please, master of darkness, just one last chance!"

"You know I do not give second chances. You are banished to the fiery pits," said Beelzebub as he swung his arm and heaved a burning ball that engulfed Mephistopheles and sent him spiraling downward into a bottomless pit where eternal damnation awaited him.

IN LOVING MEMORY OF

JEFFREY S. MC CARTNEY
VALERIE CLARK

ACKNOWLEDGMENTS

Rob Bignell, my sole editor on *Mikey's Absolution*, also formatted the novel. Rob is a former English teacher and author of many books on Amazon and other online outlets. He completed his work on both books speedily and professionally. His tireless attention to *Mikey's Absolution* was exemplary, and his best-selling volume, *7 Minutes a Day to Mastering the Craft of Writing*, was an invaluable reference tool.

Andrew Castrucci of upstate New York, formerly of Cliffside Park, is the enormously gifted artist of all three novels. He has long been hailed in the East Bergen arts community for his remarkable talent, regularly displayed at Manhattan art galleries.

Daniel Velle, an ace graphic designer and SVA student from New York City, was receptive to all last-minute changes.

Bill Kamberger, creative advisor and co-editor of my first two novels, *Paradise Atop the Hudson* and *Irish Jesus of Fairview,* achieved high literary excellence. He also found time to read a few chapters of *Mikey's Absolution.*

Tony D'Ambra, of Sydney, Australia, is the longtime proctor of the premium film noir site *FilmsNoir.net,* which he founded. His writing has been exemplary, and he's served as a technical advisor for *Wonders in the Dark*, the art site where I serve as editor. Tony has proofread and made vital suggestions for the novels.

Anthony Lucibello, of Montvale, New Jersey, is a dear lifelong friend who has enthusiastically followed the publications and has generously contributed his interpretation of the novels in discussions and book readings at the Fairview Free Public Library. His ongoing involvement has been an inspiration.

485

ABOUT THE AUTHOR

Sammy Juliano, author of *Mikey's Absolution,* was born and raised in Fairview, New Jersey, where he lives with his wife Lucille and their five children: Daniel, Jeremy, Jillian, Melanie, and Samuel IV. He has taught English, literature, creative writing, and American history to junior high school students and children's literature to elementary school students in a still-running 38-year teaching career in his hometown system. He is stationed at Number Three School Annex, where Lucille serves as principal. Before his teaching tenure, he was twice elected to the Fairview Board of Education in 1980 and 1983 and is now serving his fifth term as a trustee on the Fairview library board. Sammy co-founded and continues to serve as editor of the online art site *wondersinthedark.wordpress.com,* where he has penned over 400 reviews — many essay-length — on film, theater, music, opera, and children's books. He was the lead actor in two short films directed by Jay Giampietro, "Best Picture" and "The Thing That Kills Me the Most," which were chosen to screen at the New York Film Festival, the Brooklyn Academy of Music, the Maryland Film Festival, and the Nighthawk Film Festival, among other venues. Juliano maintains a vigorous presence on social media, coordinating many film-related ventures. His first novel, *Paradise Atop the Hudson,* was published in December 2021, and his second, *Irish Jesus of Fairview,* in 2023. Juliano is working on his fourth novel, *The Glorification of Sarah Furano,* due in the fall of 2025.

Made in United States
North Haven, CT
21 January 2025